Food

By Linda P. Kozar

Published by Linda Kozar, CreateSpace Edition
Copyright ©2015 Linda Kozar

God is wiser than all of our whys.

II Corinthians 4:16-17 "This is the reason we never lose heart. The outward man does indeed suffer wear and tear, but every day the inward man receives fresh strength. These little troubles (which are really so transitory) are winning for us a permanent, glorious and solid reward out of all proportion to pain."

JoBeth Tomlin loses everything—her family, her job, her figure and the man of her dreams, all before her thirtieth birthday. And just when she thinks things can't get any worse, she has to move in with her eccentric aunt, two feisty cats and a flatulent old dog named Roscoe. With all the sorrow snacking going on, JoBeth's food baby is starting to show. Will she turn to God or Little Debbie for answers?

* * *

Dedication

First—many thanks to Lisa Godfrees, who edits with mad, Jedi skills. To Michael, my dear husband; to Katie and Lauren my darling daughters; to "Patches" my Rat Terrier Princess; to my friend, author/speaker and Christian comedian, Karen Mayer Cunningham, whom I consulted for the proper "delectables" a food addict might imagine and enjoy; to my wonderful friend Dannelle Woody who did me the honor of reading all the various incarnations of this book and offering pinpoint feedback; to my dear friend Jenny Mitchell Kent; to my critique partners Joanne Hillman and Louise Looney; *and* to my sweet "Mama Rose," whose indefatigable spirit could not be quenched by a diagnosis of Dementia.

Table of Contents

Chapter One
The End

"The hatchet must fall on the block; the oak must be cleft to the center. The weight of the world is on my shoulders. Here is the pen and the paper; on the letters in the wire basket I sign my name, I, I, and again I." — Virginia Woolf, The Waves

A warped vanilla candle sputtered and spat as JoBeth Tomlin snapped a dishtowel at the lingering smoke. Wheezing, she perched herself on a wobbly stool by the kitchen counter, hoping there was enough scent left in the thing to mask the acrid tang of burnt pasta.

Her stomach churned at the sound of tires crunching against the driveway. She listened for the familiar creak of the garage door and the cadence of determined footsteps tapping against the floor.

"Hi, sweetie! I saw your car outside." Susan Tomlin paused in the doorway, keys dangling from her free hand, the other hand grasping a couple of canvas grocery bags. A youthful, attractive woman in her late fifties, an uncharacteristic frown dominated her mother's face. "What's that smell?"

JoBeth bit her lip. "Sorry, I burned the lasagna." She glanced at the sink. "The pan is — is soaking. I thought I'd come over and surprise you guys with dinner, but I guess I got distracted."

"Oh Jo . . ." Her mother hefted the groceries onto the counter in one swoop, depositing the keys next to them. She cracked open the oven door and winced. "I was hoping I'd have it easy tonight. It's been a rough day at the shop. Dad and I had our share of troubles. Plus we had a customer come in and try to return a stack of books purchased three years ago! Dog-eared and highlighted too. Can you believe the nerve of that woman?"

"No worries, Mom, I'll cook something else. Where is Dad, anyway?"

"I mean, I realize the economy is tough, but it's tough for all of us." Susan blew out the candle and started emptying the bags on the counter. "He had an appointment at the bank, but he'll be along soon."

Avoiding her mother's eyes, JoBeth slid off the stool, opened the fridge and bent over to scan the interior. "Hmmm, there's a package of chicken." She reached in. "And a head of lettuce. We could have a nice salad. I think there's a box of instant mashed potatoes in the pantry too." She stood up. "What do you think?"

Her mother pushed the refrigerator door closed, and propped her right arm against it. "Sounds delicious honey, but I wouldn't let *you* near a stove or oven in the state you're in."

"What do you mean?"

Her mother paused, a smirk on her face. "Tell me what's going on."

JoBeth slipped underneath her mother's arm and creaked back down on the stool. "Nothing." Her mouth scrunched into a scowl. "Why do you always do that? Why does anything have to be wrong?"

Her mother stared back as if she could see right through her. Then she glided to the trashcan, paused and stomped on the lever. She reached for a pencil on the counter and peered in using the eraser end to flip items on the surface. "Hmmm. What have we here? Twinkies. Cream puffs. Indian take-out. An empty carton of French fries. A burger-wrapper. Two burger-wrappers? Should I keep going?" She looked up, concern on her face. "You ready to talk?"

JoBeth clasped her arms together. "No."

Her mother lifted her foot and the lid on the trashcan clonked shut. Hands on her hips, she moved in closer. "JoBeth Tomlin, something's wrong. Are you having trouble with Kyle again?"

She tried to meet her mother's eyes — steel versus steel — but soon turned her face away.

"I knew it." Her mother shook her head, disappointment registering on her face. "You know how your father and I feel about that relationship." She pointed. "You're wasting your time with him."

JoBeth looked up, certain the rind of red around her eyes had given her away. "You only think you know. For your information, Mother, I'm worried about my job. They laid off twelve people last week."

Her mother's mouth opened and closed before she finally spoke. "So you think you might be on the short list?"

JoBeth shook her head. "How should I know? I just told you that I'm worried. If I felt confident, I wouldn't be worried."

"You can always move back home with us. We're your parents. You know we'd love to have you. I'd cook all your favorite foods, and we could watch movies together and lots more. If we weren't in such financial straits right now, your father and I would take you on at the shop. You know that, right? But we've got a skeleton crew as it is."

"I know, Mom. I'm hoping things won't come to that, though. Even so, I have a bit of money squirreled away." She took a deep breath. "And by the way, I happen to love Kyle."

Her mother's eyes ignited. "Do you? Do you really?"

The blood rushed hot into JoBeth's cheeks. "What's that supposed to mean?"

"I think you know." Her mother brushed a strand of hair away from her face as she paced from the counter to the fridge and pantry putting groceries away. "I understand you're a grown woman and you can make your own decisions, but the truth is the truth. Kyle doesn't treat you right, honey. He never did. And I don't believe that buffoon feels the same way about you."

"He does too!"

She stopped pacing to lock eyes with her daughter. "Then why are you binge-eating again?"

Responses, from snarky to serious, whirred through her mind, but before JoBeth could answer, a familiar voice rang out. "Well, look who it is."

Frank Tomlin stood at the dining room archway. JoBeth wondered how much of the conversation he'd heard from the front door to the kitchen.

Perfect timing, Dad. JoBeth rushed to wrap her arms around his neck.

Tall and thin, her father looked the picture of health. But she'd noticed subtle changes about him over the last couple of months, enough to cause her concern. The stress of trying to keep the business afloat had taken its toll. In her opinion, the weight he'd lost had tightened flesh against bone, giving him a gaunt, unhealthy appearance.

Alarmed at the lightness of his body, JoBeth pulled away to look him in the eyes. "Daddy, how are you doing?"

"He's fine." Her mother interrupted. "You're just in time. We're about to cook dinner."

JoBeth and her father shared a knowing look.

"You must have read my mind, darling. I'm starving." Frank Tomlin approached his wife and planted a kiss on the side of her head. "What's for dinner?" He sniffed the air. "Smells like something . . . "

Her mother smiled. "Burned?" She shifted her eyes. "JoBeth managed to scorch a pan of lasagna."

He winked at his daughter, a tender expression on his face. "Well, that's a relief. I didn't feel like lasagna today. I'm in more of a meat and potatoes mood."

"You're out of luck if you want beef." Her mother set the package of chicken on the counter.

JoBeth reached for her purse. "I could run to the store."

Her mother whirled around. "You'll do no such thing. I just came from the store remember? We'll make do with what we have."

He scrubbed his hands together. "What can I do to help?"

Her mother pointed to a fresh bunch of carrots on the counter. "You can slice those for me." She glanced from JoBeth to him. "Oh Hon—" She smiled and batted her lashes at her husband. "Would you mind emptying the garbage for me? It appears to be full."

"Sure." Her father stepped toward the can. "That's my only real job around here."

JoBeth jumped from her stool to intercept him. "No, ah—ah, I have my own apartment. I'm used to taking out the garbage, you know." She lifted the lid. "I'll take care of it." She shooed him away. "You go—chop."

"Okay, okay." He lifted his hands and winked. "I'll step out of the way for our strong, capable daughter."

As soon as he turned around, she rushed to bunch the burgeoning sack together into a tight knot.

He glanced back. "Wow, you're fast."

She gasped as she lifted the sack of garbage. "Well, ah, I have to be quick taking the garbage out in my neighborhood. It's kind of sketchy, you know."

Without turning away from the counter, her mother commented. "Believe me, we know."

Halfway down the driveway, JoBeth stopped and let the heavy bag fall beside her. *Why would she do that? It's like she wanted him to see what was in the can.*

She turned to look back at the house and to her surprise, her mother waved cheerily from the window. An influx of bad words and thoughts clung like burrs to her conscience. She and her mother were always at odds for some reason. Nothing she ever said or did seemed to please the woman. JoBeth sighed a prayer. *"Lord, help me!"*

She hoisted the bag over her shoulder and carried it Santa Claus-style to the curb. As she let it fall, her cell buzzed. *Kyle.*

"What? I don't see — where are you?" She squinted and craned her neck in search of his car. He told her he was parked halfway down the block. *Out of sight.* She glanced toward the kitchen window. Satisfied that her mother was no longer watching, JoBeth casually strode to the sidewalk, and began to pick up the pace once she was out of her mother's line of vision. *Why would he do that?*

Kyle leaned out the window of his sporty black Nissan. Arm resting on the sill, he greeted her with a pouty, but somehow adorable, smile.

"Hey, babe."

Smooth-skinned and tan, his blue eyes betrayed a melancholy mood. She leaned in for a quick kiss. "What are you doing here?"

"I figured you'd be at your parent's house. I drove by and saw the cars."

JoBeth narrowed her eyes. "Why didn't you come over? We're cooking dinner."

He fiddled absently with the side mirror. "Because."

"Why?" JoBeth studied his face.

"Because you and I need to talk." He glanced down, and as he did, a shock of whitish blond hair fell across his face.

JoBeth did a double take. "About what? Look, if it's about what I said before, I'm sorry." Their argument had been about nothing, just another stupid falling-out in a long daisy chain of disagreements. She continued. "And why this? Why are you in such a rush to talk to me? You could have called or come by my place later."

He brushed at the corner of one eye, as if wiping a tear away. "I can't wait that long. Like I said, we need to talk."

Nice try. Her cell phone buzzed. She glanced down at the text. "It's mom. They're wondering what happened to me."

He clutched her arm. "Can't you text her back and tell her you're with me?"

What's up with him? He's being selfish, and as usual — always trying to have his way.

She shook her head, her mother's comments about Kyle still echoing through her mind. "You know what? No! For once, *you* can wait. I'm always jumping through hoops for you. Not this time." She pointed back toward the house. "I'm going home to have a nice, quiet dinner with my parents. You and I can talk tomorrow."

He stared back at her like a sad little boy. "Well, how about tonight? You said I could come by later."

JoBeth lifted her chin. "That offer expired. Tomorrow."

Kyle started the engine, his eyes pleading. "Are you sure?"

She raised her brows. "I'm not changing my mind."

He nodded and popped the clutch. "Okay Joey, if that's how you want it."

She watched him drive away, and as he did, an odd feeling grabbed the pit of her stomach — likely all the junk she'd noshed on earlier.

* * *

JoBeth could already hear the confession playing and replaying in her head: "Yes Mom, as a matter of fact I did binge on a whole plate full of double fudge brownies, but it's not every day a girl gets text-dumped by her fiancé."

Well, almost fiancé. After three years of dating, everyone expected them to get married. Was it only yesterday her mother had honed in on the fact that she and Kyle had been having troubles? But the woman was right about him, as much as JoBeth hated to admit it.

Her index finger hovered over the cell phone, thoughts ping ponging between keep and delete, call and don't call. She stared at the number "one" on speed dial, faded from frequent use, the hotline to Kyle Kowalski—her "ex." The word "ex" would take some getting used to.

The sudden retro ring rattled her. The phone slipped from her hand and she caught it after an awkward juggle.

"Kyle?"

"Sorry, it's me. What's going on?" Rayne Caraway's voice, mellow and melodic, somehow cut through the gloom. Her best friend since second grade, Rayne was the only one who would truly understand.

JoBeth paused a moment, voice raspy from crying. "Actually, a lot."

"You sound terrible. What's wrong?"

"I was going call you about it later."

"About what?"

"It's Kyle—he broke up with me."

"No!"

A ragged sob escaped. JoBeth reached for a bag of mini donuts and ripped it open, releasing a cloud of powdered sugar into the air.

"This morning he . . ." She took a deep breath. "He text-dumped me." She stuffed two in her mouth and inhaled.

Rayne drew in a breath as well. "What did he say? And I hope you're not sorrow snacking. You know how I feel about that." She continued. "Did he give you a reason why? What's wrong with him?"

The words stuck in JoBeth's throat as she tried to choke them out. *Of course, the donuts and powdered sugar didn't help.* She popped open a diet soda and took a long swallow. Breathless, somewhere between a sob and soda bubble, she pulled up his text and forwarded it to her friend.

"Did you get it?"

Rayne answered. "Hold on — okay. Got it."

"Are you reading what I'm reading?" She read the message to Rayne. "I'm b-r-a-k-i-n-g up with you, Jo. It's over, S-o-r-y."

Rayne gasped. "He never could spell. The university should issue him a refund."

"Yeah . . ."

"Wow, he really cut right to it, didn't he?"

"When I talked to him on the phone later, he said he needed some time to himself — said things didn't work out between us like he thought they would. He w-wants to be friends."

Rayne cleared her throat. "Hmmm, that explains a lot."

"Do you think it's because I put on a few pounds?"

Her friend snorted into the phone. "Do you really think it matters what size you are to someone who is supposed to love you?"

"No, I guess not," JoBeth agreed.

"But since you brought up the weight thing."

Okay, here it comes.

"Jo, you're like some kind of Indie 500 dieter — gaining and losing, gaining and losing. It's nothing but peaks and valleys with your weight. Last year you were down to a size twelve and now — well — that's hard on your body, you know. I think you're eating so much because you're unhappy. And Kyle is the reason. You're medicating your hurt with food."

"Look, I don't need an amateur psychiatrist right now. I need a friend."

Rayne continued, "You know what real friends do? They tell the truth. And I'm telling you the truth."

"You made your point." JoBeth rested her chin on her hands. "I still can't believe this happened. Last week we went to his parent's house for Sunday dinner. And I didn't call and tell you this, but Kyle said he really cared about me."

"Did he mention the word love?"

JoBeth paused. "Well, not exactly. He told me he really liked me, that he'd never felt such intense feelings about anyone before."

She heard Rayne snap her gum on the other end of the phone. JoBeth knew her friend pretty well. The girl had something on her mind.

"I guess that's nice, but he probably says the same thing to that monster dog of his."

JoBeth sputtered her response. "Are you? Are you comparing me to Krull? Because if you are — I think I mean more to him than that Rhodesian Ridgeback."

Rayne sniffed. "You're right. I guess there's no comparison. Kyle *cares about* you, but he *loves* Krull. I hear him say that to the dog all the time. He doesn't seem to have a problem saying the 'L' word, at least to a dog."

"That's cold." JoBeth's voice vibrated emotion.

"That's why I called you."

"To tell me my boyfriend cares more about his dog than me?"

"No, I figured there was a problem."

"What? You knew? Is — is that what you meant when you said, 'that explains a lot?'" A mist of powdered sugar puffed out with the words. The room started to spin, but she managed to reach for a few more.

"No — I didn't know anything for sure."

She held the phone away for a moment to take in the words. "What are you talking about? Stop being so mysterious and tell me."

After a rapid-fire cluster pop, Rayne started talking faster than usual, a far cry from her usually low-key personality.

"Well, you know that new funky kind of store that just opened down the street from my place? I went to check it out. By the way, did you know they have necklaces made from myrrh? I bought one and because it's a resin, when you wear it close to your skin, your body heats it up and releases the fragrance."

"Rayne." JoBeth's patience, stretched as thin as an old rubber band, was ready to snap.

"When I left that shop, I walked past the MotorMouth Grille and what did I see, but Kyle canoodling with a tall blonde. You know the one you and I make fun of? The girl who looks like a life-sized Bratz doll, only she's smart too — and rich?"

"Sophie? Sophie Perkins?" JoBeth doubled over in her chair, suddenly nauseous. Kyle cheated on me?"

No way. I had my whole future planned. How could this happen? God, why? Why? WHY?

"Jo, are you there?"

"Yeah . . ."

But all she could think about was the fact that Kyle Kowalski had broken it off with her for the most perfect woman God ever made.

Suddenly everything made sense. They rarely went out on dates anymore — opting instead to order pizza and watch movies at her place or at his parent's house. But how could she miss something so obvious? Kyle didn't want to be seen with her. Was he — could he be ashamed of her?

JoBeth reached for the donuts and simultaneously hung up on her friend.

Some people turn to a bottle. Others turn to a little happy pill, or to the bedroom. But what does a good Christian girl turn to when she's down?

Food.

Ever since she could remember, she'd always turned to food. And over the years, food had certainly turned on her. She'd ballooned to a persistent plus size. Not exactly the delicate flower she wanted to be.

She closed her eyes, imagining being blissfully in love and married to Kyle with a couple of kids, a pool, a dog, a goldfish or two and a perfect Mary Poppins life in the suburbs.

But the dream disappeared faster than a puff of powdered sugar.

And on the verge of a very big, ugly demographic change — her thirtieth birthday on April third, to be exact — she found herself over-and-out with Kyle, overweight, almost overdrawn, and way out of luck.

She glanced around the room. Besides all that, she lived in a dirty, dumpy rent house that would make Mary Poppins hurl if she saw it.

Of course, maybe Mary Poppins might be onto something. A spoonful of sugar might be just what she needed. While she waited for Rayne's inevitable knock on the door, she finished the bag of donuts and started on the Little Debbie's, cotton candy, salted peanuts in the shell, corn dogs and potato chips.

Sorrow snacking, Major League style.

Chapter Two
Lil' Debbie Debacle

"The container IS the serving." — Karen Mayer Cunningham

The takeout beat Rayne to the door by five minutes. JoBeth had ordered Chinese, enough for both of them, or just one if her friend wasn't hungry. And she wasn't counting on Rayne being hungry.

Fuchsia hair in two Princess Leia-styled buns — Rayne adjusted an electric blue tank top to cover her white bra strap. "You look terrible." Rayne released her heavy shoulder bag next to the door as usual. She waved her hands around, a sliver of worry on her narrow face. "Your aura's all polka dotty and spotty. Not good."

She followed JoBeth to the sofa, but threw open the maroon velvet curtains to let in the sunlight before sitting down. Squinting at JoBeth in the light of day, her blue eyes projected concern. "It's worse than I thought."

"C'mon, you know how I feel about that spooky stuff."

"Hmmmpf, it's not spooky. What you're really saying is, it's on your no-no list because you're religious."

"Touché." She forced a smile and reached to hug her friend. "Look, I don't feel like arguing right now. Kyle dumped me, *remember?*" She managed a half wink from a tear-swollen eye. "I promise to tackle this conversation another time."

"That's a promise I know you'll keep because I'm going to hold you to it." Rayne sniffed the air. "Is that Chinese?"

"Yes, want some?" She pointed to the coffee table in front of the sofa.

She frowned. "I'd love to, but I'm juicing this week. Can't." She eyed the Styrofoam containers and sniffed. "Of course the food smells good, but Styro releases toxic gases when you heat it in the micro. Did you know that? I won't eat anything served in one. I like the classic Chinese take-out boxes, myself."

"Guess I'll just have to eat it all on my own then."

As JoBeth took the first bite, Rayne grabbed the clicker and started channel surfing. "There's a Twilight Zone marathon. Or do you feel like an old movie? 'It Happened One Night' comes on in thirty minutes."

As JoBeth shoveled the sweet-and-sour into her mouth, she was aware of Rayne eyeing her.

Aiming the clicker with exaggerated flourish, Rayne began switching channels, rapid-fire. "How about one of those dumb talk shows? Those can be funny — sometimes. And if you like, I'll even watch one of those old scary Christopher Lee movies. Just for you, my friend." She blinked. "I'd never do that for anyone else, you know."

JoBeth grunted her approval.

"Jo?" Rayne grabbed her wrist. "Jo!"

Fork poised in mid-air, JoBeth stared her down. "Let go. What are you doing?"

Rayne's chest heaved. "No, what are *you* doing?"

"Trying to eat." She leaned forward and closed her mouth over the chopsticks and chewed.

"You need to stop eating and start dealing with what happened."

JoBeth continued to shove the food into her mouth, chomping rebellion.

Rayne opened her mouth as if to answer, but inexplicably cocked her head to the side instead. A weird expression came over her face. "Do you — do you hear something?"

"Nice try. I'm not putting my sticks down." She raised another spicy spoon of Szechwan.

Rayne stood up, craning her neck to the right, then to the left. "I'm serious."

She stopped chewing and rolled her eyes. But when she stopped chewing, she heard something. There *was* an unfamiliar noise, faint, but distinct.

JoBeth put down the container and leaned against the arm of the couch to stand. "What is that?"

Eyes wide, Rayne pointed towards the kitchen. "Sounds like it's coming from the basement or something."

They both looked toward the basement door.

The chopsticks fell from her hands. "Oh no."

Rayne sprinted over her to fling the door open. And the second it opened, they were greeted by the scent and the sound of water. Lots of it.

Rayne flipped the light switch by the door. From the top of the stairs, JoBeth could see her dirty clothes floating on the surface of a pool of bubbling black water, rapidly swallowing the basement steps.

A break in the main pipe fanned out water like a sprinkler at a kiddie pool. JoBeth pounded the wall with her fist. "Is my name Jobette or something? First Kyle dumps me, and then this happens? I should just go to bed and stay there. Just stay in bed all day."

"Jo, unless we can stop the water, you might need a life raft instead of a mattress. Where's the thingamajig that shuts it off?"

"I don't know. I have no idea. Am I supposed to know that?"

Her friend blinked. "Ah, yeah. When you rent a house, you're supposed to be aware of these things."

JoBeth leaned her back against the wall. "Well I don't know where it is. Kyle always helped me with that kind of stuff. All I had to do was call and he'd be here." She threw her arms up. "God, why do you hate me?"

"You can sit around talking to the ceiling until your whole house floats away or we can do something about it." Rayne folded her arms and strode into the kitchen, her walk purposeful. She grabbed the phone. "What's his number?"

She shook my head. "No! I-I can't face him. No way."

"Okay, not him, but isn't his best friend a plumber?"

She snapped her fingers. "Sam. His number should be in the address book in the drawer to your right. See?"

Rayne thumbed through the Holly Hobby address book. *Vintage Chic.*

"It's under 'M' for MacManus, plumbing, that is."

Rayne nodded, punched in the number, and looked at her, slack-jawed. "Your phone is dead."

"Of course it is. Great, that's just grrreat." JoBeth grabbed her cell phone and punched in the number.

One ring. Two rings. Sam picked up on the third. Though she felt awkward asking him, she went for it anyway. "Sam, I . . ."

His deep voice hesitant and surprisingly gentle, Sam got right down to it. "I heard all about it, JoBeth. I don't know what to tell you. He's my friend and he makes his own decisions even though I don't agree with . . . "

"It's okay, Sam. I mean, it's not okay, but that's not why I'm calling."

"Really?"

Rayne started mumbling something to her about a bucket, but JoBeth waved her off. Her friend threw up her hands and ran out of the room.

"I have a situation."

"What kind of a situation?"

"My basement is flooded with water to the fifth step."

"Sixth," Rayne yelled from the basement door.

"*Sixth step.* And, and I would appreciate your help even though I know it's weird for me to ask, given the circumstances. But you're the only plumber I know and trust."

"I'll be right over." *Click.*

Rayne yelled from the basement door. "Is he coming?"

"I think so. He said he'd be right over."

Ring. Ring. She looked at the number on the phone. Sam again?

"Sorry about that. I hung up before I could tell you."

"Tell me what?" His voice higher pitched than usual, "Sam the Man" as he was called, seemed hesitant, though he'd never seemed hesitant about anything.

"Well, for the record, Jo, I think Kyle's crazy for breaking up with you."

"Uh, thanks. That really means a lot. Now get over here, please or we're going to need an ark."

Click. But before she could even process that bit of weirdness, the phone rang yet again. *What's with this guy?*

"Sam?"

"JoBeth?"

"Mr. Richards?" The tone of her voice changed. "Oh, hi, can I help you, sir?" *Stupid! I sound like a cashier at a fast food place.*

Her boss had always been sort of a nice guy, but this time his voice had that, "I have bad news" tone to it.

She'd worked for Newhouse Shipping for the past three years, not exactly a dream job, but she'd always thought of it as a stepping-stone to some greater calling.

A few minutes later, Rayne ran into the kitchen to empty a bucket into the sink. JoBeth licked some runaway ice cream melting off her finger.

Rayne stopped in her tracks. "Really? What are you doing eating ice cream at a time like this? You have an indoor swimming pool thing going on."

"Mr. Richards called. I just got laid off. They're in some sort of financial crisis or something." JoBeth managed a shaky smile. "It's ironic, really. Between the flood and being dumped two times in one day, it's almost funny."

Without saying a word, Rayne lowered the dingy aluminum bucket onto the table, made a beeline to the silverware drawer and the fridge, and set a tub of Butternut Brickle ice cream right next to the Rocky Road JoBeth had already started.

She warmed at the sight. Rayne was the kind of BFF who would sorrow snack with her without a second thought, despite her own lactose-intolerant digestive system. Who could ask for a better friend?

* * *

Sam MacManus put the phone down and held on to the edge of the kitchen counter. His prayers answered? JoBeth called. She'd actually called him.

True, it wasn't exactly what he'd prayed for though. He'd hoped for the opportunity to apologize for Kyle, and maybe counsel her though the breakup. Heaven knows he'd done enough of that sort of counseling before. But if fixing the plumbing in her rent house was the help she needed right now, well—have wrench, will travel.

He gathered up a few tools to add to his metal toolbox and headed out the door, grimacing as he passed the caricature of him on the side of his work van. The words, "Need Plumbing help? Call Sam the Man." The artist had painted his head onto a cartoonish toilet with his smile as the toilet seat. A cash-poor friend had done the work for him, a trade in services. Business art for couple of leaky toilet fixes. He sighed and loaded the tools. Next time he would make sure someone who wanted to trade services actually had some sort of skill worth trading.

On the way to her house, he glanced at himself in the rear view mirror, mostly for reassurance that he looked nothing like the image on the side of the van. His dark brown hair needed a trim. He stroked his chin, wishing he had time for a shave.

A loud noise plucked his attention away — somebody laying on a horn. He swerved just in time to avoid a head-on with a beat-up truck approaching in the opposite lane. Besides the sound of the tools clanking together in the back of the van, an obscenity from the driver's open window cut through the air as the two drivers passed. Sam white-knuckled the wheel and exhaled. Close call.

But his thoughts soon drifted back to Jo. Who was he kidding? Why worry about the way he looked? He might as well look like the Captain Commode on the side of the van. She wasn't interested in him. Not anymore. She'd never given him a second look after their first date. Not after she set eyes on Kyle.

Chapter Three
Off To A Blue Start

"When you have a fat friend there are no see-saws, only catapults." — Demetri Martin

"Thanks for letting me move in. It-it's only temporary." Head down, JoBeth pushed a mop of light brown hair away from her face and into a loose bun.

"Honey, your father and I love to have you home with us. We didn't understand why you moved out in the first place." Her mother pulled a couple of sweaters out of the suitcase and placed them in a bureau drawer. She paused, elbow resting on the dresser. "You know, I've always felt guilty that I had to work so much while you were growing up. You know, my favorite thing in the world is spending time with you."

"Me too, Mama." JoBeth grinned.

Susan laughed. "You haven't called me that for a long time. It's sweet to hear."

Though people said she resembled her mother, JoBeth couldn't see it. Highlighted hair in a smart bob, thin and muscular, a dynamo of energy, her mother seemed to be everything she was not.

She glanced around. Her room was just as she'd left it when she went away to college, all pink and frilly. There were posters of outdated film and music heartthrobs plastered along one wall, ribbons and corsages draped across her vanity mirror, an old cassette/CD player on a shelf — her parents hadn't changed a thing.

She grimaced. The longer she stayed with her parents, the sooner they'd start treating her like their little girl again. Mom would start ringing the dinner bell. Dad would remind her to brush her teeth. And there would definitely be chores. Of course as the latest statistic to join the ranks of the unemployed, she could sure use the fifty-cent weekly allowance.

By now her mother had moved from putting sweaters away to hanging a few shirts in the closet. "You really did lose a lot of clothes, honey."

JoBeth shrugged. "Less to wash."

Her mother sighed. "You could be saving oodles of money living here with us instead of squandering it away paying rent on that dumpy place. Why don't you just stay with us permanently?"

JoBeth held up her index finger. "First, there's no way I could save oodles of money because I have zero money coming in. And second, my rent house is not dumpy."

The look of shock and disgust on her mother's face forced JoBeth to burst out laughing. Soon, she and her mother were tumbling over each other on the bed giggling.

"S-seriously? You don't think your place is d-dumpy?" Her mother doubled over.

JoBeth pictured the tiny galley the landlord called a kitchen with its cracked tile countertop, miniscule oven and burners that worked when they wanted to. The cabinets were falling apart at the hinges and she kept a container of Drano near the kitchen sink for the perpetually stopped-up drain. As for the bathroom, the toilet cover was cracked, her ceilings had wads of plaster peeling off and the wood floors squeaked like crazy.

"Okay, okay," she nodded. "The place is a wreck, but it's all mine."

Laughing hysterically, her mother batted the air with her hands and took deep breaths. JoBeth had seen the move time and again over the years.

Eyes watering, she used the hem of her shirt to blot them. "Honey, thanks for the laugh. I needed a good one, especially today."

"Why?" JoBeth studied her mother's face.

A shadow of emotion changed her mother's demeanor.

She reached for her mom's hand. "What's wrong? Tell me."

They sat on the edge of the bed. Silent a moment, her mother shrugged. "The store is in trouble. But I'll bet that's no surprise to you."

Her parents owned the only Christian bookstore in town. Though they'd enjoyed a modest measure of success over the years, certainly enough to put her through college, the business had taken a nosedive over the past five years.

"Again?" The struggle to keep the business from going under was ongoing. But her parents always seemed to find a way to keep the doors open.

"This time is different." Her mother dabbed a sleeve to one eye. "Our financial situation is declining—fast. And I don't think we're going to pull out of it."

"We'll be okay." Her father stood at the door to the bedroom. *How does he always manage to sneak up on us like that?*

A reassuring smile cut across his jaw line. "How's my Petunia?"

"Daddy." She rose and wrapped her arms around his neck, then stepped back for a better look. He'd picked up a tan, probably from helping her move, and it went well with the ice grey in his hair.

"Sorry, I couldn't help hearing. Please let me assure you, things are going to work out. We have an appointment tomorrow afternoon at the bank to talk about some options. Phil Nesbit says we might be able to take out a second mortgage on the house and . . ."

"Another mortgage? No way." Her mother hopped off the bed, eyes blazing.

"Now dear, we've already discussed the possibility. He spoke in a low, calming voice.

"And we decided it was a bad idea, a very bad idea." She stood toe-to-toe with him, hands on her hips. "What kind of inheritance are we going to leave our daughter if we're in debt to the hilt? We should have set up a trust for her. That way, even if we declared bankruptcy, creditors couldn't touch it."

JoBeth backed away to avoid being in the middle of one of their "conversations," the family code word for arguments. He whispered something in her mother's ear, eliciting a nod.

He spoke out loud. "Darling, maybe you and I could discuss this later. After all, our Jo hasn't even finished moving in."

Her mother stole a glance at JoBeth, offering an unconvincing smile. "You're right, dear. How thoughtless of me. We need to welcome our little sweet pea back home, which reminds me, I need to start on dinner." She made an A-OK sign with her fingers. I'm making your favorite, honey bunny."

JoBeth patted her stomach. "What isn't my favorite?"

Her mother wagged her finger. "No negative affirmations."

She wagged her finger back playfully. "Mom, I'm a grown woman, not a sweet pea or a petunia, or a honey bunny anymore. And besides all that, you know I'm on a diet."

"Nonsense, honey—I mean, Jo. We're celebrating your return." She winked. "You can start another diet tomorrow."

Her parents held their arms open beckoning her into a group boa constrictor hug. Her mother kissed the top of JoBeth's head. "You'll always be our little girl."

* * *

Sam MacManus checked his phone and stared at the bible scripture in front of him. Kyle was late, as usual. They'd agreed to meet at a neighborhood coffee shop. His friend wanted to talk about *the breakup*.

Genesis 29: 4-6 "It is well, and behold, Rachel his daughter is coming with the sheep." From the moment Jacob set eyes on her — on Rachel — she'd captivated his heart. Exactly how Sam felt about JoBeth. He closed the cover.

A twinge of guilt nagged at him. *Why am I glad about the split?* He balled his right hand into a fist and released it. He and Jo had dated briefly, happily, until he made the mistake of introducing her to his "best" friend. And that was that. JoBeth dropped him for Kyle.

Kyle and JoBeth had asked his forgiveness. And what else could he do but forgive them? Over time, he and Kyle had worked things out. Although Sam was glad they'd managed to salvage their friendship, remaining friends with Kyle meant he'd have to see them together. A lot.

"Hey man."

Sam looked up. Immersed in his own thoughts, he'd failed to see his friend walk through the door. Kyle reached for his hand and squeezed it.

"Thanks for coming."

Sam watched as Kyle took a seat. "No problem." He gestured to his latte. "Do you want to order something?"

Kyle shook his head. "Naah."

Sam nodded, waiting for his friend to speak.

Kyle pressed his lips together. "Sam, I want you to know — I never meant to hurt her. It's not like I was looking for someone else." He continued. "I mean — Joey — she's a great girl. *You* know that. But one day I ran into Sophie. She was standing by the fountain outside the library, talking to some friends of mine and I went over to say hi, and before I knew it, she and I started talking, and something clicked, you know." He snapped his fingers. "Like that."

"She captivated your heart." Sam stared back.

Kyle leaned forward in his chair and pointed. "Whoa, man — you nailed it."

Sam measured his words with care. "As your friend, part of me is happy for you."

Kyle's forehead tensed. "What about the other part?"

"I'm upset that you would do this to JoBeth."

He hung his head. "I know, but I — I couldn't help it. I'm in love." Longish hair parted to the side, he brushed away a few stray locks. "When you fall in love, you do crazy things."

"Like breakup with your long-time girlfriend for a — "

Kyle's eyes narrowed. "Don't say it, Sam. She used to party a lot, but Sophie's not the same girl. She even said she'd go to church with me this Sunday."

Sam rested his hands on his bible and smiled. "Well, that's a start. Why don't we read some scriptures and pray together? Let's put God in the middle of this situation, eh?"

Kyle grinned. "Sounds good."

* * *

Silver foil squares neatly folded all over her head, hair a mash of highlight and bleach, the stylist had nestled JoBeth under a janky hairdryer to process. For the next twenty minutes, she would be a prisoner under a downdraft of warm, chemically infused air.

Her mother had given her a gift card and sent her to the salon for a makeover, perhaps sensing a downward emotional spiral on the way. After two weeks of ambitious attempts to find another job came up empty, JoBeth had sequestered herself in the house, keeping mostly to her room. Her parents persisted in offering her a job at the bookstore, but she'd refused with the same determined resolve. They could barely scrape up payroll for their existing employees much less add someone new. On the upside however, the chances of getting approval on the second mortgage looked good. The business would survive, for now at least.

Mani. Pedi. Cut and color — the works. JoBeth held her hands up to inspect the manicurist's work. Ombre nail wraps started from the cuticle as deep raspberry and lightened to a hot pink towards the tips. *Pretty.* Besides losing her job and her apartment, the whole breakup with Kyle had weighed heavily on her heart. She'd finally come to the realization that she and Kyle were done. He'd made it abundantly clear he wasn't interested in getting back together. Not with Sophie in the picture.

JoBeth busied herself thumbing through beauty trade magazines, gawking and giggling at all the crazy haircuts. With the hair dryer going full blast, it was hard to hear, but she caught bits and pieces of conversation from people around her. Bored, she leaned to the right, positioning her ear outside the edge of the dryer, and listened.

A client had whipped out her cell phone to show baby pictures to her stylist. "And I'm entering him in a beautiful baby contest. My neighbor told me about it. Truth is, and, I hate to say this, but my boy is so much cuter than all those other babies, especially that little sea monkey she's entering."

Mean. JoBeth shook her head and shifted her body to the left, hoping for a better conversation to listen in on.

" . . . I can't believe she gambled away all that money."

Hmmm, interesting. JoBeth craned her neck to listen.

The stylist paused, comb in hand. "And you said she's the PTA president? You're kidding? She stole all the money you raised?"

The woman nodded. "Every last cent. Do you know how many fundraisers we had? The money was earmarked to buy computers for the kids, and now it's all gone. I heard she lost it at the Blackjack table."

JoBeth was so engrossed in listening she didn't even hear her cell phone ring at first. If the phone hadn't vibrated on her knee, she would likely have missed the call.

The female police officer had to repeat the sentence a couple of times. More like six. And the officer kept mentioning her parents' names.

" . . . drunk driver."

But they're on their way to the bank — the mortgage.

She punched the dryer helmet away and slid from the chair to her knees, screaming. Her cell phone skidded across the floor, shattering as it hit a nearby wall.

A second later, her body was sprawled on the cold, hard floor. And there were people bending over her, faces gawking — mouths moving — and voices, all jumbled together.

She opened her eyes wide and looked up, instantly recognizing the woman who'd bad-mouthed her neighbor's baby. The PTA mom too — only she was on her cell calling the paramedics. JoBeth turned on her side and curled up. Curlicues of snipped hair dotted the salon floor, the last thing she saw before everything went dark.

Chapter Four
Loco Relo

"Those who get too big for their pants will be totally exposed in the end." Author Unknown

"Here's something I'll bet you've never heard of." Rayne's voice shattered the silence with a forced bubbly tone. "If you lick a Jolly Rancher, and stick it to your windshield, and then try to pry it off later it'll crack the glass. I'm not kidding or anything. It's true."

"Really . . ." JoBeth listened to Rayne making small talk and a monotone voice reminiscent of her own, responding. But the words seemed to bounce around her cranium like Monopoly dice.

"So you don't mind if we try it on your windshield later, right?" Rayne glanced over to the passenger seat, a hopeful smile on her face, the square shape of a Jolly Rancher visible inside her cheek. "Jo? Jo?"

JoBeth ventured a smile. Somehow, her friend's dulcet voice pushed past the gloom. Instead of responding to the question however, she stared at the dusty dashboard of her ancient Chevy "Loser Cruiser," packed to the gills with almost all of her worldly possessions — rattling and shifting with every bump and turn.

Moving day.

With the recent, and surprisingly rapid sale of the house, she was officially a nomad again. Her landlord had informed her that the rent house was still trashed and torn apart with a growing list of code violations, repairs, and renovations. He figured she'd be able to move back in about four months. Maybe six. And besides all that, he was trying to blame *her* for the deluge in the basement.

Which brought her back to the day her life began its downturn. The flood.

In the midst of the broken pipes incident, Sam took on hero status. The night of the flood, he'd arrived, waded right into the basement, and called up from the bone-chilling water to tell them he'd located the leak. She and Rayne stood at the top of the steps elbowing one another. The man was totally soaked by then and head-to-toe *gorgeous*, an observation JoBeth shook off at the time with some degree of difficulty.

Later, Sam told her that all the plumbing in the house was circa 1945. He promised to support her if anything went to small claims court. As far as she was concerned, Sam was a decent guy, a lot nicer than his cheating friend.

Jarred from her daydreaming by a bump in the road, JoBeth turned to her friend and put together a shaky smile. "Thanks for driving me and, for packing. For everything."

Her friend's hair, now dyed sleek-black, was braided, piled on top of her head and fastened in place with two colorful chopsticks. "No worries." Rayne shifted an eye towards her. "By the way, I noticed another card from Sam in your mail. Why don't you read it?"

"Really?" *Sam again.* JoBeth looked out the window, her eyes tracking corridors of shifting scenery blurring by. Ever since the breakup, Sam called or asked about her every other day, like he was worried or something. Probably doing damage control for his little friend — always cleaning up after Kyle's mess-ups. "Did you read it? What did he have to say?"

Rayne shifted her bottom on the grass mat seat cover. "Of course. He said something about the singles meetings at your church for a long time, and they were having some kind of hotdog roast-y thing once a month and he wondered if you were going to go to the next one."

"Oh."

"I guess I already know the answer." The Jolly Rancher clicked and clacked on Rayne's teeth as she shifted the candy from cheek to cheek, the tantalizing scent of sugary watermelon infusing the interior of the car.

JoBeth grabbed two out of the bag but had to work hard unwrapping the sticky things. *Was Rayne serious about the windshield thing?*

She cleared her throat. "I went on that interview at the TV station."

Rayne stole a quick glance. "Oh right, I forgot about that. How did it go?"

She shrugged one shoulder. "I dunno. There are probably a gazillion people wanting that assistant producer's position. Besides, I probably bombed it."

"Oh c'mon, be positive. You're just as qualified. Look at all the places you've trained and interned. It would be nice for you to work in a job that has something to do with your major for a change. I've been telling you to get out and apply for other jobs for a long time. This lay-off is probably the best thing that could have happened to you."

"You mean compared to losing my parents?"

Rayne sucked in her breath. "Jo, I didn't mean — I'm sorry. I didn't mean for it to sound how it — sounded."

"I get it." JoBeth nodded, blinking back tears. Instead of giving in to a fresh deluge though, she reached for a bag of pretzel sticks and a jar of Velveeta Cheese dip. What they both needed was a change of subject.

"Vel-veeeeeta. She held up the jar. "How did they come up with that name anyway? Sounds like some kind of exotic cheese from India." She dipped the first of many pretzels into the yellow goo in spite of the candies still in her mouth.

Rayne turned up her nose. "That stuff is total Chem cheese. Not even close to real."

JoBeth smacked her lips. "Chem cheese?"

"Chemicals."

"Um, but it's sooooo good."

Rayne's hands clenched against the steering wheel. "Is your Aunt Ada ready for you?"

With her free hand, JoBeth drummed her fingers on the dashboard. "I guess." In spite of her best efforts to the contrary, she found herself mired in a melancholy state.

Open countryside whirred by, a hypnotic slide show of greens and browns, cows and horses and log fences. Aunt Ada literally lived a bit off the beaten path, *in Beeton*, a small town roughly sixty miles away. Moving from a thriving college town to a small, quiet town with her aunt would be a radical change, but there was no other option at the moment.

Without warning, the car squealed to a sudden halt in the middle of the highway, the smell of burnt rubber more powerful than smelling salts. The seat belt held her in a powerful sling. She glanced at the driver's seat. Rayne — death grip on the steering wheel, was hyperventilating, eyes wide open. A big brown and white moo cow stared back at them through the windshield, unaware of how close it had just come to becoming fast food.

"It's okay. It's okay. It's okay." She patted her friend on the back, hoping to calm her or at least get her own heart beating to a calmer rhythm.

A quick look told her they owned the highway in one direction. One car slowed on the other side of the road to gawk at the situation. However, the cow and her herd of three moved off suddenly, as if on cue. Arms shaking, Rayne drove ahead until she was well past the animals, and pulled to the side of the road.

Her friend puffed her cheeks and blew out a few of what she liked to call "cleansing breaths."

"Wow. We came pretty close." Rayne fought back tears. "I'm so sorry Jo." She let out a nervous titter, a shaky one that passed for a laugh. "We almost had a cow-llision."

Rayne rested her head on the top of the steering wheel. "I think I was starting to doze off a little. You were asleep and I—well—I'm sorry."

"That's okay, my friend. Don't worry about it. And for the record, I wasn't sleeping. I was thinking."

"Thinking about what?" Rayne transformed her traumatized talons into hands with a few shakes.

JoBeth sighed and turned her face to the window.

Her friend stared ahead and started the engine. "Sorry, stupid question."

JoBeth turned to her. "No worries." She paused. "Are you sure you're okay behind the wheel? You're shaking like a compass needle. I could drive."

"No, I'm fine."

She watched her friend check the rear view mirror and take off a little faster than she should have. JoBeth slid an instrumental CD in the player, and Rayne's emotions seemed to even out. The music had a definite calming effect.

Satisfied her friend had returned to a better state, JoBeth turned her attention to the passenger window again. For some people, it might have been hard to pick up a train of thought so violently derailed. But she had no problem doing so. Not with so much to think about. Soon mesmerized by the swirl of scenery whizzing by, her mind turned back to her problems.

Family and friends stood by through the process of funeral arrangements, the viewing and burial. After that, most people stopped calling and checking in on her. She got the distinct impression that they expected her to pick herself up, and go on with life — business as usual.

But she wasn't near ready to hang up her sackcloth and ashes. Rebuilding life after tragedy was like trying to sort things out after a natural disaster like a tsunami or a tornado. Could a life affected by such cataclysmic damage be salvaged? A counselor told her it was possible, but she'd have to rebuild a new life from the ground up. Too bad she couldn't afford to keep her insurance. There would be no more visits.

Rayne had initially invited her to stay at her place, but she was already sharing a small rent house with *three* other people, and *one* bathroom. Plus, her roommates were weird. Guy and girl geeks into cosplay. Grown people playing pretend in full costume — as Middle Earth folk, knights and knaves in medieval battles, or little green men from outer space. Rayne knew her too well — she wouldn't have lasted a week.

Her friend broke the silence. "I think we need to hit some garage sales or resale shops. Don't take this wrong, Jo — but I'm tired of seeing you in the same clothes. I know you haven't been able to replace all the ones you lost in the 'great flood'."

Glad she'd whittled a new mouthful of candies down to more manageable sizes, JoBeth maneuvered the Jolly Ranchers around so she could speak. "I guess."

"Hey, it sure is nice of your aunt to take you in." Rayne glanced over.

JoBeth slurped her candy to the side of her mouth. "Because she *is* nice. She paused to clear her throat. "At the funeral — when Aunt Ada spoke — do you remember how she kept repeating herself?"

Rayne nodded. "Maybe it's because she lives alone. Since your uncle died, I mean. Who knows? Maybe she's forgotten how to act around people, which is why this arrangement will be good for both of you."

"Maybe," JoBeth answered. "Rayne, I'm really, really glad you volunteered to stay the night. I don't know what I would do without you."

Her friend laughed. "It'll be like a like a slumber party, right?"

JoBeth reached for the bag of BBQ potato chips and tore it open. "Right."

Rayne flashed a disapproving look and shook her head when JoBeth offered her the open bag.

"I'm glad we'll get to drive back together too." Rayne sighed. "Maybe saying goodbye won't be so hard."

JoBeth blinked, voice shaky. "Yup."

The business had gone completely bust, and all the books and merchandise were sold at a loss. Her parents had gambled on the store's success, and come up empty. The second mortgage didn't go through, of course. Her parents never made it to the appointment. The bank took possession of the house, and most of the furniture was sold to pay bills, though JoBeth had managed to save a few sentimental pieces.

JoBeth's voice fizzled to a whisper, then climbed to a high note. "Hey, I have an idea. Since you're so tired of looking at me in the same clothes, how about we stop at that thrift store on the way? You know, the Hand-Me-Up Shop on Fifth Street?" She glanced at Rayne.

Her friend's eyes lit up. "I've heard good things about that place. And I've been looking for a big comfy sweater and some leg warmers." Rayne liked nothing better than to peruse through second-hand clothes and goods. Her furniture, kitchen items, in fact, Rayne's entire wardrobe was handpicked from rejected and discarded items. One woman's trash was *her* treasure.

The two slowed and came to a stop at an intersection. The light turned green almost immediately. No traffic to speak of. Blink and you'd be through the whole town.

"The store is two blocks away." Rayne nodded. "You might want to put your shoes on."

"Right." JoBeth scrunched the chip bag closed first, then tried to reach down for her shoes and found she couldn't bend far enough. Her stomach got in the way. *Surprise.* So she fished for them with her feet.

Rayne kept quiet. By the time JoBeth got both of her shoes on, they were pulling into a metered parking spot.

Why did a town this small have a meter? Seriously.

A sigh of relief escaped JoBeth's lips. Glad for the opportunity to postpone the move to Podunk, USA, even for an hour or so, she felt a sense of freedom and calm.

A bell on the top of the shop door made a pleasant tinkle-y sound when they walked in. JoBeth sniffed the air — encountering a top note of musty clothes. Not unusual for a thrift shop. The blotchy beige walls complemented the floor, cracked, greenish Formica common in old institutional-style buildings. The look was somehow familiar, comforting even. Glittery hats, fancy dresses, and costumes lined a back wall. Racks of wrinkly shoes on shelves lined another. Classic.

They separated and started picking through the racks. JoBeth pulled out three tops to try on, a floral explosion with a Coldwater Creek tag, a not-so-gently-used basic burgundy from Banana Republic and a black top with an obnoxious southwestern design, probably a Wal-Mart special.

Rayne met her at the dressing room with an armful of hopefuls for JoBeth to try on. How she managed to grab so many clothes in so little time both intrigued and amazed her. Her friend was a true samurai shopper. The best.

"Thanks." JoBeth smiled and kicked her leg up backwards ooh-la-la style.

"I want to see them on you," Rayne demanded.

"Okay, okay." Sliding the brass shower curtain rings across the bar, JoBeth made sure there were no gaps in the smudged privacy curtain, though there was a slight tear in the middle that disturbed her. Satisfied that no one could see in, she started to undress in front of the full-length mirror, but midway though, thought the better of it and gave it her backside instead. Which turned out to be a bad idea. Staring at her pudgy white thighs in a full-length dressing room mirror with dim lighting? *Ughhhh.*

Of course, department stores were no better. They wrote the book on bad lighting. It was almost like they went out of their way to make women look their worst when they tried on swimsuits or even just regular clothes. And she always had the feeling of being watched in her little dressing cubicle. As if perverse security folk were chillaxing — feet up, dipping Lorna Doones into glasses of milk — making fun of all the women in their dingy bras and torn underwear. *Am I crazy to think that way?*

To her surprise, she could barely squeeze into the first outfit or the second.

And the third? No way.

"Lemme see." Rayne clawed the curtain.

"Not yet. Just a minute." She barked back at her friend, frustrated with struggling. She wiggled backwards, a slight panic creeping up her throat. The headline?

Woman Dies in Resale Shop Changing Room

Trapped in Two Sizes Too Small!

Rayne must have heard the irritation or notes of sheer panic in her voice. She knocked on the wall. "You decent?"

Voice muffled under the clothing, she tried not to lose control. "No." Frantic and swatting her body back and forth against the cubicle walls, she could feel a really big cry coming on. It was obvious what was happening. Size 18's — the usual — didn't fit anymore.

"Open the curtain, Jo. Just a crack, please!"

She reached out, batting the air like a kid swatting at a piñata. The blouse stuck halfway over her head. Caught in an unlikely straitjacket, she swatted and bounced off the dressing room walls. Rayne reached in and handed her another speed stack in her "free" hand, which promptly fell to the floor. After some serious wiggling, JoBeth maneuvered the shirt up and over her head. Relieved, she took in a deep breath and sat down.

Finally able to take a look at the new stack of clothes, she noted the larger size. Skeptical, she wiggled into a pair of jeans. To her surprise, the zipper went up easily, and the button fastened without having to suck in her stomach.

So far, so good.

According to the dingy mirror, the blouse, a small print with a white-collar detail, fit perfectly. *And* was she actually having a good hair day too? JoBeth flounced her hair with both hands, currently free from struggling with clothing for the moment. Her honey blonde highlighted hair must have picked up a few extra sun streaks. Whatever the cause, the girl in the refection looked pretty good, in spite of everything she'd been through.

JoBeth threw open the curtain and stepped out. "What do you think?"

A startled man, face half-conquered with a scruffy grey beard, responded thumbs up. "Hubba Hubba!"

"Uh, thanks." She broke eye contact with the guy, and scanned the room. "Rayne, where are you?"

The bell tinkled. "Here I am." She blew a stray hair out her face. "Sorry, I saw a squad car outside. Figured I'd better feed the meter. Oh, and guess what? You have a broken taillight. You'd better get that fixed." She circled, a look of approval on her face. "Hey, that looks nice on you."

"Sure does." His voice cig-raspy, the man with the beard gave JoBeth the thumbs up again, this time, accompanied by a smile revealing rows of Halloween pumpkin teeth.

Creeper alert.

"Uh, thanks." She pointed to Rayne, then back to the dressing room. "I'm—ah—gonna try a few other things on."

Ducking back into the dressing room, she unzipped her pants but decided to remove her shirt first. So, before she *"dropped trou,"* JoBeth tugged at her shirt. With the shirt halfway over her head, she heard a commotion outside the curtain. She pulled the shirt back down and ripped open the curtain just in time to see Rayne chasing the scruffy bearded man out the store with a rolled up newspaper. The cashier was yelling something at him and into her cell phone simultaneously. The creeper slammed into the doorjamb on his way out, and the tinkle-y bell tinked its last tink as it fell to the floor.

Huffing and puffing, both women looked her way.

"Please tell me he didn't do what I think he just did."

They both nodded.

A thrift shop "peeping tom?" Not exactly the "welcome wagon" she was expecting. And the way things were going her expectations couldn't sink any lower.

Chapter Five
Right As Rayne

"If you can't tell a spoon from a ladle, then you're fat!" — *Demetri Martin*

They pulled into Aunt Ada's dirt and gravel drive, the old Chevy knocking a few times as the sedan's engine shut off.

"I'd better get that checked."

She watched as Rayne bit her lip, not an easy feat with a piercing, and nodded her agreement.

The front door flung open. Aunt Ada stood at the top of the steps dressed in a faded housecoat, red lipstick slathered across her lips, and a cat under each arm. She called out, voice raspy as a cheese grater. "JoBeth. Darling. And is that you, Rayne? Come here and give Aunt Ada some sugar."

As they hugged, she dropped the cats and reached up to pinch JoBeth's cheeks. She smacked a big, wet kiss on each. "You're a good healthy girl, my Jo. I know *you're* eating right. But you," she turned her attention to Rayne, "You're skin and bones. Why, we'll have to tie you down in a high wind."

JoBeth hazarded a glance at her friend. The two of them were in the same state, barely able to contain their giggles.

With that, Ada welcomed them inside. They followed her through the entry and down a long hallway.

"We'll unpack your things later. C'mon in and get a bite to eat."

JoBeth took a first step and almost stumbled over something. "Roscoe?" Her aunt's beloved pug, shambled towards them. Old, cranky and almost blind, he poised between them. Reaching over to pet his head, he answered her attentions with a low growl.

"Roscoe, what are you doing? You know it's me."

His response was to waddle on past, swaying *left/right, left/right* down the steps. He stopped next to the car door, pawed it a couple of times and looked back, with a pitiful little whimper.

Ada laughed. "Roscoe, the girls just got here. They can't take you for a spin right now."

"He likes to ride in the car?" Wide-eyed, Rayne sputtered an amused giggle.

"Oh honey, besides eating and sleeping it's his favorite thing in the whole world. He doesn't get to do it much anymore though." Ada called to him again and though reluctant, he obeyed. The trek back into the house seemed slower, stiffer, as if the dog were acting out his disappointment.

Ada leaned toward her. "He's a little feisty these days, girls. My Roscoe's almost fourteen and he . . ."

Suddenly a strange expression came over her aunt's face. And then it hit *her!* JoBeth got a waft of a putrid stench permeating the air, and instinctively took a step back.

"What is THAT?" Rayne cowered, her nose scrunched into her sleeve.

Ada recovered enough to laugh, her voice high-pitched. "I was just starting to tell you about Roscoe's little problem. He gets gassy after he eats, poor dear. Poor thing's up in years and just about anything he eats these days gets his *widdle* tummy bloated." She reached down to pet her pooch. Roscoe seemed to light up at her touch. It was obvious that "Flatulent Roscoe" only had eyes for one person.

A quick glance over at Rayne revealed the sleeve still covering her nose. Was there a look of doubt or panic on her face? Was the look on JoBeth's face a mirror image of her friend's pained expression?

Once they settled down for lunch in the kitchen, JoBeth started feeling more hopeful. Though the room was a bit of a mess and dusty too, the beauty of the original architecture remained. Bright yellow cabinets with glass peek-a-boos and scalloped detailing on the inner shelves gave the room a cheery look. Sunbeams dappled through cut lace curtains billowing over a large white porcelain sink. The porcelain, marred by a few dark spots where the enamel had chipped away, was otherwise in decent shape. The floor was an old black and white mosaic tile. Totally 1920s, likely the decade the house was built.

But in spite of the cheery atmosphere, she noticed there was some kind of funky smell going on somewhere in the room. JoBeth made a mental note to check it out later. *Much later.*

Her aunt sat across from them at the table, favorite cat in her lap. "Say hello, Petey." The grey-and-black kitty turned his cheek to them, either aloof, disinterested, or both.

In the sun-infused kitchen, JoBeth got a good look at her aunt. Ada's face, powdered to a pale parchment, contrasted sharply with the two perfectly round spots of pink rouge on each cheekbone. Though ten years older than JoBeth's mother, she bore a striking resemblance, arousing bittersweet emotions.

However, the woman at the table was far different from the glamorous aunt she remembered as a child, or even the past year. Her aunt was tired-er, gray-er, and somehow shorter too. She hadn't seen Ada since the funeral. A pang of guilt hit. Her aunt had grown older in such a short time and she hadn't thought twice about visiting her or even calling. Yet the woman was kind and gracious enough to take her wayward niece in at a moment's notice.

At any rate, JoBeth was looking forward to eating. As she suspected they would, the three lunched on canned vegetable soup and grilled Cheez Whiz sandwiches. Not too terrible, that is until JoBeth fished a car hair out of her sandwich. And she couldn't help wondering if Ada had prepared lunch with a cat under one arm.

"Rayne." Ada pushed a plate of chocolate chip cookies toward her friend. "Have some of these, child." She winked. "I have fig cookies too."

"Uh, no thank you, Ada. I . . . "

"Nonsense, you'd better eat up and get some meat on those bones of yours."

Next, she turned to her niece. "Honey, we're having your favorite for dinner tonight—succotash."

JoBeth forced a smile. "Oh, succotash, really? Aunt Ada, you shouldn't have." At the age of nine or ten years, and only in response to her mother's prodding, she'd told her aunt how much she'd enjoyed her succotash—a forced exercise in being polite.

Seriously, who likes lima beans?

Ada rearranged the bluebird salt and pepper shakers on the table. "Oh, no trouble at all."

JoBeth cleared her throat. "Aunt Ada, thank you for letting me stay with you for a while. I don't know what I'd have done if . . ."

"Nonsense, Jo." She reached across the table for her hand. "Of course you can stay here. You're my niece, my only sister's child." She paused. "So tell me how Susan's doing. She must be busy. I haven't heard from her lately."

JoBeth drew in a breath, heart revving. "Huh?"

But the blank expression in her aunt's eyes told a different story.

Confused, she looked over at Rayne who seemed just as perplexed, then back at Ada. "Don't you remember? I mean, don't you remember what happened?"

"What do you mean?" her aunt asked.

"Well, Mom and Dad were, were in an accident. Don't you remember?"

"An accident?" She stood up. "Are they all right? What hospital are they in? I've got to go to her."

"They're not in any hospital, Aunt Ada." JoBeth shook her head, tears welling. "They—they passed away. There was a funeral. You attended the memorial service."

"What? Oh no, no, no. My little sister—dead?" Ada buried her face in her hands, sobbing. "Not my Susan. She's so young. It can't be. It just can't be."

JoBeth rushed over and wrapped her arms around her aunt, surprised at her fragile state. Hugging her brought back memories and tears. The pain of losing both parents in one day, the day she'd stopped believing.

But holding and comforting her aunt seemed to help stave off her own emotions. Suddenly her grief didn't seem so important. Maybe Rayne was right. The truth was now painfully apparent. She needed Aunt Ada's help, but her aunt needed *her* help even more.

Chapter Six
The Clean Plate Club

"An optimist is a person who starts a new diet on Thanksgiving Day." — Irv Kupcinet

One minute, Ada was crying uncontrollably and the next she was back to normal, whatever normal was. She'd forgotten all about what she'd heard mere seconds ago, a blessing to her aunt, but a shock to JoBeth and Rayne.

Before they could process what happened, the sound of thunder shook the windows. They left Ada playing solitaire in the kitchen, and scooted outside to unpack the car. The sky looked downright menacing, an evil-looking chocolate parfait towering above.

JoBeth turned her face to the clouds and teased, "I smell Rayne in the air."

Rayne stuck her tongue out. But as she did, thunder rolled across the sky. "Those clouds are going to let go any minute. Hurry up."

JoBeth rushed forward and grabbed an armload of her new thrift shop clothes on wire hangers. The hangers tangled in with the other stuff packed in the car though, and she had to jiggle and coax the mess around to free them. As she pulled, tears began to stream down her face.

Rayne rested a hand on her shoulder.

"Why did she react that way?" JoBeth squinted out a fresh rush of tears. "What's wrong with her?"

Her friend winced. "Could be old age, possibly Dementia. Or . . . "

"Or what?"

She bit her lip. "Maybe Alzheimer's."

Ada called from the porch, "You girls'd better hurry and get inside. I prayed for rain this morning and God always answers my prayers. So you'd better come in. Sugar melts, you know." She winked and disappeared back indoors.

Rayne offered a playful wink. "Should we hurry? Sugar melts . . ."

JoBeth grimaced. "No worries here." How could her aunt suddenly remember what she said this morning, but not remember her own sister and brother-in-law's passing? Lightning suddenly stabbed through the clouds. The bright flash startled them to action.

They finished the first of three hauls into the house before the first drops fell. JoBeth had put most of her furniture in the cheapest storage facility she could find. And due to the money situation, there was no chance of keeping it in storage for longer than six months. The storage unit was paid up for that long, anyway. If the situation didn't change soon, she would be having a very big garage sale somewhere. Maybe out on the sidewalk, her future residence.

But she'd brought a few small pieces to Ada's for a touch of home. Somehow they'd squeezed and eased them into the car. Getting the pieces out was a little trickier though, like playing Pickup Sticks with large objects. But they managed it.

While it poured outside, she and Rayne cleared out the guest room closet and chest of drawers, moving an odd assortment of items to another bedroom. Then they unpacked the suitcases, rearranged the furniture and made the bed. And just like that, even before Ada rang the dinner bell, JoBeth was settled into the faded robin's-egg-blue guestroom she would share with her aunt's creepy doll collection.

Not that she didn't like dolls. Distinct memories flooded back of her admiration for Ada's collection as a child. And her aunt had definitely added on many more over the years, of all kinds.

The dolls, once pampered and treasured, were now wallowing in neglect—merely dusty, cobwebby shadows of the bright polished faces and glimmering agate eyes she remembered. The bisque profiles lined a double row of shelves around the high-ceilinged room. Composition dolls too. Ada used to tell her the dolls that came after World War I were made of glue mixed with sawdust, but they lasted a lot longer than the porcelain ones from Germany. At the time, of course, she was just a girl; a girl who liked dolls and didn't care much about what an adult told her they were made of.

JoBeth knew these were special though, complete with mohair wigs, gold slippers, painted-on eyelashes and brows, dressed in jumpers or dotted organdy dresses, even wedding gowns in tiered skirts and embossed crepe. Pink cheeks and red lips, pink cheeks and rosebud lips. Blue eyes. Green eyes, gray, violet, brown, black.

There were Kewpie dolls, American Girl dolls, and genuine Hiawatha dolls with shoes made of oilcloth and wearing flannel, fringed gowns and headbands. American Indian dolls dressed in authentic hide with beaded headdresses, shiny braids and tiny woven baskets. Baby dolls of every size and shape in various stages of dress or undress. Rag dolls in cute kitschy outfits, Holly Hobby dolls, and iconic "Barbies" galore, some vintage ones too. She even spotted a "Midge" doll with the trademark freckles. She remembered adding more onto her doll with a pencil. *Because you can't have too many freckles.*

There were Cabbage Patch Kids. *Ugh.* And a shopping network collection of Madame Alexander dolls in ornate historical dress too. A shame, a crying shame to see them so dusty and neglected. A fit of coughing interrupted her thoughts. *Speaking of dust.*

While the rain pinged off the roof, JoBeth tried to open her bedroom window, but the pane stuck to the frame like glue. The glass, partially opaque with years of dirt, would need a good cleaning. She yanked upwards a couple of times before Rayne joined her, adding her muscles to the task. The sash shot upward. JoBeth immediately brought her face up close to the screen and breathed deeply between the fluttering cobwebs. She squeezed her eyes shut. "Ahhh."

Rayne touched her shoulder. "You look like you're about to pray or something."

JoBeth opened her eyes and stared at crystal raindrops trampolining off the gloss of dark green magnolia leaves. "Naah."

"Well, maybe you should. I-I sort of liked when you used to pray. Even though you could be obnoxious at times, you were happier when you did."

Shrugging off her friend's comment, JoBeth asked, "So what do you think about this place?"

Rayne frowned. "You can't avoid the subject forever, Jo." She started towards the bedroom door. "I'm going to go straighten out all the stuff we transferred to the closet in the other bedroom. Be back in a little bit."

"Okay." She turned back to the fresh vista outside her window and sniffed the air. The distinct odor of ozone lingered in the atmosphere. A smell akin to bumper car sparks. Curiously alluring.

Then something odd caught her attention; a fat, yellow-and-black caterpillar outside the glass. Nestled in the top left corner of the window frame, the insect was slowly spinning a silky thread around itself, forming a chrysalis.

She whispered. "I wish I could do that." JoBeth drew closer. "Daddy used to tell me that believers who died are like you guys. Wrapped in a shroud for a time—until Jesus resurrects us. And then we fly away. Like beautiful butterflies . . ."

* * *

Sam struggled to loosen a rusted joint on a pipe. Head and half his body under a sink, he used his sleeve to swipe at beads of perspiration on his brow.

"How's it coming?"

He stopped what he was doing and eased his head partway out from the kitchen cabinet. Sophie Perkins, Kyle's new girlfriend, leaned against the counter staring down at him. Clad in a low-cut blouse and short denim skirt, she blocked what little light there was in her stark kitchen.

"Good."

Hit by the overwhelming scent of perfume, he squeezed his eyes shut for a moment. His allergies were sure to kick in if the woman hung around his workspace much longer.

She flipped back a swatch of silky hair. "Is there anything I can do to help?"

Leave? "Not really."

"Are you sure?" She flashed an inviting smile.

"Well, there is one thing."

She leaned forward.

"You could reach in my tool bag and hand me that flashlight." He pointed with the wrench in his hand.

"Oh . . ." The smile turned into a pout. Regardless of her obvious disappointment, she found the flashlight and handed it to him. But instead of releasing her grip on it, she held on.

Seriously? What kind of game was she playing?

"I just want to thank you, Sam. For coming here on such short notice, I mean."

"No problem." He rubbed his nose, suddenly fighting the feeling that he had to sneeze. *Did the woman dump an entire bottle of perfume on herself?*

She released her grip on the flashlight and he turned it on. Flashing straight into her face for a moment. "Sorry."

He slid backward to his former position near the pipe and coiled the flexible flashlight to shine on the joint. Aware that her eyes were on him, he felt an acute sense of discomfort. He wondered what Kyle saw in the woman. Flighty and flirtatious, she seemed to thrive on attention, especially from males. Her provocative attempts to secure his attention proved how shallow and self-absorbed she was.

Though he felt bad about the breakup, he was hopeful that JoBeth might one day consider going out with him. Her friend seemed to think so. He'd run into her several times. Though Rayne was a different sort of woman, she had a remarkably level head on her shoulders.

"So, did you know her well?"

"Who?" He calibrated the wrench to fit then gave it a half-turn. *No give at all.* He took a different tack, tightening instead for a quarter-turn, then loosening the opposite way, which worked.

"His old girlfriend."

Voice straining as he untightened the joint, he replied, "Her name is JoBeth."

"That's right. So what's she like?"

He stopped what he was doing. "Why do you want to know? Maybe you should ask Kyle."

She stomped her flip-flop on the kitchen floor. "I have, but he never wants to talk about her."

Good for him. "If Kyle doesn't want to talk about her, then maybe you should let things be. After all, you're the one he's dating now."

"But my friends are dying to know."

He pulled off the joint, set it aside and began to install the new one. *Easy as pie from this point on.* "Dying to know what?"

"Why he dated her."

A sick feeling rose in the pit of his stomach. Where was she going with these questions? He slid out from under the sink. "Why wouldn't he?"

She began to giggle. "Because she's so humongous. We're like night and day. No one can believe a hottie like Kyle would even give a fat-a-potamis like that a second look."

He put the wrench down and pulled himself to a sitting position on the floor. "Sophie." Sam glared. "Would you do me another favor?"

Voice breathy and seductive, she answered. "Anything."

"Would you mind leaving me alone while I work?"

* * *

A hand bell clanged from the front of the house, a sound that brought a smile to her lips and joy to her heart. The sound of the big silver bell clanging reminded her of home. Ada and JoBeth's mother shared an affinity for dinner bells.

Hard to believe I used to be annoyed by that clanking sound.

Rayne darted back into the room, pushing past her, extended both arms out the screen less window. She closed her eyes and took in an extended breath.

JoBeth watched Rayne heave in air. "What's going on? Are you okay?"

Rayne whispered. "Mothballs. Now that you're living here you won't have to worry about moths eating your thrift store finds. This place reeks. The chemicals are making me sick. I'm glad you opened the window."

Voice lowered to a respectful whisper, JoBeth responded. "I agree. Tomorrow is Mothballgeddon! We'll search and destroy every mothball we can get our hands on."

"Hmmmph, that won't be easy. There's probably a gazillion of them in this house."

"You girls ready for dinner?"

They jumped at the sound of Ada's voice. Accompanied by Petey on her shoulder like a living mink stole, and Roscoe, slow as an old crocodile, she pointed towards the window and smiled. "God did that for me, you know."

JoBeth tried to hug her but Petey hissed a warning. "We know, Auntie."

"C'mon girls," she beckoned.

The two followed Ada into the kitchen. But the first thing her aunt did was spoon cat food into a dish for Petey and Zoomba. Then she set out a special dish on top of a couple of old books for Roscoe so he didn't have to dip his head so low to eat. "Here you go, Sweetie, it's your favorite." She spooned some discolored glop into the dish.

"What's that?" JoBeth asked.

"It's Roscoe's favorite — leftover burritos." She smiled. "Here you go, darling. Chow time."

Roscoe obliged, digging into the chopped-up, cold burritos with more enthusiasm than she thought he had left in him.

She cleared her throat. "Well, he certainly seems to like Mexican food. But I have to tell you Auntie, that's probably why he has such a problem with excess gas."

"Gas? What are you talking about? Is there a gas leak?" She sniffed the air, fear in her eyes.

Rayne reached for her arm. "No Ada, there's no gas leak. Everything's fine. Your niece was just talking about Roscoe's little problem."

Ada cocked her head backwards and laughed. "Oh, *hehe.*" As if she'd forgotten the whole incident, she reached down to pull up her knee-hi stockings, the tops visible from the hem of her housecoat.

They grabbed some plates out the cabinet began a search for paper napkins and silverware.

"No need for any of that, girls. We're all set up on TV trays in the living room. That's where your Uncle Fritz and I always ate. Every night for supper, we'd settle down in front of the Tube and watch our shows together. We used to eat Swanson TV dinners back then, every Friday night."

They followed her into a small room in the front of the house with maple-hued paneling, framed needlepoint art, and a multi-colored rag rug. An ancient TV set in a carved wooden cabinet was the focal point. By the thick layer of dust on the surface, JoBeth guessed that particular set hadn't worked in years.

Her aunt continued, "Sometimes we'd play Crazy 8's or Rummikubs." A slight tremor in her hand, she held it up to her heart. "I was better at Rummikubs."

On the right wall was a shrine to her only son. Every picture of Seth, from the moment he opened his eyes was framed, pasted, tacked or taped directly onto the paneling. But on the left wall was a different cluster of framed photographs—JoBeth's parents, a stern-faced Uncle Fritz, and shots of a very plump little girl.

She gulped. There were more. Of course there were more. Pictures of JoBeth—as an overweight teen, with blotchy zits, graduating from college, and JoBeth with one of the worst haircuts of her life standing beside Kyle. The *piece de resistance*? An 8 x 10 of a larger-than-life JoBeth. Not even one of her skinny pics though. Not a one.

She noticed Rayne stifle a laugh.

The "working set" was on top of the old TV cabinet, a clunky thing with a dirty doily on top. In front of the sofa and an easy chair were three trays set with paper towels torn in half, Ada's answer to napkins, vintage silverware, and colorful Fiesta ware plates piled high with bright green succotash, a concoction of corn, lima beans, butter, milk, and a sprinkling of nutmeg. Informal, 50's-style dining at its best. JoBeth raised her fork warily.

"Wait, dear. We've got to thank our Father first." Ada folded her hands in front of her. "Dear Lord, thank you for this meal set before us . . ." She hesitated a moment.

"Ada?" Rayne asked. "Are you okay?"

"Where was I?" A confused look surfaced on her face.

"You were saying a prayer." Rayne reassured.

"Oh that's right. I was saying Grace." Ada heaved what sounded to JoBeth like a sigh of relief. "And thank you for my darling niece JoBeth coming to live here and keep this old woman company. And for her sweet friend Rayne that she will ask You into her heart one of these days — in Jesus' name. Amen."

JoBeth held her breath and looked at Rayne, wondering what her friend would say. But Rayne, a professed agnostic, just smiled back at Ada. JoBeth and Rayne had parried back and forth on the issue of salvation for years, and come to a truce of sorts. And that truce was an easier solution in the present circumstance.

Ada took a bite and flicked on the TV. No ordinary clicker, the giant-sized keys were set to her favorite home and retro channels. She liked to hop back and forth between shows. Along with home makeovers, the three watched old episodes of Gunsmoke and Gilligan's Island as they dug into succotash, which at some point during the day had probably been warm.

Just like the glass of milk next to each plate had probably once been cold. The milk was warm and tasted sour, the kind of sour that made JoBeth suspect it was way past the expiration date. And surprise, surprise, another cat hair turned up.

She looked up at the ceiling, concocting an excuse to duck out to the kitchen and dump the cat-hair-infused plate into the garbage. *Cough. Cough.* JoBeth grabbed at her neck. "Feels like something's stuck in my throat."

"Are you okay?" Rayne's eyes widened.

Ada put down her fork. "Dear, are you all right?"

Waving the napkin, JoBeth stood and in the finest rasp she could muster, reassured them, "I'm okay. Gonna get some water." She jumped up singing yahoos in her head and sprinted to the kitchen. Relief flooded over her. A temporary escape at best, she decided that living in the moment worked just fine.

Listening for footsteps from the other room, she was relieved the neither woman had come after her. She opened the pantry door for a peek. The floor-to-ceiling shelves were packed with food, but she could see from the dingy packaging that most of it had been there for a very long time.

Shocked, she picked up a box of cereal and read the expiration date. Two years ago? And a can of green beans with an expiration date five years ago? She shook her head in disbelief.

The outside lid on the vegetable bin, stained with some kind of black gunk did not bode well, but JoBeth lifted it anyway. Rotting potatoes and onions in a sea of rotty black juice. *Ugh.* Likely the weird smell she'd detected earlier.

It seemed she would be on the Ada diet plan for now, probably the only plan that had a shot at success. In the meantime, her stomach was already doing some thrill ride twists and turns. There was absolutely nothing in Ada's pantry or Icebox that excited JoBeth's taste buds in the least. She would make a trip to the grocery store in the morning, but with limited funds, food- shopping-sprees were going to be few and far between.

She mouthed the words. *I need a job crazy bad.* Without one, she would certainly waste away around the waist.

Back in front of the TV tray with a glass of water, she watched her aunt clean her plate first, with Rayne not far behind. Of course it was expected, even predictable that Rayne would eat the succotash. She was a Vegan after all, but JoBeth was willing to bet her friend didn't enjoy it cold. Vegans have taste buds too. All the same, she was impressed.

"Somebody didn't join the clean plate club." Ada gawked at JoBeth's plate, a disapproving look on her face.

Oh no. She looked down at her plate, the corn and lima beans now in a state of rigor mortis. In the haste to escape, she'd forgotten to bring the "suffering succotash" to the kitchen where she could have buried it — at the bottom of the garbage can.

"It turns out that I'm not all that hungry after all." Her stomach growled loudly in response. *Traitor.*

"Looks like your old auntie's going to have to feed you." Ada got up, pulled a chair close to JoBeth's and sat down.

"Oh no," JoBeth cringed.

Horrified, she looked to Rayne. Her friend's arms crossed, Rayne leaned back, a wide smile on her face. There would be no cavalry to the rescue. Her friend was planning to enjoy every moment of this.

A slight tremble in Ada's hand, she lifted the first forkful to JoBeth's mouth. "O-o-open the barn door."

Chapter Seven
A Job For JoBeth

"If you're happy, you eat. If you're sad, you eat. You lose a job — you eat. You get a job — you eat. It's, you know — it's addiction." —
Barbara Cook

Bright and early the next morning, JoBeth set out to do two things — find a job and go grocery shopping. Not necessarily in that order. Blame it on the mothballs or the cat hair, but Rayne found she had suffered some sort of an allergic reaction and took some strong meds before she went to bed. The slumber party they'd planned was a bust.

And JoBeth's attempt at sleep had been restless as well. She went to bed hungry and feeling sort of "succotash sick-y," soon realizing she wasn't really sick, just hungry. In the middle of the night, she'd remembered the snack-attack bag in the car and tiptoed in slippers to fetch it. Not an easy task. Almost all the floorboards in the house squeaked. But once back in her room, she had her own personal pork-rinds-and-pixie-sticks party, just the ticket to lull her gurgling stomach to sleep.

But sleep eluded her afterwards. Maybe it had something to do with the unholy army of porcelain dolls on the shelves above, or Petey and Zoomba, who decided to be inquisitive in the middle of the night.

There's nothing more conducive to a good night's sleep than a couple of cats suddenly pouncing on your chest.

To top it off, the unpleasant scent of mothballs and wisps of cat hair floating in the air, as well as the monster dust bunnies under the bed, made her eyes water — so much so, that when she woke up the next morning, they were red, runny and itchy.

Convinced that she and her friend were suffering from mothball poisoning, JoBeth was also certain that the methane polluting the indoor air — compliments of Roscoe — was a major contributor to their misery as well. Whatever the cause, she found Rayne sitting on the porch swing in the early light — the bags under her eyes, a sad testimony. Her friend looked miserable.

Her voice nasal-y, Rayne asked. "So, the job search begins. Tell me about Beeton. All I know is that it's a miniscule town in the great state of Texas."

"Miniscule is a good word." JoBeth pursed her lips. "Beeton is so small, GPS is all in lower case. But seriously — there's lots of farmland, farm animals, and farm folk. Plain sense. No nonsense types. And besides the resale shop and its resident pervert, there's a little factory or two, and some small storefronts, a grocery, and clinic, as well as a few places to eat. And there's a dinky little town square some mayor built. Oh, and you can thank that same ambitious mayor for the useless parking meters too. But that's about it."

Honestly, we didn't hang out much in town. Our family had dinner at Aunt Ada's house when we visited. The grown-ups talked and played board games and my cousin Seth and I used to play out in the yard. But he was a strange ranger from the get-go."

"How so?" she asked.

"He followed all the rules, *all the time*. I couldn't convince him to throw a stick sideways. Talk about boring."

She cocked her head. "That doesn't sound normal."

"Maybe it was because he used to bruise so easily. I heard Aunt Ada talking to my mom one time about how they thought he might be anemic. Seth bruised like a Georgia peach. I guess he's okay now though. The last few times I saw him, he didn't look bruise-y or anything."

Rayne stuck the corner of a tissue in her runny nostril. "What about your uncle? You hardly ever mention him."

JoBeth smiled. "Sometimes I forget that you and I met in college. I feel like I've known you all my life and you already know everything about me."

Her friend laughed. "The more I think I know you, I don't."

"Well FYI — I didn't like Uncle Fritz. He was the stern type. I stayed out of his path."

She grimaced. "No wonder your cousin wasn't any fun." She checked the time on her phone. "We'd better get going. Times-a-wasting, 'Lula June'."

"Very funny." JoBeth stuck her tongue out.

Rayne headed to the kitchen to make coffee and JoBeth returned to her room. She closed the door behind her and leaned against it, heart pounding. *What am I doing here?*

The little twin bed, the hooked rug on the floor, dusty dolls lining the shelves — all shouted failure. But spiraling into an emotional miasma right now wasn't an option. She raised a fist in the air, like Scarlett O'Hara, having an epiphany with a radish.

No matter what I have to do to survive, I'm doing it. Whether I have to fill potholes in the street, manage a janky Laundromat, or groom dogs for a living, I'll do it. Whatever it takes.

With new resolve, she shimmied out of her pajamas and put on the resale jeans. A freebie t-shirt from a burger joint and her hair clumped into a loose ponytail completed the look. The mission of the day — to find a job, buy food and cleaning supplies, return to Ada's house and get to work scrubbing the place from top to bottom. There were years of neglect to catch up on.

After coffee and a bowl of cereal, they said goodbye to her aunt and headed out. JoBeth floored the car through standing water pooled near the curb. Thankful for the morning sunshine, she nudged Rayne who looked up from filing her nails.

"You okay?" JoBeth asked.

"I think you're aunt's place is Krypton to allergy meds."

"No—besides that. What's up?" JoBeth pressed. "I can always tell when there's something on your mind."

Rayne made a face. "Besides wondering how you and your aunt are going to live in her toxic hovel, or how I'm even going to manage visiting you, I'm thinking we need to find a good geriatric doctor for Ada, ASAP."

JoBeth took a deep breath. "Wow, you're full of ideas early in the morning, aren't you? I agree, but I'm not bringing my aunt to a doctor here in *Hickshire*. I want to take her to the big medical center back in Abilene."

Rayne pointed the nail file towards JoBeth. "There's a woman I know, a friend of one of my roommates who's a radiologist at the hospital. I'll ask if she knows someone good."

"Thanks." JoBeth gunned the engine and took off for Main Street, only a couple of blocks away.

Rayne looked down at her nails, a slight smile on her face. "Look, I'm your *best* friend. And if you don't snap out of this woe-is-me gloom soon, I might be your only friend. I know it's one more problem in a long line of recent problems, but we have to talk more about your aunt's condition."

In answer to that comment, JoBeth swerved a hard right. Rayne's nail file flew out of her hands.

As she bent down to pick the file off the floorboard, Rayne spoke. "Nice driving. But it'll take more than that to shut me up. Your aunt needs proper medical care and I don't think she should live alone anymore."

"Okay," JoBeth replied. "Sorry."

"And what about your cousin? Where's he?"

JoBeth settled deeper into her seat cushion. "The sheet metal manufacturing plant he inherited is here in Beeton, but Cousin Seth lives in Houston. He has people running the plant and he takes care of the sales end of the business there. Mom was always upset that he didn't visit Ada much."

"Is he married? Does he have a family or something?"

"Oh look." She screeched to a halt in the middle of Main Street. "Look." JoBeth pointed to a '*S-e-c-e-t-a-r-y* Wanted' sign in a law office window. "Write down that number for me, will you?"

Rayne scrunched her nose. "It's misspelled. Do you really want to work in a law office where they can't spell such a basic word?" She snapped her fingers. "Hey, maybe Kyle posted that sign for them. He's certainly qualified."

"Rayne, humor me, okay? I need a job. Besides, it's obvious they don't have high standards, which gives *me* higher odds of success."

With a disapproving sigh, her friend scribbled the number down on the flipside of a silver gum wrapper she fished off the floorboard. JoBeth veered back onto the road.

"And Seth's single, by the way. Not much of a conversationalist, though."

Her friend squinted. "And not very nice to his mother either," Rayne added. "How old is he anyway?"

She shrugged. "About five years older than us."

Rayne whistled. "No offense, but he sounds like a loser, or maybe a bruiser. Even a mama's boy would be better."

"Watch it now. That's my cousin you're dissing," JoBeth cautioned. "Besides, why does something have to be wrong with him? Maybe he just hasn't met the right woman."

"You said it yourself. He's a strange ranger."

"And boring, but people can change, can't they?"

Rayne's right brow lifted, a *bona fide* Spock skill. "He doesn't visit his mother. There's no evidence of change. You can forget about fixing me up with that loser. I'm setting my sights higher these days, and so should you. Of course, *you* might be ahead of me on that."

JoBeth did a double take. "What do you mean?"

"Sam, maybe."

JoBeth tightened her grip on the steering wheel. "I'm not interested in anyone right now. My boyfriend dumped me a hot minute ago. Remember? My heart's all tattered and torn."

Rayne folded her arms. "I know you need time. But you should give him a chance. He's, he's a good guy. If anyone knows that, you do. Sam's the kind of guy you really want."

"And how do you know what I really want?"

She shrugged. "Because I'm your best friend. That's why."

Spotting another help wanted sign nestled in a café window, JoBeth screeched to another sudden stop at the curb. "Write that one down too, will ya?"

Wide-eyed, Rayne dutifully wrote the number and handed it over. "Now I know you're desperate."

JoBeth smooshed her lips together. "Yup, I am — totally desperate. That's me." The more she stared at the door to the Last Chance Café, the more a mustard seed of courage started growing inside. Maybe the sign *was* a sign. On a whim, she opened the car door and dashed out. Maybe dash wasn't the right word. She walked as fast as her legs could carry her, which wasn't very fast at all. Rayne followed at a noticeably slower, reluctant pace.

A little bell tinkled when she opened the light blue door, paint distressed from frequent use, she hoped. *And what was with all the bells on the doors in this town?* The ten people inside looked up from their food and conversation when the two walked in. Three of the men wore bib overalls, never a good fashion choice — big men who gave them a corner-of-the-eye once over. The rest were women, backcombed beauties with big hair and blue eye shadow.

The waitress, an older gal with crispy, permed hair gave them a judgmental scan before she smiled. "Have yourself a seat girls." She could tell by the woman's expression that Rayne's gold lip ring was going to go over big in town.

"Actually, Kit," she read the nametag, flashing a hopeful smile. "My name is JoBeth Tomlin. I'm Ada Davidson's niece living with her here in Beeton now, and I'm here to apply for the job advertised in the window."

A nervous glance to the other customers and back to JoBeth spoke volumes. "Well, ain't that sweet. I'd be happy to take your application honey, and we'll fer shore git back to you real soon."

Suddenly, the swinging doors to the kitchen opened a crack, and a keyhole view of a face peeked out. Dark eyes blinked a couple times before a male voice bellowed. "Tell her she's hired." With that said, the swinging doors danced shut.

The same could not be said for JoBeth's mouth.

And the crispy-haired waitress's eyes were wide as muffin tins. She held up an index finger. "Why don't you young ladies have a seat in that booth over there? I'll be right back." Her lips clamped together as she stormed into the kitchen.

Beyond the swinging door JoBeth and Rayne, and the rest of the customers heard a one-sided argument fomenting. Kit was apparently arguing with herself.

Rayne leaned over to whisper. "Reminds me of that Hitchcock movie you like, *Psycho*. There's probably no one back there. No one alive, that is . . . "

They giggled together until Rayne grasped JoBeth's wrist. "This is a tragic choice for a job. You know that, right?"

JoBeth shook her head. "No way. People in my situation can't be picky. Don't rain on my parade, Rayne. I have a job. I followed my whim and here I am — gainfully employed."

"Are you kidding me? That not-so-hot mess of a waitress already hates you and you have been here a total of five minutes."

"But the mystery man in the kitchen does. At least, I hope someone with a voice that deep is a man. Besides, has it occurred to you that maybe God wants me to work here for some reason? Otherwise getting the job wouldn't have been so easy."

She whistled. "Wow, are you suddenly okay with your God again?"

JoBeth decided not to answer. Actually, she wasn't sure how.

The door swung open and Kit, her knees stiff as corn stalks, walked to the booth, white leather waitress shoes squeaking all the way. The dour expression on her face was hard to read.

"Well, young lady." Kit eyed her with undisguised disgust. "Looks like the owner see's some *poe-tent-shul* in you. You're hired." She plopped some paperwork down in front of her. "Fill these out."

"When do I start?"

"Tomorrow." She turned on her squeaky shoes and walked off to help the other customers.

"That went well." Rayne snickered.

The trip back to Ada's house seemed shorter, even though they made a trip to the town grocery store along the way. Maybe attitude had something to do with it. Gleeful. *The* word for the way she felt. They unloaded about ten bags of "celebration groceries" and cleaning supplies in the kitchen. With the promise of a job, she'd spent more than originally intended. *Splurge* was the word for her reckless shopping spree. The two started emptying the bags and looking for places to put everything.

"My, my girls, I see you've been to the market."

"Auntie." JoBeth twirled her around in a playful dance. "I have good news to share. I'm celebrating. I got a job."

Ada clapped her hands together. "Really? Oh that's wonderful dear. Where at?"

Rayne pulled out a can of peaches and box of Little Debbies. "At the Last Chance Café."

Ada's face lit up for a moment, and dimmed as fast. "Really? I think I know somebody there."

An expectant silence fell between them. But her aunt said nothing.

JoBeth cleared her throat. "Um, Auntie, who is it you know?"

"Who?"

"At the Last Chance Café."

"Oh . . ." Her eyes roamed to an ancient calendar on the wall. "I'm not supposed to talk about that. Fritz wouldn't like it at all."

JoBeth could feel a furrow developing between her brows. "Why not?"

A wistful smile came over her face. "Because of Grizzwald."

A smile bowed across Rayne's face. She crept forward till she was close to Ada. "Who's that?" JoBeth held her breath.

Ada giggled, her cheeks blushing crimson. "The Last Chance Café is his place. He always dreamed of having his own diner. We used to date when he was a soda fountain jerk. My, my, that was a long time ago." She smiled, her expression soft and dreamy. "He was so handsome."

JoBeth swallowed hard. The owner, the deep-voiced mysterious man in the kitchen went by the name of Grizzwald? A man Aunt Ada used to date?

Questions chirped around in her head. *Was she ever in love with this man?*

Rayne spoke what JoBeth was thinking. "Something's cooking in that kitchen besides greasy comfort food."

Whatever the case, she and the new boss would soon meet.

JoBeth let out a sigh and held out an open palm towards her friend. "Rayne, where did you hide those Little Debbies?"

Chapter Eight
Housework Is Evil And Must Be Stopped

I've decided that perhaps I'm bulimic and just keep forgetting to purge." — Paula Poundstone

Sam rinsed his face in the sink and dried it off with a small towel. He stared at his reflection in the bathroom mirror. *Why would she want anything to do with you now? You were weighed in the balance and found wanting . . .*

He wiped down the mirror and the sink, and threw the towel in a hamper. Then he picked up his toolbox and headed to the living room. "The tub is good as new."

Pastor Yau, s short, fit man in his early thirties, looked up from his laptop. "It's unstopped? Already?"

Sam smiled. "I told you the clog wasn't that serious."

"How much do I owe you?"

Sam shook his head. "Nothing."

"But I have to pay you."

Sam smiled. "Consider this visit my welcome gift to our new pastor."

Pastor Yau stared back, a surprised expression on his face. "Then, I must confess, I feel *quite* at home now." He stood and shook Sam's free hand. "Thank you, Sam. You've been more than kind to my family for the four months we've been here."

"It's an honor, Pas—"

"Please call me George."

"George. Well, it's an honor and a pleasure to help you."

The pastor gathered up some papers next to the computer and sat down. "I was going to let you know in a couple of days, but since you're here, I'll tell you now."

"What's this about?" Mystified, Sam lowered his toolbox to the floor.

"I've submitted my recommendation to the church board. I want you to be our new assistant singles pastor. Now, it's strictly a volunteer, part-time position for the first few weeks, but I hope to be able to offer you a part-time position with a salary as soon as I get approval. If you're interested, that is. And I'm not sure about how you feel about a career change, but a full-time position could open up in the near future."

Sam rubbed his hands across his cheeks. "Me?"

"Yes, you." Pastor Yau's eyes danced. "Granted, I haven't known you for very long. But I consider myself a good judge of character. You've shown yourself to be an able and caring volunteer in the singles ministry." He flipped over a paper. "I checked up on you, and asked around too. You have a couple of years of seminary training. You've served faithfully for over three years, and have a sterling reputation. I'm looking for someone who has a heart for young people: someone who isn't there for the title, or the money, or the status. And that's you, Sam."

Pastor Yau extended his hand. Tentative at first, Sam's hand clasped his, and the two men shook on it.

Seated back in his work van, Sam turned on the ignition and rested his forehead on the steering wheel. Though he'd gone into the plumbing industry out of necessity, his heart had always been in ministry. He'd dropped out of Bible College after his father was injured and couldn't go back to work. Somebody had to pay the bills. He brushed a few tears away and looked up. "Thank you, Lord."

* * *

Though they pressed Ada to answer more questions about "Grizzwald," she either evaded them or had completely forgotten what they were talking about. And soon her aunt began to yawn. Apparently, they'd interrupted her normal naptime, so JoBeth and Rayne put off pressing Ada for answers. Before long, Ada quietly shuffled off to her bedroom.

JoBeth and Rayne spread out the cleaning supplies like a weapons arsenal on the kitchen table. Locked and loaded, they set to work cleaning, scrubbing, dusting and mopping.

JoBeth thought all the "ings" were covered until they decided to tackle the fridge. The few times JoBeth had opened the refrigerator door previously, she'd detected a super funky smell. She'd already discovered the source of the foul odor in the pantry, but was apprehensive about what was lurking in the fridge.

A testament to neglect, the refrigerator was filled with an assortment of expired foods — a veritable Petri dish of food poisoning and fermentation. There were at least a couple dozen tiny dollops of food saved in twisted, fig-shaped sections of plastic wrap. Apparently, Aunt Ada never wasted a thing, even if there were only two bites or a spoonful of something left on her plate.

JoBeth closed the fridge and thought of poor Roscoe eating month-old burritos. Speaking her thoughts aloud she commented, "It's a wonder that old dog lived this many years."

"What?" Rayne blew hair out her face as she looked up from a vigorous attempt at scrubbing the kitchen floor.

JoBeth coughed. "I was thinking about all the expired, rotted food in Ada's fridge and wondered whether she was eating expired stuff and feeding it to the animals too."

Rayne scrunched up her nose. "Duh."

Another look in the interior of the fridge and a hesitant sniff was all it took. "Rayne, call me a procrastinator, but I just made an executive decision. We're going to tackle the fridge last."

Sweat beading her forehead, Rayne glanced up and nodded.

Since JoBeth was slated to re-enter the working world tomorrow, there would be precious little time for deep cleaning. She resolved to get as much done as possible.

Dust bunnies proliferated throughout the house. The doll collection in her room was connected with a vast network of spider webs, barely tackled by dishtowel-covered brooms. JoBeth was certain that colonies of various and perhaps as-yet-undiscovered species of insects lived in and among the poor neglected dollies.

A proper cleaning would involve taking them all off the shelves and attending to each doll individually, which would have been an excellent excuse to get them out of the room. The dolls would have to wait for another day, though. There was too much to do and too little time to do it.

Eliminating the mothballs turned out to be sort of fun, like a twisted, toxic Easter Egg Hunt. Bound and determined to get rid of every one of the smelly balls of chemical doom, neither of them was prepared for the volume. There were so, so many. They counted over five hundred before calling it quits. Of course, that tally didn't include Ada's room, which was off limits while she was sleeping.

And the bathrooms, the bathrooms . . .

What they really needed to clean them properly was a small nuclear device. Instead, detergent, cleansing powder, bleach and lavender-scented cleaner would have to do.

After they finished scouring the first bathroom, they tackled the second, but the room left them puzzled. The toilet looked like it hadn't been used in years. The lid was closed and there were faded magazines stacked on it, topped by what looked like a feather boa of cat hair. Did Petey or Zoomba nap there regularly? And the old claw bathtub had been transformed into a library of magazines and paperback books. Thankfully, both tub and toilet still worked.

"Rayne," JoBeth asked, a grimace contorting her face, "Have I ever told you how much I hate cleaning toilets? It's really my least favorite job out of all the household chores."

Her friend attempted a weak smile. Even her lips looked tired.

Rayne threw down her cleaning rag and struggled to her feet. "There's one last thing to do before Ada wakes up. Let's finish up with the fridge, Jo. After that, you've got to drive me home so I can shower and get my tired body into bed so I'll have an iota of creative energy left for work tomorrow."

They had agreed to finish by four so Rayne could get back to her place at a decent hour. Rayne's job was light years more interesting than waiting on tables in a cheesy diner. She did graphic design for a small ad agency. The money wasn't great, but the job provided her friend with great experience and exposure. People liked her work and she'd won some awards for it too. Though the same age, her friend had managed to distinguish herself in her career—something JoBeth had failed to do thus far.

Of course, Rayne was doing something she loved and JoBeth had settled for a job at Newhouse Shipping to pay the bills. And tomorrow, she'd be waiting tables at the Last Chance Café, yet another instance of taking any old job to keep the lights on and food on the table. Maybe she'd get a call back on the assistant producer's job she'd applied for. Maybe. She blinked back tears.

Still in a crouching position next to the toilet, JoBeth paused, knees bent. "Just give me a sec, okay? I keep trying to think about what that *sicknasty* smell in the fridge could be."

Rayne yawned. "You won't find out just sitting there. C'mon." She picked up her cleaning cloth and snapped it. "I'm going in."

JoBeth rose to her feet, knees creaking in the process. "All the same, I wish we had HazMat suits."

Familiar, yet foreboding, the fingerprint-stained fridge door held secrets. Armed with all-purpose cleaner, window spray, baking soda, and spray bleach, they were determined to search and destroy. Whatever fortitude this job was going to take, they were bound and determined to get it done. Rayne opened the door and sure enough, the nostril-pummeling smell knocked them backwards for an instant.

JoBeth held up a gargantuan black plastic garbage bag and the two began reading expiration dates, looking for bulging cans, green blooms on cheeses and other foods, and using their noses to test for the stench factor. If it was hairy with fungus or mold or any other form of hair especially cat hair, they tossed it. Most of what they did was intuitive, utilizing the gag reflex, which turned out to be a great decision-making tool.

They decided to take a short break from the fridge and open the freezer instead. The top-loading freezer was easy. Mostly everything had serious freezer burn and had to be tossed. The food, covered in such a layer of permafrost, made JoBeth 99.9% certain she'd find wooly mammoth bones at some point in the extraction process.

But after that short foray, they turned their attention back to the fridge. Now deeper in, they discovered juicier, more decayed items. Soon, the main part of the fridge was empty — twist-tied into big black garbage bags deposited at the curb for garbage pickup. What could be salvaged was salvaged and what had to be thrown away was pitched.

But there were a few items they put to the side, waiting to be explored — the ancient Tupperware bowl for instance. JoBeth guessed it must have once been pink. Now, a sallow salmon hue, the container was stained and scratched. After she popped the lid and a whiff of what looked like fermented cabbage hit, she slammed the top back on and threw the whole thing away. Next, a container of what looked like leftover lasagna, pockmarked with black slimy spots. And after that, Rayne found something that raised a lump in her throat, another salmon-hued Tupperware container.

"You don't think . . ."

"I don't know," She gulped down the acid she felt coming up.

A pop of the lid revealed, of all things — succotash, only with a green film on top.

JoBeth dropped the jar of five-year-old pickles in her hand and ran out the back door hollering. Rayne joined her, yellow plastic gloves ripped off, bare hands now covering her mouth. JoBeth thought of Edvard Munch's "The Scream," and wondered if a moment similar to this one might have been the artist's muse. Rayne did look kind of like the woman in the painting, with the exception of her big yellow rubber gloves.

After her friend arched over a few times, and there was nothing left in her stomach, she began to dry heave.

"Girls? What's going on?" Ada came down the back steps wiping her eyes. "Sorry, I guess I'm no good before my morning coffee."

Did Ada really have no sense of time?

"Oh Auntie, you're up from your nap." JoBeth rose and took her by the arm, then looked back at her gagging friend. "Let's go back in the house. Rayne's just feeling a little under the weather. Isn't that right?

Rayne, her face pale, eyes glazed over, tried to smile like everything was okee dokee.

"We're going to give her a minute to get herself together." A quick wink at her friend was all she could offer in the way of comfort.

She led Ada back inside the kitchen, then down the hall to the TV room. A flick of the clicker and her favorite retro station was on. "You relax and I'll go make you a nice cup of tea, okay?"

"Really? That would be lovely." Ada sniffed. "The house smells so clean. You girls tidied up for me? You didn't have to do that." She planted a kiss on JoBeth's cheek. "Thanks anyway."

JoBeth started to leave the room, but snapped her fingers when a thought hit her. "Auntie, could you tell me where your teapot is?"

"Oh dear, I don't know where I put it. But hold on a minute." She disappeared down the hall and came back holding something blue. "I found you a teapot. Isn't it cute? I don't know why, but it was in the bathroom. Isn't that a funny place for a teapot?" She brought her hands together and smiled as The Lucy Show caught her attention.

"Thanks, Auntie." JoBeth bit her lip. "I'll be right back." But Ada was instantly immersed in TV land.

Back in the kitchen, lips still pressed together in a vise, JoBeth burst out laughing. She put on a pot of water in a freshly scrubbed saucepan instead, took a good look at the "teapot" her aunt had given her — Rayne's Netti pot. Her friend used the contraption to cleanse her nasal passages, which is why the "teapot" was in the bathroom. JoBeth couldn't stop snickering.

She threw a whole packet of tiny link maple-syrup-infused sausages into a grill pan and broke eggs into another pan greased with liberal pats of butter. When the eggs were done, she cut away the whites and deposited them into Roscoe's dish. As far as JoBeth was concerned, whites were the throwaway part of the egg. Then she plated the eggs with the sausages, yellow yolk melting into the maple syrupy goodness of fried sausage syrup and grease. *Pure decadence.*

Back in TV land, Ada had no problem opening the barn door and JoBeth's stomach, definitely on empty, was growling for grub.

Rayne on the other hand, ate zilch, retreating instead to her bedroom with a cold washcloth across her forehead. Her friend was still so green around the gills she didn't have the heart to tell her about the Netti pot incident. That would have been downright cruel.

After dinner, with Rayne with Ada watching Gunsmoke, JoBeth slipped back into the kitchen, washed the dishes and turned her attention back to the fridge.

Holding her breath, she dumped the last of the gunky, mucky foods into the trash bag. Then the veggie bin caught her eye. There was something ominous looking about it. She knew in her "knower" that the veggie bin would be her true nemesis — a vision quest — the source of a stench so foul it would knock a buzzard off a bag of rotten kielbasa.

With one fluid movement, JoBeth pulled open the vegetable drawer. *Maggots.*

Chapter Nine
Suffering Succotash

"If life gives you a lemon, make lemonade. However — if life gives you a pickle, you might as well give up, because pickle-ade is disgusting." — Clifton J. Gray

At first, they were silent on the trip back. JoBeth surmised it was either because the two of them were too exhausted to say anything, or overwhelmed by the sheer grossness of the day. But there was an unspoken agreement between them to avoid waking Roscoe.

Note about Roscoe. He wouldn't take no for an answer anymore when it came to riding in cars. Sure, they got away with it a couple of times, but the wily canine would not let the opportunity to cruise in a car pass him by again. The old dog bolted into the vehicle as soon as the door opened, and bared his teeth at all attempts to remove him. Besides, picking up the old gassy dog was like playing a bagpipe. Not an option.

Ada was right about the pooch — he loved him a car ride. Ada hadn't driven her old Grand Marquis in quite some time. The tires were completely flat. Her neighbors and friends drove her to church on Sundays and to the store when she needed to go. At least that's what she'd told them.

JoBeth was glad to be the one who cleaned out the infamous veggie drawer and bleached it. Rayne was in no condition to help. She would have yakked all over the kitchen. *And the succotash…*the stuff was totally rancid. It's a wonder all three of them didn't get food poisoning.

JoBeth took a bite of dill pickle and dipped the chomped end into a plastic cup filled with orange Tang powder.

Rayne turned her head at the sight. "How can you eat that stuff?"

"Easy. It's tangy. Get it?"

"Ugh."

She chomped down the rest of the pickle in a few calculated bites, and licked the sweet orange flavor off her fingertips. "All the years I've known you and I had no idea you had such a delicate stomach."

Still looking kind of pale, Rayne waved a weak hand her way, "Please, don't talk about it."

"Okay, okay. No worries." JoBeth opened a bag of red licorice and stuck a few strings of it out of the corner of her mouth to nibble while driving without taking her hands off the wheel. She held up a can of diet soda and dipped a strand of licorice inside, using it as a straw. *Clever — no?*

Sweaty, tired, hair messy, clothes wrinkled, spotted and stained from cleaning, the two of them smelled *and looked* heinous. But it wasn't like they were on their way to a beauty pageant or anything.

She stole a glance toward Roscoe on the floor in the back seat. Earlier, she'd noticed patches of grey on his coat and a few wilder grey ones sticking out his ears like an old man. Fast asleep and burrowed deep into one of Ada's old plaid picnic blankets, his tail was curved into a charming parenthesis. But his tail was all she could see. Roscoe seemed to be a happy camper. Course it was hard to tell with the pug. His expressions were pretty much the same, awake or asleep.

The sound of a siren startled them. Unnerved, she swerved right, then to the left and screeched to an abrupt halt on the shoulder. Heart thumping, the words tumbled out. "Oh no. What did I do? What do I do?"

Right behind them, a cop on a cycle waved her over to the curb.

"Calm down, Jo." Rayne, now animated, ordered. It's probably that broken taillight I told you about. Now I guess you'll really have to get that fixed."

Hands shaking, she fished through her wallet for her driver's license and insurance card. "Maybe I can sweet talk him. Hope I can. Or I could use the cry card. Men hate seeing women cry."

"WHAT'S THAT SMELL?" Rayne covered her nose and mouth with her sleeve and gagged.

"Aggghhh." JoBeth clawed at the air, half blind, eyes mere slits.

A knock on the driver's side window interrupted. JoBeth squinted at Rayne, desperate.

Her answer, though muffled, resonated urgency. "Roscoe must have . . . " She coughed. "Quick, open the window before we get thrown in jail."

"For what? Bad smells?" JoBeth hit the electronic window button and even before it was down all the way the policeman took a step back.

And if she had been standing instead of sitting, JoBeth would have taken a step back as well. The trooper was super. Gorgelicious. She could have lost herself in those blue eyes. But how could she even let a thought like that cross her mind at a time like this? Kyle's electronic games were still in the rent house. Well, used to be, anyway. Now, they were in storage along with her common sense.

"Driver's license, insurance card and regist — whoa!" He jerked his head, as if trying to shake off the sour expression on his face. "What's that?" He waved his leather-gloved hand back and forth.

     This had to be one of the worst moments of her life, the kind of moment most people dread, hoping the scenario will never ever happen, especially in the presence of a really cute guy. JoBeth always took great care to avoid situations like this. For instance, she never ate corn or spinach in public because, sure enough, corn and spinach would somehow adhere to every nook and cranny in her teeth. Problem solved. And in school, she avoided drinking too many beverages in between classes so she wouldn't have to get up and go in the middle of a lecture. But how could she have ever imagined that a flatulent pug in the back seat would so thoroughly embarrass her in the presence of such a dreamy guy?

     Nervous, JoBeth handed the officer her license and insurance card. She began talking fast, accentuating every word with crazy hand movements. "It's Roscoe. You see, he has this-this problem and it's really, really bad only we didn't know how bad until just this moment and we're really sorry."

     "Roscoe?" His eyes moved to the empty back seat.

     By that time, Roscoe had burrowed deep inside the blanket and slept through it all like he was in a coma.

     "All I see are you two." He looked at her license. JoBeth Tomlin and . . . "

     "Rayne Caraway," her friend finished, removing her sleeve from her nose just long enough to speak.

     He tried to speak, but instead covered his mouth and nose with a kerchief hastily pulled from his pocket and coughed.

     Rayne leaned her head forward so he could see her better. "It really is him. I mean, Roscoe. My friend is telling the truth. Roscoe's responsible for the terrible odor in here."

     Rayne always has my back.

     His eyes lit up like he'd suddenly caught on. "Ohhhhh, I see."

     The friends shared a look of relief.

     Good, he gets it.

He did an air quote with his fingers. "'Roscoe 'ate too many tacos or burritos' today, didn't she—I mean he?"

Horrified, her lips started moving but nothing came out. The policeman thought— WHAT? Could anything be more disturbing? "Noooo. No, let me explain this to you, Officer."

He held up a hand and smiled. "No need." He shook his head. "I—ah, come across this sort of thing more than you think. Don't be ashamed. It's a natural .·. ." He coughed, locking eyes with JoBeth. "Bodily function."

"But."

He handed the license and insurance cards back. "Just thought you should know you have a broken taillight on the passenger rear."

'Officer, I . . . "

He backed up and put his pen and pad away. "Now, I'm gonna let you off with just a warning this time, Miss Tomlin, but if I see you with a broken taillight and stop you again, I'm going to have to give you a ticket for sure." He touched his right hand to his chest like he was making a solemn pledge. "And believe me, I'd sure hate to have to pull *you girls* over again. But I will if I have to and let me say it one more time—I sure hope I don't have to."

JoBeth started to speak, but he interrupted. The officer held up his black leather-gloved hands. "Don't thank me. I'm just doing my job." He started to walk off, but paused and pivoted. "Oh and, word of advice ..." He grimaced. "If I were you, I'd leave the windows down for a while." With that he mounted the motorcycle kicked it to life and zoomed past their car, a big grin on his face.

They turned to one another at the same exact moment. "He thinks we?"

"I know."

"How could he?"

They lifted their faces, voices calling out in unison. "Roscoe!"

Just when she thought things couldn't get any worse, her cell phone vibrated. JoBeth glanced at the caller and pressed her lips together. "It's Sam."

"Aren't you going to answer it?" Rayne squinted. "Well?"

Though reluctant, JoBeth did.

"How are you, Jo? I thought I'd call and check on you."

"Hi Sam. I'm tired from cleaning my aunt's house all day."

"Sounds like a big job."

She laughed. "It was—a monumental task." The snap decision not to tell Sam about the new job fed directly into her pride. How could she admit to the people who knew her back in town, that she'd taken a job as a waitress in a greasy diner?

"Yeah, I'm pretty tired. Plus I'm driving right now."

"Oh—okay. Well, don't wear yourself out too much. Before I let you go, I wanted to ask you something. I don't know if Rayne mentioned this to you, but I was wondering if you would like to come to town for the singles hot dog roast. It's going to be fun. We do it every month, you know."

"Sorry Sam, I don't think so. Not this time. I have a lot going on."

"Are you sure? Because I could come and get you if that's an issue."

Come and get me? Are you kidding?

"No, no, that's not it. I'm just not ready to go to one of those things yet."

"Well, that's okay. We'll miss you. Maybe next time." His voice betrayed more than a hint of disappointment.

"Yeah, maybe." She raised her voice to a happier notch. "Thanks for the invite, anywho."

"No problem."

"Bye, Sam."

"You take care, bye."

"Why were you so rude?" Rayne's disapproval seemed to be all the 'perk' left in her friend after an unbelievably eventful day.

"Rude? I wasn't rude."

"Yes, you were."

JoBeth stared straight ahead at the road. "Okay, maybe I was a little less friendly than I could have been."

"Why?"

She looked over at the passenger seat. "Because he's interested in me."

Rayne tilted her head. "And that's a bad thing because?"

"I dated his best friend. Why would he be interested in dating someone that dated his friend? That's just weird, don't you think?"

"Wait, wait, wait. Technically, you dated Sam first and Kyle stole you from him."

She laughed. "You don't know what you're talking about."

Rayne nodded. "Oh yes, I do. I was there. You dated Sam first and you two really connected. But when you saw Kyle that was it. You went for the shallow end of the gene pool."

She hated to admit it, but her friend was right. Sam was a nice guy, and certainly good-looking, but Kyle took her breath away.

"Who knows?" Rayne lifted a hand. "Even though you broke his heart, maybe Sam never stopped loving you all these years."

JoBeth frowned. "That's crazy. Why would he?"

Rayne bent her knees on the car seat and wrapped her arms around her shoulders. "There's no logic to love. That's why people *fall* in love. There's no control in a fall. It just happens."

She stared from the road to her friend, then back to the road. "Are you kidding me? You think he still has feelings?"

Rayne nodded. "Yes, I do."

JoBeth dug her nails into the steering wheel. "Rayne, you're such a romantic. It's never going to happen. I couldn't care less how he feels about me."

Rayne turned her face to the passenger window. "Suit yourself."

She dropped Rayne off and as soon as they said their goodbyes, JoBeth drove through a few fast food windows to keep her tummy happy. The return trip might have been uneventful from that point on, but JoBeth kept looking over her shoulder, expecting to hear police sirens. Though happy she got away earlier without a ticket she couldn't afford, the fear of being pulled over again was ever-present. Unfortunately, Roscoe wasn't done with his diabolical doggie deeds. There were more "episodes" along the way. Per Officer Hunky's advice, she drove with the windows down. On the flip side, Roscoe was happy. At least somebody was.

A sinking feeling in her heart kept reminding her of the finality of it all. She would never go back to her family home for dinners or holidays or celebrations. Never again ask her mother for advice or cry onto her shoulder. And her father — her father would never walk her down the aisle if by some miracle she were to ever get married. Tears flowed from her eyes like open spigots, so much so that she found it hard to see the road.

Chapter Ten
Strange Dreams

"Forget love — I'd rather fall in chocolate." — Theophile Gautier

Aunt Ada was already in bed snoring when she returned. Good thing she'd thought to ask her for a key before leaving. She wiped her face against her sleeves, wishing she had windshield wipers for her eyes.

JoBeth fed the kitties first, then filled Roscoe's dish with some dry doggie food, a special food she'd purchased for senior dogs with sensitive stomachs, and topped off his water bowl. He looked up at her for a moment before burying his face in the food. Gratitude perhaps?

"Roscoe, you can thank me by having a healthy digestive system. Good night, boy." She stroked his back, turned out the kitchen light and made her way to the bathroom. When she turned on the light, she paused to take in the fresh smell of bleach, scouring powder and lemon cleaner. A good soak in a clean tub was exactly what she needed.

And oh how the tub sparkled! She filled it with hot water and soothing lavender bath salts — another grocery store purchase.

Stretched out in the deep claw-footed tub, JoBeth stole at glance at her semi-submerged body. Her thighs were gigantic, and her stomach — ugh. The way it poked out made her look huge. Blubborous. Bloaty. She frowned. And there was a definite food baby thing going on.

Time to get her mind on something else. Anything else. All she could find to read was an old Farmer's Almanac somehow left behind when they'd emptied the tub. She did an exploratory leafing through it. Not bad — lots of interesting facts the average person would never care to know, but enough to keep her occupied while her skin pruned.

She checked the headlines. "Hmmm. Dirt cures a winter cough . . .For a headache try leeches on your forehead or cow dung with molasses on your temples" Hah.

She read on. "When your name is called, don't answer the first time-it may be the devil calling you . . .Whatever you do, don't let a lizard count your teeth." *No problem.*

As she was about to slap the book closed, she noticed a banner headline, "How to Find the Perfect Mate," and couldn't resist taking a look at what the almanac farm folk had to say about the subject. After all, it was obvious she needed all the help she could get in that area.

"Walk around the block with your mouth full of water; if you don't swallow it, you will marry within the year." *Right.*

"Pick an apple, prick it full of holes, carry it for a while under your left arm, then give it to your lover." Seriously?

She closed the book and set it on a little wicker stool by the tub.

JoBeth took a deep breath and closed her eyes. An overwhelming silence, a silence louder than all the other sounds she was used to hearing. That's when it hit her. Aunt Ada's house was set way back from the street, her nearest neighbors two lots away. The absence of city sounds would take some getting used to.

JoBeth put on her favorite flannel jammies, the buttons now busting at the closures. Size eighteen no more. She put on the matching slippers and padded straight to the kitchen. It was definitely time for a midnight snack — a reward for a hard day's work.

Banana-Fana-Fo-Fana! She peeled a banana, removed the foil from a handful of Hershey's Kisses, and patiently studded the "nanner" with them. Next, she poured chocolate sauce over the whole thing, rolled the banana in chopped nuts, and then sprayed ripples of whipped cream on top. JoBeth finished the masterpiece off with a maraschino cherry. So yummy and delicious, she had two.

Satisfied, satiated, or both, JoBeth turned off the kitchen light, made her way back to her room and slid between the sheets. She let out a big yawn and did a bear stretch. This was the time she used to say her prayers. Used to pour her heart out to God before she turned out the lights.

She reached over to set the alarm for 4:00 am, and clicked off the lamp. Though she couldn't be sure, it was likely she was out as soon as her head hit the pillow. Sometime, soon after that, she began to dream.

Walking, or was she floating? JoBeth found herself on a cloud or a mist steadily drawing her to a clearing. Little scurrying sounds from all sides pricked at her ears. Sounds like the scuffles and squeaks of rodents. She shuddered.

A small shape emerged, but remained partially in the shadows of the deep green foliage. "JoBeth. JoBeth-h-h-h-h." Other shadowy shapes came into view, their voices joining the one. "JoBeth. JoBeth. JoBeth."

One by one they stepped forward into the light. Dolls. Perfect porcelain faces. Eyelids flicking open, flicking shut. Blue eyes. Green eyes. Violet eyes.

"W-what do you want?" JoBeth took a defensive posture, arms out in front, hands up. Then for some inexplicable reason, she did a Karate Kid praying mantis move. Like she would be some kind of threat to a herd of demon dolls!

Of course the alternative thought, that a herd of dangerous dollies had her trapped in some fourth dimension was just too weird to consider.

Note to self: stop watching creepy movies.

"What do you want?" Frightened and angry, she thrashed her arms in front of her. "Go away. Leave me alone."

"Come with us, JoBeth Tomlin."

A doll with glossy brown pigtails stepped forward. "We have something to show you. Follow us."

JoBeth shouted. "How do you know my name? I'm not going anywhere with you—you Bride of Chucky."

The piggy-tail dolly shook her index finger at her. "Don't be afraid."

"This is some kind of sick joke." JoBeth yanked at her own hair in an attempt to wake up.

Note to self: Stop eating junk food late at night.

The dolly motioned with her little arm. "Follow me."

Now in normal life, JoBeth would never have followed that hellacious thing anywhere. When she watched scary movies she was always the one who yelled out, "Why would you go down those dark stairs to the basement? Are you out of your mind following those ghostly footsteps? Why would you explore a haunted castle?" But since she was dreaming, she had no control over actions that called for common sense.

Cautious, JoBeth followed the doll, poised in praying mantis stance. She continued to follow the dolly down a twisted path until they came to a larger clearing. In the center was a huge, frilly, pink, four-poster doll bed piled high with a mountain of popular junk foods.

But the pile of food opened its mouth. "Waaaah."

A baby?

In the dream she jumped back ten feet. No way she could have done that in real life. A body of sorts, its parts made up of donuts and Little Debbie's, big glossy pretzels, French fries and onion rings, burgers, shakes, cookies, chips, Hot Pockets, Italian Cream Cake, Brownies, ice cream, M&Ms, Sno-Caps, Fruit roll-ups, Cheese puffs, and dozens of other delicious foods and candies JoBeth had desired and devoured over the years.

She summoned up the courage to address the thing. "Who are you?"

"Waaaah. Waaaah." It opened its mouth to cry, revealing a whole mouthful of perfect pointy rows of candy corn teeth—like some kind of high fructose corn syrup-drinking kind of vampire.

"What do you think it is?" the dolly asked.

JoBeth wagged her head. "I don't know. And I'm not sure I want to know."

That's when the little piggy-tail dolly stepped in closer and leaned in. "Don't you recognize her?"

JoBeth backed up. "No I don't. Why should I? It's a truckload of talking groceries. Look at it. Hair made of cotton candy, face a buttermilk pancake, fingers—actual candy bars."

"She's your food baby."

"My what?"

"Your food baby." The other dollies stepped out of the shadows and stood next to the piggy-tail dolly. High-pitched baby doll voices, repeated the maniacal mantra. "She's your food baby. She's your food baby. Your food baby—your food baby—your food baby."

JoBeth bolted upright and screamed, chest heaving.

"Child, what's wrong? Are you all right, dear?" Aunt Ada leaned over her. The elderly woman must have heard her crying out in her sleep, and her mother's instinct kicked in. She rested a hand on JoBeth's temple. "You're all clammy."

She thought of the—the thing she'd seen in her dream—the image forever burned into her psyche. How could she even try to explain something that weird to anyone?

Ada circled her arms round, nestling JoBeth's head to her shoulder.

JoBeth murmured. "I guess I just had a bad dream. A very bad dream." Her eyes focused upward to the shelves. Thankful the dolls were still there, spider webs and all.

Ada stroked JoBeth's hair. "Don't you worry, child. It'll be all right in the morning. This is what I used to tell my Sethie. Remember, when you wake up from a nightmare, it's already over."

She eased backwards and Ada began to tuck in the covers. "Now go back to sleep, honey. Everything's okay." Ada kissed her forehead and smiled. "Good night." She paused. "And sweet dreams." She flicked off the light.

JoBeth listened to the gentle pad of her aunt's footsteps before opening the nightstand drawer. Still rattled by the demon doll dream, she needed something tangible to help her cope. S.O.S. Snackage.

Chapter Eleven
Whine Not

"The only time to eat diet food is while you're waiting for the steak to cook." — Julia Child

JoBeth woke to the sound of finches chirping in the soft light of early morning. The first thing she did when she rolled out of bed was look at the floor. After the first midnight jaunt to the car, she'd decided to keep snacks handy for emergencies. And the nightstand was the perfect place to store those goodies. And last night after the bad dream, she'd let the wrappers fall with abandon.

She reached down, picked up all the cupcake and candy wrappers, and chip bags and tossed them in the trash. Reluctantly, she forced a glance up at the dolls. Piled on the shelves in the same pattern of neglect, the spider webs and dust still in place, she relaxed and took a deep breath. Nothing more than a dream, only a silly dream.

The next thing she did was check out the caterpillar's chrysalis on the window. Yesterday, the chrysalis was white, but this morning it seemed the color had turned a darker, grayish shade — but other than that, no change.

Fresh from a shower and a waffle-and-whipped-cream breakfast, she pulled the Loser Cruiser into a parking spot near the Last Chance. The great thing about owning a beat-up car was the ability to park anywhere without worry or concern. Another dent? So what? A scratch? Big deal.

Was there a uniform she was supposed to wear? A glance down at her simple white shirt and pants made her wonder. Kit wore a pale yellow outfit yesterday, a classic waitress uniform. JoBeth tried to picture herself wearing one too. But she decided the all white theme she had going on was pretty cool too.

Four forty-five on the nose, a full fifteen minutes early. She was sure to make a good impression. Maybe Kit would grow to like her too. She was sort of nervous about meeting her boss.

Her cell vibrated. "Rayne?"

"Morning. Hey, just wanted to send positive feelings your way this morning."

"Aw, I appreciate that. You been doing *yogurt*?'

Her friend laughed. "Yeah, and I meditated some positive thoughts your way. The universe is going to send you good things. You'll see."

JoBeth laughed. "Rayne, if I had time, you and I would have a nice little discussion about this spooky kooky stuff."

"I know." Her voice calm, relaxed, "centered" as Rayne called it. "You have a problem integrating other modes of thought into your concept of God, though even by your own admission you've lost touch with what you thought you believed."

JoBeth drew the phone away from her ear. If ears could taste, what her friend said would have left a very bad taste indeed. "Okay, that's enough for now. I've got too much going on. What with demon dolls in my dreams and the food baby, and my elderly aunt having some kind of forbidden love affair, and me starting a new job working for the man side-by-side with a woman who already hates me, I can't handle any more."

Once outside the door to the Last Chance, she ended the conversation. "Gotta go. I'm here. Talk to you later."

"Okay." Rayne's voice sounded a little too calm, the way a counselor's voice sounds when a client utters something a little too over-the-top. Or maybe her friend was just plain disappointed. She was always trying to show her spiritual side, and how much more "advanced" her idea of religion was. Like she was competing, or something. But Rayne was right about her. A familiar twang of guilt began to resonate from deep within.

"You're going to have to tell me more about all you've been going through lately, especially the part about the demon dolls. Sounds intriguing."

"Later. Promise." JoBeth clicked the phone shut and reached for the door handle.

The bell announced her arrival. "Hello, helloooooo? Anybody here?" Her words broadcast to empty booths. She surveyed the room. Empty. She walked to the restrooms, "Helloooooo?" She opened the door to the ladies room. Empty. Then, after an awkward moment, decided not to open the door to the men's room. She put her ear to the door. *Nothing.*

The door to a big storeroom was unlocked. She stepped inside. "Hello? It's me, JoBeth Tomlin, Ada's niece." But her voice fell flat. The walls of the stockroom were lined neatly with mega-sized canisters of pickles, mayo and mustard and ketchup and such, the kind of foods one would expect in a diner. Her eyes settled on the canisters of pickles, imagining the crispy, slippery vinegary crunch. She swung the door shut and covered her face with her hands. *Be strong.*

She placed the papers Kit gave her to fill out on the counter by the register. There was one more room to check out, the kitchen. The first thing she saw when she walked in, besides all the usual stainless steel counters and tile and pots and pans, commercial stovetop and griddle etc. was the door to the freezer — wide open. When she looked closer, she noticed the backside of a very large person bent over a box, dragging it out. Suddenly, a man with a head the size of a Bison turned and looked at her. In spite of the cigar stub in his mouth, he spoke a legible sentence.

"Well girl, what are you doing standing there? I could use some help."

She imagined her mouth formed a perfect circle, like a pie bird. But she overcame the initial shock fast. "Okay, yes. Of course." She forced her body forward and stepped beside him at the open edge of the freezer. Together they began to drag a few boxes out. One contained frozen hash browns, the other, meat patties.

When they were done dragging, she stood straight and so did he. They looked at each other in the eye. Huffing and puffing, she pointed to her chest. "I'm JoBeth."

He pulled the cigar out of his mouth and pointed to his chest. "Me Tarzan."

She laughed. "Good one."

"Big Grizz."

He held the smoking, smelly brown cigar in between his thumb and forefinger. His fingers were wide as hotdogs. Between that anomaly and the bison head, it was no wonder they called him Big Grizz. *I'll bet Ada and his mother are the only two people who ever called him Grizzwald.*

"I know who you are." He waved his hand. "You're Ada's niece. Saw you through the porthole in the kitchen door." He smiled, revealing tobacco-stained teeth.

"How did you know what I looked . . .?"

He interrupted before she could finish. "I heard you mention her name. She and I — we go way back."

He must have noticed from her expression that she still didn't understand.

"You're Ada's niece. That's all the reference I need." He took a short puff on his cigar.

"So, Big Grizz?"

"All day every day." He wiped the sweat over his mouth on his sleeve.

"Is that really why you hired me? Because I'm Ada's niece?"

Grizz blinked. "Yup." He brought the cigar up to take another puff. "Did she, uh, mention me?"

Before she could answer, a shout echoed through the kitchen.

"Grizz!" Kit strode into the room, a dynamo in a yellow uniform.

"Furious" wouldn't have done her mood justice. She grabbed the cigar out of his hand and mashed it into a nearby sink. "You know better than that. Honestly, you know you're not supposed to smoke that thing in here. Not to mention your health. You know what the doctor said."

"All right. All right." He waved her off. "Don't get your liver in a quiver."

"Good Morning, Kit." JoBeth smiled her brightest, hoping to make a better impression.

The woman scowled. "You'd better get your uniform on. Folks'll be arriving here any minute." Kit pointed at Grizz. "And you had better get cooking." She handed him an apron. "Put this on and don't forget to wash your hands."

JoBeth raised her hand like she was in grade school. "Ah, ma'am, where exactly did you say my uniform was?"

Her lips twisted in a funny way. "You mean you don't have one?"

"I didn't know I was supposed to have one."

She looked her up and down. "You're wearing pants. That's a no-no. Waitresses don't ever wear no pants when they're waitressin' here. Got that?" She stomped over to a closet and picked through the racks. "We have uniforms, but not for anyone *your* size." She snatched an apron off the rack. "Here, put this on for now." Then Kit handed her a nametag and a black marker. "And don't call me ma'am. My name's Kit, got that?"

"I'm sorry, I will. I mean, I didn't know about the uniform."

Big Grizz interrupted. "Kit, the girl didn't know. Ain't it obvious? She's never waitressed before. Give her a break."

Kit squinted her eyes at him. "Why should I? You already did." With that, she stormed out.

JoBeth leaned backwards against the wall—relieved Kit had left the kitchen. "I'm sorry to have caused you trouble, Mr. Grizz. I can call you that, can't I? M-maybe I should just quit. She doesn't like me and she sure doesn't want me here."

He plunked some pans onto the burners and shifted his eyes toward JoBeth. "You can call me Grizz or Big Grizz, but don't ever call me Mr. Grizz." He winked. "And in spite of Kit ordering me around like that, I'm still the boss of this here place. Get it? If I say yer hired, yer hired and that's that." He pointed to a tray of condiment bottles. "Fill those up, willya? You'll find the canisters—"

"In the stockroom," she finished. "I checked it out already."

"Good." He pointed to a big pot. "Then boil a full pot of water and make some iced tea concentrate. Use exactly 100 of them big bags. That'll get us through the day. And add half a cup of baking soda to the concentrate while it's hot."

"Baking soda?"

"The secret ingredient to a perfect glass of iced tea."

She nodded calculating how long brewing the tea would take.

He continued. "After that, go ask that harpy which booths you're gonna get. An' don't be surprised if she gives you the ones with the least customers. She's got rank on you. You're number two in the pecking order for the breakfast shift. Don't be offended or nuthin.'"

"Okay, thanks." JoBeth set the tea water to a boil and threw the bags in, then covered it with the lid. Done. She would add the baking soda after she turned the fire out.

She had no problem filling the yellow and red squeezy bottles either — standard stuff. She filled the salt shakers too. No problem until it was time to fill the pepper shakers. While she was holding the funnel over the very last one, JoBeth had the uncontrollable urge to sneeze. A black cloud of pepper soon settled over the whole counter. Her eyes watered, throat burned, and she kept sneezing into her sleeve.

"*Gesundheit.*" Grizz looked over from the stove where he was frying up a mess of bacon.

The smell of the bacon nearly drove her out of her mind. Her stomach screamed.

Kit stomped into the kitchen, eyes blazing. "Look at this mess. You'd better clean this up right now and get out on the floor with me. We got customers."

JoBeth used her arm to sweep the pepper into a trash bin next to the counter. But she kept sneezing.

Kit clipped two orders on a carousel and whirled it over to Big Grizz. "Two eggs sunny, two strips o' piggy, Texas toast, one egg salad on shingle down. Drag it through the garden." Then her nose squinched up for a second and although she fought it, the woman let out a monster sneeze. Madder than a hornet, she pointed to JoBeth. "Soon as you're done messing around with that, get out on the floor." Her voice carried forward as she pushed through the swinging doors.

What had Kit rattled off to Big Grizz? And what did "drag it through the garden" mean?

"Don't mind her," he said, voice compassionate but strangely shaky. His hand went up to his nose, hotdog finger flat under his nostril. His attempt to stop the hurricane sneeze that came out was totally unsuccessful, a real window-rattler.

"Thanks," JoBeth called back on her way through the kitchen doors. Apparently, Big Grizz didn't have time to cover his mouth. She wondered if he ever did.

From that moment on, JoBeth resolved to avoid eating bacon in the Last Chance Café.

Chapter Twelve
Can I Take Your Order?

"Thou shouldst eat to live, not live to eat" — Cicero, *Rhetoricorum LV*

After a crash course in diner lingo, Big Grizz told JoBeth she was ready to go out on the floor. It was a good thing he was confident in her, because she sure wasn't. And it was a given that Kit didn't have a lick of confidence in her.

One thing she never knew about the restaurant business. Correction—one of the *many* things she never knew about the restaurant business was that it was a lot of hard work. Kit introduced her to waitressing like a swim instructor throwing someone in the water and yelling, "Swim!" Her idea of mentoring was handing JoBeth a pad and pencil and pointing to a couple booths and a table in the worst spots in the café. The booths Kit gave her were straight-up shabby or "tore up from the floor up." The cushions were ripped, initials scratched into the tabletops, and the seat on one of the booths was broken. Anyone who sat there was going to dip way down in the center—rear ends likely swallowed into oblivion.

And the table for two Kit assigned her was right next to the bathroom door. Big Grizz was right about the woman.

But JoBeth was determined to win Kit over. The woman had taken an instant and total dislike to her. Maybe it had something to do with JoBeth's weight. She hoped not.

An Elvis tune played on the tinny sounding ancient jukebox in the corner. *Love Me Tender*.

The bell tinkled and an old couple shuffled through the door. To her surprise, they headed toward JoBeth's station. The place wasn't even packed out and they were heading toward the broken-down tables assigned to her. JoBeth shifted from foot to foot waiting for the erstwhile customers to approach. And of course, they headed right for the booth with the broken seat. The second thing she noticed about them, besides the age observation, was that the woman was short—5'1" she guessed, and the man towered over her—had to be at least 6'4". An odd couple, for sure.

"Oh, excuse me." She ran up behind them. The woman wore a synthetic pants suit, a large print floral number in Peter Max colors with flare legs, and the man wore what could only be described as a seventies disco shirt. Silk, with a very busy design. "This booth has a broken seat. If you don't mind, maybe you could move to the other one." She flashed a wide smile.

The old woman's eyes narrowed. "Elmer, what's she saying?"

"Huh?" Elmer turned to JoBeth in slow motion. "What?"

Under the circumstances, she thought it best to repeat herself. So pumping up the voice volume a bit, she pointed to the alternate booth. "Maybe you should sit here instead, if you don't mind. The booth you wanted is broken. The seat is, anyway."

The old couple didn't budge. Instead, they slid into the broken booth, and sat across from one other.

"Well okay then." JoBeth shrugged. "Apparently, you want that booth for some inexplicable reason. If you're happy, I'm happy I guess. What can I get for you?"

"Girlie," the woman frowned. "Ain't you heard? This here booth belongs to me an Elmer. We been coming here for years. In fact, this is the very same booth where he proposed to me forty-two years ago."

She struggled for words. "Sorry, I didn't know. That's so — so romantic." She tried to imagine them as a young couple sitting in the new red Naugahyde booth.

"What?" Looking a bit confused, Elmer held a hand to his ear.

"I said I didn't know."

"What? You don't know where to go?" He shook his head, a wide smile across his face. "Well, young lady, maybe you should take our order an get it into the kitchen. That's where you need to go." He cackled like Precious Pup and winked at his wife.

Stunned, JoBeth shook her head. What was it with the people in this town? "No, no." She raised her voice to boom box setting. Using hand movements, as if those were going to help the man understand, she formed a huge X. "I didn't say I didn't know where to go, I said . . . "

"Is there a problem over here Miz Martie?" Kit gave JoBeth a judgmental sideways leer as she chomped and popped her gum a few times, which reminded her of Rayne, who she wished was with her right this moment for moral support.

Martie pointed. "This here girl tried to make us sit in that there booth."

JoBeth tried to explain the situation to Kit, but she just made a face and looked the other way. Meanwhile, the musical stylings of Pat Boone sauntered through the atmosphere with *April Love.*

"I didn't know." The words fell on deaf ears.

"Young lady, you oughta keep that information to yerself 'stead of broadcasting it on the evening news." Elmer resumed his cackling, half cough-half chuckle.

Kit made sure the couple settled into the booth comfortably. Pen poised over pad, she asked, "What kin we git you Mr. and Mrs. Grimble?"

Martie's face relaxed. "The usual."

She nodded. "Okee dokee. Be back in a minute." Kit pulled JoBeth to the side and rattled. "Coffee, OJ, Flop two, hockey pucks, piggy, Georgia ice cream—that's the usual fer the Grimbles. They come here 'bout every morning, so you'd best memorize their order 'cause they don't like repeatin' it none and neither do I."

"Okay," she gulped. Hmmm. If memory served, 'Flop two were two eggs over easy, hockey pucks were—were biscuits, piggy was bacon (the easiest one to remember), but Georgia ice cream?'

A frustrated Kit fanned her hands at her. "Well, what are you waiting for? Go place the order."

JoBeth broke into a sweat rushing to the kitchen, writing the order on the guest pad as fast as she could. Pausing, she practiced rattling off the order in her head. Flop two, hockey pucks, piggy and Georgia ice cream. She was relieved to see Big Grizz hard at work, sweating vigorously over the stove. *Ick.*

He didn't answer, so she spoke the order again in plain English and clipped the nickname order onto the carousel. "Ah, two eggs over easy pleas-y. I mean please, and some bacon with each order and biscuits and, and—"

Without turning around, Big Grizz answered, "Grits." A big smile, he explained. "Georgia ice cream is grits. This is for the Grimbles, right?"

"Right, the Grimbles," JoBeth answered eying the toast that popped up.

He noticed where she was looking. "You hungry?"

She bit her lip and nodded.

"The Grimbles almost always order the same thing. You can just say 'the usual,' and I'll know." He grabbed a couple slices, slathered some butter on the Texas-sized toast and handed them to her on a napkin. "In between customers you can come on in and grab a few bites, but you have to keep an eye on your tables and take care of your customers. Got it?"

"Yes, sir. Thank you, sir." JoBeth smiled, grateful for the food and the kindness. Piling the toast one on top the other, she took the biggest bite her mouth would accommodate. She put what was left next to the condiment tray and walked back to the table still chewing. A short swipe with a dishtowel dispatched the crumbs off her face. She swallowed just as she reached the table with a fresh pot of coffee.

"Coffee?" She forced her mouth into what she imagined was a good semblance of a smile. The old woman stared.

"You bet." The man held out his cup and she poured.

Mean Martie kept staring. She pointed. "What's that on your teeth?"

JoBeth brought her tongue up to her front teeth and her tongue found the problem right away. A rather big chunk of toast stuck in between her two front teeth. Through sheer suction, she wrenched it out of place and did a half smile. "Thanks."

The old woman held out her cup without saying a word and JoBeth filled it. "You got any cream?"

She knew from experience that most servers carried cream, straws, pencils and other stuff like that in their pockets, but since she wasn't wearing a proper uniform there was no place for those items. JoBeth looked down—pants with an elastic waistband and no pockets and a blouse that hung down far enough to cover her tummy. "Be right back."

Near the coffee station she'd noticed a little bowl of tiny creams in a stainless steel bowl of cracked ice. She fished out four and carried them to the Grimbles. "Here you go."

"These ain't fat free, girlie." Martie slid them to the edge of the table back to her. "We only used the fat free ones cause I'm watching my figure and Elmer's watching his heart." She made sure she accented the fat free part by looking JoBeth up and down.

On the way back to the bowl of cream she'd already come up with the very first nickname for her very first customers. Once she deposited the new cream on the table she turned around fast to avoid any further complaints from "The Grumbles" and went to check on their order. Back in the yummy-smelling kitchen, she finished off the toast in one bite, checked her teeth in a tiny mirror hanging on the wall and grabbed their plates. Big Grizz winked, a look of approval on his hairy face. *This waitressing thing isn't so hard after all.*

When JoBeth emerged from the kitchen, the place was packed, including the two other tables. She put the plates in front of Elmer and Martie and turned to the other booth. *Lean On Me* was playing, but she couldn't remember who sang it.

"Waitress. Ketchup please." Martie scowled.

JoBeth snapped her fingers up in the air as she came to two conclusions, Al Jarreau sang it, and this woman had to be one of the meanest, orneriest old people she'd ever met. Besides Kit, of course.

"Be right back." She rushed into the kitchen, grabbed one of the squeeze bottles she'd filled but forgotten to put out, and hightailed it back to the table. "There you go."

One of her other booths was occupied by a normal-looking middle-aged woman who wanted scrambled eggs, but was picky about where they came from. JoBeth had to quiz Grizz about whether the eggs were from free-range chickens and whether the wheat used for the wheat toast had chemicals sprayed on it and if the coffee was organic. Whether his answers were truthful or not, JoBeth couldn't be sure, but far be it from her to question her boss's integrity. She dropped off the order. "Two cackleberries—wreck 'em, brown down."

Of course, between the twenty questions game and filling the needs of the other customers, she took the order at the one remaining table in her section. The man seemed to be about her age—kind of cute. Brown wavy hair, he sported a soul patch on his chin. He was thin yet fit and moderately muscular. The guy had a nice expression on his face too.

"You're new here." He looked her up and down. By this time, JoBeth was sweating like a racehorse. Large strands of hair had escaped from the pristine ponytail she'd started the day with. Her hair hung like a wet shower curtain, around her face.

"Yes, I am. What can I get for you?"

"What's your name?" He squinted, trying to read the nametag.

She glimpsed down at it, the ink now smeared and illegible. "Sorry — I'm JoBeth."

"And I'm Bobby. I used to come here a lot, but not so much anymore." He peered once more at the menu and cleared his throat. "JoBeth, I'd like a bowl of Georgia ice cream, an English muffin and a large glass of orange juice."

Scribbling fast, she nodded. "Got it." On the way to the kitchen, his order bothered her. How did the guy know about Georgia ice cream?

Back in the kitchen, she placed the order. "Georgia ice cream 'n Burn the British." By this time her stomach was growling, knees and feet ached and she was tired too. Kit joined her in the kitchen to place a couple of orders. She guessed from the look on Kit's face that she must've looked a sight because the woman's eyes widened the size of HoHo's, JoBeth's favorite cupcake. *Heaven knows how many I gorged on last night.*

There was something different about the woman though. Not the usual acerbic attitude. JoBeth eyed her cautiously.

"Why don't you take a minute to freshen up? Pull your hair back or something. We gotta keep up to code around here and you might git some of that in somebody's food." She pointed to the sink and mirror in the far corner near the freezer.

From the corner of her eye, she noticed Kit and Grizz glance at one another. Now it made sense. Grizz must have given the woman a good talking to.

"Thanks, I will." She dashed over to it. "Oh Lord." Her face, red and sweaty, hair stuck to her cheeks. What a mess. She combed her hair back using her fingers as rakes and secured the ponytail with an extra twist. Then she washed her face at the sink with soap and cool, clear water.

To JoBeth's surprise, Big Grizz handed her a little plate of scrambled eggs, a couple slices of bacon and a kiddie orange juice that was so cold, she guessed it had come straight from the freezer. Blocking out her earlier vow to never eat bacon at the Last Chance Café, she thanked him, downloaded the food into her stomach in less than thirty seconds and washed it down with the juice. Sacrifices would have to be made.

On the way back to her tables, feeling refreshed *and fuller*, she grabbed the earth mother's plate and poured a large glass of OJ for her newest customer, delivering it to his table first. She heard a thank you from behind a newspaper, and moved on to the earth mother.

"Here you go." She put the plate down in front of the woman. "Can I get you anything else?"

She shook her head slowly behind the open book hiding her face. JoBeth noticed the woman was reading a romance novel, a real bodice-ripper with the kind of cover that should have some sort of warning on it. *Who knew?*

So she checked on the Grumbles. "How was everything? Can I get you some more coffee?"

Elmer answered. "That's okay, Girlie. You weren't around. Kit took care of gitting us a second cup."

"Oh." She swiveled. Two tables away, Kit caught the glance and gave her a sarcastic smile that sent chill bumps down her spine. Was this the same woman who bent over backwards to be nice in the kitchen? Or was Kit only making a pretense of being nice to her in front of the boss?

JoBeth scribbled on the guest check. "In that case, I hope you enjoyed your meal." She placed the guest check on the table and smiled at them nicely the way she'd seen so many servers do before.

"Hmmmph." Martie slurped on her coffee.

Guessing there wouldn't be much of a tip coming from that table, JoBeth turned her attention to clearing the dishes away as the two maneuvered out of the booth. Elmer laid some bills and change on the table. His arm entwined in Martie's, he handed something to Kit on their way out. JoBeth looked down at the table. Exact change. She looked back at Kit, but this time the woman didn't return her gaze. The Grumbles must have given *her* the tip. Just for pouring a second cup of coffee? JoBeth wanted to scream.

"Excuse me."

"Huh?"

She looked back where the voice came from. A police officer was already sitting in the Grumbles booth, his motorcycle helmet on the table. Must have slipped in during the smoldering glance. Had to be those quiet shoes they wore, good for sneaking up on people.

This guy wasn't just any officer though, this guy was THE officer, the one that pulled she and Rayne and Roscoe over. *Muskrat Love* trilled over the speakers. The fight or flight reflex kicked in right about then. JoBeth thought of something crazy, like trading in her car for a baby blue Vespa and driving cross-country to random destinations, sleeping in KOAs along the way — leaving all her problems and embarrassments behind.

He leaned his head to the side, a studied look on his face. "Don't I know you?"

She let out a tiny forced laugh. No use denying it. "Well, come to think of it, I think I recognize you too." *Cue nervous titter.*

He pointed. "The broken taillight." A wide grin came across his tan, chiseled face.

"Can I get you something?" she interrupted, hoping to stifle the reference.

He pressed his lips together, likely to hold back an outright laugh, but his eyes betrayed his amusement. Opening the menu slowly, he scanned through it while she waited, tapping her foot. "Hmmm. I didn't know they served Mexican breakfasts here. Do *you* like Mexican food? I don't know about those refried beans though. He patted his stomach."

She blew a stray wisp of hair out of the way. "You ready to order yet?"

He must have heard the serious tone in her voice. So what? The man already thought she lacked any kind of social grace.

Faster than it takes to shake an Etch-a-Sketch, the grin was gone off his face, for, the moment at least. "Yeah, some coffee to start and the—ah, blueberry pancakes."

"I'll have them out to you in just a minute." JoBeth turned to go, but had the uncontrollable urge to look back. When she did, she saw him jabbering into his hand held radio gizmo and laughing. And if the cop hadn't been in a restaurant full of people, she'd be willing to bet he'd be rolling on the floor laughing.

Roscoe, what have you done to me?

Chapter Thirteen
Waiting On Tables, Waiting On God

"The second day of a diet is always easier than the first. By the second day you're off it." — Jackie Gleason

Three months of waiting on tables had definitely made JoBeth lighter on her feet, which seemed to ache more and more each day. She'd found a pale yellow waitress uniform at the resale shop, pants and a top — no dress — much to Kit's dismay. But the outfit *so* worked. There was no way she was going to squeeze herself into a dress every day. And pantyhose? Forget it.

Funny thing, waitressing kept her on her toes — so far the only exercise program that had shown any results. Now a couple sizes smaller, she sported a better self-image, at least for the time being.

Besides their trips to the grocery store and her aunt's insistence on a once a week sprucing up at the beauty parlor, she drove Ada to church every Sunday. She never missed a service and seemed to know everybody in the congregation. Every time she asked JoBeth to come with her though, she found an excuse not to. Little pangs of guilt hit, but nowhere near hard enough to make her want to go.

Rayne came in every other weekend to visit and hang out. The two of them took over the cooking for Ada, though Rayne liked to add tofu to everything.

Tofu — probably the worst food item ever. The consistency of white school paste, although the school paste tasted *better*. But JoBeth's hate affair with Tofu was just beginning.

As much as she disliked the stuff, there was no way she was going to have to suffer through her new least-favorite food, "succotash" again. Today being Saturday, Rayne was due to arrive at the end of her shift. JoBeth still worked the breakfast crowd, which was fine, but she had the same lousy tables. The bright side was that the place packed out every morning during her shift with regular customers, so the lousy tables didn't make that much difference. The rest of the time she spent applying online for jobs back in the city, following up on applications with phone calls, and having daily epiphanies about avoiding careers in the food industry.

She'd just finished putting on a new pot of coffee when Kit called out to her.

"Pay attention, girl."

Kit leaned over the counter, crispy hair almost in JoBeth's face.

"Really?" She peered over the woman's shoulder for a glimpse at the Grumbles. "Maybe you should wait on them since they're slipping you all my tips."

Sure the words were inflammatory, but totally true. For all the months she'd worked, the Grumbles had stiffed her of rightful tips and slipped them to Kit instead. She guessed they hardly gave more than two bits most of the time, but nevertheless, JoBeth was the one doing all the fancy footwork and Kit was reaping the reward.

Not that she considered herself much of a good Christian these days, but if it wasn't for her upbringing, she might have a few taboo words with the woman.

She accented the pithy remark with a finger snap and an arm arc, and walked off. On the way of course, she fancied a peek at Kit's mouth falling open. *Choice moment.*

The first thing JoBeth did was bus the earth cookie's table. The woman had come in extra early this morning and left. She was disappointed to see her regular hadn't left a tip. What she did leave was a coupon for a free sample of goat cheese at some kind of health food store. JoBeth couldn't believe a town as tiny as Beeton even had a health food store.

She took out her green order pad and pulled the pencil off her ear.

"Where were you?" Martie squinted as she stepped up to the booth.

"Now honey, let the girl be. Can't you see she's busy?"

JoBeth couldn't believe her ears. Was Elmer actually defending her?

Maybe there was a way to win one-half of the Grumbles over. She fluttered her lashes the way she'd seen girls like the infamous Sophie Perkins do. "Why thank you, Elmer. As a matter of fact, I was busy making a fresh pot of coffee just the way you like it."

"Hmmmph," Martie tightened her lip.

"Would you like me to fetch a cup of coffee for you two?" She smiled.

"Sure," Elmer offered a gummy smile in response.

Martie drew in a vortex-like breath. "Old man, where are your teeth? Don't tell me you forgot to put 'em in this morning." She slapped her hands down on the table. "How could you fergit yer dadgum teeth?"

Elmer held up his hands, palm up and shrugged. "Must-a slipped my mind." He tapped his forehead. "I was watching that morning show and I think I left 'em on the coffee table. I shore hope Grady don't think my teeth are a chew toy."

She snorted her disapproval, and then picked up a menu. "Well let's just see what the old man can eat today." Martie pointed at the menu. "Give him a bowl of grits and scrambled eggs. He can gum that down okay. And give me the breakfast special with bacon and eggs over easy. Two orange juices too, and more coffee when you come back with the juice."

She scribbled furiously. "Okay, anything else? She glanced over at Elmer, who held his hand up. "I want some bacon too."

Martie pounded the table with her fist. "If you wanted bacon, you shoulda remembered to pop in yer teeth, old man." She looked up at JoBeth. "None for him."

"But Dear Heart . . . I want bacon."

"Who's plucking this chicken?" she shot back at him.

It was easy to see who ruled the roost in the Grumble family. If JoBeth was going to win them over, it was going to have to start with Martie. "Okay, no worries." She turned to rush the order to the kitchen when she heard the woman call out her name *sort of.*

"An' Jell-O."

"Whaaaat?" She rocked her head to the side.

"You stick to being a soup jockey and keep those roving eyes off of my husband. He's a respectable man in this here town and he don't need no floozy makin' goo-goo eyes at him. *Comprende-vous?*" Martie's face narrowed into a sneer.

Unbelievable. This woman was obviously off her rocker. Plus she didn't know her Spanish from her French. But, aside from those issues, JoBeth had reached her tipping point. "The name's JoBeth, not Jell-O, and I'm not making goo-goo eyes at your husband. I was just being nice and trying hard to extract some niceness out of you too. Is being kind a concept so foreign to you that you can't understand it when other people are?"

Elmer looked down at the table.

She was actually glad when Kit showed up to poke her nose into things. JoBeth used the excuse about turning in the order to skedaddle to the kitchen. Still shaking her head about what she'd just heard. Like she'd be desperate enough to fall for an old fossil like Elmer.

Note to myself: Leave the eye-batting moves to women like Sophie.

Big Grizz turned to acknowledge her when she walked in and gave him the order. "The breakfast special and a bowl of —" She stopped mid-sentence. "Grizz, why do we use three words to describe a one-word item? Saying Georgia ice cream is just a waste of time. No problem doing the rest of the silly lingo stuff, but not the Georgia thing. If it's okay with you, from now on it'll be grits for the Grumbles."

A wide smile on his face, Grizz tipped his spatula her way. *The favor of the King . . .*

* * *

The grocery store was a madhouse by the time Sam got there. The dinner-dash rush hour was on full throttle, with people streaming into the store on their way home from work. The bouquets in the floral department were slim pickings by six-o-clock, but he chose the best of what was available, hoping his date wouldn't mind.

George had encouraged him to start dating again. He'd begun counseling Sam on a weekly basis, and persuaded him to consider moving on with his life. According to his pastor, Sam's inability to let go of his feelings for JoBeth, were holding him back.

On his way to check out, Sam passed through the produce area and saw something slip from a woman's hands to the floor. He scooped it up.

"Excuse me. You lost something." Sam handed the pomegranate to a young woman with fuchsia hair.

She reached out to take it from him, her eyes focused on the fruit. "Uh thanks, it got away from me."

"Rayne?"

She glanced up, her face registering surprise. "Sam?"

He exchanged the bouquet of flowers to his other hand and shook hers. "It's good to see you. How have you been?"

She smiled and twisted the vegetable bag over the pomegranate before placing it in her cart. "Good. I'm super busy at work, and visiting JoBeth every other week."

"So, how is — ?"

She finished. "She's okay, I guess. Going through some rough times. I mean — that's not news to you, though."

He nodded. "She's living with her aunt now. How's that going?"

"Life in Beeton. Need I say more?"

"She mentioned that she has a job. Where does she work?" He noticed her looking at the bouquet.

"Are you going on a date?"

He felt his face flush. "Well, as a matter of fact, I am. A first date with a girl I met at church." He gestured to the wilted flowers. "Do you think she'll like these?"

Rayne smiled. "If she has absolutely no sense of style, taste or self-respect — then yes."

He bowed his head and laughed. "You're right. These are terrible."

"Well, now that we have that settled . . . "She put her hands on the cart handle. "I hope you have fun. It was nice running into you. Thanks again."

He shifted the flowers to his other hand. "I'm glad I could help you wrangle that runaway fruit."

She nodded and rolled the cart past him.

He called after her. "Rayne, wait a minute."

She stopped the cart and looked back, a puzzled look on her face.

"Would you mind doing me a favor? Maybe you could tell JoBeth hello for me. And, ah, maybe tell her we really miss her at church too."

Rayne leaned against the cart and studied him. "You don't give up easily, do you?"

He gulped. "I just want her to reconnect. She used to love being a part of the singles ministry."

Eyes locked on his, she replied. "That's not what I was referring to."

Heart thumping, his chest rose and fell as he met her gaze. *She knew. Rayne knew.* He decided to come clean. What did he have to lose? "No—I don't give up easily. I guess my heart won't let me."

Rayne grinned. "Good. I was hoping you'd say that." She gripped his shoulder with her right hand. "Keep listening to your heart, Sam MacManus."

Chapter Fourteen
Romeo And Julienne

"The biggest seller is cookbooks and the second is diet books — how not to eat what you've just learned how to cook." — Andy Rooney

The following Monday, she brought Ada in to work with her. Big Grizz insisted as soon as he found out about the appointment.

Rayne had helped her locate a topnotch geriatric doctor at the University hospital. She'd scheduled an appointment to take Ada into town and planned to leave as soon as her shift ended. JoBeth was looking forward to the trip as a much-needed break from small town monotony.

Except for one nagging thought. She'd decided not to tell Seth. Not yet anyway. For one thing, the guy never even called his mother. In fact, he'd called her a grand total of *no* times since she started living at Ada's house. And second, she wanted to find out what was going on with her aunt's health so she'd have something concrete to tell him.

On the bright side, or sunny side up as they like to say in the diner biz, JoBeth was socking away money for an apartment and to get her things out of storage. Things were going well between her and Ada. They had lunch and dinner together at home every day and JoBeth was even beginning to like retro TV shows too—especially Gilligan's Island.

They arrived at the Last Chance Café a half an hour before her shift. JoBeth opened the tinkle-y door and held it for Ada. Her aunt surprised her that morning when she came out for breakfast already dressed. Most mornings, she needed a reminder to change out of her nightgown—and a second reminder not to wear the same outfit as the day before.

But today her aunt was dressed to kill. She wore a cute summer frock that had probably been hanging in her closet for years. Though Ada wore nice clothes to church every Sunday, she'd never gone to this much trouble to look good.

JoBeth paused to smile at her. "Auntie, you really look nice today."

Her aunt did a slow-motion swirl. "This old broom can still sweep."

At Ada's request, JoBeth had helped set her soft gray hair the night before with something called Dippety Do, a pinkish jelly-like styling product with a scent reminiscent of Jolly Ranchers. After breakfast, she watched Ada apply pearly pink lipstick and bite down on the corner of her napkin. This reunion was promising to be some kind of serious rendezvous.

As they entered the café, Kit walked over to help, a big smile on her face. JoBeth had never seen a smile of that magnitude on her before.

"Hi, Miz Ada. How are you today, darlin'? You look wonderful." She took the elderly woman's arm. "Lemme help you to a booth."

JoBeth watched in surprise as Kit led Ada to one of her booths. "Now hold on Kit. Ada's my aunt and she can sit in one of my stations."

Kit lifted her chin "No, Grizz wants her to sit at this one cause it's the nicest booth in the place."

Right then, JoBeth noticed a basketball-sized head in the porthole of the swinging door. Grizz pushed through, untying his apron at the same moment. The man had on a dress shirt and pants. He'd trimmed his rat's nest of a beard and —." She sniffed the air. "He was wearing some kind of stinky bay rum cologne that old men favor.

Grizz smoothed his hair back with his palms and approached the booth just as Kit helped Ada settle in. JoBeth stayed her distance. Kit backed off too.

"Ada." His normally grizzled voice had never sounded so soft and gentle.

Her aunt smiled back at him. *And blushed?* She took one of his bear paws in hers and stared into his eyes. When tears welled up in his, she kissed his hand and held it to her cheek.

Kit motioned a retreat into the kitchen, though it was doubtful Grizz or Ada noticed their departure.

"What's up?" JoBeth asked.

Kit windmilled her wrist at her to come closer. "I think we're gonna need to get all the prep work done an' maybe the cookin' too."

"Really?"

"You saw the way he looked at her. The man is going to lose all track of time an' everything. Did you know that he sits on the bench across the street from her church every Sunday to catch a glimpse of her?"

JoBeth drew back. "What? The neighbors used to take her but I drop her off every Sunday and I've never seen him."

Kit surveyed the stainless steel kitchen. "Like I said, he's there every Sunday." She put her hands on her hips. "It's no use trying to snap him back to reality as long as your aunt's here."

JoBeth made a mental note to look out for Grizz on a bench the next time she dropped Ada off at church.

"You know him pretty well, don't you?"

Kit looked away for a moment and nodded.

A thought began to tug at her. "You like him, don't you?"

Kit drew away and pointed toward the freezer. "Let's haul out the stuff we need first and then git to it."

JoBeth rested her hand on the woman's shoulder. "You really do like him, don't you?"

Lips quivering, Kit pulled a handkerchief from her pocket. "I do—have for years."

Face-to-face, JoBeth could see the pain Kit had been holding in. "But the only woman he's ever loved is her."

JoBeth nodded her understanding.

"I've stayed here waitressing all these years so I could be close to him. Truth be told, this was supposed to be a temporary job."

"Like mine?"

Kit answered with a tearful nod.

Without saying a word, the two of them walked into the freezer and began pulling the heavy boxes out, like JoBeth had done the first day with Big Grizz. The two women groaned and grunted under the strain, but Kit resumed talking.

"I kept thinkin' he would forget about trying to get her back, since she was married and all and didn't give him a second look or offer him a shred of hope. Ada stayed away from the café like Superman from Krypton."

"So they never saw one another?"

"No, until now, she kept her distance from him, and he respected that except for the church bench thing."

"Why?"

"Her daddy didn't approve of him."

"My grandfather?"

"Yup."

"I don't understand. You don't have any idea why?" She shook her head.

"I guess that was pretty hard for him, huh?" JoBeth pulled at a box of beef patties with all her might.

Kit, normally cool as a cucumber, had little rivulets of perspiration rolling down her temples, and JoBeth could feel the sweat rolling down her own cheeks.

"He never stopped loving her." She sighed. "I think he'll be in love with her till the day he dies."

The two spent the next half hour pulling out all the frozen food items they would need and transferring them to the industrial refrigerator. The kitchen doorbell rang and they accepted the fresh produce delivery, then the eggs, dairy and meat.

Kit took off her apron and started to don the chef's apron. "Look JoBeth, you go ahead and wait tables and I'll do the cookin'."

"Are you kidding me?" JoBeth's heart thumped at the thought of waiting all of Kit's tables and her own. She knew there was no way she could keep up with all those customers.

"I'd be swamped."

"Well, what else can we do?" Kit asked, a look of exasperation on her now-tired face.

JoBeth reached out. "Hand me that apron."

"Why?"

"I'll cook."

"You?"

"Yes, I've watched Big Grizz. I know how he works. I can do this. Trust me."

She shook her head. "I don't know. It gets mighty hot in here. You'll be cooking nonstop too. On your feet the whole time."

JoBeth wrapped the apron around her waist. "I know."

Kit tapped her foot. "And what about tips? You won't have your tables . . ." She kept tapping while JoBeth started seasoning the grill.

"I'm going to do my best." She patted her belly. "You don't get this big without knowing a thing or two about cooking good food. Besides, I take care of Ada every day, and used to cook for my parents too." Her voice caught.

Kit paused. "Tell you what, I'll do the waitressing. It's the one thing I'm good at in life and even though I'll be 'in the weeds' today by myself, I've done it before. The girl whose place you took was gone a week and I'd been doing it all. So why not today?"

"If 'in the weeds' means you'll be super busy, then okay, it's decided." JoBeth smiled and threw a pile of bacon strips on the grill. The sizzle and pop momentarily deafened her, but the instant smell of bacon was enticing.

Kit tied the perky waitress apron back on. "And I'm gonna split half the tips I make today. It's only fair. "

She smiled back at Kit through the cloud of bacon grease. "Sounds like a deal."

"Look, I know I been a real . . . "

"No need," she gestured with a greasy spatula.

"I'm sorry, okay. You're gonna see a different side of me now. I promise." She rolled and unrolled the apron strings in her hands. "I'm not perfect or nuthin' though, so don't expect us to be best friends. I'm a military brat and making friends don't come easy. But when I do . . . " She whistled. "It's for life."

JoBeth flipped the bacon. "Deal."

As Kit swished through the kitchen doors, JoBeth wondered what she'd gotten herself into. How was she ever going to keep up with all the orders?

Frantic, she focused on prep work. She lined up the bread slices, melted the butter on the edge of the stove in a square stainless steel container and spread out the utensils. JoBeth fried up some sausages halfway, so she could finish them on the stovetop per order and cooked up some grits, keeping them warm over a double broiler. She pulled the eggs out and set them on a shelf over the stove — ready to go. Before long, Kit was back in the kitchen with the first three orders.

She pointed to the first ticket. "This here one's for Grizz 'n Ada. They look real happy. After they eat, Grizz is going to take her for a walk and they're going to sit in the town square and watch the birds like they used to." The woman tried to look happy when she said it, but she wasn't going to win any Oscars. As she started to walk out, Kit added, "You're doing good, girl."

The orders kept coming and JoBeth kept turning them out in the sweltering heat. She messed up on a few orders because her diner lingo was off. Her face now a vast oil reserve, she commanded Kit to speak the King's English when she ordered. No more fancy lingo, except the logical ones like "piggy" for bacon. JoBeth didn't have time to second-guess.

Sweat poured down the front of her pastel yellow waitress outfit, rendering it see-through, though she was not aware of this fact until Kit came through the door and uttered a stifled scream. "I kin see your drawers!"

JoBeth swiveled around, mouth unhinged.

Kit's head rocked up and down. "Pink flowers."

She looked down at herself. Her clothes, now plastered to her body were indeed see-through. "Oh no, Kit. What am I going to do? Why isn't there a window in this place so I can cool down?"

The gears in motion, Kit was as quick-minded as she was fast on her feet. First, she opened the back door and disabled the alarm by calmly taking a hammer to it. Then she handed JoBeth two of Grizz's big aprons from the uniform closet and told her to change in the freezer. She obeyed and the quick-change time in the freezer revived her, though she was clueless about what to do with the aprons at first. Kit peeked in and told her to tie the aprons back-to-back.

As Kit flipped the pancakes, JoBeth emerged from the freezer a new woman, cooler and less on the verge of indecency.

Kit handed her the spatula. "You look better, I guess." She tick tocked her index finger. "I told you it was gonna be too hot in here."

"How does Grizz do it?"

"I don't know. I guess he's used to it."

"How can anyone get used to that? He needs to install some ventilation in here or knock out a part of that wall and put in a window or a fan or an air conditioner, something. Just having that back door open like that is making all the difference in here. Thanks."

She picked up her orders and placed them on the tray. "Don't mention it."

JoBeth looked at the greasy industrial clock over the range, ten-thirty. Almost time for her shift to be over. Grizz would be heading back with Ada. He knew about the appointment. She hoped and prayed he was ready to get behind the stove again for the lunch crowd.

At 10:45, there were only two orders left. Ready for the breakfast-to-lunch changing of the guard. JoBeth set the orders under the warming lamp and ducked into the freezer where her uniform was laid out, now stiff as a board. She peeled off the aprons and pulled the uniform apart enough to slip her legs in, which wasn't difficult because her body was so hot. The uniform felt good—nice and cool.

She stepped out of the freezer, hung the aprons on a nearby hook and ate a small plate of bacon and eggs she'd set aside for her second breakfast. In spite of the four chocolate chip waffles she'd snarfed that morning, her stomach growled and complained. She'd hit the ground running and went without her usual mid-shift snack. Imagine that.

Grizz came into the kitchen, whistling a tune and walked right past her. "Hello, Jo." He continued whistling as he set up the grill for lunch, only offering a passing glance at the open door and smashed alarm.

Stalling, she drew out every word. "Well . . ." She pointed toward the swinging door. "I'm off now — off to town to do those tests; the ones for Ada." Hand on the swinging door, she paused and glanced back. "Well?"

"You want to know about our reunion, right?" He chuckled. "We ate breakfast and sat on our old bench in the square. Ada even spotted a blue warbler."

"Really?"

He continued, eyes moist with emotion, "I think she still cares about me." He covered his face in his hands. "More than I could hope for."

"Oh, Grizz." JoBeth threw her arms around him. "That's so wonderful."

"Thanks." His head tilted off to the side, a strange expression on his face. "Why are your clothes so cold?"

She looked at her watch. "I'll tell you later. I've got to get out of here."

"Wait." Grizz pulled out his wallet and pressed some money into her hands — a wad of green. "This is for you, Jo." He kissed her forehead. "Thank you for covering for me today."

"Thank you, but —"

"I insist." He swirled around in an impromptu dance. A white rosebud pinned to his shirt, hung all askew. "Today was such a wonderful day, like old times. That's what it was like."

"I'm happy for you."

"You take good care of her, okay? And let me know what the doctor says." He reached for a spatula. "I mean it."

JoBeth pushed through the swinging door. She imagined how bad she looked, but had no idea until she saw the reaction on some of the diner's faces. The romance reader earth cookie dropped her book. Some of the guys in bib overalls paused their forks in mid-air, and the big-haired wives actually stopped talking. Thankfully, the place was in transition, between breakfast and lunch, so there weren't as many customers.

She waved at Ada sitting in the same booth as before. But before she could take another step, Kit intercepted her from behind the pie counter, steering her by the shoulder behind it.

Kit pulled her hand away. "You're colder'n a well digger's bottom."

"Feels just great to me," JoBeth answered.

Her nose scrunched up. "An' you kinda smell funny too, all sweaty n' stuff." She reached into her crisp pocket and balled something up in her hand. "Here's your half of the tips today." She paused and reached into the other pocket and pressed something else into the other hand. "And, well, here's all the tip money the Grumbles, I mean the Grimbles —" She looked around, mouth gaping open. "Gave me."

Thankfully, the Grimbles were long gone.

"It rightfully belongs to you. I should'na took it. Sorry." Her eyes cast down in self-imposed penance.

Intrigued, JoBeth blinked a few times. "How did you know I call them the Grumbles? Did Grizz tell you?"

Her eyes widened. "I call 'em that too." Kit raised a hand to cover the smile on her mouth and whispered. "They really do grumble a lot, don't they?"

They shared a giggle until the old black phone on the wall began to ring. "Hold on." She pulled a pencil out from behind her ear and began to write a number on the wall, next to hundreds of other numbers and doodles.

But JoBeth was already whistling happy tunes inside her head. Old crispy-haired Kit had done right by her. JoBeth eyed her watch.

Frantic at the hour, she got Kit's attention, pointed to the watch and waved at her as she headed out the door with Ada. Kit nodded, the phone wedged between her shoulder and ear. Nothing more needed to be said. Just like that.

Ada had a pretty corsage pinned on her shoulder, a fragrant gardenia and some sweet-smelling jasmine blossoms framed by a spray of baby's breath and tied with a white satin ribbon. Grizz had gone all out.

The smile on her aunt's face spoke volumes, until she got a good look at JoBeth and held a hand to her mouth.

"Are you all right, Honey? You look like you have a fever." Ada placed her hand on JoBeth's forehead, the other on her shoulder.

"You're hot." She felt JoBeth's shirt. "But you're cold too."

"Auntie," she sighed. "It's a long story. We'll talk about it on the way."

When she positioned Ada in the passenger seat, JoBeth looked at herself in the rear view mirror. All she could do was gasp. The makeup she'd applied that morning had long ago melted away and left patches here and there of mascara and foundation. Her face was still red from overheating and her hair clung to her scalp like a palm to a basketball. There were curious splotches on her neck too. When she swiped at them with one of Ada's tissues, she figured out the butter had splattered while she was cooking. Might have happened when she painted the toast. Big Grizz used a paintbrush in the melted butter. Did the job quick.

JoBeth took a quick look at the change of clothes she'd brought along in the back seat, and the makeup. Yes, she'd thought to bring makeup, but for a quick touchup, not a complete overhaul. Too bad the car didn't come with a showerhead too. She was beyond sweaty. Grimy.

Ada sat in the passenger seat. "Where are we going, Jo?"

She leaned over to buckle her aunt in. "We're going to see a doctor for a checkup. You and I talked about it yesterday and this morning too."

"Oh," she looked out the window. "We did? I feel perfectly all right."

Ada reached for JoBeth's hand and placed it on her forehead. "See, I don't have a fever. I don't need to go to the doctor." She shook her head and began wringing her hands together.

All JoBeth needed to round out that day was for Ada to become agitated, so she decided to try and calm her down. "Auntie." She started the engine and turned the AC on higher. "I'm sorry, but we have to go. It's a routine checkup, like when you go to the dentist to have your teeth cleaned."

Suddenly, her eyes lit up with understanding. "But JoBeth, I don't have any teeth. See?" She pulled out her dentures and showed them to her — midair.

JoBeth threw the gear in park and sat back. This was going to be a little harder than she'd thought. Her voice calm and even-keeled, she spoke. "Well that's nice, Auntie, but maybe you should go ahead and put those back in."

While her aunt was doing that, JoBeth pulled out a makeup remover from her case and cleaned her face, neck and hands, the back of her neck.

She talked to Ada while she wiped and swiped herself clean. "This is a different kind of checkup, you know. It won't hurt or anything."

Ada looked out the window and then back, her face visibly more relaxed. "All right, dear. I trust you."

JoBeth smiled. "Okay then, let's get going." Tossing the used makeup remover sheet in the backseat, she threw the gear into drive and took off.

The drive to University Hospital went faster than she expected. Of course, driving a bit over the speed limit helped, actually, a lot over the speed limit. Funny, she wasn't even worried about getting stopped by the police, even though her taillight was in its same sorry state. And why? Because she knew Roscoe wasn't in the car. If he was, God bless him, she'd have been stopped before leaving the Beeton city limits.

They arrived at the hospital fifteen minutes early, without much lead-time, but it was the best she could do. After a few circles around the parking lot, JoBeth found a good spot not too far away. She didn't dare drop Ada off at the door by herself. She might not remember why she was there and wander off before JoBeth could get to her.

JoBeth zipped into the first bathroom she saw and had Ada hold her good clothes while she stripped down in a stall. "Ada, I'm ready. You can hand me the clothes." She opened the stall door wider. "Ada? Ada?" No Ada.

In a panic, she pulled the damp shirt back over her head and bolted out of the bathroom. "Ada. Ada."

"Yes." The door behind her opened. Ada poked her head out of the rest room. "Jo, what's wrong dear?"

JoBeth exhaled in relief. "Ada, where were you?"

"Why, I was right here in the powder room with you."

"Really? Because I didn't see you."

"I was in—I had to powder my nose, dear."

Puzzled, she asked, "Powder your nose? Well why didn't you do that in front of the mirror?"

Ada's eyes shifted to the right and then to the left before she answered. "JoBeth, I had to powder my nose." She placed greater emphasis on the words this time.

Oh . . .

Her aunt was speaking in a code of sorts—Ada's genteel way of saying she had to use the facilities.

JoBeth checked the time on her phone. "We're out of time." She looked down at her rumpled soggy, smelly outfit and felt like crying. She could only imagine what another glance in the mirror would reveal. "Let's go."

"What should I do with these?" She held out JoBeth's clothes.

She looked longingly at them. *If I only had more time!* "I'll hold them."

They made the transfer and JoBeth draped the clean clothes on hangers over her arm with a wistful sigh. She wished she could make herself invisible. Being invisible would certainly solve her image problems for the present. And it would certainly be the answer to bad hair days for women the world over. If only she had the option of sending Ada in without her. But there was no other way.

The appointment with Dr. Brenham was perfectly punctual—no delays, which was kind of refreshing for a doctor's office. She'd filled out the paperwork online ahead of time, so she could avoid fishing through her purse to look up elusive tidbits of information that weren't imprinted on her brain.

Dr. Brenham, a man in his early 40s, seemed pleasant enough, though he looked at her kind of cross-eyed. Who could blame him? She looked like a dirty wrung-out dishrag and smelled like one too.

Ada seemed a bit nervous at first, but he put her right at ease, by talking about the history of Beeton. He started talking about the town like he knew it.

She interrupted the conversation. "You seem to know a lot about the town. Are you from there?"

He frowned. "Yes, I'm originally from Beeton."

Ada took a closer look at the man. "Why, I think I remember you. Sandra's boy, aren't you?"

Dr. Brenham smiled. "That's right."

"And you married that nice girl. What was her name? Deal—dealy?"

"Delia."

"That's right. Sweet girl. How is she?"

"Fine, I suppose."

JoBeth's ears perked up when she heard him mention Delia's name—one of her steady customers, the romance-reading earth cookie woman.

"So, you're married to Delia?" JoBeth asked.

"Was."

"You're divorced?"

"People who used to be married generally are," he answered, a condescending tone in his voice.

The vibe he put off was a tad between touchy and snarky, but JoBeth kept on talking. "She runs some kind of organic grocery store or something. I haven't been there yet but I see a lot of people going in and out. Guess they like that healthy stuff, eh?"

He pushed his glasses up the bridge of his nose. "I understand the shop opened not long ago and does quite well. I hear her customers are mostly from surrounding towns— people who appreciate organic, pesticide-free produce, antibiotic-free meat and food items she offers."

JoBeth nodded. "She gave me a coupon for a free sample of goat cheese, but like I said, I haven't been there yet. Wonder where I put that coupon? She likes to read too." *Why do I sound like such an idiot?* Maybe the heat from the kitchen had overheated her brain.

He stared back at her, scanning her like an MRI. With one difference, however—*an MRI isn't judgmental.*

"You should definitely visit her shop, Miss Tomlin." The doctor gathered some papers and straightened them with a tap-tap motion on the flat surface of the desk. "Now, maybe we should get on with the examination."

The man had insulted and dismissed her in the worst way. Was she supposed to pretend everything was okay? But a glance over at Ada, and she knew in her heart she would do whatever needed to be done for her aunt's sake.

Dr. Brenham did some memory tests, cursory examinations and blood work, which Ada wasn't too fond of. He grimaced as he listened to her heart.

Concerned, JoBeth asked, "Anything wrong?"

"The rhythm is a bit off."

"What does that mean?"

Dr. Brenham offered Ada a reassuring smile. "Probably nothing. We'll schedule some further testing to be sure."

Besides the tests he did, the doctor put in orders for more—with a cardiologist, gynecologist, and endocrinologist.

In the most pleasant voice she could muster, JoBeth asked him some questions. "Gosh doc, I thought you were more of a one-stop shopping kind of deal. Why do we have to go to all these specialists?"

Elbows resting on the desk, he tapped his fingers together. "Basically, because I can't specialize in all these areas, but I can refer you to those who do and take those results and link those findings all together and come up with a specific treatment plan for your aunt."

"Oh, I see. I guess that makes sense." From her angle, JoBeth could see glimpses of his freckly scalp through the obvious comb over on top of his head. Focusing on *his* imperfections somehow made her feel better. With that kind of view, it was hard to concentrate.

He stood up and walked around the desk. "Ada." He held out his right hand and took hers. "It's been a pleasure getting to know you today. I hope to see you again soon so we can chat more."

"Oh yes, doctor." She held out her index finger. "But keep those needles to yourself, young man."

He smiled. JoBeth wasn't sure whether he was just being pleasant or he was sort of tickled that she called him a young man. "I'll certainly try." He turned and held out his hand, at a visibly greater distance to shake JoBeth's. "A pleasure meeting you, Miss Tomlin."

"Doc, I want you to know that I don't normally look this way. I had to fill in for the cook today and-and things were kind of crazy."

He squeezed her hand like she needed another dose of Prozac. "No need to explain, Miss Tomlin. You look fine, just fine." He returned to his desk, sat down and scribbled something on the chart.

Heinous. He thinks I'm heinous. They all do. The doctor, his nurses . . .

On their way out, Ada turned and smiled. "You have a nice office."

He looked up from behind his desk and glimmered a weak smile.

Something awful was happening to her reputation now. Not that it was JoBeth's fault. All the circumstantial stuff was totally out of her control.

Could she control the way she looked after melting in a hot as Hades kitchen? Could she control a flatulent dog with a talent for rendering himself invisible to police? And finally, could she control a cheating boyfriend who'd weighed her in the balance and found her wanting?

Chapter Fifteen
True Grits

"In the Middle Ages, they had guillotines, stretch racks, whips, and chains. Nowadays, we have a much more effective torture device called the bathroom scale." — Stephen Phillips

That night JoBeth had another dream, or more like a continuation of the same one. And this time, the food wasn't to blame. After a quick shower, her tired body collapsed like a brick wall onto the mattress.

The nightmare would be the only downside to an otherwise perfect doze. Back in the recurring nightmare scenario, she found herself walking, again toward the clearing in the mist. Cooing sounds came from a little cradle.

"JoBeth. JoBeth." This time a fancy Victorian doll dressed in rich blue velvet emerged from the grey. Her eyes, the color of purple hull peas, opened and flipped shut faster than the answers on a Family Feud board.

"What do you want?" JoBeth demanded.

"Hello." The dolly, a single expression on her bisque features, stared. "Do you see the cradle?"

"Yes, I mean the thing is less than five feet away from us. *Duh*. But listen up, I don't want to be here in this dream anymore, so I'm going to wake up and all this stuff will be gone, including you. No offense, but you're just a figment of my imagination."

"Waah. Waah. Waah."

It was obvious whatever was in the cradle wanted her attention. JoBeth shook her head, and took a few steps toward it. The delicate dolly followed and stood on her tippy toes to look over edge.

"The baby seems smaller. Don't you agree?"

JoBeth blinked a few times to focus better. After all, this was a dream and she was supposed to be sleeping. She stared down. "Okay, so the thing does look smaller. And it's made up of different foods this time. But who cares?"

"What kind of foods?" the dolly asked.

"Well." JoBeth rolled her eyes. "The head of lettuce is, by the way, so typical. I would have expected something more creative." She pointed. "The arms are carrots and the feet are potatoes, the body — a watermelon. And yes, there are rice crackers and grapes and all the . . . "

"All the foods you've been eating lately," she finished.

"Waah." Suddenly agitated, the food baby demanded. "Feed me, JoBeth. Feed me."

Instead of answering, JoBeth backed away, an icy wave of chill bumps overtaking her.

"It talks?"

The doll crept up closer. "Do you know why she's hungry? Do you have any idea why?"

"She?"

The doll leaned in. "Do you?"

"No, am I supposed to know or care? This whole thing is crazy — just a stupid recurring nightmare. And I'm standing here like an idiot talking to an imaginary Chucky doll and an equally imaginary baby made of food, both of whom are somehow able to talk."

The food baby fell silent. The dolly stood still, eyes wide open. JoBeth took the opportunity to back off during the eerie pause.

She held her palms up. "I've had enough of this dream. Enough." JoBeth woke up breathing hard and shivering, forehead damp, her pajamas clinging to her skin. Reaching for her cell phone on the bedside table, she speed-dialed her friend.

Her voice cracked as she spoke. "I-I'm so glad I caught you."

Rayne yawned, her voice scratchy. "Caught me? It's 2:00 in the morning. Where else would I be but in bed, sleeping?"

"Oh—sorry. But I had that nightmare again."

"The one with the Chucky dolls?"

"Yeah, but they're not exactly Chucky dolls even though I call them that to their little porcelain faces. They keep trying to tell me something."

Rayne yawned again. "Probably your subconscious mind trying to reveal the source of your obsession with food. Tell me more about the food thing, the baby."

"The baby was smaller this time. I don't know why. The doll was trying to get *me* to say why."

She cleared her throat, but her voice was still rough and scratchy. "Like I said before, this dream or nightmare, depending on your point of view, is rife with symbolism. You're obviously tired or bothered about stuff before you go to bed, or perhaps developing self-awareness about the source of your problem. Sometimes, and I know this for a fact, you eat a lot of food right before you go to bed, and that's not good. Your poor stomach has to work overtime when it should be taking a much-needed break."

"Thank you Dr. Rayne. But FYI, this time I didn't have anything to eat before I went to bed. Not a bite."

She yawned. "Okay, whatever. Look, we'll talk more about this later, okay? And you'll have to catch me up on that doctor's appointment, too." Rayne yawned long. "I'm going back to sleep now." Without so much as a goodbye, her friend hung up.

Now that the recurring nightmare was out of the way, JoBeth sighed and tried to fall back to sleep, but couldn't. So she wrapped herself in her favorite old quilt and made her way to the front porch swing.

Little droplets of dew, cradled in leaves and blades of grass, sparkled in the first streaks of light filtering through the waning darkness. Birds chirped singsongs as she watched the sky turn shades of pink and butterscotch cream. Between two immense puffy clouds, she spotted the morning star. Fading in the watercolor wash of dawn, it twinkled bravely between the evanescence of night and the bloom of a new day.

Her thoughts turned to her situation and how much easier it would be to go to God with her problems instead of trying to solve them on her own. She'd had her come-to-Jesus moment at the age of fourteen. Salvation — fast as hitting justify on a heavenly typewriter. But now she felt stuck between two worlds, as out of place as that little twinkling star.

Since she was already up, JoBeth decided to go in to work early. Before she left, she made a bowl of oatmeal with brown sugar, cinnamon and fresh berries for Ada and set it in the microwave with a note taped to the outside with instructions to warm it. A smile bloomed across her face. Ada had grown accustomed to having a nice breakfast.

Before JoBeth moved in, her aunt had more than likely skipped meals, or ate leftovers. Taking care of Ada made feel her good, like she was definitely making a difference in her aunt's life. Not to mention Roscoe, Petey and Zoomba.

Going in early proved to be a good move. She was able to *catch-up* on her *ketchup* duties — filling all the squeeze-y bottles. Mustard too. And all the salt and pepper shakers. Filling the glass syrup containers was her least favorite job — too messy.

The Grumbles came into the café as soon as Kit unlocked the door. They headed over to their booth and JoBeth met them halfway with a warm hello. *When I Fall in Love* played, creating a romantic atmosphere. Martie and Elmer looked into each other's eyes. *Likely one of their favorites.* JoBeth noticed a change, a soft look in Martie's expression she'd never noticed before.

Martie rattled off the order before they even sat down. "We'll have the special, two coffees, two OJs and don't forget to bring the nonfat cream."

"JoBeth wrote fast in her secret code. The one Big Grizz suggested. He told her to just write 'The Grimbles' on the ticket, an easy-peazy solution.

Elmer smiled wide, rows of white visible. "I have my teeth today."

"Good." JoBeth praised him.

Martie sneered. "Quit yer flirtin' old man." Then she turned her attention to JoBeth. "Ain't you got work to do?"

Elmer called after her. "I'm having bacon today, young lady. Now don't you forgit."

Delia slid into her booth. A slight woman, she carried a huge natural hemp bag. The first thing she did was pull out a hardback, another steamy romance. JoBeth decided to chat with her this time, now that she knew a little more about her.

"Good morning." She flashed her sunniest smile. "What can I get for you?"

"I'll have a glass of grapefruit juice, two poached eggs, a slice of whole wheat toast, no butter and a small bowl of oatmeal."

JoBeth wrote "Delia" on the ticket. She almost always ordered the same thing.

"Got it." In an effort to spark conversation, she pointed the pencil to the book cover depicting a scantily clothed couple. "Hey, ah, I'm always looking for an interesting book. Is that one a good read?"

Delia's features warmed instantly. JoBeth saw what almost looked like a blush bloom across her face.

"Definitely. This is one of the better ones. Lots of romance and well-written." A wistful expression replaced the blush. "Can you tell I have a love affair with romance novels?"

JoBeth squeezed her thumb and index finger together and smiled. "Just a teeny bit."

The woman smiled.

"I could use some romance in my life too. Things didn't turn out the way I expected with my previous relationship."

"Really?" The woman looked interested.

The icebreaker a success, JoBeth continued. "We've never formally introduced ourselves. You're Delia, right?"

"Why yes," she answered, flipping her dark hair back. "I suppose one of the other wait staff told you?"

She shook her head and leaned closer. "No, funny story. I brought my aunt to the University Hospital."

Delia's skin blanched. "And you ran into my ex."

"That's exactly what happened."

She leaned back against the booth. "What did he say about me?"

"Well, he was telling my aunt about the history of Beeton and said he used to live here for a time and was married to someone who owns the health food store in town."

Delia rested both elbows on the table. "Valley Organics is an organic food co-op, to be more precise. What did he say about it?" The tone of her voice changed from soft to methodical as soon as JoBeth mentioned the guy. What a difference.

"He said he heard it was doing well."

"Hmmmph." She turned her coffee cup right side up on the table. "I think I'm going to need some tea today. Just bring me the hot water though." She reached into the sack. "I've got my own tea."

"Sure thing." JoBeth bolted off to the kitchen to place the order first. Big Grizz was sweating up a storm as usual. The back door was closed, a new alarm installed.

"Two deadeyes, a dark shingle and a bowl of oatmeal."

He looked back at her when she said 'oatmeal' and winked. "Delia, right?"

She winked back, picked up the Grumbles order and delivered it to their table first. Back at Delia's table, she poured hot water into the cup. Curious, she looked to see what kind of tea the woman pulled out of her bag. Chamomile—a calming tea. Guess what she'd told Delia about her ex husband upset her.

"Look, I'm sorry about making you unhappy. Divorce is a hard thing. I didn't mean to pry into your business or anything."

Silent, Delia bobbed the tea bag in the hot water.

"I've had a lot of things go wrong in my life lately, and I guess misery loves company."

Delia stopped the bobbing and glanced up. "That's okay. I'm obviously still sensitive about it. My husband and I chose different career paths. That's all. We lost sight of one another and I—I wish him well." She took a sip of the golden-hued tea. "And I hope things will start looking up for you too."

JoBeth sighed. "I don't know about that."

"At least you're losing weight."

JoBeth looked down at herself in disbelief. "You can tell?"

Delia nodded. "Sure, you've been dropping weight quite steadily."

She looked down at herself again, this time with a more discerning eye. True, she had lost a bit. Her pants weren't as tight, for sure.

"Have you been on a diet?"

"No."

"Eating differently though?"

JoBeth thought about all the things she'd been doing lately. The job was physically demanding and she worked long hours. Plus, she didn't have time to eat the way she used to. Every morning for breakfast, she prepared two bowls of oatmeal, one for her and for Ada.

Before moving in with Ada, she would never have come close to eating a bowl of oatmeal for breakfast. And healthy food? Forget it. Her idea of greens was a package of mint Oreos, a big bag of Funyuns, and a Mountain Dew.

And there had been another lifestyle change—she wasn't eating a lot before bed like she used to.

"You know, come to think of it, I have been eating better food most of the time, and not as much."

Delia smiled. Reaching into her bag, she pulled out a card and handed it to her. "Come by the shop and I'll help get you started on a healthy diet and supplements. No charge. It's on the house. You've already started to make positive changes in your life. Let's keep it going in the right direction."

They shook hands. "Thanks."

On the way to top of the Grumbles' coffee she thought about what Delia had said. Had she really changed enough for people to notice?

Close to eleven a.m., Kit asked if JoBeth could stay a little longer than usual. The lunch staff was running a little late.

"Good, I'll finally get to meet them." JoBeth was always gone by the time the two waitresses showed up to man the lunch bunch, but she'd heard a lot about them. They were like super waitresses, legends among the clientele who frequented the Last Chance.

Hello Young Lovers ran on the jukebox, but barely sifted through the crowded room. She hoped someone would play another tune more in keeping with the energy of the place. Plus, after working at the café for three months, she wished Grizz would add something other than love tunes to his repertoire. The whole love song thing was getting a bit tired.

Kit practically ran into the kitchen with her orders. Things were popping at her booths. JoBeth glanced over at her own area and noticed a man, face hidden behind a newspaper at one of her single tables. Since she and Kit had come to an understanding, JoBeth had acquired more tables and thus, more opportunities to bring in money from tips. Hurray.

And the dreamy policeman who pulled her over was sitting in his usual booth. *Please God, please keep him from making more burrito jokes . . .*

She stopped in her tracks. *I'm praying?*

Right on the nose at 11:30, Betty and Cecelia, the lunch shift, sauntered into the Last Chance, giggling like schoolgirls. Veteran servers, these two were armed and dangerous. Uniforms crisp and pressed, pocket hankies embroidered with their names, sheer hose and white rubber-soled shoes. Hair teased to high heaven and spray-lacquered to a high gloss like Chinese furniture.

Just as warriors prepare for combat, the two women had loaded straws, peppermints, toothpicks, extra cutlery; green order pads sharpened pencils, Band-Aids and packages of gum for clean, fresh breath when they conversed with customers. JoBeth watched awestruck as Betty stuck a pencil over each ear.

Lock and load baby! Lock and load!

Betty's hair, the color of hell's flames, would have made Lucille Ball cringe.

"Hi, I'm JoBeth." She extended a hand.

Betty unwrapped the silver foil on a piece of gum and popped it in her mouth. "Hello there, darlin'." She chomped and squeaked hard, trying to stretch out the new stick. "I heard about you." She and Cecelia tittered together.

So much for first impressions . . .

"And Cecelia." JoBeth extended a hand. "Pleased to meet you."

Cecelia's hair was the intense kind of black you only see on people into Goth, or Bollywood starlets, or like Ruth Buzzi on Laugh-in, another of her new favorite retro shows. Of course, she was probably the only woman in her generation who watched reruns like that, thanks to Ada.

"Charmed, I'm sure."

Totally retro. JoBeth had heard that expression in old movies, but had never heard anyone actually say it before.

"Well, I guess I should be getting back to work."

"Nice meeting you." Cecelia called after her. *You've Lost That Lovin' Feeling* clicked on just then. Off the top of her head she couldn't guess who sang that one, but his voice sounded familiar.

JoBeth took an order for the man behind the newspaper first. He never lowered the paper to tell her what he wanted. She scurried off to the kitchen with the order, just so she could delay going to the officer's booth. But it was so dreadfully hot behind the swinging doors, she had no choice but to go back and do her job.

She approached the booth with a glass of ice water to start. "Good morning, Officer." She forced a smile for "The Force." "What can I get you?"

A ridiculous grin on his face, he went through the exaggerated motion of looking up and down over the laminated menu, which she noticed had an ugly smear of jelly across the front.

"I think I'm in the mood for a Mexican breakfast. You like the Mexican breakfasts here?"

JoBeth had really had enough with the same sorry jokes and the whole gastrointestinal array of tasteless puns and she made it known with what she imagined was no-nonsense expression on her face. "You ready to order?"

He frowned, likely realizing she was having none of his foolishness — yet again.

After placing his order with Grizz, she circled back from the kitchen with the grits and English for the man behind the newspaper. Out of the corner of her eye, she saw the officer now had company. There were two of them. They waved at her. "Be right over." She managed an anemic smile.

Lord, help me. There it was. Another prayer.

The newspaper accordianed down revealing his face, and the *mystery* man smiled up at her. But he wasn't a mystery man after all! She recognized him as the skinny, semi-muscular guy who'd been in once before — her first day on the job.

He folded the paper and glanced over at the other booth. "Don't mind them. I was listening to those two talk. They're tickled about something involving you."

She ventured a half-smile. "Is that so?"

"I only heard bits and pieces, but it's something about how one of them pulled you over for a broken tail light and your car smelled bad. Does that ring a bell?"

She put the bowl of grits and the plate down along with a little dish of foil wrapped butters.

"Thanks." He looked up. "Sooooo?"

She snapped her fingers. "Tom Jones."

He blinked.

"Sorry, I keep trying to guess whose singing."

He swiped at his mouth with his napkin. "You're right about the singer, but you were about to say something else, weren't you?"

"Right." She leaned in a bit to whisper. "If you must know, it was Roscoe."

One brow arched. "Roscoe?"

"My aunt's dog. He's really really old and he . . . "

"Has a little problem with bloating?"

"Right."

"And you were just taking him for a *ride*?" Now he was looking at her like she was truly beserko.

How could she make him understand? The whole thing didn't even sound normal to her. "He likes going for rides in the car."

"When Aunt Ada told me, I didn't believe it at first."

"Ada?" His eyes seemed to glaze over. "Ada Davidson?"

"Um, yeah. How did you know?"

"Ada Davidson's your aunt?"

Uneasy, she took a step backwards. "Okay, I'll get back to you in a sec. I've got to take some orders. Enjoy your breakfast."

He grabbed her arm. "You're her niece?"

Fear tingled along the nerves in her arm and clanged up and down her spine. Now *she* was the one wondering if *he* was a couple of side orders short of a Blue Plate special.

But as suddenly as he tensed, the man relaxed. Maybe the change had something to do with the proximity of the cops.

"I'm sorry. Don't mind me." He tapped his finger on the table. "Can we, ah, talk when you get off?" The guy tried to smile in a non-crazy, non-threatening kind of way. But his freak flag was already flying as far as JoBeth was concerned. Like Rayne always said, "you never know about pervs and stalkers. They're everywhere."

She kept backing up. "Uh, maybe." Of course, she had *no* intention of getting back to him on anything. She held her breath and swiveled.

By now, JoBeth had backed away from her creepy customer so much she was face-to-face with the law. She worked her facial muscles into what she thought was a good representation of a smile. "I see you have company." She looked at the other officer who pulled aside the menu. He was grinning wide, eyes watery, cheeks red like he'd been laughing. "What can I get you, Officer?"

He rattled it off faster than Morse code. "Some blueberry pancakes, two sunny side up eggs, a couple of sausage links, biscuits and gravy."

"Got it." Before they could say another thing, she walked to the kitchen as fast as she could without running and placed the order. The other order was up, so she quickly rattled off the new one.

Grizz was sweating up a storm. By now, he'd stripped down to a white tank, prodigious chest hair springing out the sides, like the fur edging on a coat. His baggy pants, soggy looking, hung low on his waist. The kitchen was a steam bath. She didn't see how the man endured it every day, especially after walking a day in his shoes, or aprons to be more precise.

A towel wrapped around his huge neck, presumably to catch the drips, he buried his face in it as she watched. When he turned around, she gasped. Kit had no doubt made him put a hairnet over his Brillo Pad-like beard. There was no way any self-respecting man was going to do that on his own. And the way the hairnet squared off his facial hair, Grizz looked like an oversized Egyptian pharaoh.

"How's it going, Jo?" The hairnet bobbed up and down when he talked.

She leaned across the stainless steel counter so he could hear her over the sounds of frying. "Well, there's a guy in there who kind of scares me."

Grizz squinted. "What's he look like and where's he a-settin'?

She told him where, but as she described the man Grizz began pacing and muttering. All of a sudden, he untied his apron and threw it down on the greasy floor. To her horror, he stormed through the doors and straight to the table.

She followed bearing the short stack of blueberry pancakes for the officer. The way things were going, she wasn't sure when the other guy was going to get his.

"I told you to stay away from here." Grizz started cussing from A to Z, stopping at certain letters more often than others. Course, the hairnet on his beard helped muffle some of the words. *Sweet heaven.*

"What're you doing here?" Grizz growled at the customer, the netted beard bobbing up and down. She'd never heard a man actually growl, but Grizz certainly came close.

The psycho man stood up. "Why? Can't I eat here if I want to?"

Big Grizz pointed right at the man's kisser. "I told you to never show your face here again!"

Kit, Betty and Cecelia surrounded them. Kit spoke up in a calming voice. "Now Boss, maybe you should . . . "

"You girls keep outta this," he commanded.

The women backed off behind the cash register. The entire café went silent.

The young man shot JoBeth a look that would have cut a dagger in half. "Did she tell you about me?"

Grizz, the whites of his eyes in stark contrast to the dark tootsie roll centers, answered, voice razor sharp. "Don't matter how I found out. I told you not to come back 'til you met my conditions. Have you? If you ain't met 'em you'd best get out before I throw you out."

In response, the young man threw down his napkin, and stormed out, slamming the door so hard behind him that the little tinkle-y bell fell off, ringing dismally as it skidded across the floor.

Big Grizz watched him leave, his chest heaving up and down. Then, without another word, he stomped back to the kitchen. The people in the rest of the café were silent for just a few moments, and went back to eating and talking.

JoBeth stood still as a statue, wondering what had happened and why. Kit came up alongside her. "Old Grizz is hotter'n a pepper sprout. You'd best bring Officer Ken his meal. Then come back over here to the register when you're done."

She walked, robot-like, to the table and deposited the pancakes and syrup. The officers were still grinning like they hadn't seen the altercation that had just taken place. She looked at Officer Ken. He now had a name. She still didn't know what the cute one was called, but what did it matter? To him, JoBeth was just one big joke.

"I'll have your order in a minute. Be right back."

Kit, Betty and Cecelia were huddled at the counter waiting for her. She approached them like a cow going on a tour at a meatpacking plant. This was going to be bad. Hired and fired. Great.

"JoBeth," Kit began. "We thought you should know."

"Okay," she interrupted, tears welling up inside her eyes. "I'm sorry I've done such a lousy job. I don't know what I was thinking trying to do a job like this. It's harder than it looks. What can I say? I was just desperate to work and make some money and then this happens. Elderly people hate my guts. Cops are laughing at me. I cause a cussing fight between my boss and a customer."

"JoBeth." Kit stopped her. "That young man Big Grizz had a fight with is his son."

"What? The man he cursed a blue streak at? His son?" She leaned against the counter in stunned silence. "But he's been in before."

She nodded. "And we kept it quiet so something like this wouldn't happen. But it ain't your fault. You didn't know."

Kit turned to Betty and Cecelia. "You two had best get started with the lunch crowd. We're finished with our shift."

JoBeth perked up when Kit said the words "we're," realizing she still had a job. "C'mon." Kit took her by the arm and led her into the kitchen. JoBeth noticed right away that the other officer's order was up. Grizz, back at work, seemed mesmerized by an array of sizzling meats.

"Hold on a minute, Kit." She loaded her tray and carried it to the table.

"Here you go." JoBeth filled the officer's coffee cup and left a handful of cream on the table.

"Thanks," he said. "Now we're cooking with gas."

The cute officer covered his mouth with his napkin and started snickering.

But Officer Ken sat back against the booth and studied her face. "You look kinda shook up."

She sighed.

"Don't worry about Grizz," he said taking his first bite. "He's all talk. That was his son. They argue all the time 'cause he won't work in the café. Truth be told, he don't want to work nowhere. Anyway, neither one of 'em means it. Nobody in town pays much attention to them two fighting." He grinned at the other officer. "Not even us."

She sighed again, this time in relief. "Thanks." JoBeth pulled some stray hairs away from her face. "Can I get you all anything else? I'm clocking out soon and just wanted to make sure you're okay."

A wry smile spread across the cute cop's face, magnified through the bottom of the juice glass he offered up to her.

"One refill, coming up. And you?"

Officer Ken looked down at his pancakes. "Some blueberry syrup would be great."

"You got it." She picked up the empty plate from the laughing officer and put it on her tray, along with the empty juice glass and returned seconds later with more juice, and the syrup. She refilled his coffee cup as well.

The cute officer had a serious expression on his face. He was listening to something coming in on his walkie-talkie thingie. Officer Ken vacuumed up his breakfast. Either he was super hungry or he figured they would be called into action any minute.

On her way back to the kitchen, JoBeth worked through several scenarios. Was Big Grizz's son the black sheep of the family or a rebel, maybe? What conditions did he make to his son and why hadn't his son met them? She was fully prepared to quiz Kit with the growing list of questions boomeranging through her mind as she swished through the swinging doors.

But instead, she froze in her tracks, shocked to see Kit on the floor leaning over Big Grizz who was clutching at his chest. She looked at JoBeth, panic in her eyes. "Call an ambulance! And get those officers in here. I think he's having a heart attack."

Chapter Sixteen
Serious As A Heart Attack

"Shall we never get rid of this past? It lies upon the present like a giant's dead body." — Nathaniel Hawthorne, The House of the Seven Gables

Face streaked with tears, Kit rode with Grizz in the ambulance. The two officers gave them an escort to the only clinic in town in the only ambulance in town, just to get Grizz stabilized. The officers had performed CPR on Grizz right away. All JoBeth or any of them could do was pray.

A grim atmosphere swallowed all joy from the café. They shooed the customers out as quickly as they could, cleaned things up and closed down the place. Not that she cared about tips at that point, but JoBeth noticed each of the officers had left her a twenty percent tip, which wasn't bad considering all the teasing she'd been through. When Grizz went down, she caught them as they were walking out the café, responding to another call.

Big Grizz's son had even left her a fiver. She didn't know what he and his dad had going on between them, but the guy couldn't be all bad if he was thoughtful enough to lay down a Lincoln — even after his father stampeded out the kitchen.

Delia left three bucks and her book with a note attached. "You need this more than I do." Made her smile. JoBeth's cell phone vibrated just as she laid down her towel.

"Rayne." Her voice broke. "You don't know how glad I am to hear your voice."

"You sound desperate. Was your day that bad?" Rayne asked

"You have no idea." She caught her friend up on the day's events as fast as she could and promised to call her back later with more details. She missed her friend, and was starting to realize how much she'd come to depend on her. But there was no time to talk.

After they closed up, JoBeth headed over to the clinic. There wasn't any semblance of a real hospital in Beeton, just a bojankety ready-clinic in a failed strip mall with a couple of doctors and staff. Kit told them they were going to be transferring Grizz to University Hospital.

Things didn't look good according to a cursory exam by a Dr. Peabody. Grizz had suffered a major one. Not that it came as a big surprise to anyone. Overweight and overworked, Grizzwald ate all the wrong things, smoked cigars regularly, and rarely got any exercise. Add in the temper factor, and you had a *fait accompli*.

It seemed as if JoBeth's career in waitressing was about to come to an abrupt end. But then she thought of her aunt. *How am I going to tell her?*

The doctor turned to Kit. "Did you call Bobby?"

Her face seemed to drop an inch. "I did. His phone is turned off. He's not picking up. The only way to get in touch with him is to knock on his door and that's across town."

JoBeth gulped. "I'll go. I mean—I would want to know if my father was in the hospital. Plus, I feel like I'm somehow responsible for this happening." How far could it be? Beeton wasn't exactly a metropolis. Urban sprawl for them meant somebody opened a tack shop or a feed store on the edge of town.

Betty pooh-poohed her. "You're not to blame for Big Grizz keeling over like he did. He and his son have been fighting for years before you ever got here. This was bound to happen."

"You serious about going out to tell him, though?" Cecelia asked. "I would go with you, but I really want to travel with the girls to University Hospital. I can't drive myself. My car is unreliable."

"Can you?" Kit asked. Her tear-swollen eyes seemed to call out to JoBeth.

"Sure, just give me the address and your cell number too." JoBeth repeated hers to Kit as she wrote, all the while trying to forget about how crazy mad the guy was when he left the café. After all, this was a mission of mercy.

She jotted the address down on an old coupon pulled from her purse and handed it to JoBeth along with her cell number. "It's kind of tricky to find. Just remember to turn left by the little white dog."

"White dog? What if the dog isn't around?"

She coughed. "He's chained up in the front yard. And he's white with black spots."

Adrenaline pumping, JoBeth fired up the old engine and took off, though not exactly sure where she was going. Robert lived on 27 Hystaker Lane. She followed the directions, a mere five miles away. She spotted the cross street hidden behind a large overgrown Mulberry bush partially covering the street sign. And sure enough, two houses down on the left was a white and black rat terrier short-chained in the front yard. It looked pretty miserable.

What kind of people would do that? Why do people like that even have dogs?

She pulled into the son's driveway and thought she saw someone peek from the edge of a torn shade. The yard was a mess, junk all over the place, empty beer bottles and garbage. The steps creaked, and not just because of her weight. She bit her lip and knocked on the door. No answer. She knocked again and thought she heard some movement inside.

"Bobby Herschelstein? I know you're Grizz's son and I have something very important to tell you. It's about your father."

The door swung open. Bobby, eyes wild, hair a mess, pointed a finger at her. "You tell my father to leave me alone. I got nothing to say to him."

JoBeth spoke over his rant, her tone matter-of-fact. "Your father had a heart attack. They're taking him to University Hospital."

His mouth hung open. "What?"

"Your father had a massive heart attack. He's not doing well. You need to go to him."

"What do you mean he's in the hospital?" He patted his pants pockets, presumably looking for keys. "Hold on." Hands to his forehead, he raked through his hair. Then, to her surprise, he swiveled and hit the door with his fist. Hugging his bruised hand — *and ego, she presumed* — Bobby let out a pitiful yelp. Seeing him bent over almost made her feel sorry for him.

Between grimaces, he spoke. "My battery died as soon as I got home. I was too angry to argue with him right then. I was going to go back later and talk."

He paced back and forth, still cradling his hand. "Do you ever feel like everything is going wrong in your life?"

Though she tried not to, she laughed. "I do happen to have some experience with that. Maybe we can talk on our way to the hospital. Since your battery is dead, you're welcome to hitch a ride with me."

"Thank you. Thank you so much. I'd pay you for gas but I-I just spent the last of my money on breakfast."

So he'd tipped her his last fiver. "Don't worry about it."

Before she hit the unlock button on the passenger side though, she cautioned him over the car roof. "No crazy business, no cursing or ranting."

"Okay. Okay."

She let him in, belted up and gunned the engine. As they drove off, JoBeth pointed to the yard next door. "Who owns that dog?"

His lips pressed together. "Shiner? He belongs to the Claytons."

As they passed, she noticed a girl at the door watching. Thin and tall, she wore a red polka dot dress. She saw a flash of long blonde hair. "You know her?"

"Yeah." The look in his eyes was somewhere between hungry and sad.

"Is that Mrs. Clayton?"

He rocked his head slowly, sad eyes lingering on her as they passed. "No, that's Candy."

"And what about the dog?" she asked.

He shrugged. "He's just a dog."

"So he's always chained up like that? Do they feed or play with him at all?"

He squinted. "What are you, some kind of animal rights activist or something? I don't care about that right now. I'm worried about my dad."

She shifted in her seat. "Sorry." For the time being at least, she put her feelings about the dog on hold. There was Big Grizz to think about—and Ada.

How am I going to handle the situation with her?

On the way out of town, she had a worrisome thought about the taillight. What if they got stopped again? She couldn't afford a ticket, not on tips anyway.

He shot a tentative glance her way. "Your car doesn't smell so bad. I don't know what that cop was talking about."

Her cell rang.

JoBeth held up her index finger. "Hold that thought." She answered the call. "Kit—on your way? So are we. Thanks."

She glanced at him. "Your dad is stable for now and on his way by ambulance and police escort."

He bent over and buried his head in his hands. "Thank you. Thank God, he's alive. I need to talk to him and tell him something."

"I know what you want to tell him." She paused. "I never got the chance to tell my parents how much I loved and appreciated them. And I never got to say goodbye. They died in a car accident."

"I'm sorry."

"And I'm sorry you're going through this with your dad."

A moment of silence passed before either one spoke again. But JoBeth had a question tugging at her. "What did you want to talk to me about? I mean, you came off as kind of a creepster in the café, which is why I mentioned it to your father in the first place." She brought a hand to her mouth, to keep from sobbing. "I wish I hadn't. Maybe he'd be okay . . . "

Bobby squeezed his eyes shut for a moment. "When I found out who you were, I wanted to ask you some questions about your aunt and her son."

"Why?" Her curiosity aroused, JoBeth was sorry she had to keep her eyes on the road.

He looked away. "Don't feel bad about telling him. Doctors have been warning my dad about his health for years. He's stubborn — real stubborn."

A fresh wave of silence between them seemed to pull the tide of emotions away. And though JoBeth wanted answers, she decided to try coming from a different angle.

"Hey thanks, for what you said about the car smelling good, but the car isn't the problem. Roscoe is."

He didn't respond. In fact, he suddenly seemed disconnected or disinterested. But curiosity spurred her to keep the conversation going. "So, ah, what do you do when you're working, Robert?"

"Bobby." He leaned back into the seat, his body tense. "Stick with Bobby." He stroked his soul patch, probably a nervous habit. JoBeth intended to hit every one of his nerves until she found out what was going on between him and his father.

"So, Bobby, what did you say you do?" She pressed on.

"I didn't say."

"Oh."

"I dropped out of college, okay?"

"What were you majoring in?"

"Business, but I hated it. My father." His voiced cracked. "It was his idea. He thought it might come in handy when I took over the café. That's what he always wanted—expected me to do."

"And I'm guessing you're not too excited about the idea."

Her stomach growled. *So much for the scrambled eggs.*

He smiled. "You're hungry? Didn't my dad feed you? He always makes sure everybody around him eats. When he was little, there was never enough food." His voice trailed off. He paused, and continued. "That's one of the reasons he went into the restaurant business."

"Grizz gave me some toast and scrambled eggs. But I didn't get this way eating tiny meals."

He looked away and laughed. "You're not so big. My dad's overweight. So was mom."

"Is she—?"

He bobble-headed a yes. Maybe because it was too painful for him to talk about, given the circumstances?

"I'm sorry." JoBeth concentrated on driving for a few minutes to give him a break from all the questions. But to her surprise, Bobby started talking on his own.

"They divorced when I was little. It's not like they loved each other or anything. I knew it. No one had to tell me. Anyway, she remarried a great guy and was happy for a long time. But she passed last year." His head hung low, like he had no strength to hold it up.

JoBeth mustered her boldness. "Do you think their marriage failed was because your father might have been in love with someone else?"

He head came up fast. "Of course." He started playing with the glove box, opening and closing it like a bored teenager. "When I was old enough, he told me that he'd fallen in love at my age with a girl down the street."

Bobby paused to stare her way. "Ada. But her father said he wasn't good enough for his daughter, or something like that."

"Why?" She slowed the car down.

"My dad always wondered. He thought it might have been because he worked as a soda jerk at the time and didn't have much to offer. He came from a poor family. Also, he's Jewish. He thought maybe your grandfather was an anti-Semite. Who knows? But if that was the reason, I guess with a last name like Herschelstein, it would have been obvious."

"I can't imagine that. My grandfather never said anything like that in front of me." The thought of her grandfather harboring that sort of prejudice was disturbing.

"From what my old man told me, he and Ada were totally in love. He gave her a ring. But her father wouldn't hear of it. Ordered her to stop seeing him. So they snuck off and got married." He laughed. "When her father found out, he was furious and got her to agree to have the marriage annulled. Then he set her up with some guy who worked for him at the tool factory and suddenly the two were engaged. She wound up marrying the guy. Had a baby right away. Broke my dad's heart."

"How sad."

"That's not the weirdest part though."

"What? There's more?"

"My mother always suspected Grizz fathered Ada's son."

My cousin? "What? Does her son—does Seth know?"

He licked his lips. "No, Mom told me everything right before she—well—it was one of those deathbed confessions." He sneezed into his navy sports shirt. "Sorry. Where was I? Oh yeah, I should give you a little background first. My mom worked at the soda fountain place with dad. She liked him a lot, but my father was crazy about Ada.

"So Mom went to Ada's father and told him Grizz was a dishonorable man who ran off and married his daughter but had already compromised her own virginity and left her with child, an unwed mother."

"That's terrible."

"Mom wasn't proud of lying about Dad, and felt bad about it after the fact. But she got what she wanted for whatever it was worth. I guess she didn't want to take what she did to the grave though."

"Wow."

"Ada's father didn't care for my Dad to begin with, but after he got an earful from my mom, he despised him. As I said, lickety split, the marriage was annulled, Ada was married to a new guy and they had a baby."

"But Grizz didn't know why all this happened."

"Nope. He was real broken up about it too. He could never have the woman he loved. Pitiful stuff."

Bobby kept playing with the glove box, open/shut, open/shut, open/shut. "Funny thing is, some people in town told me they knew Ada really did love my Dad and only married that other guy so her daddy would approve."

"That other guy you're talking about was my uncle."

"Sorry."

"Your father wound up marrying too?"

"Mom got the wedding band, but what she wanted most was his heart."

She gripped the steering wheel tighter. "Grizz was still in love with Ada, so his marriage was destined to fail."

"That's it in a nutshell. But the same isn't true of your aunt. She stayed married, even stayed away after her husband died. And now history is repeating itself."

"What do you mean?" she asked.

"That girl, the one you saw outside the house with the dog, we're in love. Big time love, but her daddy don't approve of me 'cause I don't have a job or a good future to offer. No job or nuthin'."

JoBeth saw a U-turn up ahead and made an executive decision, churning up gravel as her wheels skidded round — like some kind of NASCAR driver.

"Are you out of your mind? What are you doing? I thought we were going to see my dad."

"We are," she said in the most serious tone in her arsenal of voices, "but we're taking somebody with us." She zoomed ahead in a new direction, finally sure of what she was doing. This was a love story gone wrong and JoBeth planned to set things right. "We're picking her up. I asked the neighbors to take care of her."

He rolled his eyes upward as if praying, frustrated, or both. "Ada." Bobby covered his face with his hands. "I can't believe you're doing this to me."

"Why? Ada's a nice lady. I mean, I guess you could consider me biased, but really, she is. Plus, she has this little problem."

He peeked at her between his fingers, which thankfully, were nowhere near the size of hotdogs. Overall, the only noticeable similarity between Bobby and Big Grizz seemed to be in the full head of hair and beard. *I'd be thanking God every day my head wasn't shaped like a bison.*

"What kind of problem?" he asked.

"I'm not sure yet, we haven't gotten all the tests done yet, but she might have a touch of Alzheimer's or something."

He removed his hands from his face. "What? Then why are you bringing her? I mean, if she doesn't remember, what's the point?"

"Because she remembers your father."

He was silent a moment, likely mulling things over in his *normal-sized* head. He coughed. "Just to let you know, FYI, people don't just have a touch of Alzheimer's. They have it in different stages. It only gets worse."

She turned the corner to Ada's street and let out a whistle. "Thanks for the encouragement, Mister Bobby."

In less than five minutes, she had Ada seated and belted in the back seat, Roscoe at her side. JoBeth tried to talk her out of bringing him, but Roscoe wouldn't budge once he jumped in the car. He growled and snapped when they tried to force him out. So Roscoe assumed his favorite position, curled up and burrowed inside his natty old blanket on the floorboard.

JoBeth braced herself for the nasal assault to come. Though she'd warned him about Roscoe, Bobby didn't know what he was in for. She had to stifle a grin threatening to erupt.

"Aunt Ada, this is Bobby Herschelstein, Bobby, this is Ada Davidson, my aunt."

The anticipated assault came later than she thought. She'd hoped the change in diet was making a positive impact. But about ten minutes into the drive, Roscoe released his gaseous offensive.

JoBeth noticed Bobby shift from side to side like he was suddenly uncomfortable or something. He looked at her and she noticed the panicked look in his eyes, hands clawing at his face.

A veteran of the bad smell blitzkrieg, JoBeth pressed the electronic window button, confident the offensive odor would soon be sucked out. But to her horror, the window control didn't work. She pressed and pressed, finally banging on the control a few times with her fist, swerving slightly as she did. *Time to panic.*

But as it turned out, Bobby was resourceful as well as desperate. He pounded the vent open and adjusted the controls. Bad air out, good air in.

"Whew." Ada stretched an arm over the front seat. "Smells like somebody tooted in a potato bin."

He opened his mouth long enough to say, "Thanks."

But the vent suddenly stopped sucking and the odor hung in the air like a green sewer cloud.

"Gaah!" Though her eyes were beginning to water, JoBeth turned her focus to driving.

Ada continued, "I've never met you or your mother before though I've seen you around town. I always wondered what you were like in person." She studied his face. "You don't really look much like your father, but I can see you have his eyes, his sweet, sweet eyes."

Did Ada actually remember the introduction? If JoBeth wasn't so miserable, she would have been high-fiving somebody.

Then Ada did something else. She pointed at Bobby. "Is this nice young man your boyfriend?"

JoBeth frowned and "quick-glanced" him, a look of distaste surely mirroring the one on his face. "Nooooo. He's just a friend. That's all."

She patted JoBeth's shoulder again. "Where are we going? To the Frosty Top?"

JoBeth swallowed hard for two reasons. The thought of food intertwined with the rotten Roscoe smell didn't do a thing for her appetite, and number two, she didn't have the heart to tell her aunt that the remnants of the old Frosty Top diner were scattered across an empty lot on the way into town. "It's a—a surprise."

Her aunt clapped her hands together. "My, my, I love surprises. But I hope we get to eat. I'm hungry." She looked down. "And I think Roscoe is too. I always feed him when I eat. And I wanted to eat something at home but I couldn't find my food."

A whimper from the back seat confirmed that Roscoe had heard and acknowledged the word "food."

"Oh, of course we'll eat. Don't worry about that. Eating will definitely happen at some point for sure. We'll eat."

Though she spoke with confidence, JoBeth wondered how she would pay for a meal out. She had twenty dollars to her name after the grocery spree. But then she remembered the meager tip money *and* the money Grizz had pressed into her palm, and there was more than enough.

"Good." Ada reached to stroke her niece's hair. "You're a good girl, my Jo."

The sound of a siren blared behind them. This time, a police car shadowed the car, lights flashing round and round.

A sinking feeling punched the inside of her stomach. *Not again.*

JoBeth's hands began to shake as she pulled over to the shoulder. "Great, now I'm going to get a ticket I can't afford to pay."

Bobby held his hands up to his mouth, muffling his voice. "We got bigger problems than that." The invisible cloud of toxic stench bombarded the closed interior of the vehicle.

"What? I can't hear you." JoBeth threw her hands up. "How am I going to open the window for the cop?"

Bobby made a gagging sound, as if he were about to lose his lunch.

A sharp rap on the window caught their attention. Officer Ken.

JoBeth leaned her head on the steering wheel. "We're doomed."

Chapter Seventeen
Emissions Test

"How can I go on a diet? The refrigerator is still full." — Unknown

The black-gloved hand rapped on the driver's seat window. In response, JoBeth held up her hands. She pointed to the window button hoping he'd understand, but he didn't. He held his hands, palm up and moved them from the bottom of the window to the top. It was obvious he wanted her to roll down the window.

She pointed to the controls, and raised her voice. "I can't. It's broken." When she reached for the door handle and cracked it open, he backed up, hand on his holster. She spoke through the crack, her voice cracking as well. "Officer Ken, it's me, JoBeth. Remember? I brought you pancakes."

"Wow, that was brilliant," Bobby snarked, "Couldn't you think of anything better than 'I brought you pancakes?' Now he really thinks you're cuckoo."

So she tried again, her voice muffled through the thick window glass. "The power window is broken. None of them are working."

Officer Ken did a double take. He grabbed the door handle, pulling it open.

"JoBeth, eh? I remember you all right. Driver's license, insurance card and . . . is that what I think it is?" His head recoiled when he got a whiff of Roscoe's cloud. "When Hank told me about it, I tried to imagine what it was like, but whew, it's way worse."

"Yeah," JoBeth coughed, trying her best to ignore the smell and his remark. "Look, I'm trying to take Big Grizz's son to see him at the hospital."

"Can we get out of the car?" Bobby begged.

Ada, a rim of bright red lipstick on and around her lips, spoke up. "Somebody left their lunch in here."

The officer held his pencil out. "Nobody gets out of the car until I say so. Stay put."

JoBeth handed him her driver's license, insurance card and registration. By now, she knew the drill. He looked it over and handed them back. Then leaned in, held his breath and took a look inside, his eyes focusing immediately on Bobby.

Bobby's eyes had a pleading, sad kind of look. *Good gravy.*

The officer stepped back away from the car's interior and spoke. "Hank gave them an escort. They left over a half hour ago."

Frustrated, Bobby pointed to JoBeth. "My car broke down and she's taking me. Can you let us go, please?"

Bobby's eyes opened wide when he took a breath.

"Okay Miss Tomlin, I'm going to let you off the hook this time." He focused on Bobby. "And I'll give you all a police escort to University Hospital. Don't worry." He started to walk away, then turned back and poked his head back in, pointing to Bobby. "Unless . . ."

"Unless what?" Bobby craned his neck to hear.

"Unless you want to ride with me."

Bobby Herschelstein was out of the car before anyone could blink.

JoBeth wished she had the option.

The two men were off in a flash of sirens.

She followed the police vehicle all the way to town and straight into the parking lot at University Hospital. Ada stayed in the backseat for the rest of the ride, reiterating her unshakeable belief that someone had tooted in a potato bin.

The officer dropped Bobby off at the entrance. JoBeth and Ada met up with Bobby inside about fifteen minutes later. Her aunt wasn't capable of speed walking. Since the evening was almost upon them, and the temperature in the forties, JoBeth decided to leave the car windows open a crack with Roscoe inside. But then she remembered the automatic windows didn't work. A swift kick to the front tire temporarily calmed the storm inside her.

Confused, concerned or both, Ada held JoBeth's arm and asked. "What's wrong honey?"

"The window's not working. It won't go down."

"You mean it won't roll down?" she asked.

"No!" JoBeth pounded her fists on the hot hood of the car.

Without missing a beat, Ada began to pray. "Dear Lord, please fix JoBeth's windows. Amen." She took JoBeth's cheeks in her hands, a wide smile on her face. "There, now you can roll them down."

JoBeth rubbed her temples, willing herself to stay calm. "That was nice of you to pray Auntie, but . . . "

The hopeful expression on her aunt's face began to tug at her heart.

"Okay, we'll give it a try." With half-hearted effort, JoBeth slowly settled into the driver's seat and turned the key to start the engine. She glanced at her aunt standing outside the car. She touched the window switch.

And the window rolled down.

Just like that. Aunt Ada prayed, God answered, and the window worked. In fact, all four of the windows went down. The broken window switch had somehow undergone a supernatural repair.

Ada's face lit up as she smiled. "See Jo, I told you. God always answers my prayers."

JoBeth's jaw came unhinged. *What just happened?* Did her aunt have some sort of special hotline to heaven?

She stared at the dashboard. *Why did my parents have to die?* Apparently, God didn't have a problem fixing a stupid window switch on a car. Why didn't he prevent the accident?

"Jo?"

Tears rolled down her face. "It's not fair!"

"Jo?"

JoBeth swiped a sleeve at her face and tried to smile. "There's no doubt about it Auntie. You've got some kind of pull in heavenly places."

Ada reached for JoBeth's hands and planted a kiss. "God loves you too, Jo."

JoBeth needed a moment to decompress, so she and Ada took Roscoe for a little walk across the surrounding grassy areas before going into the hospital. Roscoe had needs. They couldn't stay long, anyway. She had to get dinner for Ada and then get her back home to rest.

In the cool of the evening, Ada's pooch would be fine in the vehicle. But even with the car window cracked open, JoBeth dreaded getting behind in for the ride back. In the short amount of time they would inside the hospital, Roscoe was sure to pollute the car's interior.

Once in the waiting area, JoBeth spotted Kit, Betty and Cecelia right away, which wasn't difficult considering they were still in their waitress uniforms. Then she saw Officers Ken and Hank.

"Where's Bobby?"

Ken pointed to the ER. "They took him right away."

JoBeth's eyes met at Kit's. She tried to decipher the older woman's expression. "How is Grizz?"

Kit brought a tissue up to her nose. "The doctors say it's real serious. Gonna be touch and go."

Betty broke in. "He needs an operation to save his life."

"A quadruple by-pass," Cecelia added. "My uncle had that and he turned out okay. Course he was ten years younger, and a runner and skinny."

"Who's sick?" Ada asked. She fussed with the top button on her housecoat.

All eyes upon her, she stood off to the side and put her hands on her hips. JoBeth's heart sank. *Should I have told her? Why didn't I at least try to prepare my aunt?*

She walked over and finished buttoning the top button on the housecoat. "Aunt Ada." She took her hands. "It's your friend, Grizz. He's had a heart attack."

Ada blinked, her mouth twitching. "Where is he? I want to see him. I don't care what Daddy says."

Officer Hank held out his arm. "Right in there, Ma'am. I'll walk you in."

Ada clung to him, arm trembling. JoBeth followed.

Bobby sat beside Grizz's bed holding his giant paw of a hand. His father was unconscious, chest heaving up and down thanks to the breathing apparatus. Hoses and wires crisscrossed his body. An IV hung over him, pushing fluids into his arm as the heart monitor graphed its every beat.

Ada gasped, tears in her eyes. "Grizz, oh my Grizz." She reached out to touch him, but everywhere she tried to touch was connected to something else. She began to stroke the tops of his feet, crying out.

Bobby soon joined her, his eyes overflowing with all the tears he'd been holding back. He buried his face in his father's hand.

"Cold, so cold." She sniffled. "We're going to have to warm up those feet of yours." She drew the hospital blanket over his feet and toes, tucking it neatly underneath. "You'll catch a chill." Tears flowed down her cheeks.

"Where's my Seth? He needs to see—" Her eyes pleaded with JoBeth's. "He needs to see his father."

"I—I'll get him here, Auntie. I promise."

She clasped her hand. "T-thank you, Jo."

A nurse approached to tell them only two visitors were allowed at one time.

"We should go." JoBeth put her arms around Ada's shoulders.

"I-I can't leave him." She leaned over grasping his feet.

"Auntie, let Grizz sleep right now. He needs to rest and recover. Come on. Bobby needs some time alone with his father."

She peered over her shoulder and saw Bobby's face still resting on his father's hand. By the rise and fall of his chest, she could see he was sobbing.

Back in the waiting room, they sat down and Ada reached for JoBeth's hands. Voice shaky, her aunt began to pray. "Lord, please help Grizzwald ask you into his heart. Heal him and make him whole." Her hands began to tremble. "He needs You now more than ever."

The waiting room fell silent as she prayed, the air bristling with emotion.

With tender care, JoBeth wiped Ada's face with a tissue. Kit sat down beside them. "Maybe you should take her home. This is a bit too much."

JoBeth kissed her aunt on the cheek and stroked her hair. "You're right. We'll go, but would you mind sitting with Ada for a minute while I place a call to Seth? She asked me to."

"You're really going to call him?" Kit asked, surprised.

"He's—I'm pretty sure he is—Grizz's son."

"Duh." Kit pursed her lips. "Boy looks just like him. People in town have been talking about that for years."

JoBeth gestured to the swinging doors. "I'll get better reception outside."

Ring. Ring. Ring. Ring. She'd made certain his number was in her list of contacts, especially since she was staying at his mother's house. It rang twice more before he answered.

"Seth?"

"JoBeth? Is Mom okay?"

"She's fine, but I have something else to talk to you about."

"What?"

"Maybe you should sit down."

A few minutes later, JoBeth returned to the waiting room, seething. Seth hadn't exactly embraced the news.

She lifted Ada's chin. "We'll come back tomorrow after the operation, okay?"

Ada's eyes were sort of blank and tired looking. "What operation?" She sat up straight. "Where are we? Are we going to have breakfast soon?"

Her short-term memory seemed to be getting even shorter. All the events of Ada's day, including the visit to Grizz, the emotion, the prayers — were erased — gone.

Kit touched JoBeth's arm, her expression sympathetic. "It's a blessing in a way." She continued, "Jo, I'm awful sorry about the way I acted in the beginning. I thought Grizz was plumb out of his mind when he hired you. But he knew exactly what he was doing. I think he hired you 'cause he considers you part of his family, the family he never got to know."

"Such a sad story," Betty whispered.

Kit patted JoBeth's arm. "And you're a hard worker. Grizz made the right decision. He was right about a lot of things."

They said their goodbyes to the others. JoBeth walked Ada out to the car. Officer Ken escorted them outside since it was early evening. Once she had Ada buckled in the back seat, JoBeth shook the officer's hand. "Thanks so much for all your help."

"My pleasure, Miss Tomlin." His eyes seemed to catch a movement in the back seat. Surprised, he gawked at the sight of Roscoe rousing from his nap. "So there is a dog after all?"

"I told you." JoBeth lifted her arms in triumph.

He shook his index finger at the animal. "You're a real stinker." Roscoe uttered a low growl in return, as if he understood.

The officer laughed. "I'm sorry Hank and I gave you such a hard time. We didn't know you were telling the truth."

"No worries." She beamed a smile his way, confident she would no longer be labeled the disgusting female offender with the broken taillight.

JoBeth opened the door, buckled in, fired up the engine and drove away. Motivated by her aunt's hunger, not to mention her own and Roscoe's, she decided to take Ada to Pearl's Place, a quiet little seafood eatery she was fond of. She chose to sit on the patio, which was surrounded by large potted plants. They could enjoy a fast, discrete meal, and most importantly, the place was canine friendly. A short wrought-iron fence separated the patio from the sidewalk.

Since she hadn't planned on going anywhere today, except to work, she still had her waitress uniform on. Ada was wearing a housecoat and Roscoe was, well Roscoe.

Their meals came fast and Roscoe set about devouring his underneath the table.

JoBeth took care to maneuver her chair so as to insure she would be partially concealed by a couple of bright green banana leaves. She noticed a few familiar people passing by, but thanks to the potted plants and an old drop-the-napkin-on-the-floor trick, she avoided locking eyes with any of them. After one such drop-the-napkin tactic, she sat back up in her seat, breathing a sigh of relief. But right in the middle of a rapturous spoonful of crab bisque, she heard someone call out her name.

"Joey?"

Only one person in the universe had ever called her that—Kyle. She looked up.

There, on the sidewalk side of the little ironwork fence, stood Kyle and Sam, "turned out" in suits and ties. All she could do was sit and stare.

Sam tilted his head as if puzzled. "JoBeth, what are you doing here? I didn't know you were in town."

She waved back, though her hand felt weak. "Hi, Sam."

Kyle took a step forward and leaned down to give her a hug. Her ex, the guy who dumped her, stood before her dressed in a killer suit, hair slicked back, wafts of his signature aftershave tickling her nose.

She resolved to exchange pleasantries, nothing more.

"Joey, you look great. Is that a uniform?"

Her worst fears, now realized! The last thing she wanted was for him to find out she worked as a waitress. JoBeth decided to redirect the conversation, hoping he would forget to bring it up again.

"Where are you guys off to?"

She gestured to Ada, almost knocking over her iced tea in the process. "You remember my aunt, right? Aunt Ada, this is Kyle."

Eyes wide, she looked from him to JoBeth, and back, confused. "Is he the skunk?"

"Hehehe, why Auntie, nooooooo. You remember K-y-l-e, my old boyfriend?"

"The skunk." Ada folded her arms, a frown on her face.

Maybe Ada's memory wasn't as bad as she'd thought.

Sam stepped forward. "I remember you, Mrs. Davidson. I met you about two Christmases ago at a family gathering. You guys called me to come fix a stopped-up sink, and then had me over for dinner afterwards."

Ada took his hand. "You're nice."

JoBeth let out a nervous laugh. "Sam really saved the day that day, didn't he though? Did I ever thank you for that? Cause, you really did a great job with that kitchen sink problem. I mean it. You really saved the day. For sure, you did."

"Joey," Kyle interrupted, "How are you?" He dug his hands into his pockets, a boyish stance she used to find charming.

"Where do I start? Well, after my apartment flooded, I moved to, I mean in with Ada. I moved in with my aunt."

Kyle cleared his throat. "I heard you moved there, to Beeton, I mean. Wow, what's that like?"

"It's a small town, but it's cool, you know. I mean there are things that go on there too, even though it's small and everything. The town's got swagger."

"Swagger, eh?" Sam latched onto the word, one eyebrow slightly off kilter. "Maybe I should come check it out sometime, 'cause *this* town is kind of low on swag."

"Oh yeah, hehe, maybe you should." While she laughed, she was mentally ramming her head into a wall, wailing. *Why oh why did I say something that stupid? Beaton's got swagger? Seriously?*

Kyle however, had not forgotten his first question. "You never got around to answering. Is that a uniform?"

"Oh this?" She looked down.

"Agh." Kyle stepped back suddenly. "What's that?"

She looked down, over the edge of the table. *Roscoe, you darling!* At that moment she could have kissed the stinky old dog.

"It's Roscoe."

"Who's that?" Kyle used his fingers as pincers to pinch his nose. "It's so bad."

"My aunt's dog." She pointed down and they both leaned over to look. Roscoe met their gaze with a soulful look, his tail lightly dusting the ground.

Sam batted at the air in from of him. "I have to agree. You sure that dog isn't part skunk?" He laughed.

Ada smiled. "That's my widdle boy."

"Hey." She held out her teaspoon in an attempt to quickly change the subject to something she knew would take Kyle in another direction. "How's Krull?"

Kyle backed up, fingers still pinching off his nose. "He's good." He looked at his watch. "Well, it was sure great seeing you, Joey, and nice to see you again too, Miss Ada, but we have to go. We're meeting Soph—meeting some people for dinner."

Meeting Sophie. He almost said it.

But Kyle stopped a moment in mid-track and turned back. "Look, I know this is weird but I'm kind of glad I ran into you because there's something I have to tell you, and it's better that you hear it from me."

JoBeth blinked. "What is it?"

"Sophie and I are getting married. Sam and I are on our way to the engagement dinner."

She couldn't seem to get a breath out at first but when she did, her voice sounded surprisingly calm. "Well congratulations. I'm happy for the two of you. I hope you have a great life together."

We dated for years and they dated for a second.

"Thanks." Kyle took a step backward.

"I'm glad we ran into each other and I got to hear the news straight from you." *I'm surprised he didn't text it.*

"Me too." He nodded.

"Bye." She waved, a totally fake smile tacked on her face.

She watched him go but was surprised to see Sam lingering behind, staring intently at her. Dressed in a sleek black suit and white collared shirt, she had to admit he looked incredible. There was an amused look on his face too. She had the distinct feeling he knew her smile was fake.

"You have a thing." He pointed, then picked up a napkin, dipped the edge in her glass of water and moved in closer.

"What?" Sam drew close, his face close to hers, and she could do nothing else but hold her breath. Full lips, chiseled jaw, muscular neck — a trio of personal space violations that set her heart pitter-pattering. She choked down her words.

As he swiped at the corner of her mouth, JoBeth could have sworn she felt a current of electricity run up and down her spine.

"A thing, it was a little piece of crab. Pearl's Place does have the best crabmeat bisque, don't they?"

She blinked. "Was that on my lip the entire time?"

He nodded. "I'm afraid so."

JoBeth sank down in her chair, hands on the side of her head. "Why, oh why didn't you tell me earlier?"

"I guess I didn't want to embarrass you."

Too late for that. "Thanks anyway."

Ada reached for Sam's hand and brought it to her cheek. "He's nice."

Sam shifted his gaze to JoBeth. Eyes twinkling, he smiled.

* * *

Ada, Roscoe and JoBeth were about halfway back home before JoBeth breathed a sigh of relief. Ada and Roscoe fell promptly asleep in the back seat. Somehow, the trip home seemed faster than the trip there. Or maybe she could attribute the swiftness of time to the state of her mind.

Frustrated by the news of Kyle's engagement, JoBeth gnawed on her lips, tears running down her face. *Kyle never even gave me a promise ring, and he gets engaged to some girl in a matter of months.* Every time she thought of that chance meeting with her ex, she felt like punching her fist through the dashboard.

She'd dreamed of seeing him again, only in one of her skinny phases, maybe even her fantasy size, double zero, and wearing something totally off the chain—makeup, hair and nails perfect, accompanied by a hot-looking guy. She'd walk by Kyle as if he were invisible, and he'd call after her.

She'd turn around, absently twirling a jeweled necklace from Tiffany's, a gift from the hot-looking male model she was dating. "Kyle? Why, I hardly recognize you."

JoBeth dreamed of a moment like this — the chance to make him regret what he'd done. Kyle would beg and plead with her to take him back. And she'd listen to his passionate entreaties until she spotted a glimmer of hope in his eyes. And right at that moment, that very moment, she'd pull out her phone and send him a "b-r-a-k-e-u-p" text. *Take that, Kyle!*

So much for all those revenge scenarios. Kyle had trumped every one of them when he said, "Sophie and I are getting married."

Finally home, JoBeth tucked a very tired Ada into bed, fed Roscoe, and apologized to Petey and Zoomba as she fed them. "Poor babies. I'm so sorry we were late with your din-din. Forgive me?" Both responded with grateful purrs. Tired, she shuffled towards her room, but changed her mind at the last second.

In spite of the late hour and her exhausted body, JoBeth wandered out to the front porch and sat on the wooden swing, launching off with a gentle push. Forward and back. Forward and back. How much sordid history could she fit into such a short period of time?

She found out about forbidden love and its consequences, discovered she had an uncle she didn't know existed, met another cousin, half-cousin, to be exact. And she'd found out more about her aunt than a niece had any right to know.

But the thoughts all jumbled together like puzzle pieces. There was no way she was going to piece things together tonight, at least not in her present state. She made her way to the bathroom and filled the tub. After a good soak in lavender bliss, she emerged from the tub thoroughly relaxed. A memory fluttered through her head as she toweled off, a recount of the morning she woke up to the butterfly.

A couple of weeks after she'd first spotted the chrysalis outside her bedroom window she woke up super early one Sunday morning to find the insect emerging. She set a chair nearby and stayed by the window as if glued there. Hours passed. After breakfast and three quarters of a boring novel, the wings slowly began to unfurl. Lovely wings, black and yellow, like delicate panes of stained glass. As the day progressed, she went about cooking and cleaning, but kept coming back to check. On one such visit, the wings began to flutter. Up and down. Up and down. She held her breath. And suddenly, the butterfly lifted off! It lighted briefly on a leaf and was gone.

JoBeth wiped a circle of steam away from the bathroom mirror and stared at her image. *Am I like that worm?* The face she knew so well was stronger, more resolved. She'd changed more in the past few months than she had in the past year.

She reached for her cell phone to call Rayne, but stopped in midair remembering what her mother always said, "Go to the throne, not to the phone."

There was something she had to do first, the only way out of her circumstance. Something she had avoided for a very long time.

Chapter Eighteen
JoBeth Meets Cain And Abel

"It's not the minutes spent at the table that put on weight, it's the seconds." — Daniel Worona

When she woke up the next morning, her whole body ached. After months of hard work and hard emotions, especially over the past few days, JoBeth had used muscles and summoned strength she didn't know existed. And all the turmoil left her wrung out and hung to dry like an old mop.

Ada was tired too. She let her aunt sleep as long as she could before rousing her and heading off to the hospital, this time without Roscoe. She ignored his whimpering. There was just no way she would allow herself to be embarrassed and humiliated like that again. Her taillight was still out, and given her recent history, the odds were high she'd be stopped.

Grizz was still in surgery according to the last call to Kit, though he was stable. Coincidentally, Ada had some of her tests scheduled at 8:00 a.m. The plan was for them to go to the hospital and spend the day doing the tests and keeping vigil in the waiting room until Seth's flight, which was scheduled to arrive at 2:00.

JoBeth would pick up Seth and bring him to the hospital. After that, they would take him home for a visit and a lot of *'splaining to do* as Ricky would say to Lucy. How would this affect Ada? She might not be ready to open up to her son about her past. And there was a good chance she wouldn't even remember. But it was high time for some 'splaining nonetheless.

On the way into town, JoBeth talked to Rayne on her cell while Ada snored in the back. JoBeth had put some thought into planning the trip; setting out pillows and a soft blanket in the back seat so her aunt could nap comfortably, yet remain safely buckled-in.

"Rayne, I'm glad you're going to be able to meet us at the hospital. Sorry I didn't tell you about what happened yesterday or call you back last night. It's just that everything went down so fast and I had to get Ada home. Trust me, you wouldn't have wanted to be around Roscoe."

Rayne whistled and double-popped her gum into the receiver as JoBeth filled her in on the events of the day before.

"Sounds like quite a day. So, I'm curious, what did your cousin say when you talked to him?"

"Not as much as you would expect from a guy who just found out his father might not be his real father."

"Wow." She accented the reply with an amazing pop.

JoBeth imagined a big pink hot air balloon-sized bubble sticking to her friend's face, a sight she'd seen happen once or twice before.

"Seth is like some kind of emotionless droid. I was so frustrated talking to him. He just listened to what I had to say and asked questions like I was talking to him about the weather. I had to beg him to take a flight out. He finally agreed."

"Jo, maybe he's on medication — some little happy pill and can't really express his emotions. Or maybe he's in therapy?"

"Doubtful."

She continued. "Or a sociopath. He could be a sociopath."

"Comforting thought, Dr. Carraway."

Rayne continued. "I'm taking off the rest of the day to spend with you at the hospital." Papers shuffled in the background. "Oh, and by the way, when I called yesterday I was going to tell you something, but then there was your emergency and all that, so I never got around to it."

"What is it?" JoBeth asked, curious.

Still shuffling papers, her voice sounded a bit distracted. "Agh."

"What's wrong?"

"I just dropped a stack on the floor." The phone sounded like it was doing somersaults. "Sorry." More somersaults and then she grabbed hold of the phone. "I-I'll just get it later. Anyway, I was wondering if you would go with me to a tournament. Not this weekend, but the next."

"I don't know. It kind of depends on what happens with Grizz. What kind of tournament?" she asked. "Basketball, golf, tennis, what?"

She snorted into the phone, which JoBeth guessed was some kind of ironic laugh. "Nooo, it's—" She coughed. "Cosplay."

JoBeth almost lost control of the car. "Oh *no*, not one of those things." Play day for geeks.

"I don't think so. Rayne, you know I can't think of anything else I'd want to do more on a weekend off then watch a bunch of nerds swing fake weapons at each other all day."

Rayne's roomies, hardcore LARPers, spent all their spare time crafting shields with personal crests, making Nerf spears and swords and sewing costumes, the whole enchilada. One of her roommates worked behind the counter at a self-storage facility, the other was a mailman, and the girl cut hair in a beauty salon specializing in edgy colors and cuts.

"C'mon, JoBeth. It'll be fun. We'll be outdoors getting tanned, hanging out with nice people." She clapped her hands. "And we could have a picnic lunch. Not the ordinary kind though, a real foodie lunch with gourmet stuff."

"And watch nerds joust and jab at each other with Nerf weapons . . ." JoBeth added with more than a hint of sarcasm.

"All right." She popped and snapped her gum. "Forget I said anything."

Now she was curious. "Rayne, why do you want to go anyway? You don't like those events any more than I do." She laughed hard into the phone. "Your roomies are total nerds."

"That's not cool. And for your information, I do go to some of the events to support them. It's only right. Besides, my roommates all pay their rent on time and keep the place clean too. I could do worse, you know."

Something wasn't ringing up right. "What's going on here?"

"What do you mean?" Rayne's voice resonated with a strange vibrato.

"Oh, I think you know what I mean. My spider senses are telling me a different story. Hmmm."

"Now who's the nerd?" She cackled. "Spider senses."

The nervous laugh, the evasive comments, the audibly louder and more frequent gum chomps, all added up — but to what? JoBeth waited, hoping the silence would prompt her friend to 'fess up.'

Rayne finally broke. "Okay, so there's this good-looking guy who's playing a knight and he's everything I've always dreamed I wanted in a man. He's perfect — like he stepped out of a modeling shoot. When I first met him through my roomies, I couldn't stop staring at him. And, and to sum things up, I think I'm in love."

JoBeth sucked in her breath.

"He's really hot." She stopped chomping. "Promise me you'll come. I need you with me, Jo."

JoBeth whistled, amazed at her friend's infatuation. Rayne and the word "infatuation" didn't go together. He friend was an even-tempered, sensible—a look-before-you-leap type. "Does this guy even know you like him?"

"Not yet."

"I knew it."

"What do you mean by that?"

"Rayne, I love you to the moon, but it's not worth wasting a day watching nerds skip around sweating and sneaking bites of hot pockets hidden in their costumes and yelling at each other in the stupid metaphorical language I don't understand."

"The guy has a smoking-hot friend," Rayne dangled the temptation.

JoBeth paused. Her friend was pulling out all the stops. "Define smoking hot."

"I mean, sizzling, volcanically hot."

"Volcanically hot, eh? Why aren't you chasing after him instead? The other guy is only hot."

Rayne answered. "Because—because the hot one is the one I like."

"Hmmm. My friend, you've given me something to think about. All I can promise is, I'll think about it."

Rayne sighed. "I know you have to play it by ear with your situation and everything." Papers shuffled again. "Look, I'm going to do the fifty-two card pickup with the stuff I just dropped on the floor and meet you at the hospital in a bit. See ya."

Ada and Roscoe slept the whole rest of the way. JoBeth was glad to have a bit of quiet time, a little peace in the midst of all the chaos.

Going to the cosplay thing would definitely be a sacrifice. But Rayne had done a lot to help her. The least she could do was suffer through a boring day on her friend's behalf. And there was the matter of the smoking hot guy. Funny. The first image that popped into her mind when she thought of a smoking-hot guy — was Sam.

When they arrived at the hospital, Kit informed JoBeth that Grizz was still in surgery. The doctors either considered him stable enough or were desperate enough to go through the bypass.

JoBeth had brought along a comb, some deodorant and toothbrush for her new half-cousin Bobby since he'd stayed there all night. Bobby looked ragged, even after he'd taken the comb to his hair and brushed his teeth.

Later, he sat down next to her in the waiting room, idly rubbing the beard stubbles across his cheeks. "He's gonna have to do a complete lifestyle change according to the doctor. No more cigars or eating too much or being on his feet all day cooking." A thought washed across his tired face. "What did you all do about the café?"

JoBeth answered, "No worries. We closed it yesterday. Kit had me put a sign in the window about your dad. The regulars all know anyway."

"Right." He nodded. "Thanks."

"If you want us to open the place, we could. I can take over the cooking until you guys figure something out. There's no doubt I know my way around a kitchen."

"Really?"

"Sure, I've already filled in for your dad before and it wasn't too disastrous, except for the way I looked afterwards. Besides, the longer you keep it closed, your regular customers are going to go somewhere else and the food's going to go bad."

"I don't know. The café's the last thing I'm worried about. I never liked that place anyway." He slumped back in the chair.

His stance reminded her of a bratty little kid.

JoBeth snapped into action. Those psychology classes she thought were worthless in college might come in handy after all.

"Really? So, what you're saying is you don't care about your father's business, a lifelong dream he's poured his whole life into? And I guess you don't give a lick about your inheritance either."

He strummed his fingers on the chair rest and looked at her.

"That's right. The Last Chance Café is your inheritance. Even if you wanted to sell it, you'd never get back what the place is worth when it's closed down and boarded shut."

Then his fingers began to strum more slowly as if reaching a light bulb moment. "Do you seriously feel like you could run the kitchen? That's hard to do. I don't know how dad did it all day every day. He let me do some cooking occasionally when I worked as a bus boy in the café in my teens. I must've watched him cook a thousand times over the years."

JoBeth answered. "I don't think I could do it all day though. It's hot as H-E double toothpicks in there. I don't know how your dad does—did it."

"Maybe, the answer is in split shifts. JoBeth, you could do the first shift and I could do the second."

"That could actually work." She smiled. "Good thinking."

A nurse walked into the waiting area. "Herschelstein family?"

Bobby stood. The room fell silent. "Yes."

She held up a hand. "Don't be alarmed. I'm just here to tell you that the patient will be able to receive visitors, family members only, in about a half hour according to doctor's orders. Two minutes each, two people at a time, okay?" She touched Bobby's shoulder. "He's critical, so when you do go in to see him, please make sure he remains calm." She lifted her chin to Bobby. "The doctor wants to talk to you. Follow me."

He swallowed hard and followed her down the hallway.

JoBeth checked her watch and turned to her aunt. "It's time for us to get those tests done."

A puzzled look fell on Ada. "What tests? JoBeth, what do you mean? I don't need any tests. I feel fine."

"The tests we talked about with Dr. Brenham. You remember seeing him, don't you?"

She stood up and tipped from side-to-side, like she wanted to run. "I don't know any doctor. Why am I here anyway? I'm missing my shows. I want to go home now." She grabbed her purse and held it close, as if it held top-secret information or was filled with cash! But there was nothing much in it except an expired drivers license, a tube of lipstick and some orange Tic Tacs her aunt was convinced were baby aspirins.

Kit stood up, concerned. Betty and Cecilia stopped talking and watched.

JoBeth steered her aunt by the shoulder. "Okay, we'll go home. I just have a little errand on the way. You don't mind coming along, do you?"

Her aunt relaxed. "Okay, I suppose not."

Although she felt bad about fooling her aunt, it was absolutely the only way she could get her to the appointment. And to JoBeth's amazement, when they signed in for the testing, Ada didn't put up a bit of fuss. She'd already forgotten about it.

JoBeth checked back in the waiting area after Ada's tests were completed to find out about Grizz. Kit was there, standing by the window holding a styro cup of coffee. There were lines on her face JoBeth had never noticed before. Cecelia and Betty had called a relative to take them home. Bobby sat a few chairs away on his cell phone. She walked Ada to a chair and sat her down, and joined Kit at the window.

"How is he?"

Her eye twitched. "Holding his own."

"What do you mean?"

Eyes watery, she continued staring, as if in shock. "It ain't too good. He'll live through this most likely. You know they done a quadruple bypass on him this morning. Doctors said it worked. But he can't cook anymore or do much of anything like he used to. He's still got a bum ticker."

"Oh no."

She continued. "The only shot he has is to git a new heart and there ain't no chance of that. He's too much of a risk. They got other people with higher chances of survival who need 'em. That's what the doc said."

"You mean he's going to die?" JoBeth couldn't believe it.

Kit's lip quivered.

"How much time do they think he has?"

She wiped her eyes with a clumped up tissue. "They don't know. Depends on when his heart decides to quit on him."

"Is he going to be able to go home?"

She nodded. "Yeah, in a couple weeks or so to recuperate." She wiped a tear away.

JoBeth hugged her, and as she did, her face brushed up against Kit's hair, a teased web of Aqua Net.

"We'll get through this." She lifted Kit's chin with her index finger. "Okay?"

Kit smiled through her tears. "Okay."

"I have to go to the airport and pick up Seth. Are you going to stay here?"

"Café's closed. I got nowhere else I need to be."

"Would you mind keeping Ada with you? After all those tests, it might be better for her to stay here with you and rest a bit—maybe even grab a bite to eat." She added, "Do you think you could get her in to see Grizz too?"

"I'd be happy to help." She wiped a fresh onslaught of tears. "I just hope she doesn't git too worked up when she sees him with all those tubes and machines around him." She buried her face in a tissue.

JoBeth reached over and cradled Kit's head on her shoulder while she sobbed.

Ada, oblivious to them, stared out the window, a little smile on her face. What was she thinking about? Hopefully, Ada was thinking happy thoughts. *Somebody* needed to think happy thoughts.

She offered Kit some money to buy lunch in the cafeteria, but the woman refused, insisting that she take care of Ada.

JoBeth timed her arrival at the airport with enough leeway for Seth to touch down and make it to baggage. His flight was on time according to the App on her cell phone. His number was on speed dial. If things worked out, she'd be seeing him walk through the automatic doors to the pick-up area any minute.

There were lots of security personnel in the area. A few policemen directed traffic. Worried about the taillight situation, she pulled in behind a red Mini Cooper. She'd have about ten minutes wait time before she reached the front of the line. Then the policeman would direct her to go and she'd have to circle back around and get back in the queue. Hopefully that wouldn't happen.

She answered the cell on the first ring. "Hello? Hello?"

"It's me."

"You at the hospital?" She asked Rayne.

"No, I was on my way out when my boss called me back. One of the clients is having a meltdown about the ad campaign and wants a whole new concept." She sighed. "Looks like I'm going to be here burning the midnight oil."

"Aw, I'm sorry you have to work. I'll miss you. Oops, there's a call coming through. I think that's Seth. Don't work too hard. See ya."

"Hello?"

Greeted by Seth's monotone, she wondered if she'd ever hear or see any emotion come out of the man. He told her he was waiting outside the door. With renewed expectation, she revved up the engine and drove straight to him. She'd described her Loser Cruiser to him. He stowed his luggage in the back seat and settled into the front.

"Hi." She looked him over with a whole new perspective, in fact, with flat-out amazement. The more she analyzed her cousin, the more she realized the boy belonged to Grizz. Head like a bison, hotdog fingers, the trademark Herschelstein look.

He stared straight ahead. "Hello, JoBeth."

She smiled. "I'll wait till you get buckled."

He clicked the seatbelt together. "Done."

"Thanks." She popped the car in drive and accelerated. "How are you doing?" JoBeth coughed and cleared her throat, the situation nothing less than awkward.

But then, without warning, she started blurting. "I mean, how are you handling all this? It's a real shock, isn't it? Finding out your dad might not be your dad. I know you loved . . ."

He stopped her in mid-sentence. "Can we skip the small talk and go to the hospital and get this over with? I really have a lot of work to do and I'm hoping to swing by the plant before the end of the day."

Stunned, she answered, her voice in "best manners" mode. "Sure, no worries." But the more she thought about the man's callous attitude and the way he treated his mother, the madder she got. Halfway to the hospital, she could no longer keep it in and cut through the silence with laser precision.

"Seth, what is wrong with you? I mean, you act like you don't care, like you're not affected by any of this news. Your whole world should be shaken to the core. You should be sitting in that seat asking me a million questions. But you're not. It's like you're disconnected or something."

He turned to her, his face a blank canvas.

"What do you want me to say? What if we start with the facts? My mother had an affair and the man I thought was my biological father was actually my stepfather. And I have a trailer trash half-brother too." He waved a hand in the air. "Wow—celebrate."

While JoBeth was still processing that slice of drama, she watched as he pulled a handkerchief out of his pocket and blew his nose.

What kind of man under the age of seventy carries a handkerchief?

He continued. "Can I change any of these facts? No."

JoBeth pulled to a stop at a red light. "That's it? That's what you have to say about all this?"

He hesitated, as if thinking about how to answer. "Yes." He pointed. "The light is green."

They drove the rest of the way in silence while she thought about what to say and he probably thought about how to dodge whatever she was going to say. She pulled into the hospital parking lot and began to cruise for a place.

"First of all Seth, what you stated as fact, isn't true. Your mother did not have an extramarital affair with Grizz. She conceived you while she was *married* to Grizz, a legal marriage that was annulled. Grizzwald Herschelstein is your biological father."

"Oh." He boinged his hand off of his head, trampoline-style. "That's soooo much better. Thanks for pointing that out."

Fuming, she voiced a comeback. "Apparently our grandfather had the marriage annulled."

"And Mom kept that little bit of information about a previous marriage from my dad, didn't she? She let him believe I was his own son, though the biological father was someone else. And she wanted this other man even though she was married to my dad. That's adultery you know. Even if it's in your mind."

"Stepfather," she corrected.

"Father. If my biological father wanted me, he should have let it be known. But I only have one father and he's dead."

"Grizz is very much alive." She stole a glance at him.

"For the time being," he snarled.

"Why would you say something like that? You're an idiot!"

"Whatever."

JoBeth's chest heaved, the anger rising.

"I visited that sorry café for years. If that greasy excuse for a man wanted to meet me, he could have walked out of that kitchen any time and said, 'Hey, I'm your dad. I slept with your mother. Glad we finally met, son. Hope you had a good life. Now I have to get back to flipping burgers.'"

"That's enough!"

He shot a sideways glance. "I'm just getting started."

Grizz could have told Seth he was his father, but he didn't, probably out of respect for Ada. Grizz had every right to hate the woman. She'd had the marriage annulled and apparently, never told him about their baby. He had to find out by watching the boy grow up in the same town, and notice, along with the rest of the residents of Beeton, the uncanny resemblance.

The more JoBeth got to know Grizz and the depth of his love for Ada, the more convinced she was that Grizz would never have acted against her wishes. Still, she wasn't sure how to answer Seth.

"Don't expect me to get all touchy-feely about the news. That man may be barely alive, but he's dead to me. Understand? As far as I'm concerned, I'm here for my mother."

Her heart sank at his words. They walked through the hospital in complete silence. When they finally entered the waiting room, Ada rose, threw her arms around her son, and kissed him over and over again.

"Oh Sethie, my baby. I missed you so much. How are you, sweetie pie? I can't remember the last time I saw you. Are you eating right? You're thin and you need some sun, but that's nothing some of your mama's home cooking and some fresh air won't fix." She grabbed his jaw with her hand and wiggled it into a sweet pucker. "That's my boy."

The sight of it wrenched her heart. Ada really missed her son. Needed him too. Even though her niece was there with her, the one face she really wanted was standing there right in front of her. How could JoBeth convince that cold, bitter excuse for a son of that?

Bobby looked on the tender scene, waiting for the right moment. Eyes on Seth, the brother he never knew, he was likely confirming the same physical similarities that she had.

"Herschelstein family?" The nurse held the door open and scanned the waiting room. "The patient can receive visitors again. Family members only at this time."

Bobby started towards the nurse, but stopped and crooked an arm for Ada.

"Would you like to come with me, Miz Ada?"

She smiled and took his arm. As the two started towards the door, Bobby suddenly stopped again. He spun around and signaled to Seth. Perhaps too stunned to object, Seth, hesitated a moment, but went with them.

"Here we are," Bobby said to the nurse, "The Herschelstein family."

"But there are three of you," she objected.

Bobby grinned and rocked his head from Ada to Seth. "Yes, there are."

Chapter Nineteen
Dog Gone It

"Nothing was a more powerful compass of my mood or a better indication of my self-worth than the number on the scale." — Betsy Lerner, Food and Loathing: A Life Measured Out in Calories

Beer cans and bottles, a rat's nest of tires, trash, and a couple of old cars up on blocks created a junkyard ambience in the overgrown yard. JoBeth held her head high and strode to the front porch. The screen door was off on one hinge, so she knocked on the wall next to the door.

She'd decided to pay a visit to the house next to Bobby's on Hystaker Lane — the one with the little white dog tied up in the back yard.

JoBeth remembered every detail of how to get there, the street sign hidden behind a large overgrown Mulberry bush. And sure enough, two houses down the street on the left, the little rat terrier was short-chained in the front yard. That dog had captured her heart from the moment she set eyes on him.

Slade Crayton answered the door, the smell of alcohol on his breath. His shirt, a wrinkled, mismatched plaid was stained and straightup shabby. Add a skipped button and the whole shirt gave an off-kilter vibe. The man didn't seem to care much about anything, certainly not the way he smelled or about the grey dirt under his fingernails either.

Though she knew his name and a little bit about the man thanks to Bobby, he was actually worse than she'd imagined.

"Hello, my name is JoBeth Tomlin."

"I ain't got no money to give none of you people," he wheezed.

"I'm not asking."

"And I ain't got no time for no religion neither."

"That's not why I'm here."

He squinted as if seeing her in a new light. "Then what're you here fer, purdy lady?" Slade ran a hand through his grimy hair, preening what was left of it.

"Like I said, my name is JoBeth Tomlin, and yours is?"

He seemed confused for a moment. "Oh, ah Crayton. Slade Crayton's the name."

"Good to meet you, Mister Crayton."

"You can call me Slade." He winked.

"I'm here to see if you might be interested in selling me that dog you got chained out back. I'm looking for a Rat Terrier."

Sly thoughts seemed to streak across the chalkboard of his dilated pupils. The man was likely thinking about how to take her for the most money.

"Well, why don't we go take us a look?" He hitched up his pants that had fallen low on his hips for lack of a belt. Gaunt, boney and gristle-faced, he walked with an unsteady gait.

They maneuvered through the tall weeds on the side of the house around to the backyard. On the way JoBeth noticed a broken Venetian blind on a window move slightly and got the definite feeling they were being watched.

The dog's short, snipped tail vibrated briefly like a compass needle, then tucked down the closer they came. He cowered at Slade's approach. Another sign JoBeth was dealing with a real scum ball.

JoBeth bit her lip. *Gotta play this cool.*

"Here he is." The man popped the top off a cheap beer pulled from his pocket. How convenient. *No wonder his pants were falling down.*

"One thing you should know 'bout this here dog is he's a real 'pure bread' animal." He wiped a sleeve across his mouth, "Shiner's worth a lot of moo-lah."

White with black spots, his body petite and undernourished, JoBeth's heart immediately went out to this sweet, neglected dog. She bent down and offered the top of her hand for Shiner to sniff—a non-threatening way for a dog to get to know a human. The chain around his neck, too heavy for his diminutive size, clanked as he moved.

Eyes moist, JoBeth spoke in a happy voice to him. "Here boy. That's a good boy." He sniffed her hand and though cautious, flicked out his tongue for a quick lick. His tail wagged a bit—a good sign.

Encouraged, she reached out and began to pet his head. But he backed off as soon as Slade opened his mouth. "So miss, looks like Shiner's taken a shine to you." When he lifted a leg to rest his foot on a dry tree stump, his pants hiked up revealing purple bruises against the pale of his ankle. "But this here guard dog is real important 'round here. He protects us from criminals an' such. This here show-dog earns his keep." He bent down to pet Shiner's head, but Shiner backed off and showed his teeth. Slade uttered a curse. He turned his mouth to the side and spit out something black.

"Shiner ain't on his best behavior today, but he's one of them fancy kinda dogs and that's how they is." He held up his hands, palms up. "What kin I say?"

JoBeth looked him in the eye, barely containing the distaste she felt for the man. "How much do you want for him?"

He stroked his chin with a grimy hand, a pensive expression on his face "Well, I 'spect since yer a dog lover and stuff, I could part with him fer about five hundred dollars." He stared back at her for a response.

She opened her purse and held out cash. "Take a zero off of that and you've got a deal. I've got fifty bucks."

He let out a string of curse words, and spit again. He brought his foot down hard on the ground. "Yer wastin' my time, little miss. You ain't gittin my prize show dog fer no measly Ulysses S. Grant. Where was you raised? That's a insult where I come from." He pointed. "A personal insult. I ain't gonna fergit that neither."

He set off toward the house.

Ah, negotiations. She watched him go and knew he expected a counteroffer from her. The problem? There was there was no counteroffer to make. JoBeth had no more money to put down on the table. And it broke her heart. This poor dog, abused and neglected by its miserable excuse for an owner, was out of luck.

She followed Slade out of the backyard to the front porch. As she started down the steps he yelled out. "You got two-fifty? It'd be a loss to me, but I like you. You're a purdy little thang and I'd be a-willing to let go part of the asking price fer you."

A sideways glance showed him how dismal her mood was. "I don't have two-hundred and fifty dollars. I have fifty."

He shuffled around, as if uncomfortable. "Seventy-five. I'll take seventy-five."

"All I've got is fifty. That's it." To accentuate the fact, she held up the money and fanned it out, waving it seductively back and forth hoping the sight or smell of it would lure him.

He shook his head. "No, no, I ain't giving the animal away. That' ain't enough cash fer that dog. I'll fetch a better price fer him with someone else." He held a finger up. "I'll put a ad in the paper and fetch a purdy penny fer him." He pointed a gnarled finger and prophesied. "You'll regret what you missed out on. You coulda had a deal, but you passed it up." He popped a fresh wad of chewing tobacco in his mouth and rained black spittle off the side of the porch.

JoBeth turned and walked back to the car without saying goodbye. Dejected, she drove off, circling round for a last look at Shiner. "Sorry I let you down, boy." He cocked his head to the side like he was disappointed. The tears flowed as she left, so much so, she had to pull over by the landmark mulberry bush.

"Lord," she cried. "I know you and I haven't talked much lately. But could you please help me? That little dog needs help. Please help me get that pup out of there. You could even give him to someone else. As long as he goes with someone who loves him and will take good care of him, that's okay with me. Help him, please."

JoBeth sat in her car and cried for a few more minutes before she felt together enough to take off again. Her sleeves were wet, mascara runny. When she pulled into Ada's driveway, she reached for the kit she kept in the car. Life had gotten so busy that most days she did her makeup in the driver's seat, before or after arriving at wherever she was headed. This time the mirror revealed something surprising though. Her face looked different. She moved her head at different angles to get a better perspective. Thinner. Her face was definitely getting thinner. Car mirrors don't lie.

Touch-up complete, she shuffled down the hallway, hoping to sneak past her cousin. He was the last person she wanted to see. After the emotional outburst in the car, JoBeth felt drained. As she walked the hallway past the kitchen, he called out to her. Ada and Seth were sitting at the kitchen table, a plate full of succotash in front of each of them. He looked up at JoBeth, like he was ready to make a mad dash out of the house. Ada was busy tucking a napkin under his shirt collar.

She stifled a laugh while depositing a kiss on her aunt's cheek. "Hiya, Seth." She pulled out her phone and snapped a picture.

Her cousin held his eyes shut for longer than a moment. When he opened them, he glared. "Don't post that anywhere. I mean it."

"Aw, Aunt Ada, you made your little boy his *favorite* dish." JoBeth smiled sweetly, "Don't worry. I intend to add this cute family photo to the other ones on the wall."

She reached for a chair and pulled it away from the table. He patted the seat. "JoBeth. Won't you please join us for lunch? We were just getting ready to dig in. There's plenty enough for all of us."

Ada pinched JoBeth's cheek. "You need to eat more, dear. You're wasting away."

Me? Was she talking about me? I could see her telling Rayne that, but never me.

"Yes," Seth added with a sneer, "you should join us."

JoBeth waved her hands vigorously. "Oh no, I really not all that hungry. Besides, you two need a little mother-son time together."

"A glass of iced tea then?" Ada poured one over ice before she could answer.

"Thanks, Auntie." She settled into a chair at the table.

"So." Seth took a tentative spoonful and stared her down. "If you don't mind my asking, how'd you get in such a bind? I mean, financially. You know — how'd you wind up having to move in with my mom?"

JoBeth could feel the smile melting off her face. *Touche' Sethie.*

He continued, "I don't want to be nosey or anything, but didn't your parents leave you some money when they died?"

Stay calm. "Do you remember that they owned a Christian bookstore business?"

"That's right. Bookstores. *Hmmmpf!*"

Ada forced another spoonful into his jaw, an adoring smile on her painted lips.

"What do you mean, by that?" JoBeth asked, her voice on edge.

In between bites, he answered. "Retail businesses are problematic. Much too risky."

Ada shoved another spoonful of limas into his mouth.

She couldn't argue with cold logic, *emphasis on cold.* "They were in a lot of debt. Mom and Dad prayed about it and decided to put all their savings into trying to keep the shop open. They were ready to take out a second mortgage. And why? Because they believed God wanted them to keep that shop open, and that they were making a difference in the community."

He interrupted, "Sounds like they made some bad business decisions." He held up his spoon. "I could have advised them." He pointed. "And you know what I would have told them? Dump the business on some moron who doesn't know any better, or liquidate the inventory and shut the doors."

She stared at him, wondering how he could be so lacking in emotion or compassion. "Gee, thanks, but like I said, my parents *prayed* about it. And no one on this earth could fault them for being faithful to God's call. Not even YOU." JoBeth pressed her lips together to keep from verbally clobbering him.

He squinted. "Then I guess the Almighty wanted your parents to go bankrupt."

She squinted in disbelief. "What?"

"Susan's bankrupt?" Ada's face registered concern.

JoBeth pressed her lips tightly together, hoping the choice words she wanted to unleash on her caustic cousin would stay put. She flashed an angry look at him.

"Aunt Ada, everything's all right with her now."

"Oh, thank goodness." Soothed by her reassurance, her aunt calmed down and resumed eating.

For Ada's sake, JoBeth decided to get away from her idiot cousin. "Sorry to bow out, Auntie, but I think I need a nap. The café reopens the day after tomorrow and I'm going to need every ounce of strength to do all that cooking to keep Grizz's business open."

"All right, dear. That's sweet of you." She placed her hands on JoBeth's cheeks and pulled her head down close for a kiss. Ada's eyes lit up when she looked over at Seth. "Darling, you should go help Grizzwald out too."

Seth's mouth hinged open and a lone lima bean dropped out.

JoBeth realized that Seth hadn't had much time to work through things, and he certainly hadn't figured out there was something seriously wrong with his mother.

"Yes, mother," he snapped. "Maybe I should go help keep that dirt ball's business afloat. Maybe I should help the man you slept with. Maybe that's what I should do."

Stunned, JoBeth put her arms around Ada's shoulders.

"What did you say, son?"

JoBeth tried to stop him, but he blurted it out.

"You had another man's baby. How could you?"

Now the emotions were flowing. But he had no idea about his mother's delicate state. How could he not see it?

She smiled at her son. "Baby? Who's having a baby? I love babies." She touched his arm. "Are you married? Did I go to the wedding?"

He stared, disbelief freezing his expression in place.

In as calm a voice as she could muster, JoBeth asked. "Seth, could I speak with you alone? Out on the back porch?"

He sat back in his chair. "About what?"

Stunned at his ignorance, she slowed her words down. "About t-h-i-s." She did a circular motion with her hands. "This situation."

He stood up. "All right." He looked back at his mother. "Make it quick."

"I'll try." JoBeth smiled at Ada. "Keep eating. Excuse us for a minute or so, Auntie. We'll be right back."

A pleasant smile on her face, she responded. "All right dear, but don't be too long. The succotash will get cold. Nobody likes cold succotash."

The back porch was no more than a neglected stoop with two old apple crates to sit on. JoBeth peeled the napkin off her tea glass and brushed off the crates. They sat down.

"Well?" His hotdog fingers formed a steeple.

"What do you think of your mother?"

He recoiled. "What kind of question is that? She's my mother."

"A legitimate one. Now answer."

He sat up straight. "If you'd have asked me that last week I would have said something positive, maybe even mushy." He put his hands over his eyes. "But now — now you don't want to know what I have to say."

JoBeth interrupted. "I wasn't talking about that particular issue. Since you brought it up however, let's discuss what came out of your mouth a few minutes ago. What you said to your mother was inexcusable and beyond disrespect. And are you seriously trying to blame her?"

"Yes and that piece of garbage she talks about."

"Ada married the man she fell in love with. Don't you get it? That formula is supposed to end happily. But instead she was bullied by her father to end that marriage and marry someone else."

"My father!" He rasped.

"Your mother is the real victim in this situation. Don't you have the slightest iota of compassion for her?"

He glared. "I didn't ask to have my life turned upside down."

Disgusted, JoBeth pounced on his words. "Really? Do you think you're the only one whose life has ever been turned upside down?"

"I didn't mean . . ."

"Are you trying to make this all about you? Maybe you should think about what you're going to say before you open your mouth. I lost everything and *I'm* still here!"

"Sorry." His voice cracked. "I know it's hard. What you've been through—I mean, losing your parents is rough."

"And my parent's bookshop and my childhood home, and almost everything in it, and my job and my apartment and my boyfriend, and more."

He interrupted. "I get it, okay? Let me tell you again, I'm sorry."

JoBeth closed her eyes for a moment to calm herself down. "Thank you."

"Now, back to the point of why we came out here." She cleared her throat. "I want to know what you think of your mother's condition."

He peeked out between his fingers and pulled them away. "Her general condition. She seems like she's in okay health for her age, if that's what you mean."

"That's not what I'm talking about."

"What then? I know she's forgetful. But she's old."

She grimaced. "Haven't you noticed anything different about her? I know you haven't been home very long, but my friend and I noticed right away there was something going on."

The look on his face told her he still had no idea what JoBeth was talking about.

"Is she sick? Does she have some kind of disease I need to know about?" Panic froze his face in a confused expression. "Tell me."

The words barreled out. "Seth, I hate to have to tell you this, but your mother might have Alzheimer's or Dementia or vascular degeneration—something on that order. Ada has a very poor short-term memory. For some reason, maybe one of the above, she can't remember what she said or did moment-to-moment."

A light of recognition began to burn in his eyes. "She keeps telling me the same things and asking the same questions over and over again."

"Bingo."

"Well, what can we, I mean, what can I do about that? Is there a pill?"

"Don't be mad, but I took Ada to University Hospital to have her checked out, and the diagnosis should be ready soon."

"What? You took her to see a doctor without asking me?"

She nodded an affirmation. "Yes, to the hospital and they ordered a lot of tests. I know I should have told you about what was going on, but I thought I'd wait until we had a firm diagnosis. She has an appointment two days from now to see her doctor. He'll have the diagnosis by then. It's the same day the café reopens, but I'm off in the afternoon. Kit's going to take over the cooking."

"You should have told me. She's *my* mother, not yours."

JoBeth tilted her head to the side. "Really? You act like I'm trying to take your mommy away from you. Are you a five-year-old?"

"No, but it's not your place to do that. It's mine. I take care of my own mom."

She sniffed. "How can you say that? You haven't been with her every day and seen what I've seen. For instance, did you know she was eating spoiled food? Did you know the house was a wreck—and that she was wearing the same clothes every day?"

He went silent at her words. Voice muffled, he finally answered. "No, I should have. I should have checked on her more." He cleared his throat. "I know I haven't been there for her much in the last couple of years. I worked hard to establish the company in multiple locations." He squinted, as if focusing in on something. "It takes time and sacrifice to do that. I used to have friends, even a girlfriend, but I'm too busy."

Seth looked out over the neglected back yard, grimacing as he did. "I didn't realize. Sure, I noticed she went through some hard times when dad died, but she seemed to be handling things as well as she could. She enjoyed going to church and getting to know the neighbors." Teary-eyed, he looked miserable.

JoBeth got up and stood next to him, her arm on his shoulder. "You're here now. That's all that matters."

"Sorry about what I said in the kitchen. I wasn't sure why you moved in. I thought maybe you were mooching off my mom or something."

"I'm shocked that you would think that about me. We grew up together. I'm not mooching. Your mom is helping me out by letting me stay here, that's all."

He wiped his hand under his nose. "I was wrong. I'm sorry."

"Sethie? JoBeth?" Ada poked her head out the back door. There's someone knocking." Ada's voice dwindled. They both sprang up, knocking the crates down as they did. JoBeth started down the hallway, her cousin in tow.

But somehow, along the way, Ada managed to shove another spoonful of succotash into her son's mouth. JoBeth smiled at the sight.

She beat Seth to the front door and swung it open. To JoBeth's surprise, standing on the front stoop was Candy, Bobby's *amore'*. Blonde hair pinned back from her face revealed perfect skin and teeth, long legs and a sweet expression. JoBeth could hardly believe Slade's tattered genes could have produced such a creature. In her right hand was a rope and tied to the collar on the end of that rope — the little rat terrier!

"Shiner?" JoBeth bent down and scooped him into her arms. Tentative at first, he flicked his tongue at her cheeks and began licking. Joyful, tail wagging a mile a minute, Shiner was like a different doggie from the sad pooch chained in the junkyard. She thought at once about the tearful prayer she had offered by the mulberry bush and whispered a silent thank you to God.

"Who's that?" Seth joined her at the door. A stunned expression on his face, she noticed another lima bean hanging off the side of his lip.

"Candy, I believe?"

She nodded.

"Bobby told me about you."

"I know," she answered.

He stood still as a board, thunderstruck.

"And Shiner? Your daddy refused to sell him to me."

"I know. My sister told me about that. She watched and listened from her room. I was gone. She didn't come out."

"Why not?"

"Daddy. When he drinks, you never know what he's going to do. He's always threatening one thing or another. Bobby bought me a lock and told us to hide there if we was ever scared."

"Where's your mother?"

Candy looked away. "She left 'bout five years ago. Took off."

"I'm sorry to hear that." JoBeth touched her shoulder.

"My daddy ain't easy to live with. It's just that . . . " She paused. "It's just that I wish she'd taken us with her wherever she run off to."

JoBeth nodded. "And you haven't heard a word from her?"

"No, nothing." She pointed to the dog. "Well, anyway, my sister said Shiner's taken a liking to you. He deserves a better life than he's got. My daddy's mean and ornery to him. He treats him 'bout the same as he treats us."

"What's he going to say when he sees the dog missing?"

"He'll figure the dog ran away again. Daddy was gonna change Shiner's name to 'Whodini' 'cause of that. He don't know I'm the one who helps Shiner escape so often."

Reaching into her pocket, JoBeth pulled out some money.

Candy took a step back. "Oh no. I didn't bring him fer no money. I brought him 'cause I know you'll take care of him. It'll do my heart good."

No wonder Bobby liked her so much. Nonetheless, JoBeth pressed the fifty dollars she'd intended to pay Slade into the girl's hand. "Take it anyway."

Reluctant at first, she finally closed her fingers around it and nodded.

In the meantime, Shiner jumped up onto JoBeth's knees and back down again, likely excited by the absence of the heavy chain around his neck.

Her cousin had the kind of vacuous grin men have on their faces when they spot a real "babe." She'd never ever seen her starched-collar cousin this way before, but enjoyed seeing that side of him. Instead of telling him he was drooling over his half-brother's girlfriend, JoBeth decided to use his present state of infatuation as leverage. "Seth, you don't mind if I keep my new dog here, do you?"

"Huh? Oh — no — that's fine. Of course." He extended his hand to the girl. "Hi, I'm Seth Davidson. And you are?"

"Candy." She blushed.

"I guess your parents named you that because you're so sweet."

JoBeth twisted her grin. With lines like that one, she had a better clue as to why her cousin couldn't keep a girlfriend, and it had nothing to do with working too hard.

Chapter Twenty
Organic Mechanic

"Inside me there is a thin person struggling to get out, but I can usually sedate her with four or five cupcakes." — Bob Thaves

Though it was hard to drag herself into Delia's organic food co-op for the first time, JoBeth did, and she even remembered to bring the coupon for a free sample of goat cheese. She was stunned to find out that Delia had dedicated one whole wall of Valley Organics just to vitamins, literally from A to Zinc. Another wall of bins contained funny looking, funny smelling stuff like grains and crumbs and beans, and stuff that looked like futuristic space food.

Since she'd finally managed to force herself through the doors, JoBeth decided to come clean with Delia about her eating habits. She told her about the snack stashes, the midnight dashes, the crazed ordering of pizza and Chinese food, and even her favorite guilty pleasure — bananas studded with Hershey's kisses.

" . . . There's something more you should know about me. My idea of a healthy diet is eating icing rosettes off a cake instead of the whole cake. My idea of healthy eating is driving through Long John Silvers and ordering the 'Crispies,' leftover bits of crunch/oily batter from the fry basket. My idea of healthy food is putting a handful of blueberries on top the peanut butter in a sandwich instead of jelly because blueberries are like nature's pop rocks."

She took a breath and waited for Delia to respond. But Delia seemed unfazed and instead offered to help JoBeth work on a "genuine" healthy diet. She suggested one that included all fresh, organic foods, juices, vitamins and weird tasting concoctions made with powdered green slime. And tofu—that white stuff that resembled custard, but tasted like elementary school paste. Rayne wasn't the only one who had a love affair with tofu.

It took some getting used to before the food tasted palatable, except for the green slime and tofu paste—that stuff would never ever feel *or taste* right.

One morning, on her way to the café, JoBeth stopped in Delia's shop. A little bell tinkled as she opened the door. By this time, she was so used to the tinkle-y bells in the town of Beeton, it seemed weird when she didn't hear one.

"Hi, Delia."

Her new friend looked up from behind the green counter set smack dab in the middle of the store. Short brown hair in an attractive bob, she closed the book she was reading. Another romance.

On the way to the counter, JoBeth inhaled the fragrance of goats' milk soaps—lavender/oatmeal, basil/lime/buttermilk, almond/berry, carrot/honey and cucumber/melon. She decided her new favorite at bath time would be lavender/oatmeal, hands down.

"Well, look at you. She walked a circle around JoBeth, leaving a faint scent of lemon verbena in her wake. "You still dropping weight?"

"Not as much anymore. I'm eating all the same good stuff, but not losing the same way. That's what I want to talk to you about."

Delia took off her glasses and nibbled on one arm. "Hmm, I think you need to add an exercise regime. You're not getting enough of the right kind of workout at work."

"You're kidding me? I work hard."

"It seems you've reached a plateau. To get past it, you're going to have to take it to the next level."

JoBeth sat down on a modern silver stool that looked somewhat like an eggcup. "Okay, tell me what I need to do."

Delia excused herself to get behind the desk. She rummaged under the counter for a time until she found what she was looking for. "Ah, here we go." She held up an 11 x 17 laminated page of exercise illustrations and handed them to her. "You can keep this. Follow the exercises in the privacy of your home. Twice a day, okay? You can do them in the morning before you go to work, and again in the afternoon when you get home."

JoBeth nodded, obedient to Delia's instruction and advice. No matter what the woman told her to do, she was determined to do it. Not that she'd started out even trying to lose weight. Losing her parents, her job, her house had been the catalyst to change her life. The lifestyle change would be totally up to her.

Delia began to explain how each of the exercises worked, and which muscles they concentrated on.

The bell tinkled. The two women looked up. *Dr. Brenham?*

Delia's expression froze for a moment, but quickly softened. She stood up. "Peter?"

His suit impeccable, shoes shiny, comb-over laminated in place, the man looked pretty decent, like he'd taken extra care. He barely took is eyes off Delia on the way to the counter. "It seems things are going well for you, Delia."

He finally noticed JoBeth and it took a few seconds before he recognized her. "You're Miss Tomlin. With Ada, right?"

"That's right, she's my aunt. I guess it's a small world."

He made a sweeping motion with his arms. "You look different." He stroked his chin.

Delia spoke up. "She's lost three dress sizes, maybe more."

His brows arched. "Really? Is she on your diet plan?"

"She is now, and I'm starting her on an exercise plan as well."

His eyes locked on Delia's as she spoke.

And Delia's voice had somehow morphed in the seconds since he walked into the store. It was softer, almost like the tinkle-y little shop bell.

"Not to change the subject, but you look well." He twirled his fingers in the air. "You've done something different with your hair. Highlights? I-I like it."

As Delia patted the back of her hair, her skin flushed pink. "Do you? I wasn't sure about the cut."

"Oh yes, the cut is attractive on you as well." He smiled.

This was getting more and more awkward by the moment. JoBeth held up the chart. "Thanks. Got to get to work. Don't forget to come to the grand re-opening tomorrow."

She held up an arm to wave to as JoBeth headed toward the door. "I wouldn't miss it. Tell me how those exercises work out for you."

"If these work, I won't have to tell you. I'll show you." With that, she opened the door.

On the way to the café, she couldn't help thinking there was some kind of spark still there between the two.

Before they could reopen the Last Chance, the staff had a lot of work to do to get the place back in shape. It was amazing how shutting things down for a couple of weeks had such a cascade effect. Food went bad, deliveries backed up, and equipment went haywire.

The "Grand Re-opening," sign on the door warmed her heart. Kit looked up from one of the tables when JoBeth walked in. Surrounded by salt and pepper shakers, she was doing the very first job JoBeth had done when she came to work in the Last Chance.

"Hiya."

"Hi yourself," she answered. "So how do you keep from sneezing when you fill those?"

Kit held up her index finger. "I'll show you." She lifted a bandana made from a cloth napkin over the lower part of her face.

"You look like you're about to rob a stagecoach."

"I may look funny, but I'm sure not sneezing like somebody else I know."

"Touche'."

Betty and Cecelia greeted her from behind the counter. They were busy slicing pies to place in the revolving pie window.

JoBeth watched, hypnotized by each cut into the mouthwatering flaky crust, the sweet red pieces of ripe strawberry revealed with each swipe of the knife. Temptation hit like a thunderbolt. "Where did those come from?"

Betty smiled and licked some stray strawberry filling off the side of her hand.

JoBeth's heart pounded at the sight. She wanted to dive into a slice of that delicious pie. No, to dive into a whole strawberry pie and wolf it down. Maybe two. Or three.

Cecelia held up her pie cutter, dripping with apple goo from the apple pie she was slicing. "Bobby's girlfriend made the pies. Can you believe it? She showed up to help, and wah-lah."

Kit's guttural laugh came out all muffled through the bandana. "If only someone else had the magic touch with cooking."

Betty and Cecelia giggled in unison. "That's for sure," Betty added.

Reeling from a fresh onslaught of temptation, JoBeth had to wipe away beads of perspiration on her forehead. "What—what do you mean?"

"Shhh," Cecelia laughed—pointing toward the kitchen doors.

Kit pulled down the bandana after she screwed the top on the last pepper shaker. Eyes toward the swinging doors at first, she smiled and lowered her voice to a whisper. Cecelia and Betty leaned forward over the pie counter straining to hear, hanging on every work.

She held a hand over her mouth to stifle a laugh. "Put it this way. Bobby still has a lot to learn about cooking. The boy went all crazy with spices that ain't got no business being in proper food."

Betty, eyes wild with laughter spoke. "He added whole cloves to the burger meat."

"What?" JoBeth gasped.

The three of them tittered into their shoulders, or napkins — anything they could find to muffle the laughter.

Kit, though doubled over, got control of herself first. "He thought them cloves'd taste real good in the burgers."

"You are kidding me?"

"Besides the burgers tastin' funny, we was picking whole cloves out of our teeth."

Betty went on. "And he added them to the chili, too." Betty rolled her eyes toward the ceiling. "And they didn't taste no better in the chili."

The swinging doors popped open. Bobby emerged holding a pie in each hand. "Hope you're all having fun talking about me." He placed the two pies on the counter in front of Betty and Cecelia. "Maybe I'm not so good with burgers, but get a load of these. Candy's latest creations — coconut marshmallow pie and berry madness."

Bobby slapped his hands on the counter. "Give me a break. I was experimenting. I had to get it out of my system."

"You'll do okay. Just keep your paws off them cloves." Betty tried to offer some encouragement.

Candy emerged from the kitchen, flour on one side of her face. "So how do ya'll like 'em?" Bobby planted a kiss on her cheek. "Your pies are a hit, baby!"

"Candy!" JoBeth gave her a hug. "I just want to thank you again for Shiner. I love that little dog."

"I'm real happy he's with you. I know you'll take good care of him."

"And your pies — they *are* amazing."

"I been baking since I was little. Mama taught us."

"Us?" JoBeth asked.

"Me and my sister."

"That's right. I thought I heard you mention you had a sister."

Cecelia dug into the coconut marshmallow pie with a spoon. Her mouth full, a look of pure ecstasy came over her face. "Um, uh, um, oh m — these are THE best I've ever had, and I mean that, cross my heart and hope to die." She steam shoveled into the pie several more times. "Candy, you have real talent."

The rest of the staff joined her. JoBeth tried to stop herself with one shovel. She couldn't. The only saving grace was the fact that she was sharing the pie with a group of equally enthusiastic tasters.

"Tell us about this other pie again," Kit urged.

A shy smile on her face, Candy replied. "Oh, that there is what I call berry madness."

Bobby smacked his lips. "It's a combination of fresh strawberries, blueberries, raspberries and blackberries. The way I see it, you can't have too many kinds of berries in a pie."

They took turns dipping their spoons. Candy's pies weren't just the ordinary run-of-the-mill creations. They were special the way Mozart wrote music, the way Albert Einstein wrote formulas. When it came to pies, there was no doubt about it — the girl could bake.

"Uh, Candy," JoBeth asked. "What about Slade? Does he know you're here?"

She looked straight at Bobby, eyes wide. "No, I . . . "

He untied his apron, took it off and folded it onto the counter. "I was going to wait till later to say this, but. . ." He gazed into Candy's eyes. "I guess this time's as good as any."

"What news?" JoBeth put down her fork.

"Candy ain't my girlfriend. She's my wife."

Chapter Twenty-One
Running The Show

"Is it better to count calories than to count chins?" — Unknown

Elected to fill Grizz's ample shoes as "Cook Extraordinaire," for the day, JoBeth left the house in the early morning both excited and dreading the ordeal she knew she was in for. Since she was ahead of schedule, she decided to visit Grizz before heading to the café and ask for some helpful tips.

His home was a couple of blocks away from the Last Chance. Propped up in his oversized wooden bed, in the early morning light, Grizz looked about as uncomfortable as she imagined he'd be.

The male nurse tending to Grizz seemed glad to see her. As soon as she walked in, he excused himself out the front door and lit up a cigarette as the door shut behind him.

Grizz chuckled. "They promised me a smoking hot nurse, and this is what I get?"

JoBeth covered her mouth, as she laughed, afraid the man might hear her.

Grizz's bed, carved with western scenes, coyotes, teepees, cowboys and the like, didn't strike her as something that would've belonged to the man. He must have noticed her perplexed expression because he addressed it right off the bat.

"I got this chuck wagon cot cheap from the man who sold me the café years ago. Had to leave town quick and didn't want to take any furniture. Not my taste exactly, but the price was right." He winked. "Besides, the design grows on you after a while."

"Sounds like the deal of a lifetime," JoBeth winked back.

She glanced around. The rest of his bedroom consisted of an oversized chest of drawers and nightstand made out of the same wood and a lamp made out of deer hide that gave off a gamey smell when the bulb heated things up. Stacks of dusty magazines and papers were stacked up against the walls. Grizz did not appear to be much of a housekeeper.

"I could tidy things up in here for you. Next time I'll bring some cleaning supplies, okay?"

"Kit's already got plans for that, girlie. She has a crew coming in here tomorrow. So many people offer to help all the time, Kit finally took 'em up on it."

"Good, I'm glad. And I would be glad to help with anything else you need. I can do errands for you, buy groceries, fix things — whatever."

He reached for her hand and gave it a quick squeeze. "JoBeth, thanks for coming to see this old man." He rested one of his big bear paws on his stomach. "I'm just glad you're here. You don't need to do anything else. You're doing enough."

She looked him over. His face without the familiar beard looked thinner. "You've lost a few pounds."

"I was on the hospital diet plan." He smiled. Not a wide happy kind of smile though. Grizz still looked pretty weak after his ordeal. A twinkle in his eyes, he looked her over, "You lost a few too. I might even hazard to guess you've lost more than a few. Is my food that bad?"

"No, silly. I've just been working hard, eating different and Delia's been helping me some."

"Oh so you're eating that squirrel food of hers, huh?"

"It's not all squirrel food. I eat regular food too, just not as much of it, and I've started exercising too."

He patted his stomach. "The doctors want me to change the way I eat, and I'm having a hard time with that. In fact, the new diet is the worst part about all this."

"I'm sorry."

He sighed. "I knew I wasn't feeling right, but I didn't want to change anything about my life. I guess that's selfish in a way. I liked eating what I wanted whenever I wanted it, and doing the things I enjoy doing."

"Like eating a big greasy burger and smoking a smelly cigar afterward?"

"You know me too well," he answered.

JoBeth noticed something else about him. Some of the kick had gone out the old mule, as they say. After his life-and-death ordeal, Big Grizz didn't have the same fire left in him.

She cleared her throat. "I know you hear this every day from a dozen different people, but how are you feeling?"

He tried to shrug, but winced instead. "Any day above ground is a good day."

"You're funny. 'A stitch,' like Ada would say."

"I don't know about that—but stitches, I've got. In fact, I've got a train track from the doctors Roto-Rootering my arteries."

"They're staples, not stitches, Grizz."

"Staples, s'maples . . ." He tried to laugh, but grimaced in the attempt.

"Not to change the subject, but what was it like meeting Seth?"

His expression softened. "I dreamed of the day. It meant everything to finally touch his hand and tell him how much I love—have always loved him."

JoBeth took a deep breath. "And how did he respond?"

"He reacted as I expected he would." He shifted position on the bed. "I suppose he's confused and still in shock."

"For sure."

"I watched him grow up and there was no doubt in my mind from the way he looked that he was a Herschelstein. The fact that I had another son was a bone of contention between me, and my wife. I wanted to include him in my will, but she wouldn't have it. She said it wasn't proper."

"I don't think you have to worry about Seth financially, at least."

"I know he's got a good situation, but I wanted my boy to have something from me." He settled back and sighed. "I wanted him to know at some point in his life that I loved and wanted him."

"I think that's all Seth really needs from you."

His eyes sparkled. "You're right. But I want us to get to know one another. I realize he needs time, but time might not be something I have much of."

JoBeth decided to change the subject and get straight to the reason she'd come. "I don't know if Kit told you, but I'm going to be doing the cooking with Bobby for a while. Imagine that—it takes two people to do your job."

He laughed. "I used to be as big as two people."

JoBeth rested her palm on his cheek. "I came here to find out if you had any advice or instructions for me."

"Advice?" He grunted. "Kid, just don't burn down the place, okay?"

JoBeth tilted her head, "I was hoping for something a little bit more practical."

He scratched his head. "Okay, here's one. Never send out a plate of something you wouldn't eat yourself."

She paused. "I like that. It sort of sounds like 'Do unto to others as you would have them do unto you.'"

He raised his brows. "That's from the bible, right? I don't read much of that," he joked. "I can't even remember the last time I went to temple—maybe as a child. I never was a religious man."

JoBeth sighed. "I used to."

He pushed himself up a little higher on the pillow. "Go to temple or read your bible?" His eyes sparkled with mischief.

She wagged her index finger. "The part about the bible."

"Ahh." His face contorted as he moved his body. "Don't mind me. It's just hard getting comfortable."

"Are you hurting bad?"

"Nah, just a little." He raised his hand. "But besides being in pain myself, it's easy for me to recognize when someone else is in pain."

Silence hung between them.

"What do you mean? I came here to visit with *you*, not talk about me."

He went on. "You're hurting, Jo. Since you lost your parents, I mean. Losing the boyfriend, the job—that's small stuff in comparison." He held up his index finger. "Hear me out. I've had a lot of time to think being trapped here in my bed all day, every day."

A sudden panic overtook her. "I have to go. Lots of work to do." She rose and grabbed her bag.

"JoBeth." His voice, sweet and gentle, wooed her back. "Listen."

Though reluctant, she sank back into the chair.

He squeezed JoBeth's hand. "One thing Ada always said to me when we were young was that 'nothing can separate you from the love of God.' Even when you're mad at him, God still loves you."

"I'm not mad at God."

He laughed. "You know, if I remember right, there's a commandment about lying."

"I'm not lying." But the truth of what he said began to seep through her protests.

He smiled. "So you only love God when things are going well? And when they're not going so well, you hate him? You know, there's a guy in the bible by the name of Job."

"I know the story. Read it a hundred times. You don't have to tell me. Besides, how do you know about him?"

He laughed. "Oh, I dunno—maybe from the original scrolls?" He pointed. "Maybe you need to read it again. My point is, in spite of all the bad, unjust things that happened to him, he never lost faith."

"I still have faith."

"JoBeth, you're mad. Admit it." He pointed an index finger upward.

Her heart felt as if it were in her throat. She was thankful when the phone suddenly rang—a friend, calling to check up on him. She tried to leave with a quick peck on the cheek, but he grasped her wrist and pulled the receiver away. "Promise me you'll think about what I said, Jo."

Chapter Twenty-Two
Somethings' Cooking

"There are two things you should never eat before breakfast: (Lunch and Dinner)." — Unknown

In spite of her best efforts, the talk with Big Grizz a few days before stuck with her, even as she prepped the kitchen. She tried time and again to shrug off what he said, but no matter how hard she worked, the truth gnawed at her.

After experimenting with the right kind of kitchen wear, she'd learned to dress for the part with a tank top, shorts, a light cotton chef's apron and Cholo bandana around her head. Before the café reopened, Kit had opened the back door and arranged for one of the customers, an electrician, to disconnect the alarm instead of her taking a hammer to it like the one before. The open door really helped a lot with the whole ventilation problem.

One important thing she'd discovered: a cook is not a chef. A cook can be any old schmuck who throws on an apron and flips burgers. And if you throw something in the oven or stir something in a pot regularly at home, you're the family cook. *Congratulations.*

Chefs are cooks who've gone to culinary school and moved up through the ranks. Chefs rule the kitchen. And though she had no aspirations to earn that title, JoBeth did acknowledge herself as the boss of her domain, at least for the time being.

JoBeth and Seth accompanied Ada to her doctor's appointment a couple of days after the discussion they'd had about Ada. And just as Rayne and JoBeth first suspected, the diagnosis was Alzheimer's. Even though she expected it, the words still came as a blow to her spirit. Something about hearing the diagnosis . . .

The doctor put Ada on some sort of medicine — a patch that was supposed to delay or suppresses the symptoms. The drug was supposed to be effective at keeping the status quo, but there were possible side effects. Seth thought it would be worth trying out on Ada, and JoBeth agreed.

She hadn't noticed any kind of big change in her aunt since she started the medication, but Dr. Brenham said it would take a while before the effects kicked in.

The biggest news though was the heart issue. Dr. Brenham noticed an irregular rhythm on Ada's very first visit. The cardiologist later diagnosed her with atrial fibrillation, or AF as he called it. Her heart beat fast with irregular contractions. She was put on meds for that too. Ada would have to see a cardiologist regularly to monitor her heart. She might even need surgery at some point.

Though the news was disturbing, JoBeth maintained a level of hope. With good care and careful monitoring, Ada would survive for many more years.

Her train of thought was derailed when she caught two slices of toast as they popped up. She was in the middle of painting them with butter when she noticed Bobby come through the kitchen doors.

"So, are you happy with your new dog?" He beamed.

"I sure am."

Bobby smiled. "I'll bet Shiner's real happy with you doting on him."

"He never leaves my side when I'm home. He's my baby." JoBeth cleared her throat. "How are you and your dad?" She stole a quick glance away from the eggs — almost ready to turn over easy.

Bobby walked over to the wall hooks and lifted an apron off. He tied it around his waist while he talked. "He's having a hard time with all the changes. He reached into a warming tray and plucked out a couple of slices of crispy bacon. "Ummm. Dad can't even look at this stuff anymore. But one thing he sure is happy about is me and Candy getting hitched."

JoBeth scooped up the eggs and plated them just as Kit breezed into the kitchen, picked up the order and speared her guest ticket on the rounder. "Two sunnys, Adam n' Eve on a raft." The dour expression on Kit's face seemed to be a thing of the past. She smiled at them, and breezed back out.

"Go on," JoBeth urged.

"He approves of her. When I told him how crazy-in-love we are, his eyes filled up with tears."

JoBeth was so happy, she high-fivved him. "What about the other stuff, between you and your dad?"

"We're working out our differences. The two of us always seem to butt heads for some reason." He drew in his lips, as if forcing back tears. "But we get to spend a lot of time together. We talk a lot." He shook his head. "My dads' a great guy. It took almost losing him to make me realize it. We made our peace with one another, that's for sure."

She reached for a piece of bacon and popped it into her mouth. "How about your new brother?"

Still holding the spatula, Bobby scratched his face with the side of his thumb. "He's okay I guess." He flashed a grin. "It's crazy how much he looks like my dad,"

JoBeth nodded. "He does look more like him on the outside, but I think you're more like Grizz on the inside. You and your dad are teddy bears."

Bobby playfully snapped a towel at her. "I ain't no teddy bear. You need to get out of here, girl. You've been working too hard."

"No arguments." She stuck her tongue out.

He grinned. "Tell me about that play stuff again."

"Cosplay is basically a bunch of grown men and women putting on costumes like eight-year-old kids who run around battling each other with Nerf swords and battleaxes, etc. I don't understand it myself, but my friend Rayne told me there are a few cute guys there this time. I have my doubts, but I'm going anyway."

She looked at the clock on the wall and Bobby followed her eye, ten-thirty on the nose. "So, can you handle yourself in here?"

"I ain't never met a kitchen I couldn't handle."

JoBeth didn't believe that for a minute, but thought she'd humor him. "Okay then, sounds like you've got it all together."

She turned to go, but instead put her hands on her hips. "Before I go, how is married life?"

His silence captured her attention even more. Bobby looked like he was about to burst.

"Whaaaat?" she asked, her curiosity piqued.

He looked around like there were reporters from the National Enquirer hiding in the cabinets. "Don't tell no one, but Candy and I found out we're gonna have a baby."

"Really?"

He blinked what she assumed was a yes.

"And you're just now telling me?"

"We just told folks we're married, even though it happened a couple months ago. How are we going to spring the latest news on everyone?"

She sucked in a breath. "I don't know. I'm shocked, but happy for you two, or three."

He started fiddling with the apron ties, which reminded her of the way he absentmindedly played with the glove box in her car. Before she could even process whether Bobby was mature enough to be married, she discovered he was going to be a father too.

"Her daddy went crazy insane when he found out we got hitched. He wanted her to marry a man with a two-year degree from the community college, not a loser like me. Slade thinks I'm a lazy no-good nuthin."

"That's the skunk calling the rose stinky." She giggled.

"That's what he says about me. I don't know what he's going to say when he finds out about the baby."

JoBeth folded another towel. Thoughts churned round and round inside her head like a Bingo cage. She pointed to Bobby. "You said you daddy always wanted you to take over the family business. Here's your chance, at the Last Chance."

He shook his head. "I never wanted to sling hash for a living. It's back-breakin' work. Look where it got my dad." He paused. "But on the other hand, I can't see myself going to school. I'm not much for hitting the books."

"Think about where *not working* has got you. This is a good, honest way to make a living and you'd be in business for yourself, not working for somebody else. Plus, it would make your father happy and you would automatically prove you're worthy of supporting your wife and child. Old Slade couldn't argue with that."

Bobby let go of the apron ties. "I'm here to help my dad out. I never wanted to do this for a living, but you're right — now I have a wife and a child to think about."

Kit slammed into the kitchen with three more orders, her eyes immediately focused on the empty stainless steel warming counter. "Bobby, where's my orders?"

"Uh-oh." He popped into action. "I'm sorry. I'll have 'em right up."

Kit shook her head while she clipped the new orders onto the wheel. "Looks to me like you two been flappin' yer jaws instead of flipping burgers. This here's a business and we got customers to take care of. Grizz always puts his customers first." She pointed at Bobby. "Remember that, son. You've got big shoes to fill."

There seemed to be no doubt in Kit's mind about Grizz's successor. And Kit was right about something else. The Last Chance had to live up to its reputation for delicious home-style food, cooked fast and fresh. Bobby did have big shoes to fill.

Chapter Twenty-Three
LARPing for Love In All The Wrong Places

"Rich, fatty foods are like destiny: they too shape our ends." —
Unknown

"Umm, this is *too* good." JoBeth savored stolen samples
from Rayne's medieval picnic basket.

"Hey, save some for the actual picnic." Rayne pushed
her away with a playful flick of her hip.

She stood next to Rayne in her friend's closet-sized
kitchen helping her pack a basket and cooler, but couldn't
help sampling some of the delicious foods she'd prepared.
Artichoke balls for instance. Canned artichoke, drained and
mashed, blended with Italian breadcrumbs, garlic powder,
and Parmesan cheese, rolled into little balls. JoBeth managed
to sneak a couple of them before Rayne noticed and gave her a
menacing look.

Rayne had done all the shopping and donated all the
supplies for their little gourmet picnic. She knew JoBeth was
trying to save to get back into her rent house again. She hadn't
told her friend about the fifty bucks she'd spent on Shiner.
Not to mention the collar and dog food she had to purchase.
But the adorable pup was worth every penny. She slipped him
a tiny bit of ham from what was left of one of Rayne's teeny
tiny sandwiches. He licked his lips whenever he caught her
eye. The little angel never failed to crack her up. Whenever
she looked at him, that big black spot over one eye and tiny
black spots over the rest of his body made her smile.

She'd brought him to town with her because she didn't want to leave him home in the yard by himself or in the house with Roscoe. Who knew what Roscoe would do with another dog in his territory? Not to mention the kitty cats. She'd kept Shiner in her bedroom with her at night and let him roam free in the yard in the morning while she was at work.

He seemed perfectly happy to be by her side or following close by her heels — for now at least. She'd set up a nice bed for him on Rayne's screen porch. There was no way she was going to take Shiner to the live action role-play event with all that fighting going on. The little fella might get scared or hurt.

JoBeth palmed off another tiny bit of ham his way. Honestly, she didn't mind spoiling him a bit. The little guy needed a bit of pampering after the kind of life he led at the Clayton house.

She took a piece of celery out the ice chest. *What's good for the dog is good for the girl.* Stuffed with feta and sprinkled with paprika.

Yum. Funny thing, the more she lost weight, the more discriminating her taste buds had become. She felt as if she could really taste food again. The celery tasted delicious. A few months ago, she would have preferred a bag of Cheetos dipped in Chem cheese dip or sour cream potato chips dipped in plain sour cream. Now she preferred celery, thanks in part to Delia — even goat cheese, thanks to the coupons. With Delia's encouragement, she'd gone out of her way to try other fruits and vegetables too.

She put her aunt on a healthy diet as well. Roscoe too. JoBeth didn't have time to eat like she did before. She ate healthy food in smaller quantities.

Rayne was right about her. JoBeth had undergone a total lifestyle change due to a series of bad events in her life. She ticked them off on her fingers: losing her parents, her relationship with Kyle, rent house, job . . . figure. And she avoided dealing with her hurt, preferring instead to stuff her emotions down and medicate herself with the comfort of food.

The move to Ada's house, getting a new high-energy, though menial job, making new friends, getting to know old friends better, even having her own dog, all worked together to change her life and attitude for the better.

As if reading her thoughts, Rayne eyed JoBeth. "You look great. It's probably due to all that hard work you do. It's better than pilates."

"Thanks." She looked down at her outfit, a new resale shop find, a loose Turquoise top, size fourteen, the Cindy Crawford collection, and a calf-length black skirt from somewhere. The tag was missing. She'd washed her hair and let it air-dry into natural waves. Minimal makeup completed the look.

JoBeth licked a bit of low fat cream cheese off her finger. She'd had something on her mind besides everything else happening in the past couple of weeks, but wasn't sure how to bring it up with Rayne. "So — have you heard anything from Sam lately? Not that I miss his calls and texts. But I noticed that he hasn't tried to contact me."

Rayne kept her eyes on the food prep. "I think he was seeing someone for a while."

"What? Seeing someone? Who?"

Rayne shrugged. "Some girl he met at that church singles group you used to go to."

"What's her name?"

"How should I know? I don't go to church."

"Right." JoBeth's voice fizzled. Then a thought occurred to her. "So how do you know?"

"Know what?" Rayne asked.

"That Sam is dating someone?"

"We ran into each other at the grocery store. I noticed the bouquet of flowers in his hand, and asked him who they were for."

"Flowers, huh?"

"Yup, for their first date."

JoBeth's heart sank. Sam had brought her flowers on their first date. Now the thought of Sam spending time with someone else . . ."

She looked up at her friend. Rayne's hair was now a very unnatural shade of pink. And she'd had it cut and shaped by her roommate yesterday—into a ragged, razor-cut bob. Smooth on the top and ripped on the edges. Cute. Except for the pink. But Rayne liked to experiment with different colors.

"That's it." Rayne closed the lid on the basket. "Let's go. I don't want to be late."

"Should we try and walk? It's so close." The sedentary version of JoBeth would never even have come up with that idea. And the park was only fifteen minutes away.

"There's no easy way to get there carrying a heavy basket and cooler, Jo." Rayne held up her keys. "I can't believe I'm saying this, but we're going to have to leave a carbon footprint today. It's only a few minutes away by car."

JoBeth made sure Shiner was settled in with his new doggie bed and toys. She set out a bowl of food and clean, fresh water for him too. A pet and a kiss on the top of his sleek head and they were out the door.

Toting the cooler, she followed Rayne to the vintage robin's egg blue VW van, pockmarked with rust spots. "You must be in a rush to see that guy." The seats, worn and torn, offered little support. A couple of springs poked her buttocks.

Rayne laughed. "When you see him, you'll understand why." She turned the ignition. JoBeth marveled at the engine because the rust bucket sounded like a toy car or soapbox derby kind of engine. Maybe even a clown car. Her friend never went anywhere far in it, mostly because it was unreliable and the tires didn't exactly hug the road anymore. In fact, the van and the road were hardly on speaking terms. The vehicle was screaming for a major overhaul but a major overhaul was major expensive.

"Can't wait." Rayne didn't usually go all school-girly over guys this way. There had to be something a little more special about this one.

"So have you talked to him at all, or is this just an eye candy thing so far?"

To JoBeth's surprise, her friend blushed. *Hmmmm.*

"No, we haven't talked yet."

As they drove the short distance, JoBeth noticed a cloud of noxious smoke leaving a trail from the tail pipe. "Rayne, I think you're leaving a carbon footprint the size of a Sasquatch."

A little worry line furrowed across her friend's forehead. "I've really got to get this thing fixed." She pounded the steering wheel. "I'm not green in this machine."

They broke out in laughter. From their vantage point, JoBeth spotted groups of "Renaissance" soldiers bearing arms and food and supplies headed toward the central gathering spot known as "The Meadow."

The Meadow was normally a nice place to play extreme Frisbee, fly kites or jog. Today though, it would be a battleground where people in period costumes pretend-shanked one another with pretend weapons.

Wonder of wonders, Rayne spotted a parking spot across the street from the park, a tricky one though. Halfway up a hill. She backed in—brakes squealing like baby pigs.

"Don't forget the emergency brake, Rayne. Remember what happened last time?"

She rolled her eyes. "How could I forget?"

The last time she'd parked on an incline, suffice to say, the van took a little ride all on its own, backwards of course.

They unpacked the van. Bearing the basket and cooler, they waited to cross the busy street. Car after car zoomed past. Rayne pressed the pedestrian button, but a gap between cars came open and they decided to go for it.

About halfway across, a couple of drivers, reckless souls who never got the memo about pedestrians having the right of way, sped past them on either side. The two scurried to the curb, gasping.

"Crossing the street around here is like playing Frogger." JoBeth giggled as they headed toward the meadow.

Through gaps between the trees they could see battles in full force. Hand-to-hand combat. Rayne waved at a couple of people.

"Sedgie! CeeJay!" Rayne quickened her step to walk next to two of her roommates. "Hey, how long have you guys been here? Where's Cada?"

CeeJay answered first. "How art thou, mistress?" He drew closer and whispered. "The 'GM', I mean, Game Master Triton, sent out a group text yesterday to meet in Mayfield Heights this morning, at 5:00 am, sharp."

"You gotta be kidding me," she said. "Five a.m.? I knew you guys left early, but not that early."

He leaned in again. "M'lady, thou must remember to speak in the native tongue."

She stopped in her tracks. "You mean I have to talk like one of you?"

Their eyes shifted one to the other until CeeJay finally spoke. "Thou art correct, Mistress Caraway." He winked.

A postal worker, I noticed how *apropos* CeeJay's costume was—a silver maile armor shirt. In his late twenties with uber pale skin, the man ascribed to the medieval code of hygiene, which was, according to Rayne, no laughing matter to his roommates, or to me since I stood in his proximity.

They'd almost kicked him out a year ago, until the group worked out a solution. If you call showering once a week a solution . . .

"M'lady, good morrow to thee." Sedgie focused on Rayne's basket. "What news? Perhaps thy basket beareth the fruit of the earth to beguile our taste buds." He whispered to the side. "I hope you brought some good food. I'm starving."

"So where's Cada?" Rayne asked again.

CeeJay answered in a low whisper. "She had to work. Had some clients scheduled for the morning. Said she'd be in just in time to play the damsel. I hope she makes it."

Sedgie, short for Sedgewick, was a name exuding nerdiness. What kind of parents would brand their kid with a name like that? A web monkey for a local finance company, he wore the stereotypical round black glasses forever sliding down his nose, which seemed out of place with the costume he was wearing. A long, green tabard with bronze trim and a wide, leather belt around his tubby waist, duct-taped weapon tucked under his arm, his hands clutched multiple bottles of water and Gatorade.

"You two remember JoBeth, right?" Rayne pointed to her.

Sedgie's face flushed embarrassment. "M'lady, thou must pardon this rogue. I am of a sanguine nature to be sure. Fair thee well. I am pleased thou couldest attend this campaign."

"Good morrow, m'lady JoBeth." CeeJay fumbled with his cap, also made of maile.

A less than enthusiastic welcome for sure. She wondered if she should try the lingo. "Can I help you with your hat?" JoBeth asked, hoping to change her image, and their opinion of her.

"Yeah, though it is a coif, Mistress." He wrangled it over his face and thin, oily hair. "Ahhh. That feeleth much better. Fie. It is as hot as Hades beneath the coif."

Her roommates weren't exactly fans, likely because she'd done a little nerd branding of her own, judging them instead of simply being nice. *Plusweird* is what she usually called them. But face-to-face with them, she felt kind of bad, probably because she'd experienced a bit of judging as well.

The boys led them to their spot, a place under two massive oaks, half in the shade and half out. They'd constructed a long river stone fire pit, complete with a grate made out of a gate from an old iron fence. A big, black, iron pot filled with water shot out a cloud of steam.
JoBeth spread out a couple of blankets a safe distance away but before they could do anything else, Rayne decided they needed an informal table.

"Guys, let's collect some wood and stones and set up a low table near the edge of the blankets. I need something to put the trays on, okay?"

CeeJay groaned.

Sedgie asked, "Mistress, may I be so bold as to inquire as to what manner of sustenance might be in the holds of thy basket carried on yon delicate arm, and whether we swarthy lads might partake of a bit of it?"

Rayne teased. "Thou art Rogues to be sure. But yah if thou wilt fetch me the planks for mine table, I may yet be of a favorable nature." She added, "Besideth, thou lads knoweth me well. I've broughteth snacks alongeth."

How impressive was that? Living with LARPers had definitely leeched into Rayne's brain. She seemed to have no trouble with the lingo.

In accordance with Rayne's demands, they gathered sticks and flat pieces of wood and smooth stones and fitted them over the gnarled exposed root system of the oaks, a perfect base for the table. They soon had an outdoor table fit for pretend king, queen, knight or peasant.

Rayne portioned out two little plates of appetizers for CeeJay and Sedgie and made them the happiest guys in the pseudo-Rennaissance world. She whispered to JoBeth. "If I didn't portion the food out, they'd have eaten it all. There wouldn't have been a crumb of food for anyone else. They've done that before, you know. Remember that party I had a couple of years ago?"

"The one with no food?" JoBeth looked over at the boys who by now were picking at crumbs on their plates. "How could I forget?"

"Okay guys," Rayne clapped, "It's time for you to pick up your broadswords and go fight someone. Lay siege or something, okay?"

Sedgie put on a pitiful look and held out his empty plate. But Rayne just shook her head and pointed to the meadow. "Go! There are damsels to slay and dragons to save." She rattled her head. "I mean, you know what I mean." She shooed them off with a flick of her wrist. "Now go." JoBeth laughed. "You treat them like little kids."

She held up a little mirror and puckered her lips. "They are as far as food is concerned. If I don't get rid of them for a while, I won't have any peace while we're getting things ready."

Though reluctant, they complied. CeeJay slipped his maile cap on and Sedgie walked off dragging the duct-tape wrapped broadsword on the ground behind him.

Rayne stood up and brushed off her canvas pants. "I'll be right back. I'm going to find a restroom. Then we'll start our medieval outdoor kitchen cooking, okay?"

"Okaaaaay," JoBeth said, glad for the tiny break in the frenetic pace of the day. She watched as fair maidens walked by wearing Ann Boleyn gowns, courtly brocades, capes, lace-up gowns with fancy trims and all sorts of odd-shaped hats. Some women were dressed as warriors as well, sporting thigh high cavalier boots, vests and knickers. JoBeth liked those outfits more than the fancy lady ones, damsels minus the dress *instead of damsels in distress.*

She reclined back on the blankets and resumed surveying her surroundings. Guys everywhere. Mostly the type lacking in social skills and basic grooming, but there were a few decent looking anomalies sprinkled in — easy to miss in a sea of eccentrics. Grown men acting out fantasy scenarios, running around in the woods or their parent's backyards, complete with capes, costumes and metaphorical language.

JoBeth noticed a line of combatants in tabards of a different color approaching the group she was watching. Shields up. She laughed to herself. The first team of soldiers had bright red shields, home projects, emblazoned with silver fleur-de-lis, and the approaching warriors held Green "something's." She wasn't sure about the image on their shields. Anyway, they faced off against each other, releasing guttural warrior cries.

"Those Greek Sea Dragons got swagger."

JoBeth looked up. Sam smiled down at her, his dark hair in an adorable wave to one side. Not in keeping with his scruffy plumber image. Was it the tabard or did the man look more muscular? He'd morphed into some kind of juiced-up lifter.

The first thing that came to mind when she saw him was one of Delia's romance books. Sam could have been one of those guys on the cover. Well, maybe if his hair was longer, or a team of crackerjack romance-book-cover-photographers sprayed a bucket of tanning oil on his chest. And of course, the wind machine — got to have the wind machine going. She blushed at the image in her head.

"What are you doing here?"

"That's not much of a welcome." He indicated the blanket. "Do you mind if I join you?"

She nodded.

He sat next to her on the blanket. "Rayne invited me." He backed up a bit and looked her over. "There's something different about you."

"You're being polite Sam. I'm not as fat as I used to be."

"Okay, how did you lose weight, if you don't mind me asking?"

"One of my customers, she owns this place called Valley Organics right down the street from the café. Delia, that's her name, put together a diet and exercise plan for me."

"Well, you look amazing," he repeated, "Amazing."

She felt her cheeks flush. "So Sam, I would never in a million years have guessed you'd be at one of these events. Are you, ah, here alone?" JoBeth glanced around. "Did you bring a date?"

"I guess Rayne told you about that." He glanced away. "It didn't work out."

Though her insides were inexplicably doing somersaults, she kept her reaction low-key. "Oh, sorry." *This is crazy. Why would I care if Sam were dating, or even serious with someone?*
She continued. "But since you are here, have you been to one of these events before? Can you tell me what's going on?"

His right brow arched. "Well, I've only been to a few. One of my buddies used to be into Sci Fi Conventions and I went a couple of times to humor him."

"Go on," she urged.

"This is actually high concept stuff. It's a battle game, it's theatrical, even a sport sometimes. But most of all, these are gamers acting and living out the scenarios they love. They write and create characters, settings, ideologies, and whole worlds with their own rules and consequences."

He gestured his arms with dramatic flair. "Role players get into their characters like actors do the total immersion thing. But it's a group immersion. Everybody's living the same fantasy. Some of them like Roman or medieval stuff or civil war reenactments and others are into futuristic battles with aliens or post-cataclysmic zombie scenarios or worlds filled with magic, monsters or non-human sentient beings." Sam looked around. "And what's wrong with what they're doing? Nothing. They have good clean fun — adventures, glorious battles and they spend all year making costumes."

As he spoke, a tired-looking young man in a tattered tabard walked into their camp. He fired off a tired message, one he'd probably already conveyed to fifty other people. "Message from the Game Master: "Stay in character. Remember, you can only know what your character knows. It's cheating if you use your own knowledge vs. player knowledge to unfair advantage. That is all." He moved on, clearly dragging his feet.

JoBeth sat up straight and crossed her legs Indian style. "Sam, tell me more."

He stretched out on the blanket and leaned on one elbow. "Okay. The players are PCs, Player Characters and everybody else is the NPCs or Non Player Characters. Today is only the beginning of the campaign. The thing could go on every weekend for weeks or months."

"You're kidding?" She unfolded her legs. Sitting that way used to be comfortable when she was five . . .

Rayne returned with a new face, and what a face. Tanned, with light green eyes, chiseled jaw, dark brown hair. As they walked to the camp, the guy began to remove his armor plating, revealing a ripped chest through a tight maile undershirt. Rayne looked like she was going to swoon. This had to be the guy she was talking about. No wonder.

"Greetings, Sam." Rayne spoke without taking her eyes off wonder boy. "Please be acquainted with Sir Logan, a knight of the kingdom."

He bowed. Charming. "Sir. Mistress. Good morrow to ye. Tis true, I serve with Her Majesty's forces and am bravely clad a knight of her highest order."

Suddenly inspired, JoBeth tried on the lingo for size. "Tis a real pleasure to make acquaintance with such a comely man of rank." She winked at Rayne who actually took her eyes off Logan for a second to smile in her direction.

Sam added, "Sir, I perceive by thine emblem thou art with the Greek forces."

"The Sea Serpent thingie?" JoBeth whispered to Sam, who nodded.

"Aye, I am sore vexed at the battle waged this day," Sir Logan answered.

Rayne handed him a small dishtowel and he used it to wipe the back of his neck. Ugh. What was she thinking?

Sedgie returned to the camp as well, mud splattered across his tabard, which JoBeth noticed bore the Sea Serpent as well, in his case, a muddy sea serpent. She also noticed he was carrying what looked like a purse.

"Is that what I think it is?" JoBeth asked.

"Mistress." He frowned. "It is a pouch."

Logan added, "With thou I must heartily disagree, young lad." He gestured. "Merely a pouch without tassels, but with, as in thy case, the object referred to, is a Sporran. It is Gaelic, of course."

"So it is." Sam laughed, eyes twinkling.

Sedgie lowered his head. "I bow to thy wisdom, brave knight."

Rayne edged her head to the side, a signal to her to move closer to the fire. "JoBeth, let's go ahead and put the mussels and endive on the grate."

"Okay." JoBeth reached into the bag and pulled out a chilled container filled with the black shells. They spread some foil, drizzled some olive oil, Marsala cooking wine and fresh Thyme on top and sealed the shells in by folding the foil over.

Rayne nodded. "These gifts of the sea shall steameth in the foil and be doneth in no time at all."

JoBeth's mouth began to water.

Her friend spread endive leaves on the grate and ordered. "Squeezeth some fresh juice of the lemon on them and sprinkleth salt from the sea and cracked pepper on top."

"How long?" JoBeth whispered. "I'm tired of talking that way."

Rayne whispered back. "In less than a minute."

When she nodded, JoBeth noticed Sam smiling at them.

"Fair maidens," he said, "May I inquire as to the remainder of our fine repast?"

JoBeth did a double take. "Translation please?"

He sat cross-legged, hands on his knees. "What else is on the menu?"

Sedgie leaned in, crowding out Sam's face. "Yes fair maidens, what is on the menu?"

"Sitteth thyself down and utter no more words." Rayne glared at Sedgie, who complied.

Logan also lowered to the blanket, enlisting Sedgie to help him shed parts of his armor.

"Hey, can I use one of those things for a pillow?" Sam asked.

She noticed he pointed to a thing that fit over the arms. "Or those maybe?" He pointed to leg coverings.

Sedgie started shaking his head back and forth, whispering something to Sam.

Logan's muscular face turned three shades of red. "What knave? Lay upon my vambraces? Or my paldrons?" Eyes blazing, he reached for his sword. "Nay, I should sooner slay thee than have you lay head nor hand upon the sacred trust of her majesty. He stood, taking up his broadsword as he did.

"What are those things, Rayne?" JoBeth asked. What's the big deal anyway? The guy was getting all up in Sam's grill for wanting to touch a part of his costume?

Mesmerized at the sight of her fair knight holding a sword with his chest muscles rippling, she answered without looking back at JoBeth, or missing a beat or making sense for that matter.

"Lower arm—armor for the lower arm armor." Her voice trailed off, then picked up again. She pointed. "Those things are called embrace—vambraces and pauldrons are shoulder armor and they lace to your gambeson which is a, which is a-a-a padded, kind of jacket that fits on the c-h-e-s-t."

I could smell carmelization happening.

From her experience as a cook, JoBeth knew the food was ready to be pulled and plattered. She used the tongs to take the endive and mussels off and plate them. Taking matters into her own hands, she decided to use food to force a détente'. Besides, she had to protect Sam from the crazy good-looking knight.

"Ah, who-*eth* is hungry?" She tried her best at the *lingua franca*.

Logan lowered his sword. All eyes looked at her as she passed near them bearing the steaming platter. Rayne came back to her senses and joined her with a platter of cold hors d'oeuvres she'd prepared earlier that morning. Now properly mesmerized by the lure of food, all squabbles ceased.

The endive, crispy burnt around the edges was delicious. She had no idea lettuce could be so tasty, and the mussels — smoky, with just the right touch of butter and Marsala. Perfect. And the cold platter of hors d'oeuvres rocked.

Logan plucked the last of a plate of mussels and swallowed, a satisfied look on his face. "Fair maidens, though hadst transformed these gifts of the sea into legendary cuisine."

JoBeth held up an empty shell. "Thanks."

Rayne stared, dreamy-eyed, again.

"Am I too late?" CeeJay burst into the camp, a panicked look on his face. But as soon as he set eyes on Logan, he shifted gears into proper form. "Ah, didist thou fine folk put aside some nourishment for this knave?"

JoBeth handed him a foil-wrapped plate. "Though absent, we didist keep thy name in our remembrance."

The look on his face was priceless. Gratitude. Joy. Relief.

From that point on, CeeJay's attitude about JoBeth changed, all for a plate of food.

Which made her think about the power of food. Her entire life had been a love/hate relationship with it. Loved to eat. Hated herself for eating. The lure of food led every move. She woke up thinking about what she would eat or not eat in the course of a day, planning the day around her favorite pastime.

"JoBeth? JoBeth?" Sam called out her name. He snapped his fingers in front of her face.

"Oh, sorry, I was, I was lost in thought. She gathered her skirt around her. The wind was picking up a bit in response to a smattering of dark clouds.

She noticed Rayne had begun to lay the next course, so she excused herself from Sam and moved closer to help. Three large salmon fillets covered in fresh dill, cracked pepper and lemon slices. The fish would take a while to cook given the size of the fillets. She helped her friend put together the savory soup too. Into the black pot, they poured the vegetables she'd pre-chopped at home, along with packaged broth and fresh herbs. No animal meat at all. Rayne didn't eat meat, just seafood, and she wasn't going to compromise by cooking it. JoBeth had to admire that about her. Rayne stuck by the things and the people she believed in.

Laughter rang out from the huddle on the blanket. Sam, Sedgie, CeeJay, and Logan seemed to be engaging in covert conversation. Definitely out of character. They joined them.

"What's this?" Rayne, hand on her hips, looked from one to the other.

Logan answered. "Your friend, Sedgewick is it? He was telling us about his—"

"Why is it suddenly okay for them to talk in the King's English?" JoBeth asked.

"Latest postal adventure," Sam finished. "And we decided to take a short break from the banter. Besides, it would take twice as long for him to tell this story."

CeeJay elbowed his friend. "Go on, tell them the story too."

Sedgie, basking in the attention, pushed his glasses up the bridge of his nose. "Well, I was on my regular route and there's this dog and it's always loose. A big ferocious mongrel."

"Oh no, does it bite?" Rayne asked.

"It has. The guy who had the route before me got bit twice before he was transferred to the main office." He continued, pushing his traveling frames back up. "The people who owned the dog complained to my super that they weren't getting their mail. But I couldn't even get close to that house armed with pepper spray. Not that they even kept the animal in the yard. It roamed the streets every day."

Logan laughed. "That's when he got the idea."

"The idea, yeah." CeeJay joined in.

Sedgie's eyes widened. "It came to me in a flash of brilliance."

"Brilliance." Sam agreed.

"I put on the suit of —"

A young man in courtly dress burst into the camp.

"Armor."

"Many pardons." He removed a feathered hat and bowed with a flourish. "Her majesty requests the presence of Sir Logan."

With that, Logan stopped laughing and sat up straight. "I?"

The young man brushed away a bit of pretend lint from a poufy brocaded sleeve. "Yes, it is so. Her majesty requests your presence, Sir Logan."

Clearly in controlled panic, Logan stood and glared at Sedgie and CeeJay who sprang into action, re-attaching his vambrance arm thingies and the leg thingie-things, whatever they were called.

"What does that mean?" Rayne asked Logan.

"M'lady, when the queen requests a knight to court, it is a position of high favor. I would wager to say that thou will not be seeing this brave knight the remainder of this campaign, fair one."

The young knave pulled absently at the dainty lace on the end of his sleeve. "I dare say thou speaketh the truth."

Logan lifted his sword. "Sir Logan, at Her Majesty's service."

"This way." The young knave turned to go.

"But when will I see you again?" Rayne, eyes wide, called after him.

Logan held the sword up, the OSHA safe police-grade Kevlar tip visible. "Thou mayest catch my stand-up act at MotorMouth Grille on Friday nights. Five dollar cover." With that, he ran after the knave and was gone.

Rayne's expression fell and from that point on, her mood changed too. She ignored the food and withdrew, taking position under a beautiful elm.

So JoBeth took care of things. She plated and served the meal, to the delight of the guys and a few stray others who happened by. Afterwards, JoBeth brought her friend a plate of food.

"You need to eat. It's time for you to enjoy the fruit of all your hard work."

Rayne took the plate, but rested it in her lap. "He left me." She snapped her fingers.

"That doesn't mean he isn't interested. He did tell you about the stand-up thing. We could go see him on Friday night. I'll even drive out to meet you."

A ray of hope lit up her eyes. "That's true. Maybe that was his way of saying he's interested. She took a bite of salmon and closed her eyes. "Yum, the salmon turned out good." She chewed, then took another bite and pointed her fork. "I could wear that new dress I bought, the blue one."

"Perfect." JoBeth agreed. "And you were right about him. He's hot. Not like most of these guys." Then she thought of something else. "Which reminds me — where's the other one? The good-looking friend you told me about? You said he'd be here too."

Her mouth opened and closed as her friend struggled to bounce the words out.

Hmmm. Sketchy.

"That's true. I did tell you there was a good-looking friend, but you've already met him."

"Who?"

She squinted her eyes and pointed her fork in the direction of the blanket.

"You're kidding me?"

Unaware of her pointed fork, Sam laughed out loud with one of the stray role players eating on our blanket.

"Sam?"

She took another bite. "He's good-looking, isn't he? It's not like I lied or anything. Except for the part about the two of them being friends."

"You lied?"

She shook her fork again. "Okay, technically. But I was right about him being volcanically-hot, right?"

"That's too weird."

"Why?" Exasperated, she threw up her hands. "Kyle's moved on. You should too."

'But I—" JoBeth glanced back at him, "I don't feel right about it. Besides, he's a plumber. It's not like there would be any future with him."

Rayne threw down her fork. "Why not? How can you say something like that? You've hit a new low. So what if he's a plumber? Wasn't your Jesus a carpenter? Huh? Maybe I should remind you that you didn't do so well with Kyle, the male model, or as I like to call him—the 'face' with a 'space' where his brain should be." She went on. "Sam, on the other hand, is smart. He's nice, and he's a hard worker. Hot-looking, too. But I guess that's not good enough for JoBeth. Face it—you dated Kyle to feed your pride!"

JoBeth closed her eyes. *Why did I say that? It came out of my mouth. Like dumping over a can of garbage — the words spilled out.*

"Rayne, what I said came out all wrong."

"I hope so." She frowned. "I don't think I could be friends with someone that shallow. And you and I go back a long way. But here's a question for you. If Sam were anybody else than Kyle's BFF, would you give him a chance?

JoBeth looked over at Sam, who at that same moment, happened to glance her way. She offered a weak wave. "I might."

"That's more like it, Jo." Rayne clearly approved. "Keep an open mind."

More like — what? Sam was all the things her friend had said, and more. Rayne was right as Rayne about him. *But were she and Sam right for each other?*

Chapter Twenty-Four
Damsel in 'Dis Dress?

Dieting is wishful shrinking." – Unknown

The wind picked up a bit. "Do you think it's going to rain?"

"I dunno." She looked past JoBeth. "What do you guys want?"

CeeJay answered first. "Forgive us, m'ladies. Couldest thou forego a moment of thy time to hear ye a proposition?"

"A whaaaaat?" JoBeth asked.

"Sorry, that didn't translate well," he laughed. "I'll speak the King's English. Some of the women didn't show for the NCP parts or some of them left 'cause it looks like it might storm. Cada was supposed to show up and play a damsel in distress, but she's swamped at work."

Cada, the missing roommate was also Rayne's stylista, the one responsible for the black Emo hair, the rainbow of colors, and all the ripped haircuts. The woman had a lot of explaining to do for all the strange hair do's and don'ts Rayne regularly turned up with. But JoBeth had to remember that Rayne *wanted* her hair to look that way.

CeeJay sank to his knees and begged. "We need a damsel in distress and a lady of the court or we'll have to shut down the game. Puh-leese?"

"No way." Rayne turned her head. "I'm tired."

"With sugar on top?" Sedgie asked.

"NO." Rayne turned her head to the side.

But the Bingo wheel began turning in JoBeth's head again. "Guys, is the court where the queen is?"

Sedgie smiled big. "Exactly. You'd be with the queen, Rayne. So will you do it?"

JoBeth grasped Rayne's arm. "And at the queen's side is where Sir Logan would be."

They shared a grin. No explanation necessary. Rayne jumped to her feet. "Where do I sign up?"

Sedgie held out his arm. "This way, m'lady. You'll have to change into the court dress. Is that okay? And you have to talk the talk too. Don't forget to stay in character."

"No problem." Rayne winked and did a "YES" pump with her arm.

Ceejay held out a hand to help JoBeth up off the ground. When she stood, she noticed Sam.

"So, you're going to be a damsel in distress?" Sam asked, a funny smile on his face. "And I've been elected to fill in as a cavalier or a knight or something." He tipped an imaginary hat. "Guess I'll see you on the field."

"To the field!" She raised an imaginary toast.

After a short walk she found herself in the lady's tent. A stressed-out woman, who reminded her of a theater mom, handed her a couple of dresses. "Taketh care with mine daughter's gowns," she accented with a snort. "Sorry," she wiped her nose with her sleeve, "the hayfevereth plagues me."

Some people were better at the lingo thingie than others.

The first dress JoBeth tried on was a blue brocade Anjou gown that laced up in the back, a good choice because it offered some "give" to a woman like herself who needed "giving" in that area. There were lovely lace details around the neck and décolleté areas that showed off way more cleavage than she was used to showing. Not in a bad sort of way, or she wouldn't have worn it. She didn't even try on the other dress once she took a look at it—a brown and cream number that screamed peasant.

Today at least, she was going to leapfrog from Hell to Valhalla and go from waitress to glamorous Lady in Waiting. "Damsel-in-distress," to be more accurate. And maybe, just maybe, a knight in shining armor would rescue her from her life.

"I am ready to present myself to thee." JoBeth emerged from behind the changing curtain.

The woman circled and let out a whistle. "You looketh good." She pointed to a full-length mirror leaning against a cardboard box.

"I hate to toot my own *vuvuzela*, but I think I have to agree with you," JoBeth smiled.

"Vah-WHO-za WHAT?" she asked, her face a complexity of perplexities.

"A horn they blow at soccer games."

"Oh," she answered like she thought JoBeth was either highbrow or mental.

The woman placed the pointy cone-shaped hat on JoBeth's head. Festooned with a long sheer blue scarf at the tip, she couldn't decide whether she looked like a damsel or a dunce.

Sedgie gasped when she came out of the tent. "M'lady, thou art—hot."

"Thanks, I thinketh." *Stay in character. Stay in character.*

The troops stood on opposite ends of the meadow waiting for the signal. Apparently, her arrival had something to do with the signal because they cheered as soon as they saw her approach. A little cheering can do A LOT for a girl's ego.

Sedgie offered his arm and walked her to the staging area with a newfound confidence. A giant fake dragon made out of a brownish tarp spewed white smoke and fake fire out its nostrils thanks to an air compressor and strips of red and orange cloth. She walked up five steps to a platform paper mache'd to look like a castle keep.

"Stand here." Sedgie ordered with a sly wink. "The dragons are the good guys. The fleur-de-lis are the bad guys. The objective for both teams is to rescue you from the dragon." He pointed towards the dragon spewing its smoke and the guys responsible for animating it stepped out from behind to wave. JoBeth waved back.

He took a deep breath and whispered, which seemed incongruous. "Now here's the best part."

"Okay, go ahead."

"You get to start the war."

Confused, she scrunched up her nose. "You mean, like throwing the first pitch at a baseball game?"

He pounded the blunt end of his spear into the ground and laughed. "That's what I'm talking abouteth." He looked around. "And when you get yourself rescued, you give the scarf that's hanging off your hat to the knight who rescues you. Some of the knights ride on real horses in this campaign."

"Got it."

"You're sure you're ready?" he asked.

"Yup." She smiled.

"Then here is your mic."

"Yeah, we have to be able to hear you scream and stuff when the dragon comes for you." His mouth fell open. "Sorry, I felleth out of character."

He lifted her cone and positioned the headset, the tiny mic near her mouth, then did a quick test to check the connection.

JoBeth took a deep breath. "Is that it? Am I ready?"

"Almost." He handed her a white brocade handkerchief. "Here is yon kerchief, m'lady."

Puzzled, she dangled it in the air. "I thought the losers wave the white flag."

"Not in this game. All thou must do is drop the kerchief to the ground and voila'. The games commence the very moment thou dropeth the kerchief."

"Okee dokee-eth."

He laughed. "Best wishes, Mistress JoBeth and," he yelled as he ran off to join the other dragons, "thou dost truly look hot."

She pondered his statement. In Renaissance times, she might have been seen as a Rubinesque beauty. *Where's a time machine when you need one?* The more she thought about it, the more she realized a time machine would cure all the ills in her life. She could go back as far as needed to make her whole life a big do-over. She would stop her parents from getting in the car, fix the pipe in the basement, change her eating habits, say no to Kyle and yes to Sam. *Whaaat?*

If food for thought were fattening, she would most definitely have put on a few pounds.

But why stop there? She could go back even further and stop Aunt Ada from marrying Uncle Fritz. Then she and Grizz would have married and lived happily ever after. Of course Bobby wouldn't be around, but there would likely have been other brothers and sisters.

JoBeth held up the white brocade kerchief between her thumb and index finger in as dainty a stance as she could position herself. Heart pounding, all eyes on her, she released the kerchief, allowing it to waft its way to the ground. But before it did, both sides sounded trumpets and battle cries. Men bearing standards, musicians playing horns and trumpets, or drums. Soldiers charged to the center, swords high and began clobbering one another with battleaxes, swords, spears, and bow and arrows. From her vantage point, JoBeth could see that not all the weaponry was Nerf quality. Some of it was capable of causing injuries. Not the way the actual weapons would of course, but enough to cause some serious welts and bruises.

The sounds of battle surrounded her — grunts and groans, battle rants, the sound of armor, and metal — sword clanging against shield; a nightmare scenario for people with attention-deficit issues.

She didn't know where to look. To the right, to the left, to the middle, even underneath the very platform/faux castle keep she stood on, knights and soldiers fought with grave intent.

Meanwhile, the dragon drew closer to her, thanks to the machinations of its puppeteers. Breathing pretend fire, smoke exuding from its fiery nostrils, it's mouth opened wide as it approached as if to devour her. She pulled the scarf attached to her hat across her mouth to hide a very wide grin and very real chuckle. This game was turning out to be more fun than she'd thought it would be. JoBeth decided to add some special effects of her own. These people obviously appreciated good theater.

"Oh noooo! Is there no brave knight to save this damsel from the fierce jaws of the evil dragon? Thou cannot allow this maiden fair to die in fire-breathed air." A pretty good rhyme for off-the-cuff.

Her special effects were a big hit. Those nearby seemed to take notice and it spurred the battle on. She fell back against the side as if ready to faint, but caught herself on the railing, which really worked out well except for the fact that the railing wobbled. Miss Godwin, her high school drama teacher would have been proud. More battle cries and horns sounded.

Then she noticed two knights in full armor and regalia fighting sword to sword on horses. The horses didn't seem too thrilled with the whole thing, especially the brown horse one of them was riding. The horse bucked his knight off with a clang and clatter right underneath her podium. The knight got up with some help from a few of his fleur-de-lis fellows, but the other knight who wore the insignia of the dragon raced forward to take advantage of the vulnerable one.

In a panic, JoBeth clutched the rail with all her might, wishing she could help out the poor guy. But as the dragon knight charged, the railing suddenly gave way and she tumbled off the side screaming all the way down. Fortunately, the vulnerable knight broke her fall with his body, though she wasn't sure how fortunate that was for him, even with her recent weight loss.

The fall seemed to cause a rout of confusion in the ranks. The other knight retreated back to his former position, while the downed knight's comrades raised the two of them to standing positions and brought the brown horse near. The poor knight seemed a bit dazed at first, like he had to catch his wind, but he rubbed his back a bit and soon shook it off. They helped the knight back on to his horse, and to her surprise, the dazed knight held an armor-gloved hand out to her.

Does he intend to hoist me up on that horse with him?

She scooped up the kerchief, calculating what kind of load horses were capable of carrying on their backs. But before she could entertain a second thought, she found herself lifted and plonked down behind the mysterious knight doing a slow trot.

As soldiers rose against them along the way, the knight urged the horse to a gallop, swished his sword back and forth, and used the blunt end to bash them away. They galloped faster. Wind in her hair, a wide smile on her face, JoBeth thought of Delia's romance novels and began to fantasize that her brave knight looked like one of the muscle men on the covers. So this is why she reads them. *Minus the raunchy part, I could get used to this sort of thing.*

Safely back in the ranks of the fleur-de-lis comrades in arms, the horse came to a slow trot and stop. Her knight lowered her to the ground with one swoop. *Impressive.* She wondered what noble profile hid behind his faceplate, what mane of hair underneath his metal helmet, what sort of rippling muscles swam with perspiration beneath his chestly armor. And more importantly, was chestly even a word?

And then he swung off the horse to the ground. Her sight reduced to mere tunnel vision, she could see nothing else but him. Her eyes, her world hinged upon his every move. First, he removed his metal gloves. She held her breath. JoBeth's heart beat so fast she thought she would faint. He pulled off the helmet. She let out a gasp.

Sam? Her Knight-in-Shining-Armor?

"Behold, thou art fair, my beloved . . ."

The knight she fancied was—Sam? And did he just quote from the Song of Solomon like they were in love or something? Her vision clouded into a sudden veil of white. She fell backward. Later, when she came to, Sam's face hovered above.

"Are you okay?"

She sat up. "I think so. Guess I'm overheated in this tight dress."

"She's all right," he told the small crowd around them. "No needith to call the physician."

"You sure you're all right?" He helped her to sit up, and rise to her feet. Sam passed her a cup of water from one of the soldiers.

"I was worried I freaked you out with my quote from SOS." He snapped his fingers. "Sorry, I always forget nobody else knows my abbreviation for the Song of Solomon. Anyway, the only thee-and-thou language I know is from the bible. Hope you don't mind."

His arm around her waist, Sam helped JoBeth to the shade, which also happened to be where the queen and her court were. He sat her in a lawn chair covered with a large piece of red velveteen cloth draped over it to make it look medievally legit. "Here you go."

The knave they had seen earlier approached looking as bored as he did before. "Sir Samuel, the queen requests you approach the throne."

Sam's strong hand still rested on the small of her back. "Will you be okay?"

JoBeth nodded. "Yes, of course. Like I said, I overheated. That's all." To emphasize her okay state, she held up the cup of water. "See, I'm hydrating as we speak." A nearby serf tipped a pitcher of cold water and filled the cup again.

Sam winked. "Be right back." But he turned and held out his hand. "Mayest I have m'lady's scarf?"

"The what?"

He gestured to the kerchief.

That's right. The scarf was a trophy, an emblem of victory for the knight who saved the fair maiden. She handed it to him.

He bowed. "Thank thee, gracious lady."

JoBeth could not deny the fact that Sam was good-looking. Whoever this queen was, she sure had an eye for cute guys. She watched him travel to the throne, which was not far off from JoBeth's present position. Under the shade of the largest oak in the whole meadow, the queen sat in splendor, or Splenda depending on how you looked at her. The blonde man-eater wore a size zero, or maybe double zero except in the *chestly* area, which seemed to hoard all the weight off the rest of her body. And of course, her queenly robes were cut low enough to showcase them. And speaking of hoarding, the woman had taken extreme advantage of her royal status and herded every good-looking guy within a ten-mile radius. In fact, she'd hoarded the cream of the nerd crop for her court.

The Queen extended her glittering scepter, which matched her glittering crown, toward Sam, who approached and knelt down. An attendant handed her a sword and she knighted him once on each shoulder, smiling a wide sovereign smile. The last time JoBeth had seen anyone knighted was in a game of chess.

So Sam really, really likes me. The secret was out. Now all she wanted to do was get away from him. Was she creeped out, conflicted or both?

The woman rose from her throne, wrapped her arms around Sam and locked lips.

"What?" JoBeth found herself standing and wondering who shouted.

All eyes were on her, including Sam and the queen.

She sank to her chair. "Sorry."

What did she care if another woman kissed Sam? But the image nagged at her.

Sam had obviously come to this event with the express purpose of winning JoBeth over so he could ask her out. Maybe he was already in love with her. Who knew? And Rayne, her best friend Rayne was in on the scheme. She was the one who'd invited him. JoBeth would never have figured her for a matchmaker.

In the midst of her musings, her eyes began to register something that took her brain a few moments longer to process. A court jester dressed in yellow and purple, the traditional multi-pointed hat hanging around his face with bells at the tips, hopped about, jingling, jangling his way through the court crowd. He made funny faces. And danced little jigs to medieval flutes and drums. JoBeth smiled, thinking to herself that the poor guy looked ridiculous.

But the more she looked at him, the more she realized there was something familiar about the way he moved.

"Rayne?"

The jester pranced before a lady of the court and her gentleman. "Why am I like a mushroom?" The couple, amused looks on their faces, listened. "Pray tell us," the woman said.

The jester slurred. "Becauseth, I'm a fun-guy."

JoBeth groaned as the jester approached.

Eyes wild, Rayne, the jester, pulled JoBeth's sleeve. "How did you know?"

"Oh puh-leese." The hair was enough of a tip off. She sniffed the air. "Is that alcohol on your breath? But you don't drink."

Rayne twirled, stumbling over herself "I'm a jesther — and jestherz drinkz."

Several strands of pink hair somehow liberated from the hat, hung limp near her face. "You don't see many jesters with lip rings." She opened her eyes wide. "Hey, loved the joke. Where'd you get that? Highlights Magazine?"

Rayne stuck her tongue out at her and almost lost her balance.

JoBeth fell off her chair laughing. Holding her sides to keep from splitting the dress, she suddenly found it hard to catch her breath. The lace-ups in back constricted breathing, which explained why she'd fainted before. Of course the earlier episode with Sam might have been the result of the whole Song of Solomon thing. But seeing Rayne as a drunken court jester was worth a little shortness of breath.

Rayne knelt down next to her and fired off a barrage of slurred words. "So you thik itz funny, huh? D'you thik itz easy being a jesssther? You have to come up with jokesth and schlapstick all the time."

JoBeth couldn't respond, only nod in between laughs.

She grabbed JoBeth's arm. "When I got to court, I 'spected them to gimme in a dress like you're wearing, which looks by the way really grrrreat on you. I wanted something that would get Logan's attention. When they gimme'd me this costume, I said, 'Are you kiddin' me?' But they were not kiddin'. So I put on thiz and played the part while Logan chased every woman here, 'cept me. Isthn't that funny?" She threw back her head and offered a very scary fake laugh punctuated by a hiccough.

JoBeth swallowed. "So the jester is supposed to be the laughing stock of the court?"

Sam joined them, a swath of lipstick across his jaw. "I just got knighted."

Rayne hiccoughed. The angry look in her eyes reminded me of the dragon. "Really? I just got rooked."

He looked from JoBeth to Rayne and in as deadpan a voice as she'd ever heard, answered, "Surely you jest."

Chapter Twenty-Five
Packing For A Guilt Trip

"A balanced diet is a cookie in each hand." — Unknown

"One Loco Moco." JoBeth clipped the ticket to the wheel and spun it around to Bobby.

"What's that again? Refresh my memory." He squinted, beads of perspiration in rivulets down his cheeks, a look that reminded her of Grizz.

"It's rice topped with a burger patty, eggs and gravy."

"Oh yeah. I'll have it right up."

Bobby turned back to the stove. The guy seemed preoccupied, though she wondered why. She hadn't even had the time to process the whole tournament thing before returning to her waitress-*slash*-cook job. She'd gone from a Fantasyland experience back to Beeton without a proper transition.

JoBeth pushed out the swinging doors the same time as Kit pushed in, but by now they had their movements down to a ballet. They smiled at each other on the way through. She plucked up a pot of coffee in one hand and a pot of hot water in the other and made her way to the first of her tables. Delia sat at her usual booth. This time however, Peter sat beside her.

"Well, well, well. Dr. Brenham, you're back in town again?"

He held up his cup and she filled it with coffee.

"I'm on Delia's diet." He patted his stomach. "So far, I've lost five pounds." He looked her over. "If you don't mind my saying so, it looks as if you've lost even more."

JoBeth turned around to model. "I fluctuate between a size ten and twelve now. My ideal weight is a size ten. Well, maybe not ideal, but my target weight. I don't want to be a zero or anything."

"It becomes you." He grinned.

"I'll say." Delia smiled. She held up her cup. "Bravo."

Surprised she had to ask. "*You're* having coffee?"

Delia looked to Peter. "I used to love it, so I'm trying it again." Delia winked. "We'll both have my usual for breakfast, okay?"

"Sure thing." She had a feeling about the two of them the moment he stepped back into Delia's shop, but now there was definitely something brewing. Were they getting back together? She had to wonder why they ever divorced in the first place.

She felt a tap on her shoulder and turned around.

"JoBeth."

Sam? She couldn't get her mouth to work right away. "What? I mean—what are you doing *here*?"

"You're always asking me that," he sighed, a mock air of disappointment in his voice.

"I'm sorry."

He pointed to a table. "Is this one of yours? I thought I'd come to the café and sample the food. Rayne tells me it's good." Rayne must have filled him in on everything. She made of mental note to ask her friend about that, and there would likely be some choice words between them. JoBeth motioned for Sam to sit and immediately poured him a cup of coffee.

"Umm, you know what I like." He took a sip. "The coffee's great."

Dressed in a blue button-down shirt and jeans, with a day-old grow of beard on his tanned jaw, her heart couldn't help beating a little faster when she saw him.

"What can I get for you? Or do you want some time to look over a menu?"

He shook his head. "No, I don't need a menu when I have you right in front of me. What do *you* recommend?"

Without hesitation, she rattled it off. "A short stack of blueberry pancakes, two eggs over easy, two slices of bacon and a fresh fruit cup."

"Is that your favorite?"

"Sure is."

He settled back in his chair. "Then that's what I want."

JoBeth tore off the order and stuck the pen behind her ear. She winked with a confident air. "Be right back."

But back in the kitchen, she freaked, pacing back and forth, talking to herself.

Bobby came up beside her, an odd expression on his face. "Jo, is a-anything wrong?"

"There's this guy, and he's a friend of the guy I used to date who broke up with me not that long ago, and he's here at one of my tables and he's a really nice, wonderful, gorgeous guy, and he likes me and I don't know if I should like him, but I think he wants to date me or he's in love with me or something."

He blinked. "Okaaay. And that's a problem?"

She clutched his shoulders in a vise grip. "So what do I do? I don't want to hurt him. I don't know if I should like him like that, but I sort of might. I'm confused. What do I do?"

He gulped. "My bacon's gonna burn."

She relaxed her grip. "Sorry."

Kit breezed in with a couple of orders and clipped them to the wheel. "What's wrong?"

JoBeth looked down at the floor. "Everything."

"Let's talk after your shift, okay?"

"Okay."

Delia's orders and Sam's were up already. She put the plates on a large tray and carried them out. Delia and Peter were deep in a conversation and barely noticed her. But Sam scrubbed his hands as soon as her saw her coming.

He said a quick prayer of thanks and tasted the pancakes first. "Ohhhh, Ohhhh, these are great." He swallowed the first bite and pointed to the plate with the end of his fork. "Best pancakes I've ever had."

She went about her business, serving the other customers, but every time she passed by Sam, the man couldn't stop crowing about the food. She stopped at his table to see if he wanted anything else. "More coffee? Orange juice?"

He pushed his cup toward her. "Definitely more of that great coffee and yes to the orange juice too."

"Okay." She turned to go but he called after her.

"Jo, I was wondering."

Great, here it comes. She tapped her foot.

"This Friday Rayne and I are going to catch Logan's act at MotorMouth. You were aware of the fact that she has a huge crush on him, right?"

"Yes, I know."

"Did you want to come? If so, and you wind up staying for the weekend with her, the church is having the Holy Ghost Weiner Roast again, the monthly singles thing we talked about before. You missed all the other ones and this will be the last one until we reconvene next semester."

JoBeth had already committed. Rayne made her promise she'd go with her to see Logan perform. She considered it a last ditch effort to get the man's attention again. Logan, when he was Sir Logan, seemed to like her well enough during the campaign, but avoided her phone calls afterward. So now they would be a merry band of three? Great.

"Okay to Friday," she answered. "Rayne already asked me."

"What about the church thing? It's a lot of fun. This one is going to be extra special. We have a new pastor. I know the split was hard, but things are a lot better now. Really good, in fact."

"I might have to come back to Beeton early Saturday morning. There are some things I have to do." The stain of a lie spread over her conscience.

"Oh." He arranged his knife and fork at a ninety-degree angle with his plate. "I was hoping you'd get to come. I didn't want you to miss out."

"Not this time." She held up the coffee pot. "Look, I have some other customers to take care of. Ah, enjoy your breakfast Sam and thanks for coming. It was good seeing you." She placed the bill on the table next to the salt and pepper shakers.

She'd talked her way out of that one. Nothing against Sam, he was great-looking and gainfully employed, clearly meeting two of her basic requirements in a man. In addition, he lived on his own, not with his mother. Still another reason she should like him.

But he reminded her of Kyle, though they were as different as night and day. And every time a stray thought of Sam came to mind, she assembled a list of reasons not to like him — though admittedly, a very short list.

JoBeth kept herself busy and used every cause and justification to steer clear from his table. When she returned ten minutes later, Sam was gone. He'd left a twenty, more than a generous tip. Guilt pinged inside, like a bell reverberating through her soul. Why'd he have to do that? Why'd he have to be so nice when she'd treated him so rotten? Why couldn't he be like Kyle? She scooped up the money and shoved it into her pocket.

At the register, she rang up his bill. Kit walked up to the counter to ring her order too.

"What did you want to talk to me about? Something pertaining to that gorgeous man you were waiting on?"

JoBeth sniffled back tears. The register rang up triple zeros for change. "I feel terrible for treating him the way I did."

"The guy?"

"Yeah." She pulled out Sam's generous tip from her pocket.

Kit's eyes lit up. "Well, that wasn't very smart, was it?" She grinned. "That fellow looked to be smitten with you. C'mon, our shift is over. I'll get my purse and meet you in the town square. Pick a bench. We'll talk."

JoBeth left before Kit and sat on the wrought iron and wood bench, weathered by the sun to a silvery hue. She scooted a little way from the end where a bird bomb stained the wood. Red bud trees, now full in leaf, waved green flags to the sun. Frisky squirrels scampered after one another in the dark quince of tree trunks, and across the deep green of the lawn. The town square in Beeton was little more than a patch of well-fed lawn, four benches and a stand of lovely trees in the center. Someone had thought to hang a set of large wind chimes from an old flagpole near the trees. On most days though, there wasn't much breeze to speak of, but today the melodious resonance of the massive chimes could be heard throughout the area.

The source of the breeze was merely a glance away. Massive storm clouds billowed, reminding her of the broad sails on wooden ships. A thunderstorm was definitely on today's menu.

"Hi, Kit." She greeted her friend. The wind picked up the pink scarf Kit had carefully tied around her head to protect her hair. However, JoBeth expected it would take gale force winds to subdue that hairspray helmet.

Kit settled down on the bench. "So, tell me all about it, hon."

JoBeth told her the whole story. Everything. And Kit listened, her attention only interrupted once by a meddlesome wasp.

"That's some tale." She puffed up one side of her cheek and blew out air. "Explain to me why you can't decide how you feel about this perfect, good-looking guy? Didn't you say something about what he does for a living?"

"Oh, that." She hung she head, almost ashamed to repeat what she'd said. But she'd told her everything, not withholding any details, even the plumber thing.

Kit was silent at first, eyes focused on the pavement below. "Why are you bothered by the fact that he's a plumber? I mean *you're* a waitress."

"For now," she reminded her. "As soon as I get on my feet, I'm going to find another job that utilizes my college degree, and things are going to change."

Kit rolled her eyes. "Good grief. God took everyone and everything good out of your life and you settled for a dumb job in a dumpy little town and poor, uneducated, unsophisticated temporary friends. Is that it?"

"No!" Jo Beth shook her head.

Kit continued. "I can truthfully say that I love you, Jo. But you're acting like a judgmental hypocrite."

JoBeth's heart skipped a beat. "I am not!"

Kit shifted position on the bench, resting an arm over the back of it. "I came to this town escaping a bad marriage." She traced a finger over the wood of the bench. "Had to run. My ex was after me."

"You were married before?"

"I was only intending to pass through this town on my way to somewhere else. It's not like I knew where I was going. But then I saw that sign on the door of the Last Chance Café. I took one look at the name of that place and knew it was meant to be. So I stayed."

"That very thing happened to me. I was here with Rayne and that's exactly what I told her too. How odd is that?"

"There ain't no co-inky-dinks with God." She tapped the wood slat on the bench with her press-on nails. "In my life before this, I was a librarian."

"You were?" Amazed, I sat still, taking in the news. "A librarian? Really?"

Kit picked at a piece of imaginary lint on her chest. "I told you some of it before. I stayed because of Grizz. He took me under his wing and protected me — gave me a safe haven."

The bright sunshine now drabbed and faded by dark clouds, the temperature began to drop. JoBeth tried to ignore the chill of the approaching storm. She rubbed her palms together. "You mean to tell me you don't miss a quiet life shelving books?"

"No I don't." She set her jaw. "I've been a thousand times happier doing this job than stacking and filing books all day. This is a people job. I get to be around nice folks. In my other career, I was holed up in a quiet building all day whispering. That's what I had to do at home too, walk on eggshells all the time so he wouldn't reach his boiling point and start hitting me again. But he did anyway, no matter what I did or didn't do."

She rubbed her eyes like she was tired. "As long as I was quiet at work, everything turned out fine. Didn't matter what I did at home though. I could tiptoe around or bang pots and pans with a wooden spoon. You never knew what would set the man off."

"Is he still in the town you came from?"

She smiled. "No I found out he died a couple years back."

"But you could have moved on. You weren't tempted to go back to your town, to your old life?"

Both women looked up at the sky in response to a ripple of thunder curling above.

"Beetons' my home now." She leaned back against the bench. "I'm not ashamed to be a waitress, I'm proud of it. I'm good at my job and I like what I do, but my job isn't who I am. It's what I choose to do."

A flash in the distance indicated lightening. More ominous rumbles followed. JoBeth thought about what Kit said. *Am I ashamed of being a waitress?* She'd certainly tried to hide her uniform from Kyle and Sam at Pearl's Place. And when Sam showed up at the restaurant today, she'd mistreated the poor guy and tried to get rid of him. Was she embarrassed to see him or anybody else she knew from her other *better* life outside of Beeton?

Sam deserved an apology. How could she have treated him that way? Regardless of whether or not she felt attracted to him, he deserved to be treated with kindness and respect. In her rush to shut him out as a romantic interest, she'd also shut out the possibility of ever being his friend. And Sam would be a great friend to have.

Kit gestured to JoBeth. "Tell me, what does your two-timing boyfriend do for a living?"

"He's a catalog model."

"And you were real proud of that, huh?" Kit squinted.

"I guess." JoBeth's voice wavered. "Especially because of the way I look. I mean—I had to pinch myself every day. Why would someone like that date *me*?"

"Excuse me, Jo. But I think *he* should have been asking himself that question. This other fella—this Sam—he sounds like a nice guy. You've been so busy thinking of reasons not to date him, maybe you should do a roundabout and think about reasons you should."

JoBeth stared ahead at the burgeoning clouds. "You're right, Kit. I'm ashamed about the way I've been acting."

"Now don't be too hard on yourself, girl," Kit reassured. "You've been through a lot."

JoBeth nodded. "I don't know why all these things happened to me. Sometimes I wonder if I'm a bad person. Do you thing God is mad at me?" Suddenly, JoBeth's cell phone vibrated. She picked it up and answered. "Bobby?"

When JoBeth hung up, Kit asked. "What's he want?"

"He spotted us out here from the window and wants me to come back to the café. Says he has something he needs to talk to me about."

Kit leaned over to give JoBeth a hug. "Darling, I don't think God is mad at you. I believe when you have some distance between these events and what happens in your life in the next few years, you're going to look back and see God's grace." She winked, "See you tomorrow."

They parted ways, and JoBeth bounded back into the restaurant right before the first huge raindrops fell. Since it was the magic hour between breakfast and lunch, there weren't many people inside yet.

She went straight to the kitchen. Sitting behind a low counter near the back door, Bobby looked up when she walked in. She knew right away something was wrong.

Chapter Twenty-Six
Yes Sir, That's My Food Baby

*"Blessed are those who hunger and thirst, for they are
sticking to their diets." — Unknown*

The rain pounded on the ceiling and against the
windows the way it does when a violent thunderstorm first
lets loose. Feeling at home in the café kitchen, she poured
herself a cup of coffee, added fat free half and half and one
package of Stevia, per Delia's instructions.

She looked up from stirring. "Why'd you call me
back?"

Bobby's face still had that odd expression she'd noticed
earlier Her heart fell.

"What's wrong? Is it Grizz? Tell me he's okay." Her
emotions in a sudden jumble, JoBeth waited for Bobby to
speak.

He washed his hands in the sink and dried them on a
fresh dishrag. "It's not my dad."

She breathed a sigh of relief. "Okay then. Good." But
she kept looking at him. "What else is wrong? Is it Candy?
Not the—the baby?"

In slow motion, he moved his head to the side. "No
JoBeth, it ain't that neither. It's about you."

"What?" She pulled the stool next to him and sat on it.

"I've been going over the books every night. Not that
I'm any better than a chimp at figuring numbers, but it's easy
to see there's more going out than what's coming in."

"And . . ." She wiped her forehead with a nearby
napkin.

"I heard what you said about making this business my business. And I got to make some decisions to keep this café afloat."

She gulped. All this sounded so familiar.

"I hate to do it." His voice broke. "But JoBeth, I have to let you go. You're the newest employee, and to be honest, one my dad couldn't afford in the first place."

The rest of his words faded to white noise, ambient sounds that rang back as familiar, yet not. She said something in response. Hopefully whatever she said came out semi-lucid. JoBeth felt amazingly calm inside, not at all like the day she was laid off from Newhouse Shipping.

She closed the tinkle-y door behind her and started walking. By now the rain had calmed down somewhat, but it was still coming down in a steady shower. At the door, she rummaged through her purse for the car keys and pulled them out, triumphant.

Venturing out into the driving rain, JoBeth was soaked to the bone in less than thirty seconds. When she walked past Valley Organics, Delia rushed out the door and tried to flag down. Startled, the car keys in her hand flew through the air and went straight through the lattice of the rusty street grate.

"Nooooooo!" She screamed and planted herself on her knees in the street. Looking down into the grate, all she could see was water streaming in from all sides. *"Why does everything bad happen to me? Why me?"*

Soaked to the bone, she pounded on the metal with her fists, mascara running down her cheeks, hair wet and clinging to her head, Delia ran out in the rain and joined her. Before she could speak, JoBeth saw another person from the corner of her eye. Sam?

He motioned for Delia to go back inside the store, out of the rain. Then he knelt down beside JoBeth. Sopping wet, his dark hair clung to his and face, down the slope of his neck.

Raising her voice she asked, "What are you doing here?"

Because the rain was so noisy, he shouted, matching her volume. "You really have to stop saying that, Jo."

She broke out in tears again, sobbing over her life, over the way she'd treated him—everything. "Tomorrow's my birthday and my life is a mess."

"I know." His eyes met hers. "That's why I came here today. I-I wanted to ask—" He took her in his arms and she began to sob onto his chest. "You out tonight to celebrate."

From the moment his arms circled her, she barely noticed the rain or anything else. For the first time in a long time, JoBeth felt safe and secure.

"Don't worry." Sam stroked her wet hair. "I'll help you." He looked from her to the grate. "I'm going to let you go for a minute while I try to get your keys out, okay?"

She nodded and leaned back on her heels, flinching as a peal of thunder boomed through the sky. The rain couldn't decide what it wanted to do. The showers gained in momentum, and slacked off. She couldn't see straight. Rivers of water drained down their faces, and a waterfall roared down through the grate. How would Sam find the keys in all that?

He pulled a hanger out of his back pocket. "Delia gave me this. Let's give it a try." He pulled it apart and formed a hook at the end.

He pressed his lips together in concentration, an act she found endearing.

She saw his mouth moving and realized he was probably praying as he lowered the hanger. He began fishing around, scraping metal against metal.

The first two times he pulled up the white hanger there was nothing on the hooked end. But the third time, he pulled up the hanger, the keys dangled precariously. She held her breath.

Slow and steady, without the slightest tremor, he pulled the hanger and keys all the way out.

Heart thumping in her chest, Sam handed her the keys just as the rain decided to come down in sheets so hard her cheeks began to sting. JoBeth leaned forward, and on a crazy impulse, hands on his chest, kissed him full on the lips.

He responded, matching her intensity. Arms curled about his neck, his coiled around her waist, he drew her close. When they pulled apart, their eyes connected.

And she panicked.

"I have to go." She staggered to her feet and he offered an arm to help her stand. She yelled above the rain. "I can't do this."

"Maybe we could talk." He pointed back toward the café.

She shook her head and backed off toward the sidewalk, her waitress shoes sloshing and squeaking as she moved. "Sorry."

She turned and noticed Delia and Peter staring out the window at them. They smiled, and Delia offered a tentative wave. Embarrassed that they had seen the impetuous kiss, JoBeth squeaked off in a gentle run to her car. Before zooming off, a glance into the rearview mirror revealed Sam still standing in the street by the grate. Was he confused more by the kiss or by her mad dash?

JoBeth took off down the road. Talk about complicating matters. On top of everything else, falling in love was not on top of her list. *Falling in love?* Where did that come from? This had to be pure desperation, definitely not love. Still, the thought of his lips, full and — the thought brought an inward glow and a skip to her heartbeat.

On the way home, she stopped at the grocery store, suffering an onslaught of stares and comments from the folks around town who knew her. Funny, she didn't care what she looked like at that point. She needed something to take the edge off her feelings.

When she pulled in the driveway fifteen minutes later, it had stopped raining and a beautiful rainbow arched across the sky. She paused a moment to look at it and noticed Ada's old car was gone. Seth probably took her somewhere. Good.

Shiner greeted JoBeth with excited yelps. He jumped onto her shoulder and stayed there like a tiny mountain goat, licking her face as she traveled back and forth into the house carrying groceries back to the kitchen. She kissed his little head and lowered him to the floor on the last trip in.

JoBeth took a quick shower, wrapped herself in a fluffy robe and twisted her hair in a towel. Then she changed into stretch pants and a comfy t-shirt and headed to the kitchen. Her fears about Roscoe getting along with Shiner were unfounded. She patted the two of them on the way through the archway into the room. The dogs got along great. Even the cats didn't seem to mind the new addition to the family. Shiner was the youngest in the bunch. Maybe that had something to do with it.

She fed the animals, and sat at the kitchen table. They gathered around, attracted to the lure of food. JoBeth could certainly relate, but the feline and canine contingency weren't getting any of it. "No guys, junk food isn't good for you." The irony of that remark wasn't lost on her.

You're a failure at everything you do. You were a disappointment to your parents. You're fat and ugly, and your boyfriend left you. You can't even keep a job as a waitress. You're no good. Worthless. Useless. Irrelevant.

Shiner sat and watched her every move. JoBeth unloaded each bag and lined up the junk food extravaganza with precision and in specific order of consumption. She started with a gargantuan glob of raspberry jelly on a sticky bun, a compromise because she craved a good jelly donut, but Beeton didn't have a donut shop. Not bad for a pseudo jelly donut or two.

She poked a straw into a couple of Twinkies and sucked out all the delicious cream, then ate the cake-y parts. Next, she pulled four slices of white Wonder bread from the wrapper and laid them out on the table. After slathering the bread with Miracle Whip, she sliced Vienna Sausages in half, and placed the sausages close enough to "hug one another" on the sandwich so there would be no disappointing gaps. The trick to a successful sandwich was to make every bite count.

As JoBeth began to slice the sandwiches into quarters, she accidentally pushed some papers off the edge of the table.

Petey approached to sniff and check things out, but Shiner chased him off the papers and licked JoBeth's hands as she bent down to pick them up.

"What an affectionate boy." JoBeth tried her best to sound cheerful.

The first few papers she picked up had something to do with real estate. Then she noticed one of them had a signature on the bottom and held it up closer for a good look. Apparently Seth had signed with a local real estate agent. Was he planning to relocate the sheet metal factory? Then a thought came to her. She scanned the kitchen. Could it be? Would Seth do something like that? Was he planning to sell the house?

A car engine outside alerted her to the realization her private little binge was about to be interrupted. She shoved everything into a bit white plastic garbage bag and stowed it in her room. Only then did she notice the other white plastic bags on the floor and the dolls missing from the shelves. What? Was Seth planning to sell the house and throw away all of Ada's beloved dolls? She picked up the doll bags and shoved them into the closet. *Not on my watch buddy.* The key turned and the front door creaked open.

"Oh Roscoe? Petey? Zoomba?" JoBeth wiped her tears and face in that order and met her aunt in the hallway, Shiner at her heels.

"Hi, Auntie." She managed a shaky smile. Ada was dressed in a crimson suit, stockings and low heels. "Wow, you look nice."

But the first thing her aunt said was, "What happened?"

"Oh." She patted the towel on her head. "I got caught in the rain."

Ada turned around to model her outfit. "I don't know where I got these clothes, but the outfit is so pretty. Sethie says he found it in my closet. Grizzwald called me today and asked me to visit." She held up a slip of paper. "See, I wrote it all down. Would you take me to see him? Sethie says he doesn't have time."

Before JoBeth could answer, her cousin came through the door wearing a black suit, starched white dress shirt and blue tie. He looked her over. "What happened to you?"

"Forget about me. You two look like you were dressed for some kind of business meeting or fancy dinner somewhere."

"Roscoe." Ada bent over to wait for the domineering doggie as he approached from the other end of the hall. His tail wagging slower than usual, he pointed his body in her direction and kept going. Roscoe growled by the door, an indication he was ready for a ride. She noticed the note in her hand again and repeated her request. "JoBeth, Grizzwald called and asked me to visit. Would you take me to see him? Sethie says he doesn't have time."

"Of course I'll take you, Auntie. Just give me a few minutes to get ready."

He motioned. "Uh, Jo, do you think we could talk in the TV room? I won't keep you long. Mom and I have something to tell you."

"In a few minutes, okay?"

"All right."

She took a two-minute shower, added some mousse and gel to her hair, and threw on some clothes. Feeling the need for a bit of comfort, JoBeth checked her nightstand stash and breathed a sigh of relief that the drawers hadn't been emptied. She ripped open a pack of Jolly Ranchers, and popped one of the watermelon-flavored candies in her mouth. She dropped a handful more in one of her pockets for later.

Seth and Ada were seated in the TV room. JoBeth sat on the sofa next to her aunt.

He clicked off the television and pulled a chair in front of it, blocking the view.

Ada reached for the clicker.

"Not now, Mother." Seth ordered, his voice stern.

She drew her hand back. Roscoe let out a low growl.

His fingers together in a modified church steeple — obviously his signature move — he gestured with his fingertips as he spoke. "JoBeth, I'm well aware you're going through a tough situation right now, but our situation is changing too. I have to do what's best for my mother and that means no longer leaving her alone."

"What do you mean?" she asked. "Ada's not alone. She has me."

He glanced over at Ada who didn't look like she understood what was going on. In fact, she looked as surprised as JoBeth felt. "Here's the thing. I've decided to sell the house and take Mom with me to Houston."

"No, you can't do that!"

"She's my mother. Don't you try to tell me what I can or cannot do for her."

JoBeth pleaded. "I understand, or I'm trying hard to. But the situation is new to you, Seth. You haven't really observed her or explored other options. Why can't you stay here where your business is? Take care of her where she's comfortable, where things are familiar." JoBeth's heart punched inside her chest.

"Those are valid points, JoBeth. But I'm not interested in exploring other options. I have no interest in moving back to Beeton, sleeping in my childhood cowboy bed and eating those nasty lima beans. My life is in Houston, and I have to move mom close to where I live if I'm going to monitor her care."

Tears rolled from her eyes. "I get that. But please, don't rush into anything."

He shook his head. "We already have a buyer. He wants to close within a month. Now I realize that doesn't leave you a lot of time to find a place or afford one for that matter. I know your economic situation is grim right now, but I'm willing to help you get back on your feet. We're family and I'm not going to dump you out on the street or anything."

And I thought things couldn't get any worse. Her heart sank.

In spite of his order, which she'd already forgotten, Ada clicked on the television. An episode of "I Love Lucy" droned in the background.

His face flushed crimson, anger seething. "I said — not now!"

Ada trembled and dropped the clicker. It fell apart on impact with the floor, batteries scattering.

JoBeth screamed. "Don't talk to her that way. What's wrong with you?"

"Mom, I'm sorry. I didn't mean to." He buried his face in his hands. "I want to get her away from that man." He shook with anger. "I hate what's happening!"

Ada stood. "I don't understand."

JoBeth squinted. "Or do *you* want to get away from Grizz? I think you want to bolt from the truth. You want to run instead of resolving things, instead of reuniting with Grizz and getting to know Bobby."

Seth's right eyelid began to jump. "I already have a family. I don't need a new one."

She nodded. "You may not need another one, but you have another one. And you're right, it's your choice to walk away and live your life just fine without ever going down that path. But what if you took the time to get to know them? What if you got used to the idea of having an extended family? What if you took a chance and listened to your heart instead of your logic?"

"JoBeth?" Ada reached for her hand. "What's wrong? Seth, stop raising your voice. You're upsetting our Jo."

He placed his hands over hers. "Mother, you remember what we talked about today, don't you? JoBeth has to leave because we're selling the house."

"Selling? No, this is my home. I don't want to leave and I don't want her to leave." She drew back from him. "I live here."

He smiled. "Now mother, you signed the papers today, remember? You gave me power of attorney of your own free will so I could take care of you, and I'm going to do what's best. Trust me."

"But I'm taking care of JoBeth. And she makes me oatmeal."

"Don't worry. The residence home will make you oatmeal."

Ada stomped her foot. "But I have a home, and I have Jo to make my oatmeal!"

"Mother, you and I talked about it. You know I can't take care of you during the day. I have to work. This is the best solution for both of us."

JoBeth narrowed her eyes. "What about Roscoe, Petey and Zoomba?"

"I-I hadn't really given any thought to what to do about the animals. You can have them if you want, JoBeth. Otherwise I'll take them to the — to the shelter."

"Are you serious?" JoBeth yelled.

Seth's expression said it all.

"I don't want other people's oatmeal. I want JoBeth's oatmeal." Ada began crying, her emotions escalating.

JoBeth put her arms around her aunt and looked over her shoulder at Seth. "You and I need to talk in private next time."

"We won't need a next time." He stood. "The plans are already made. I told you—my realtor says he might have a buyer."

JoBeth glared at him and led Ada to the kitchen to make her a cup of tea. She started telling her aunt stories and reminiscing. The first story she told her aunt was the one about the caterpillar turning into the butterfly. Then they talked about blue warblers, which reminded her aunt of Grizz and how she much she wanted to visit him. Soon enough, Ada seemed to relax. The situation somewhat diffused, JoBeth made the decision to load Ada and Roscoe into the car.

But as they stepped outside, she noticed a different car in the driveway—a pristine blue BMW. Seth stepped out the door and joined them on the porch.

"Like my car? I had one of my Houston employees drive it down and fly back to the office. I realized that I'd need my car to move mother's things—hopefully, very few things."

JoBeth didn't say a word in response. She reached in her pocket and popped the other two candies in her mouth. "Ready to go, Auntie?"

"Sure," Ada smiled. "Ah, where are we going, again?"

JoBeth laughed. "To a party."

"Oh, I love parties." Ada looked down at her clothing. "Am I—Am I dressed right?"

"You sure are," JoBeth answered.

Seth shook his head, turned and opened the front door. Without saying a word—even goodbye—he was back inside the house.

"C'mon now, Auntie." Blood boiling, JoBeth rested a hand on her aunt's back and helped her into the car. But before JoBeth could sit in the driver's seat, she had one more thing to take care of. She casually walked over to Seth's prized BMW, took the Jolly Ranchers out of her mouth, and stuck them to the middle of his windshield.

Chapter Twenty-Seven
Photo Op

"When you have a food issue, you only want the things you cannot have." — *Karen Mayer Cunningham*

Grizz and Ada, overjoyed to see each other, connected at once in happy conversation.

Lucky for JoBeth, Rayne called, so she stepped outside to talk while the two of them made, in the words of Martie, "goo-goo eyes" at one another.

"Are you coming?" Rayne asked.

"To MotorMouth Grille tonight? I don't know. A lot has happened. You wouldn't believe it."

An uncomfortable silence screamed through the phone. "Rayne, are you there?"

"Yes, I'm still here. It's just that I—I'm having trouble understanding you."

JoBeth bit her lip. "It's about Sam, isn't it?"

"You know it is."

"I was terrible to him."

"I know."

How could she answer her friend? A deep breath helped her to share it all in one long sentence.

"There's nothing wrong with Sam. There's something wrong with me. I'm trying real hard to figure out why I've changed, and how to fix it. I really don't care about what he does for a living. And I no longer care that he even knows Kyle. But I'm not sure about much of anything anymore."

JoBeth decided not to tell her about the kiss, not just yet anyway.

"Fair enough." Rayne's voice had an aggravated tone. She imagined her friend tapping out frustration with her foot, arms folded. "So are you coming tonight? Sam backed out though he didn't tell me why. I pretty much figured it out. He told me he was going to see you today and ask you out to celebrate your thirtieth birthday."

"I feel bad about that." JoBeth closed her eyes.

Rayne shot back. "You should. Anyway, I can't go alone tonight. I need some support from my friend. My best friend."

It was abundantly clear that Rayne needed her and though she wanted to tell her everything, she couldn't, not just yet. If she did, she'd surely to fall to pieces. And right now, it was important to keep it together for Ada's sake.

"Okay, I'll be there. Can I bring Shiner? I don't want to leave him alone and I'm sleeping over too. It'll probably be late if Logan's comedy act goes on after the band."

Her tone lightened. "Sure, Shiner can stay." In fact, she laughed, "He can sit and stay."

"Very funny."

"I already planned on you both staying over. I set up the inflatable bed. Be here at 7:00. I'm making stir-fry. My roomies are out doing the endless tournament again."

"The campaign is still going on?" Surprised, though I shouldn't have been. Sam had told her that. She remembered their talk under the oak tree. She wished he hadn't cancelled.

"Yes, into the night this weekend and last. It should be over sometime tomorrow if all goes well."

"I can't believe they invest so much time and energy."

"They love it. And why shouldn't they? I totally understand their passion. I have a passion for graphic art and I put my whole heart into my work. What are you passionate about, Jo?"

She hesitated to answer. But the first thing that popped into her mind — the very first thing that occurred to her stood out. *Food.*

* * *

MotorMouth Grille was packed by the time they arrived at eleven. The opening band had come and gone and the featured band, "Dumpster Juice," had just finished their set.

JoBeth and Rayne found a table near the stage covered in empty beer bottles. Rayne never looked better. She wore an electric blue dress that complemented her figure perfectly. The girl was jittery with nervous excitement. JoBeth had seen this behavior before, but never to this extent.

The first thing JoBeth did was to push the disgusting plastic ashtray to the side. She noticed a few cigarettes still smoldering, so she poured some leftover beer juice from one of the bottles on it. When the waiter came by to remove all the junk, she ordered a burger and fries. But Rayne, far too on-edge to eat, shook her head.

Visions of all the delicious junk food back home in white plastic bags loomed before her. *What I wouldn't give to dig into some Andy Capp Red Hot Fries or Chili Cheese Fritos. Or those lovely cans of jumbo black olives.* She had a ritual to eating those. JoBeth slipped an olive on every finger, and ate one at a time, bathing each olive into pimento dip first.

The emcee stepped up to the mic as a new set of gel colors lit the stage. JoBeth nudged Rayne with her elbow. "The comedy hour approacheth."

Her friend was a real basket case, a state she rarely exhibited. Rayne usually had a laid back attitude about things, even when she applied for a job, like it didn't matter one way or the other. But this time was different. She'd invested emotion in this guy. The girl was fidgety. Was he worth it? JoBeth hoped so, for Rayne's sake. And she hoped he was into purple hair. Rayne had been through Cada's revolving door, *or color wheel.*

"He's supposed to go on first." Rayne took out a compact mirror from her purse for a quick look. "I don't know how you can eat after dinner. I'm stuffed."

JoBeth shrugged.

All of a sudden, the whole place erupted in "clapter," a word JoBeth coined to explain the enthusiastic claps preceding the laughs the audience expects to experience from a standup comedian.

Logan stepped out wearing corduroy pants and a tweed jacket with leather patches on the elbow, circa 1980. A lone black stool and mic stand occupied the stage. He set a bottle of water on the stool and faced the audience. Thus began his comedy routine.

"I hate going on dates. Women want to be so independent men don't know how to act around 'em. Do I open the door for her? *Cause I'm a doorman.* Can I order her dinner? *At the drive-through.* I'm so confused."

Some people were loaded enough to laugh at the jokes. Rayne tried her best, but her laughter sounded more polite than anything else. She kept trying to make eye contact with Logan since they were so close to the stage. Not that she and Rayne had been to many comedy club acts, but normally, they stayed away from the stage. Any idiot knew that the people closest to the stage are fair game for ridicule. But tonight, Rayne had insisted on being close.

Logan was on for a few minutes before JoBeth noticed Sophie Perkins with her gaggle of gal friends across the room. She nudged Rayne who managed to tear her eyes away from Logan for a nanosecond.

She brought her hands up to her cheeks and mouthed, "I'm so sorry."

Sophie was obviously having a bachelorette party at the place. How romantic. The little bridal veil tiara her head was a dead giveaway. Maybe it was the alcohol, but Sophie seemed to think everything out of Logan's mouth was hilarious. She even slapped the table a few times.

Right about that time, when Logan was clearly dying a slow comedic death, he decided as all no-talent comedians do in such situations, to heckle the audience.

He pointed to Rayne. "Look at this one." He lifted his hand and drew the audience with him. So did the spotlight. And there she was, under the bright light, smiling and excited—clearly overwhelmed that Logan had finally noticed her.

But then he spoke. "What's with the purple hair? Are you trying to look like your fairy godmother?" He looked around hoping for laughs and he got a few, mainly because some people laugh at purple hair, or pink hair or Mohawks, anything different for an easy laugh.

"Did Billy Idol open a hair salon?" He flipped his hand to the side. "Get your money back, girlfriend."

Her face flushed, Rayne opened and closed her mouth. "What's your name, honey?"

"R-Rayne."

"What's that?" He drew closer and made her repeat her name into the mic. "HeeHee." He bent over laughing as if it was the funniest thing he'd ever heard. "Now I get it. Purple Rayne." He sneered.

JoBeth's heart thumped, anger clouding her vision. She knew her friend wanted to melt under the table. People were laughing, just the reaction he wanted. Sir Logan would continue attacking her because he had zero else to offer. Instead of waiting for that to happen, she and Rayne took one look at each other and dashed. With good friends, words are not always necessary.

The hasty exit brought down the house, by far the biggest laugh Logan was ever going to get. When the two reached the exit however, JoBeth remembered that she'd neglected to pay for the meal. Rayne was halfway out the door when she yanked her back.

"What?" Rayne had that fight or flight look in her eyes.

"We can't dine and dash. I've got to pay the bill. You go to the car."

JoBeth recognized the cashier, a nice girl she knew in high school. After getting the waiter to pluck the bill off the table and bring it up to the register, JoBeth took care of it. Thankfully, Logan's act was soon over. She watched him and his career as a stand-up comedian disappear behind the curtain backstage. On impulse, she made up her mind to give Logan a piece of hers.

She made her way to the edge of the stage near the wall. The second comedian came out and while the spotlight was on him, JoBeth slipped through the side curtain. Down a dim hallway, she spotted a dark-haired woman talking to Logan. There was something odd about her hair though. As she drew closer, *so did they*, and JoBeth got the shock of her life. A front-row view of Sir Logan kissing someone with a white veil on her head — Sophie!

JoBeth pulled out her cell phone, faster than "Quick Draw McGraw," and snapped a photo of them, then scooted off down the hall before they could de-pucker.

The run through MotorMouth was a blur. She powered through the entrance and out into the night. Rayne sat in the passenger's seat crying her eyes out. JoBeth ripped open the driver's seat door, turned on the ignition and was about to pop the car in reverse. But she didn't. Instead, she wrapped her arms around Rayne. "I'm so sorry."

"H-he didn't r-r-remember m-me." She gasped between sobs, blue eyeliner in dribs and drabs at the corners of her eyes.

JoBeth rooted around her purse and pulled out a sorry looking tissue. Rayne took it and blew her nose.

"Logan's not worthy of you."

"I t-thought he liked me. He seemed like he did." She cradled her head in her hands. "That's it. I'm done with this look. P-people make fun of you when you're different. I'm done. No more purple hair. No more pink hair."

"Rayne." JoBeth put her arm around her. "I understand that you're tired of people making rude comments but let's be honest, that look attracts attention be it positive or negative. On the other hand, I totally get that the whole crazy-colored hair thing is an expression of your individuality. I can't believe I'm saying this, but I don't think you should switch to a normal cut and color just to please other people or to avoid the bullying. If you change, you should do it because you want to."

JoBeth scrounged another tissue and gave it to her friend. "Besides, if you decide to change your look, you can express individuality in so many other ways. I don't know anyone more creative than you."

She nodded, swiping at the globs of mascara and blue pencil under her eyes. "I don't know why I thought he'd ever like me. He's just so, so. . ."

"Hot." She shrugged. "Yeah, he's *hot*, but he's *not* the one for you. Let's get out of here."

She adjusted the rear view mirror and backed out. "By the way, aren't you wondering what took me so long?"

Rayne blubbered. "What happened?"

"I'll tell you what happened. I went backstage intending to give Logan a piece of my mind, but instead I found him and Sophie locked in a big kissy-kiss." JoBeth started the engine.

Her friend's hands covered her mouth. "Nooooo?"

As she took off down Main Street, JoBeth handed her the phone. "See for yourself."

Chapter Twenty-Eight
Business As Usual

"A diet is the price we pay for exceeding the feed limit." — Unknown

What remained of the night and early morning morphed into pure fun. After an emotional cry session and one full box of tissues, JoBeth and Rayne had a bit of a slumber party. They ate popcorn, watched an old movie, looked at some old photo albums and laughed at the ugly newspaper picture of Sophie and Logan's engagement. Shiner sat on JoBeth's lap the whole time, perfectly content to commandeer any stray popcorn that fell whenever they started giggling.

Rayne disappeared into the kitchen for a few minutes and came out with an Italian Cream Cake lit with a gazillion candles and sparklers. "Happy thirtieth birthday, Jo." She set the cake down on the coffee table in front of her. "You thought I forgot, didn't you?"

"Well." Happy tears rolled down her cheeks. "I wasn't sure."

"Go on. Make a wish." She laughed.

JoBeth closed her eyes and spoke it to her heart.

"What did you wish for?"

"A bigger plate for my cake. What do you think I wished for?"

She unwrapped an assortment of presents from Rayne, a cute collection of resale clothes to show off her new figure. A pang of guilt unfurled within as she thought of all the junk food she'd eaten lately. Of course, if Seth and Ada hadn't come home, she would have put away a whole lot more. Still, she wondered if the clothes would fit after all the sorrow snacking and the birthday cake on top of that.

She sent "the picture" via wireless to Rayne's flat screen television. Right before them, larger than life, Sophie and Logan shared a giant grainy, forbidden smooch.

JoBeth munched and crunched on popcorn and got tired of reaching in and out so many times, so she held the dish under her chin and flicked her tongue out.

"What are you doing?" Rayne laughed.

"Something new. I'm going to call it, 'aardvarking'. You stick out your tongue in the bowl and pull in the popcorn that sticks to it, like an anteater. Can't wait to try this at the movie theater."

Rayne threw back her head and started laughing. "You're a mess."

"We haven't been to the movies in a long time. Maybe we should go tomorrow. I mean, this afternoon, since it's way after midnight."

She nodded. "Sounds good. We're celebrating your birthday. Let's go for it."

"Rayne, I really appreciate everything you did for me. You don't know how much it means to me."

"We're best friends, silly." Rayne cupped her chin in her hands. "What do you think we should we do with it?" she asked.

"What do you mean?"

"The picture."

"Nothing. We had a good laugh. That's what we did with it."

"Maybe we should send it to her. Or him. Or both." She pointed to JoBeth. "We should soooo send it to Kyle." Rayne's mood had improved considerably since her meltdown in the car.

"Are you kidding me?" JoBeth asked between crunches. "No, that would be cruel."

She folded her arms. "Which is worse, not telling the guy you used to be in love with that the woman he's engaged to marry is already cheating on him, or telling the guy and saving him from making a very bad mistake with lasting consequences?"

"You know. . . " JoBeth crunched. "When you put it that way it almost makes sense." She put the popcorn bowl down on the coffee table. "But no way am I telling him that. That would crush him. And even though he hurt me, I — I don't wish that on Kyle."

"You're better than I am. I'd be all over that." She tapped the table like a set of bongo drums, not something her normally calm and low-key friend would do. "Then maybe we should tell Sam. He would know what to do. Sam's a levelheaded kind of guy. He'll do the right thing."

True, Sam always seemed to do the right thing. He'd know what to do with the information.

"You're the one who told me about Kyle and Sophie together at the MotorMouth Grille."

"I was wondering when you were going to bring that up. Isn't it weird that their beginning ended you and Kyle as a couple, and now the picture of Sophie and Logan kissing is probably going to end Kyle and Sophie as a couple? It's come full circle. Have you thought of that?"

The irony of the situation was not lost on either of them.

"Kyle needs to know. Maybe I should call and tell him." She reached for her cell, but Rayne grabbed her wrist in mid-air.

"That's incredibly nice, considering what he did to you. But maybe we should stick to the plan and run it by Sam first," she suggested. "He invited us to that wiener roast thing at your old church, which is tonight by the way. Why don't you stay another night?"

JoBeth looked up at the clock on the wall. Two in the morning—already? "Okay, it's not like I have to rush back into town to work or anything."

"What do you mean?" she asked.

JoBeth sighed and told her the whole sordid story about getting canned from her job and kicked out the house.

"Oh, Jo." Rayne embraced her in a long heartfelt hug. "Here I am worrying about me and my obsession with Logan and you'd just suffered two more devastating blows. Not to mention the thing that happened with Sam. And all in time for your birthday."

Shiner, fast asleep, nuzzled his nose into JoBeth's side. "Nobody else knows."

"Not even Big Grizz?"

"I'm not sure. My gut tells me no, and I don't want to upset him in his state."

"I'm so sorry." She brought her knees up to her chest on the sofa. "To make it up to you, I'll go to the church thing."

"What?" Shock waves. JoBeth had to do a double take. "Really?" She'd invited her friend to church many times over the years and to every notable church event too. Once she'd come to a church picnic because she found out they were going to have old-fashioned potato sack races. But that was it. She'd heard no so many times she didn't expect Rayne would ever say yes. This time, JoBeth didn't even have to ask. Go figure.

JoBeth peeked out from behind a sofa pillow. "Do you think Sam sort of likes me?"

"What?" Rayne coughed up a piece of popcorn.

She repeated, "Do you think Sam kind of likes me?"

Rayne pulled away the pillow and threw it on the carpet. "Nooooo, the man obviously haaaates you."

"He and I—kissed."

Rayne's eyes widened. "You what?"

For the next hour, she told Rayne the story about how it happened, why she did it, etc., stretching something that took less than a minute in real time to talk about endlessly. However, they did eventually go to bed. She heard Rayne's roomies trudge in sometime afterward.

* * *

Although she went to bed super late, JoBeth woke up super early for two reasons: the air mattress was doing wicked things to her back, and her body was used to waking up early for work.

Rayne's roomies looked exhausted, even in sleep. Sprawled across their beds, still in costume, weapons and shields littered the living room. Muddy boots crusted the kitchen floor. JoBeth had to tiptoe around the place to avoid waking the sleeping beauties.

The first thing she did after feeding Shiner was to have a peaceful breakfast of cereal and milk on the front screen porch. With Shiner back on her lap keeping a vigilant eye for cats and squirrels, JoBeth decided to call Ada.

"What are you doing, Auntie?"

"I'm tidying up," she said. "Sethie woke me up this morning."

"What?" she asked. "Why did he wake you up early? The place was pretty clean when I left. Why are you doing that?"

"Sethie, bless his heart, has been such a good help to me. He's been cleaning out the garage." She laughed. "It's nice to have a man around the house again."

"Sure is." JoBeth tried to sound convincing. All she could think of was Seth throwing things out and packing her stuff in preparation for a move she didn't want.

Ada continued. "Sethie told me he's having a friend over today. I might even make them some succotash."

Her heart sank. "Really? An old friend?" She wondered who that "old friend" was—probably the real estate person.

"That's a great idea, Auntie." *If anyone deserved succotash, it was Seth.*

She paused as if lost in thought. "What were we talking about?"

"Auntie, Auntie." A lump rose in her throat. "I was just saying goodbye. See you again soon, okay." When she hung up the phone, JoBeth felt like crying. And an uneasy feeling wallowed in her gut. If JoBeth hadn't heard Rayne promise to go to church with her, she would have gone straight back to Beeton to find out what was going on.

With the promise of a play day before them, the two had a nice lunch, window-shopped and went to a movie. JoBeth had more popcorn and again demonstrated the art of aardvarking. Rayne wasn't half bad at it either.

They returned home to Rayne's place to change and freshen up for church. Sedjie, CeeJay and Cada had the place cleaned up spic 'n span—smelling like bleach and pine-scented liquid. The weapons were put away and the muddy shoes cleaned and stacked on the porch to dry. No wonder she liked them. The best, though, was how they doted on Shiner, spoiling him like an only child. And Shiner sure took a shine to them.

Chapter Twenty-Nine
The Holy Ghost Weiner Roast

"The first thing you lose on a diet is your sense of humor." —
Unknown

Clad in jeans and casual tops, they left for the church a little after seven. Though JoBeth had fallen off the wagon as far as her healthy diet was concerned, she hadn't fallen that far. In fact, she fit into her smaller sized jeans by the skin of her teeth.

An anxious feeling came over JoBeth on the way to the church. She'd been back a handful of times after her parents died. At first, she told herself she was tired of people asking so many questions about the accident. Then she was tired of people asking about her to the point that it made her want to vomit! *How are you doing? How are you feeling?*

But the real reason she'd stayed away had nothing to do with any of that.

The parking lot started to fill with singles chattering, laughing, clique-ing. A few people remembered her, but most were new. Singles turn over that way. They get married and get out, and younger singles take their place.

In the sanctuary, the first man she saw was Sam. She knew him by the back of his head, the gloriously thick, wavy hair, and the way he stood tall and straight. He was wearing black denim and a long-sleeved shirt with flames running down the sleeves, which she guessed was some kind of homage to the wiener roast event. He was talking to an attractive woman with dark hair about the same mahogany tone as his. Thin and pretty, probably in her mid-twenties. *The girl he went on a date with, maybe?*

Rayne grabbed her arm. "Aren't you going to say hi?"

"No, I don't want to interrupt." JoBeth fought back a twinge of jealousy.

She watched the two talking and laughing, her eyes like lasers on them, but the girl, whomever she was, finally broke away and continued on toward the courtyard area.

Hands on her hips, Rayne looked at JoBeth and shook her head. "Well?" Rayne marched right over and threw her arms around him. "Hi, how are you, Sam?"

The surprise on his face evident, and happy to see Rayne, he hugged her back.

"Is it you, Rayne? Is it really you? I can't believe my eyes."

"I know, right? It's hard for me to believe too."

He laughed, but his eyes searched over her Rayne's shoulder settled on JoBeth.

"JoBeth, you're here!"

She approached. "In the flesh."

He and Rayne let go of one another and he walked over to give her a hug, so warm and comforting she could have melted into it. He extended his arm and pulled Rayne into the hug as well. "C'mon girls. Let's go outside and join the party."

JoBeth's heart ached. She'd chased him away, without explanation and still he greeted her with such warmth and kindness.

About fifty singles stood or sat around an enormous blazing fire. A few rows of crude benches constructed from tree stumps and wooden beams surrounded the flames. A station for hot chocolate, coffee and other beverages were set up on tables a short distance away. A s'mores table set with chocolate bars, huge puffy marshmallows and grahams was right next to it and another table for hot dogs, buns and condiments a short distance further.

About ten people already had their hotdogs on metal skewers. JoBeth guessed they were waiting for the singles pastor to give the blessing first. She wasn't familiar with the man. He came on about the time she stopped going to church. Sam found a place on a bench close to the fire for the three of them. As they were about to sit down, the pastor approached to give the blessing, so they stayed vertical.

Hand on his chest he introduced himself. "I'm Pastor Yau and if you don't know me already, you will." Cheers accented his introduction. The man seemed popular enough.

"I'm the pastor here at Crowne Point Church and I want to welcome you all here tonight. It's going to be fun. Also," he held out an arm towards Sam, "I want to introduce our new assistant singles pastor, Samuel MacManus. Let's give him a big hand. All eyes turned to him.

"He's also known as 'Sam the Man.'" He held his index finger up in the air. "If you ever have a plumbing issue, he's your man." Pastor Yau opened with a short prayer, and gave a rundown on the order of events.

"First, we'll eat our dogs and desserts." He grinned wide. "Then we'll move off into small groups of two to four. Each one of you will be given two slips of paper now so you'll have time to pray and write something down. On the first piece of paper, write down something you need to let go of in your life. It's okay to write down more than one thing if you want, but the focus really is to pinpoint one thing in particular that you need to let go of."

He continued. "On the other slip of paper, write down your most fervent prayer, the desire of your heart before God, the thing you need an answer for most. Then, we're going to pray over these two things in our small groups. Afterwards, whatever you wrote down on the slip of paper that you need to let go of, we'll toss into the flames and let it go forever before God. The thing you wrote on the other slip of paper, we'll pray for. That one you keep. Don't put it in your pocket; put it between the pages of your bible so you'll remember to thank God for it each day until God answers your prayer."

"So." He rubbed his hands together. "Is everybody ready to chow down?" He bowed his head. "Let's pray." Immediately after he said the blessing, a small crowd surrounded the fire, metal forks in the midst of the blaze. Wieners on sticks were thrust through the flames, like a fiery pincushion, sputtering — sending out a sizzling invitation to eat.

Rayne and JoBeth sat and watched at first. Sam returned with forks, hotdogs already skewered, two apiece.

"Oh Sam," Rayne excused herself, "I'm sorry you went to all that trouble but I don't eat meat."

"No worries." He handed her a special skewer. "We have vegan hotdogs."

"Really?" She smiled.

"And here's yours, Jo."

Why was he so nice? Kyle would never ever have done something like that, especially after the way she'd treated Sam. The differences between the two were nothing less than epic.

JoBeth looked into his eyes, searching for a hint of hurt or sarcasm, but found none. "Thanks." She smiled at him, and he smiled back.

They held their forks on the edge of the fire, and the hotdogs soon plumped up, sputtering grease into the flames. Preferring her hotdogs on the burnt side, JoBeth left hers in the flames slightly longer than Rayne or Sam who were already on the bench eating. Before she joined them she held the buns just under the red-hot tines and slipped the dogs between the buns. She thrust the fork into the ashes at the edge of the pit and took a short walk to the condiment table for some relish and yellow mustard and ketchup. Back on the bench, she polished one hotdog off in a couple of bites and started on the other one before she took a seat.

"Are you having a good time?" Sam asked Rayne.

"Sure." She beamed. "It's a wiener roast. What's not fun about that?" Hotdog juices sizzled in the background against the heat of the flames.

"How was the comedy thing? Sorry, I couldn't go."

JoBeth shot Rayne a look before her friend answered. "It was—it was interesting. I'd like to tell you about it later."

"Okay, I'm intrigued." He smiled.

A girl wearing a cowboy hat came round with paper and pencils for each of them and a recap of what the pastor just said. A fresh sense of angst filled JoBeth. What to write? What to write?

She noticed Sam's lips moving, his eyes closed. Praying. She looked over at Rayne who seemed to be going along with the program. Busy writing something already.

JoBeth bent down over her papers and tried to think. No good. But she sensed it was time to be completely honest with herself and with God. On the first paper she wrote, "I'm mad at God because He let my parents die."

She folded the paper and put it into her shirt pocket.

Next they moved on to the s'mores. Although JoBeth liked her hotdogs crispy, she preferred her marshmallows only slightly toasty, browned, not burned. She planned to treat herself to three s'mores since she hadn't made them in a while, but stopped halfway through the first. She took out the slip of paper and looked at it again.

Do I have the right to be angry?

She'd progressed from doubting the existence of God, to being angry with Him, if you could call that progress.

After they finished the dogs and desserts, Pastor Yau stood up and addressed the group again.

"Okay, we're ready to begin. Before we pray and release these slips of paper into the fire, would anyone like to share what they've written? You don't have to. These are completely private, but some of you might want to share, and I'm leaving the option open." He looked around. Six people stood. One needed to let go of unforgiveness, another jealousy, another, loneliness. But then, to JoBeth's surprise, Rayne raised her hand and stood.

Her voice shaky, she spoke. "I-I wrote something I'd like to share. I want to l-let go of a guy I thought I cared about."

"Good." The pastor asked, "I assume the relationship didn't work out?"

"That's right."

JoBeth squeezed her arm and gave her a pat on the back, which she noticed was pretty tense. "I'm so proud of you."

"And I did something bad." She stood perfectly still, her chest heaving as she spoke. "I—I sent a picture of him kissing someone else's fiancé."

JoBeth lost her balance and found herself knees to bare earth. "Please tell me you did not do that."

Pastor Yau looked confused and was about to ask her another question when a group of people by the beverage table parted and Kyle emerged.

What's he doing here? JoBeth seethed. Why would Sam invite me here if he knew Kyle was going to show up?

"You did it?" Kyle stood alone. Wearing a pair of rumpled khaki pants and a white oxford — one shirttail tucked in and one out. His blond hair tousled and dirty, he looked like he hadn't slept all night.

Sam cocked his head to the side, as if surprised. He looked to Rayne, and then moved to stand next to his friend.

Kyle continued. "I thought the picture came from JoBeth. I figured it was sour grapes about our break-up. But I didn't know they were in it together." He pointed.

Meanwhile, Kyle held up his phone for Sam, who by the look on his face got an eyeful.

Kyle, eyes ringed by red with dark circles underneath, stared at JoBeth. "Are you happy? The engagement is off." A vein at his temple throbbed.

She started to shake her head, but Rayne stepped in between. "It wasn't her, it was me." She pointed to her chest. "Don't look at her like that. It's my fault. She didn't know anything about it."

Heart sinking moment by moment, JoBeth wanted to run — somewhere, anywhere but where she was. But instead of running, she looked up at the sky. A blanket of stars above twinkled back at the earth, as if waiting for a response.

Rayne's breath formed a frosty ectoplasm in the chill of the night. "I was mad about what Logan did to me, and angry about what Kyle did to my best friend. I just wanted a little karmic justice, that's all."

"Why did it come from JoBeth's phone?" Kyle asked.

"I-I took the picture." Hands up in the air, JoBeth calmed the explosion she saw behind his eyes. "Let me explain before you say anything." She related the entire story.

Afterwards, his voice ragged, Kyle questioned her. "So you didn't know Sophie was backstage?"

JoBeth shook her head. "I was as surprised to see her as she would have been to see me."

Sam gave him a nod. "Kyle, I think you owe JoBeth an apology."

Pastor Yau added. "And Rayne, I think you owe JoBeth and Kyle an apology."

"What about Sophie?" Kyle asked.

"Sophie definitely owes you one."

Rayne yelled out. "What about Kyle apologizing to JoBeth about text-dumping her?"

A collective gasp issued from the singles crowd. Kyle looked around for support, but found none.

Kyle fiddled with his phone like he was thinking *or something akin to that process.* "Okay, I'm sorry if I've have done anything to hurt you, Joey."

Pastor Yau whistled. "Wait."

Sheepish, Kyle put his phone in his pocket.

Pastor Yau asked. "Do you all want to continue this discussion in private, or finish it the way it began?"

Kyle shrugged.

Rayne swallowed hard. "I want to finish it right here and now."

Except for the crackling flames, the rest of the group was silent, perhaps mesmerized by the drama playing out in front of them.

"Very well then, if there are no objections, let's continue." He directed his next comments toward Kyle. "The word 'if' doesn't belong in an apology. Is it an established fact that you text-dumped your former girlfriend?"

Hands in his pockets, Kyle kicked his shoe into the ground. "I guess so."

"You guess so?" Sam asked.

He yelled back. "All right, I did it. Are you satisfied?" He met JoBeth's eyes. "I tried to tell her face-to-face that day, but that didn't work out."

"Much better." Pastor Yau clapped his hands together. "Now you should apologize the right way to your ex-girlfriend. But hold on. Don't do it right this moment." He let out a whistle. "Everybody else—now for the surprise. Head on over to the corral we set up over there. He pointed to an area now lit by white Christmas lights. Buzzy and the Buzzards are calling a square dance."

Most of the singles roared their approval and immediately began the short trek to the corral, but some hesitated, perhaps preferring to linger and listen to the drama playing out before them. Pastor Yau shooed them away.

Before he left, Pastor Yau trained his eyes on the little group. "Why don't you guys stay here for a bit and try to work things out? I think that would be best." He took off after the others.

Fiddlers were poised on a riser about thirty yards away. When they began to play, people began to dance. The last of the onlookers soon joined them.

With everybody else gone, that left Sam, Rayne, Kyle and JoBeth standing by the fire.

"Kyle had his phone up to his ear and was talking. JoBeth heard a woman's voice screeching at him from the other end.

"What do you mean she's lying? I have the picture." He chopped the air with his free hand. "No, it's not photo shopped. Okay, I'll come over." His face red, Kyle took a seat next to JoBeth. "You're sure, you're absolutely sure it was her?"

Chest heaving, she answered. "Not a shred of doubt. I was there, remember?"

"I'm sorry about everything. I never meant for things to turn out this way or for you to be hurt. I did care about you, Joey. You're great. You really are. When I met Sophie—well—I knew she was the one."

An ache in her throat, JoBeth's voice cracked. "You broke my heart." Though she had tried to form the words many different times before, the words always stuck in her throat on the way out.

"Let's have a seat." Sam motioned for Kyle to sit down as well.

But Kyle shook his head. "I've got to try and work things out with her." He pulled out his keys and took a few steps.

"Hold on, a minute." JoBeth called after him.

Kyle stopped in his tracks.

"You called me 'Joey' at the restaurant the night of your engagement, and even tonight."

"What about it?"

"I'm JoBeth to you from now on. Don't ever call me 'Joey' again."

Lips pressed together, he nodded. Kyle turned on his heels and walked away.

Rayne, JoBeth and Sam sat in silence for a while, listening to the pop and crackle of the flames against the raucous sounds of square dancing in the distance.

Finally Rayne spoke. "JoBeth, I'm sorry I got you in trouble. I shouldn't have done it." She pushed a lock of hair behind her ear.

"Don't worry about it. After we talked last night, I went to bed thinking we'd agreed to tell Sam and let him decide whether or not to tell."

"Gee, thanks." Sam shifted on the bench. "Put it all on me."

Rayne bowed her head. "I couldn't sleep. My heart kept beating faster the more I thought about it, so I got up and sent the picture from your phone. I mean, your phone was right there on the coffee table. If you had it next to you on the air mattress, I probably wouldn't have done it." She grinned. "Besides, Shiner would have growled."

JoBeth held up her right hand. "Wait, let me get this straight, Rayne. You're saying it's my fault because I trusted you, my best friend, enough to leave my non-password protected phone unattended? Is that what you're saying?"

She leapt to her feet and began pacing. "No, I'm not blaming you. It's my fault. I said it, and I meant it."

"Okay."

Silence again. A log collapsed into the fire, sending a volley of ashes upward.

"I'm curious, Jo." Sam traced through the ashes on the edge of the fire pit. "What was on your paper?"

Her hand instantly rose up to her shirt pocket, though she didn't pull it out.

"Would you like to share it?" He looked around. "It's just us."

JoBeth pulled the paper out and handed it to him.

He read it out loud. *"I'm mad at God because He let my parents die."*

Before anyone could respond, she added, "And I think I overeat and binge so I won't have to deal with things."

Rayne threw her arms up and looked towards the sky. "Finally."

Sam's eyes, kind and compassionate, met hers. "JoBeth, you need to repent of that anger toward God. It's destroying you."

Pastor Yau returned to check on them just in time to hear.

Rayne, her face red and contorted, shouted. "Why should she be sorry?"

"What do you mean?" Pastor Yau asked.

She pointed her finger at him. "Why should she? The church wasn't there for her when her parents died. When she cried night after night, who stayed with her through it all? Who came to her house and peeled her off the floor? Did any of you even think to call or come by with meals? Or talk her through it? You just went on with your nice little sermons and God talk and left her behind. Left her in the dust."

An uncomfortable silence followed. And to JoBeth's surprise, Rayne had more to say.

She pounded her fist on her chest. "I was there for her. And I'm the kind of person you hate. I see the way you all look at me. Like I'm the poor little pagan with piercings and tats who needs Jesus."

"I'm sorry." Pastor Yau touched her hand. "Nobody hates you."

She lifted her face in a defiant stance. "And nobody loves me either."

JoBeth stood, still clutching the papers in her hand. "She's right. The church wasn't there for me. I thought people would care more. Instead, it seemed like everyone wanted all the details about what happened so they could talk about me. After they lost interest, people just expected me to move on and forget about it like losing my parents was no big deal."

A sob forced its way out. "I used to pick up the phone and call home to hear the answering machine. Just to hear their voices. I'm so afraid I'll forget . . . "

This time, tears joined the sobs as they came. "I asked God why He would do this. And all I got was silence—from Him, from the church." She looked around.

Pastor Yau drew near and took JoBeth's hands in his, voice tender, breaking as he spoke. "We're not perfect and you're right, we failed you. I'm new here. If I had known about this, I would've come alongside you and helped. I guess all this happened during the transition. People were hurting and distracted and you somehow fell through the cracks. I'm sorry."

He went on. "I'm not excusing anyone, including myself, but people will always fail or disappoint you if you're looking to them for answers. Jesus is the only one who will never leave you or forsake you. God loves you, JoBeth. I think you already know that though."

Her body began to tremble. Tears pushed their way up and out. JoBeth knew in her heart what he said was true, but she couldn't help herself. There were things inside that needed voice. Thoughts deeply entrenched. She'd packed them down as far as they would go and there was no more room left. She cried out. "But He let them die. He could have stopped it from happening. He's God. Why didn't He?"

The pastor paused before answering. She could tell the man was trying to be sensitive, extra careful. "Did you ask Him that?

"No."

"Why not?"

She glanced over at Rayne for support and noticed her quiet sobs.

"I wanted to believe my parents were in a happy place somewhere. Who wouldn't? But how can you love a God who takes away the people you love?" Her eyes on Sam, she asked the question again. "Why did He let them die?"

Sam opened his mouth as if to speak.

Pastor Yau, voice gentle, continued. "JoBeth, we don't know the answer. I don't know why God allows things like this to happen, but I do know that in all things He works for the good of those who love Him, who have been called according to His purpose."

"Pointless." Rayne clutched at her temples. "This is all so pointless."

Rayne's words cut straight to her heart. Who needs fairy tales? Rayne and her roommates sure did. Rayne lived a fairy tale about Logan. She fell for the noble knight, but the real Logan was a nightmare. Her roomies lived to LARP, longing for excitement and escapism, but were stuck in the mire of mediocrity. Not one of them had a real relationship with anyone special, and instead of saving for the future, they spent every extra dime on cheesy costumes and weapons to further their fantasy lives.

On the other hand, JoBeth had settled on the implied promise of a future with Kyle, when she knew in her heart, that there was no future with him. She ignored little signals and cues, and focused instead on her ideal of a perfect life. She'd settled for a job at the shipping company, one she didn't like or want and stopped actively pursuing her dreams. And even before her parents died, she'd turned wholeheartedly to food instead of turning her whole heart to God.

In fact, her faith faded into the background and she made food the focus of every thought and ambition, her husband, best friend — and idol.

JoBeth looked up at the sky and mouthed the words. "I'm sorry. "A blanket of hands covered her back and shoulders. Comforting, warm. Prayers — penetrating through skin and bone and soul, straight to the heart.

Some of the singles group gathered around her and began to pray. And those prayers began to quicken and stir something inside. As the prayers waned, JoBeth, Pastor Yau, Sam, and Rayne sat down on a log near the fire. JoBeth stared as flames licked against dry wood, burning hot and fast. Flames lifted high in the updraft. They talked late into the night, until the fire began to die down.

Another hour passed. Kind faces drifting in an out. Illuminated by firelight, glowing and going. Sam and Pastor Yau stayed with her and talked. And wonder of wonders, Rayne was suddenly engrossed in conversation with a guy on the worship team.

When they had a moment alone, Sam slid closer and placed a package on her lap. Wrapped in glittering silver foil paper with a white bow on top, "Happy Birthday" was scrawled across it.

"Oh, Sam. You didn't have to."

"I wanted to give it to you on your birthday. Or rather, I planned to."

"I don't deserve anything after the way I treated you."

"Of course you do. And it's your thirtieth, a milestone. Open it," he urged.

She tore at the wrapping and pulled it off, revealing a beautiful book bound in raspberry leather, her name inscribed in gold lettering across the cover. A bible?

Inside the cover, she saw that he'd signed it with an inscription. *"Thou art all fair, my love; there is no spot in thee."* From the Song of Solomon, chapter four, verse seven.

"I hope you like it."

"I love it. Sam. Thank you." She clutched the bible to her chest. He'd given her the best, most meaningful, memorable birthday present she would ever receive.

She leaned in and kissed his cheek. "I mean it — thank you."

But her conscience kept tugging and pulling at her. JoBeth knew she had something else to confess, and she dreaded doing it. "Sam, do me a favor and don't say anything until I'm done." Lips trembling, she volleyed out the words. "I've wasted so much time making excuses about why not to like you; I even told myself not to like you because you're a plumber, not a PhD. That was stupid and shallow, and the dumbest excuse I ever thought of not to go out with you, and I don't deserve your forgiveness, but I'm asking."

His eyes widened. "That's a lot in one sentence."

"Well?"

"So that was it? I thought maybe Kyle was better looking or charming."

She shook her head. "I was a college snobette, which is funny in retrospect because Kyle is sort of an idiot, and he graduated." JoBeth wiped her eyes with a napkin. "I've made some really bad decisions in life, but that one was the worst."

He paused, a curious look on his face. "Do you mean it?"

"I do."

His face softened into a wide smile. "Of course I forgive you, Jo."

"Then I have another question." She tugged at his sleeve.

"What?"

"Do you date ex-waitresses?"

Sam wrapped an arm around her. "I'll have to think about it."

JoBeth pulled away and gave his arm a playful punch.

The two sat next to one another for the remainder of the evening. In time, the fire turned to coal, white-hot. Perfect for roasting. But the music and the square dancing were over, and the crowd had dwindled to less than ten people.

She slipped her hand in her pocket, rolled the paper into a tight scroll and let it fall onto the coals. As the paper curled, browned and fell apart, she followed the tiny embers as they rose in the updraft, upward toward the midnight-blue sky.

Past the dark lace of leaves — past all earthly light — past the stars — to the throne.

Chapter Thirty
From Here To Eternity

"The leading cause of death among fashion models is falling through street grates." – Dave Barry

That night, JoBeth had the dream again. Sucked from her not-so-comfy air mattress into the darkness of night, the swirling mist, wet grass underfoot — all the same as before. And once again, she followed the trail to the clearing she knew would be there. But things were different.

In the middle of the clearing was a fire. Dolls of every shape, size and dress held hands in a big circle around the flames singing. *"Here we go round the mulberry bush, the mulberry bush, the mulberry bush. Here we go round the mulberry bush on a cold and frosty morning."*

The first doll she'd spoken to, the dark haired one with the piggy tails, and the Victorian doll came forward and stood near. The piggy-tailed dolly spoke first, her eyes clicking open and shut as she finished every couple of words. "Hello, JoBeth."

"Hi, creepy dollies."

The dolly responded with a mechanical blink. "Aren't you going to ask where your food baby is?"

JoBeth looked around. No sign of a big doll bed with pink ruffles or a crib or anything.

The Victorian doll approached and spoke next. "Yes, aren't you curious?"

She scanned the perimeter of the clearing. Nothing. The food baby was definitely gone. "Sure, I'd like to know. Where is the thing?"

The two dolls looked at one another, then at her. They answered in unison. "She's gone."

JoBeth craned her neck to see get an even wider view around. "Well, where did she go?"

"Where you sent her, of course," answered the Victorian doll.

Piggy-tailed dolly spoke. "You created her and now she's faded away."

"But how?" JoBeth asked.

"You called her into being. With every bite of food, with every binge and craving, she grew and grew—always crying for more—growing bigger and bigger with every passing day."

The Victorian doll blinked. "And you fed her when she cried."

"You mean I made her? Have you been talking to Rayne?"

The Victorian doll tilted her head. "How does one speak to the rain?"

"Guess that answers my question." JoBeth gulped. "But I'm not doing that anymore."

"That's why she's gone," said the Victorian dolly.

"For good?" JoBeth asked.

The dolly answered. "That's up to you."

JoBeth pointed at the dolls gathered around the fire. "What's going on?"

"We're celebrating. You saved us from the garbage heap."

"From Seth?"

"Yes."

JoBeth swiped away tears and put her hands on her hips. "Tell me, what should I do with all of you? I can't take you home. Technically, I don't even have a home."

Piggy-tailed dolly blinked. "You'll know what to do." She and the Victorian doll joined hands with the other dollies around the campfire and began to sing. *"Here we go round the mulberry bush, the mulberry bush, the mulberry bush. Here we go round the mulberry bush on a cold and frosty morning."*

* * *

JoBeth tried to get her taillight fixed on Sunday morning. Not that she had the time or the money, but she wasn't keen on getting stopped again anytime soon. Really it should have been done a long time ago. Regardless, the auto shop had to special order the light which would not be in till the following week. Fine, the gears to the repair were at least in motion. She tucked the order receipt in her glove box in the event she was stopped again.

She and Rayne said their goodbyes early before her friend went off to work. No matter what she'd done, she couldn't be mad at her for long. Besides, she totally understood why.

The events of the night before still resonated through her. JoBeth kept seeing that slip of paper igniting in the fire. In spite of all the wood smoke she'd inhaled, she felt like she could breathe again. And she actually whistled on the drive back to Beeton later in the day.

Other women in her position would definitely not be whistling happy tunes. Without a job, and without a home, her eyes should have been spinning like pinwheels. But she didn't care. Letting go of all the hurt and unforgiveness felt good. Letting in God's love felt even better.

"How's my good boy?" JoBeth reached an arm behind her toward the floor of the back seat. Shiner had appropriated Roscoe's old nest. Her little pup lifted a wet snout and kissed her hand with his tongue. Poor baby. Rayne's roomies spoiled him with lots of attention, walks and one-too-many goodies.

She decided to get Shiner on a proper, healthy diet too and stop trying to make up for the past by rewarding him with treats. Her new way of thinking and living would soon have a trickle-down effect. There would be no diet of love, affection and attention though. Her pup would have a banquet of that every day.

Her cell interrupted with a new ring tone — "Esau Was A Hairy Man.". Apparently, Rayne had done more with her phone than send that infamous picture.

"Sam? Really? I'll take you up on that offer. Rayne and I had trouble moving all my stuff the first time around, and when I leave Beeton, I still have some things in storage waiting to be picked up here. Okay. Thanks so much. I really appreciate your help. I'll be in touch soon. And Sam, thanks again."

Whenever she heard his voice, JoBeth felt her face flush warm. She thought of his eyes, his face — lips. But she shook off the urge to daydream.

Her cell announced a new text but the text was the size of a research paper, so she pulled over to the shoulder. Sent out as a group text, it read:

> *Please come to an impromptu reception at the Last Chance Café on today at 5:00 pm to celebrate all the recent happy news concerning Robert "Bobby" Herschelstein, and Candy Clayton Herschelstein. Bring a friend. There's plenty of food.*

Well, well, well — Bobby finally decided to have a little celebration. Part of her was still angry with him for letting her go. But she understood that he did what he had to do.

JoBeth forwarded the text to Rayne and was about to pull back onto the highway when she had another impulse. She picked up the phone and forwarded it to Sam.

Interested? JoBeth.

Back on the road, she started setting her personal agenda. The first order of business back in Beeton would have to be damage control. She had to find out what havoc Seth had set in motion and somehow fix it. He'd probably found a buyer and arranged for an expedited sale of the house. She doubted Seth wanted to hang around Beeton any longer than he had to.

Why wouldn't Seth let Ada stay with him? She did fine around the house during the day. As long as he kept the cable on a retro TV channel, Ada would be relatively happy. If he planned to put Ada in a nursing home in Houston, it would surely be the end of her. With no family, friends or neighbors to support her, no Roscoe, Petey and Zoomba to love on her, and now most importantly, no Grizz, Ada would go downhill fast. Maybe he didn't care. Or maybe, she shuddered, he was counting on that to happen.

And she had to stop by the Last Chance for the party and to pick up her paycheck and say goodbye to everyone. That was going to be hard. She'd developed quite an attachment to the place and the people, both co-workers and customers, even the Grumbles. Working at the Last Chance had helped her develop a new work ethic: whatever job you do, you should do it with all your heart. If you work as a waitress, be the best waitress you can be — the best cook, the best mailman, the best hairdresser, or the best *plumber*.

Big Grizz gave her a chance at the Last Chance and she owed him. After she packed all her stuff, the final order of business would be to visit Big Grizz and say her goodbyes, a thought that broke her heart, on top of all the above.

Life after Beeton would follow, but what kind of life? What to do? Where to go? Move back into the refurbished rent house or find a new apartment and pray hard for a job? At least she could get a job cooking or waitressing, something she could now do without shame or embarrassment. Not like before. She was so over that stuff. The only downside of course would be the money. How could she live on that kind of income? She and Shiner might be sharing a doggie dish if things didn't work out.

JoBeth pulled into the gravel drive behind Ada's Grande Marquis. The first thing she noticed was a "For Sale" sign in red letters stuck in the back window of the car. Wow, her cousin sure didn't waste any time. Jingling her keys, she walked past a "For Sale By Owner" sign in the yard too.

She creaked open the front door. "Auntie?" JoBeth walked in, with Shiner on the leash next to her, and started down the hallway. The familiar framed prints of flowers and wishing wells were gone. The rag rug runner in the hall was missing. "Auntie?"

"JoBeth, is that you?" Sitting in a kitchen chair, wringing her hands, Ada stood when she entered the room. Deep creases, etched across her forehead, the once happy smile now gone.

Roscoe and Shiner greeted one another, nose-to-nose, tails wagging furiously. "JoBeth, what's happening? I can't find my things. Someone's stealing from me."

"Where's Seth?"

"I don't know. But there was a man."

JoBeth wrapped her arms around her. "Auntie, calm down. I'm with you now. Tell me about the man."

Her brows drew together in anguish and she clutched her temples. "I caught him red-handed. He was in my house, stealing my things."

JoBeth looked around and noticed certain things were indeed missing. The vintage piggy cookie jar, the kitty wall clock with the tick-tock tail, the Fiesta Ware canisters on the counter, and more. "Where is he? Did he leave?"

Ada reached down next to the chair she'd been sitting in and pulled up an umbrella. "I smacked him good on the backside and he left."

About the same time, JoBeth noticed a clipboard on the floor and picked it up. A quick survey of it and she realized what was going on. Suddenly it all made sense. The man was taking inventory of Ada's possessions. Seth planned on doing an estate sale.

"Have a seat, Auntie, and a nice cup of tea." She walked to the stove, filled the teakettle and put it on the fire.

"Oh bless you dear. Maybe that will help my headache."

JoBeth searched the cabinet for the perfect tea. Chamomile. *That should calm her nerves.* She laid the bag in a china teacup, the one with the tiny pink roses, her aunt's favorite.

"Would you like some cookies with that?"

She clapped her hands together. "You know I love cookies, Jo."

A quick search through the cabinets told her Seth had been snooping around. He'd thrown out a lot of the food. JoBeth's as well — anything that was open, cookies, chips, crackers. He assumed whatever was open had to be old or stale. Then she remembered the junk food stash in her room. Brilliant.

A quick dash to the bedroom was a real shocker. First, Petey and Zoomba were fast asleep on her pillow. The kitties had appropriated the room in her absence. She made note of the horrifying fact that the two white plastic garbage bags filled with glorious junk food were gone. Not that she really cared anymore. Maybe a little . . .

But there were no less than seven kinds of cookies, regular pretzels, chocolate-covered pretzels, five kinds of chips, a giant bag of popcorn, pink cotton candy, Cracker Jacks, HoHo's, Dum Dums, Pixie Sticks, jawbreakers, Charleston Chews and on and on with the candy. All gone? Unbelievable.

How convenient, that the food was already in trash bags. But then she had a thought. The shelves he'd emptied of dolls. He stuffed those without a lick of care or concern into two identical trash bags that, thank God, she had thought to stow in her closet. He would have thrown them out without blinking an eye if she hadn't rescued them. Her junk food had saved the dollies. Ironic.

She ran over to the closet and threw open the doors. The bags were still there. The only saving grace for those dolls was the fact that she hadn't moved out yet. Seth would stop short of going through her personal belongings, but he was surely chomping at the bit to get to the rest of the stuff in the room that didn't belong to her. Apparently, he didn't see any worth in the dolls. But he could have fetched a lot of money for them on eBay if he'd done a little research.

Now that I've saved the dolls, what am I supposed to do with them?

Before she left the room, she did a quick change into a form-fitting blue top with crisscrossing straps and added a diamond heart necklace her parents had given her one Christmas.

The phone in the kitchen rang once. A little lip gloss and a spritz of lemon cologne and she was done.

"JoBeth? JoBeth, I found some cookies." She had to blink twice when she heard Ada call her name that way. Took her back to the doll dreams.

She walked back to the kitchen. Ada held a brand new box of vanilla wafers in her arms. "Look, I found these."

"Auntie, how did you know?"

Ada laughed. "You just said you were looking, that's all."

How did she remember JoBeth was looking for cookies? Her short-term memory scarcely lasted thirty seconds. JoBeth poured the tea and they sat munching while the steaming hot tea cooled in their cups. JoBeth set a personal cookie limit at two, a reasonable amount.

A newfound determination motivated her. Food would no longer be JoBeth Tomlin's pacifier, the cure-all for every crisis, or the comfort food to replace the real "Comforter" in her life.

She planned to check through the entire house to find out what else old Seth had been up to.

Shiner barked. Roscoe, not to be outdone by the young'un, followed with a howl. The front door swung open and JoBeth walked to the kitchen archway to peer down the hall.

He carried a stack of flattened cardboard boxes in with him, an angry look on his face.

"Shut up, already!" he commanded.

Shiner cowered, tail down. JoBeth scooped her dog up, kissed his head and hugged him close. Voice low, but deadly, she commanded right back. "Don't you ever talk to Shiner like that! He's had enough abuse to last a lifetime."

"I hope you came back to start packing your stuff."

"Hello to you too, cousin." She gave him a deadeye stare.

He lowered the boxes and leaned the stack against the wall near the door. "You have to understand my position. I've had to make a lot of hard decisions. What else can I do?"

"Seth Davidson." Ada walked in wagging her finger. Roscoe uttered a low growl, joined by Shiner.

"Mom?"

"I'm very upset with your behavior, young man."

"Mom, you don't understand."

"I understand what I see and what I hear. You're behaving badly. I can't believe the way you talk to our Jo." She gestured to JoBeth. "That isn't the boy I raised."

He stared back, face frozen in a scowl.

"I taught you to do the right thing, son. Do unto others. Why aren't you?"

"I-I'm making smart business decisions."

"Your business is mankind!" She pointed. "That's from 'A Christmas Carol.'"

JoBeth and Seth shared a surprised glance.

"Mom, how did you remember that?" he asked.

Her expression registered puzzlement. "What do you mean? Why wouldn't I?"

JoBeth spoke up. "It's just that—that you haven't been remembering things very well lately."

"That's silly, Jo. My memory's fine." She rubbed her temples. "My problem is this headache. I can't seem to shake it."

"Seth," JoBeth lowered her voice, "you and I can talk later—alone. Right now, I'm going to give Ada something for her pain first and then drive her to the reception, and I don't want to hear any arguments. She wants to go."

His large bison-sized head moved slowly to the right and to the left. But he didn't argue with her. Instead, he followed them into the kitchen and watched as JoBeth gave Ada some medication for her headache. Then JoBeth placed a call to Ada's doctor.

"Okay, thank you. Ten thirty in the morning? We'll be there." JoBeth hung up. "Dr. Brenham wants to see her on Monday. Apparently, headaches can be some kind of side effect. They said we should hold off on more of the pills."

Tears welled in Ada's eyes. "Is Grizzwald going to be there?"

"You bet he'll be there," JoBeth answered. But, just to be sure, she decided to give Grizz a call first, and when she did, he asked a favor of her.

Chapter Thirty-One
Marry, Marry, Quite Contrary

"Exercise is a dirty word. Every time I hear it, I wash my mouth out with chocolate." — Unknown

JoBeth helped Ada into the car and set off for Grizz's place. "Auntie." She hastened a glance as she drove. "Can I ask you a question, Auntie?"

"Oh certainly, my Jo. You know you can ask me anything." Ada beamed.

"Um, I wanted to know about you and Grizz."

"Dear me." Ada's eyes took on a dreamy quality. "Grizzwald is a wonderful man." She opened her purse, reached in and pulled out a wedding ring. "Look, he saved it all these years." She held up her hand. "And I kept the engagement ring hidden in my jewelry box."

She held the wedding ring up to the light, a simple band with a miniscule diamond. "I loved him so much. We ran away to a Justice of the Peace. It was so romantic." Her expression clouded. "But it wasn't meant to be."

"I'm not sure I understand. Didn't your father make you get an annulment after you married Grizz?"

Ada looked at her and blinked. "Yes, he didn't approve."

JoBeth gasped. "Why not?"

She dabbed at her forehead with a tissue. "He said Grizzwald was a womanizer who took advantage of me."

"Did you believe what he said?"

"No, I loved my Grizzwald." Her hands began to tremble. "But Daddy wouldn't listen to me. He had the marriage annulled and introduced me to Fritz, who worked for him."

Her aunt's thoughts were remarkably lucid for the moment. JoBeth decided to keep asking questions. She had no idea how long Ada's golden moment of memories would last.

"But you went through with it, anyway?"

Ada brought her hands to her temple. Head down, she bobbed her agreement. "I knew it wasn't true about Grizz. But Daddy thought he was doing what was best for me."

"Did you know about the baby?"

"What baby?"

"Seth."

"What about Seth?"

JoBeth reworded the question. "Did you know you were pregnant with Seth when you agreed to marry Uncle Fritz?"

"Oh, yes dear we found out right before the wedding."

"You and Uncle Fritz?"

"And Daddy." She shook her head. "Fritz promised me he'd raise the baby as his own."

"But you didn't tell Grizz?" JoBeth asked.

She shook her head. "They told me I couldn't, that I could never tell. But I insisted on naming my baby. Grizzwald and I had talked about what we'd name our children. Seth was his favorite name. Daddy and Fritz didn't know that or they would have made me change it."

Another reason Grizz knew Seth belonged to him.

"You realize Grizz still loves you, right?"

Her eyes clouded over with emotion. "Yes, I do." She clutched the ring in the palm of her hand, turning it over and again. "All these years, I couldn't let my heart feel the way it wanted to feel. I made the best of my life, but it was hard. Fritz was a good to me and he tried to be the best father he could." She yawned.

"He tried?"

"He was hard on Sethie. I tried my best to protect him."

So that was it. Uncle Fritz took out his resentment on Grizz's child. No wonder Seth was a mess.

"Dear me, I've said too much." Ada opened her purse, dropped the rings inside and clicked it shut. "I'd better hide these. Heaven knows if Fritz finds them, he'll be mad."

The window of opportunity was swiftly closing.

Ada stared straight ahead. "Our lives took a different turn, that's all."

* * *

They arrived at Grizz's house as JoBeth received a text from Rayne, telling her she was on her way. No word yet from Sam.

Still stunned by her aunt's words, JoBeth escorted Ada to a very happy man sitting in a wheelchair. The curtains were wide open and sunlight filled the room. Kit and her cleanup crew had transformed the room.

He kissed Ada's cheek, gave her a long hug and whispered something in her ear. JoBeth drew a chair close to his wheelchair for her to sit down. JoBeth hugged Grizz and sat down on the edge of his empty bed.

"I'm the happiest man in the world."

"Grizz, I wanted so badly to tell you about Bobby and Candy."

He brought his palms together. "I'll bet you did. I'm full of joy for my son and his new wife. I'm going to be a grandpa!"

JoBeth jumped up off the edge of the bed and threw her arms around him.

"Congratulations!" She leaned on the bed and stretched backwards into a sitting position.

She could feel him watching her.

The tone of his voice suddenly different, Grizz asked, "Be honest with me Jo, are you mad about Bobby letting you go? He told me today."

She raised her shoulders. "I was upset — yes — but I'm a lot better now. And I understand."

"For the record, young lady, I would have gone bankrupt before canning you." He sighed.

"I know." She squeezed his hand. "But Bobby made the right decision for the business. I think he'll make a go of it. I really do. The boy's got a good head on his shoulders."

"He does. But I wish he hadn't hurt you. Bobby feels terrible about what he did."

"I figured he would."

He laughed. "You know, I had my doubts about you when you first started, but you've become a fine waitress. I'm proud of what you've accomplished in a short time."

Ada began to mumble. "Sethie was always such a good boy. Fritz didn't think so, but I always knew he was." She clutched at her temple. "I'm praying for him. And God — God always answers my prayers."

Grizz shot JoBeth a worried look.

"He does, Auntie." Concerned, she touched Ada's forehead. *No fever, thank goodness.* "Do you still have a headache?"

Ada's eyes were half-closed. "Thanks for asking, Jo. I suppose I do."

"How about another ibuprofen? I have some in my purse."

She answered. "No thanks. I'll be okay. All I need is a little rest."

JoBeth leaned forward and stroked Ada's cheek. "You look tired."

"No dear, I'm fine." Head nestled against the chair Ada closed her eyes, as if to sleep.

JoBeth started to say more, but Grizz held his finger to his mouth to shush her.

Eyes still closed, a slight rasp to her voice, Ada asked. "Grizzwald, would you mind if I take a little nap? I can't seem to keep my eyes open."

"Of course you can, darling."

JoBeth had forgotten this was the usual time of day for her aunt to retreat to her bedroom for a snooze.

"Jo, there's a guest room over there." He pointed. "Could you take Ada and settle her in, please? She has time for a short nap before we have to go."

"Sure." She helped Ada to her feet. As JoBeth led her to the room, Ada turned and waved.

He waved back and blew her a kiss.

The guest room furniture was much nicer than Grizz's. She guessed Kit had something to do with that. Bless her and the cleaning crew. JoBeth turned down the sheets on the antique bed and helped her aunt settle in. "Sweet dreams."

Ada opened her mouth wide to yawn again.

JoBeth kissed her on the forehead. "A little rest will do you a world of good, Auntie."

Ada reached out for JoBeth's hand and kissed it. "You're so good to me, my Jo. I love you." She caressed JoBeth's cheek. "You make good oatmeal too."

Ada smiled and closed her eyes as she turned on her side. JoBeth lingered and watched the gentle rise and fall of her aunt's chest. Then she closed the door and tiptoed down the hall to Grizz.

He was about to speak, but she held a finger to her lips and whispered. "She's out."

"Good." He gestured for her to come near, so she sat in Ada's chair. "Thank you for everything you've done for us. You mean so much to me, Jo."

"It's my pleasure."

"Go ahead over to the café and have a little fun visiting with everyone. Bobby and Candy called and they told me they wanted to come over in about a half hour and pick us up. I'll surprise everyone with Ada at my side. We'll make a grand entrance. It's going to be wonderful."

"Are you sure?"

"Yes, yes, go on ahead. I'm writing down what I'm going to say."

JoBeth stood. "All right." She walked over to the door and opened it, but remained a moment between the bright daylight on the other side and the soft interior light. "You're sure?"

"Go on." He smiled. "Have fun. We'll be there soon."

She closed the door until and until it clicked shut. No sense in waking Ada with a loud noise.

She drove the short distance to the café, her heart beating a little faster the close she got. The last time she was there, she got canned and left in a daze. A surge of anxiety flowed through her.

As she reached the door, she immediately noticed a sign. "Closed for a private party." She held her breath, turned the handle and walked in just as she did that very first day, to the sound of a tinkle-y bell.

Chapter Thirty-Two
Playing My Song

"My wife is on a new diet. Coconuts and bananas — she hasn't lost weight, but she can climb a tree!" — Henny Youngman

The first person she saw when she walked in was Sam, and the song playing on the jukebox? Elvis Presley singing, "Can't Help Falling in Love With You."

He must have floored it all the way to Beeton. Sam stood at the counter, laughing with Kit as she arranged a bouquet of spring flowers in a big glass vase. Without thinking, JoBeth ran into his arms.

Dark eyes focused on hers as they embraced. "I got your text and thought I would surprise you."

He brought his hands up to the back of her head and drew her to his lips. She couldn't speak right away. Sam engulfed her with a *wow* kind of kiss, the kind of kiss that takes a girl's breath away. The one kiss a girl stores in a special memories vault in her heart and never ever forgets.

Kit let out a whistle. "Well, I'll be." She pointed at Sam. "You put the MAN in roMANtic. And JoBeth, my girl, I didn't know you had it in you, but I sure am glad you decided to let that boy know how you really feel."

She noticed movement out of the corner of her eye. Martie and Elmer waved from their booth. Martie elbowed her husband as she and Sam approached. "See, I told you she was a hussy."

"Oh Martie." Elmer took out his teeth and planted a big kiss on her. Her eyes wide open she turned back and planted a big one on him. He smiled. "Hey, this is our song." A new song began on the jukebox: *"I Only Have Eyes For You."*

Martie perked up. "That's the song you picked. Let's dance."

Kit plugged two chords together and a disco ball hanging from a chain on the ceiling began to turn slowly. Martie and Elmer began to twirl and slide across the floor.

Sam pulled something out of his pocket — the tournament scarf? The one she wore as a damsel in distress. Sam bowed, "Lady JoBeth, may I have this dance?"

She curtsied. "'Tis an honor to dance with thee, Sir Samuel."

Without saying another word, they held onto one another through the slow dance. She was struck by how comfortable it felt to be near him. No stress. No drama. Peaceful, except when their eyes met. Then she felt the way a skydiver feels jumping out a plane for the very first time.

She couldn't take her eyes off him while they danced. "I love you, Sam." *Did I just say that?*

He drew close and whispered into her ear. The gentle swish of the words tickled as he spoke. "And I'm completely, thoroughly, wholly, and perfectly in love you too, JoBeth Tomlin."

He didn't say *like*, or *intensely like*. Sam said the "L" word right off the bat, and so did she. Was it possible they had a real romance thing going?

At Last, by Etta James began to play. All the romantic songs Grizz insisted on in the Last Chance had never bothered her much before. At work, she heard them so much she hardly noticed them after a while. But now, now the words, and the melodies struck a chord in her heart.

They began as two couples on the dance floor and were soon joined by Delia and Peter. JoBeth couldn't help asking. "Are you two a twosome?"

A smiling Peter twirled Delia to the other side. "Yes, and it seems as if you two are as well."

He twirled Delia next to her. "Peter is moving back to Beeton and plans on working part-time. He's opening a small practice next door to the shop."

"And?" JoBeth asked.

"We're getting married. We got divorced because we were too busy working and not paying enough attention to each other." She cupped his chin in her hand. "That won't happen again. We won't let it."

Peter twirled her around.

"And next week, we're flying to Scotland to be remarried in an old castle." Delia shrugged. "What can I say? I read a lot of romance novels."

JoBeth threw her arms around them. Sam shook Peter's hand and hugged Delia as well. Somehow, she knew this would happen. Once Peter visited Delia at the shop, it was obvious they still loved each other.

Sam and JoBeth danced their way across the room, laughing as Kit, Betty and Cecelia lined up behind the checkout counter just like the daughters on Petticoat Junction.

Thanks to Ada, JoBeth was a fan of the show. She waved at them and they waved back.

The tinkle-y bell sounded the alarm yet again as Rayne pushed the door open, holding a package wrapped in pink foil, tied with an iridescent pink bow. But all JoBeth could see was a head full of rich brown hair, highlighted with gold, a pretty, flirty skirt in pink polka dots and a tank top.

"Rayne? What is this?" JoBeth ran her hand through the back of her shiny new "do."

"Like it?" She turned around. "I told Cada I needed a new look."

"I love it!" She threw her arms around Rayne, but noticed a sparkle coming off the side of her nose. "What's that?"

"My new piercing. I took the lip ring out and had my nose pierced instead. It's pretty small. Just a little diamond chip."

Backing off for a better look she beamed her approval. "I like it. It's subtle, you know."

Rayne continued. "I want to be noticed, but not for the wrong reasons."

"Oh you will, trust me." JoBeth showed her where to put the gift and where to sit.

The door opened again and more people showed up, among them Candy.

"What are you doing here? Weren't you helping Bobby with Grizz and Ada?"

She held out her hand. "I'm not Candy, I'm Cassie."

Her brows rose. "Cassie?"

"Candy and I, we're twins."

JoBeth drew on memories of what Candy told had told her on the front porch of Ada's house — the day she'd dropped off Shiner. "I knew she had a sister, but . . . "

She nodded. "We're twins. Most folks around here don't know that. We moved here a couple of years ago but Daddy never let us out much."

JoBeth gulped and shifted her gaze around the room. "Sorry, your father isn't my favorite person. Slade's not coming, is he?"

"Oh no," she answered, her eyes wide. She lifted her hand to her mouth to mimic a drinker. "He's had a little too much. You know."

A veritable banquet of food stretched across the diner counter. Bobby and the girls had been busy putting the celebration together earlier in the day. Kit pulled her aside. "We sure miss having you around. We were heartbroken when we found out about Bobby firing you."

"I know, but I'm okay now — really."

Kit shook her head. "I knew you'd land on your feet. You're a survivor. Don't ever forget it."

"You're right." JoBeth grinned. "I am."

The front door swung open again, and to her surprise, Seth walked in and hastened over to her.

"We need to talk now. I can't wait till later."

JoBeth folded her arms. "All right. Let's go to the kitchen." He followed her through the swinging doors.

As he settled on the lone stool in the kitchen, JoBeth spoke up first. "Your mom said something in the car today. Something about you and Fritz. She told me he was hard on you when you were growing up. She told me that your father and grandfather knew that Grizz was your father."

He looked away, the glint of tears suddenly visible in his eyes. "She told you the truth." Seth took a breath. "He was a hard man," He threw his hands up. "I'm not his child. And I'm glad."

Shocked, JoBeth's heart raced. "I had no idea."

"He never showed that side of himself to the rest of the family. Mom took the worst of it. She had to cook what he said, clean the house the way he wanted it cleaned, fold his laundry a certain way, do whatever he said. She couldn't have friends over, only the couples he invited. She wasn't allowed to speak to neighbors and couldn't go anywhere without him driving her. And she sure wasn't allowed to go anywhere near the Last Chance."

"That's unbelievable . . . " JoBeth flipped through memories for clues and came up with a few. That time Ada and Seth had come to stay at her parent's house for a couple of weeks. The late night phone calls between mom and her sister Ada. In retrospect, she realized a lot had been going on behind the scenes.

Remembering Ada's car, she posed the question. "She knows how to drive, though. Are you sure about that?"

"Am I sure? The only reason she knows how to drive is because of me. When I got my license, I taught her what I knew and took her to the DPS office to get her driver's license." He took a deep breath. "It was our secret."

JoBeth felt her mouth come unhinged. "Then all these years, Ada was, *was* abused. And so were you."

He clapped his hands together. "Call it what you want. That was our life."

"Seth—I'm sorry."

"It is what it is." He wiped his bear paw hands across his face, a move eerily reminiscent of Grizz. "When he died, I didn't have to worry about protecting her anymore. I opened an office in Houston to get away from this town. Mom seemed happy too. We were free."

How could she not know? The clues were all there—Seth's anger issues, and Ada still so fearful after all these years she wouldn't set foot in the café or contact Grizz.

"Did you try to tell someone?" JoBeth wrung her hands.

"Once."

"What happened?"

"The teacher called my father." He closed his eyes. "You can guess how that turned out."

Voice tender, she touched his shoulder. "Seth, what are you going to do now?"

He shrugged. "I don't want to stay here. There are too many bad memories. But you're right about me rushing to get everything done. Mom's been upset with all the changes. I'm upset too. The way I've been acting—that's not who I am. I'm going to slow down and help mom make the transition. I'm worried about her."

JoBeth patted his shoulder. "Maybe you should try counseling. I saw a counselor a few times after my parents died, and it really helped me."

He dusted his hands together. "Maybe."

Kit drew away from the window suddenly, hopping up and down. "Hey ya'll, I think it's them."

They hurried to the door only to find Candy, her voice drowned out as an ambulance rushed past, flashing red lights.

"What is it?" The grin on JoBeth's face collapsed.

Wheezing, Candy grabbed JoBeth by the shoulders. "It's Ada."

Everyone ran the two blocks to Grizz's house. Bobby met them at the door. Grizz, his head buried in a towel, was bent over in the wheelchair sobbing. The red flashing light of the ambulance twirled round the interior of Grizz's room, mimicking the disco light in the café.

JoBeth ran to the guestroom. Chest heaving from the run, adrenaline pumping, she warbled. "What's wrong? What happened? Tell me!"

But before the EMTs could answer, Grizz cried out from the other room, his voice hoarse. "She was tired. She said she was tired."

"She," Bobby approached, his voice soft, "must have passed away in her sleep. We tried to wake her, but she was gone."

Seth burst into the bedroom door and pushed the emergency personnel aside. He let out a wail at the sight of Ada's body on the crash cart, and sank to the floor. Bobby knelt down to comfort him.

In spite of everything, the expression on her aunt's face told a story. Ada seemed at peace, her face serene and free of worry or care. JoBeth glanced away and noticed a fresh gardenia corsage on the end table — the scent of the blossoms infusing the room with sweetness in the midst of — tragedy.

Sam took JoBeth in his arms and held her close as she began to sob, and it felt as if the gentle comfort of the Holy Spirit cradled her heart as well.

Chapter Thirty-Three
The Beginning

"If hunger is not the problem, then eating is not the solution." —
Author Unknown

"Are you ready?" Sam stood next to her. "Take a deep breath."

Seven months before, she'd walked out the door of the café and never returned. After the viewing and funeral, they shared dinner and memories of Ada at the Last Chance — a bittersweet time, but a lovely tribute for everyone who attended. It was hard to see Seth and Grizz so broken. Life is full of lasts, but most people don't realize it until it's too late.

The peaceful look on Ada's face stuck with JoBeth. Dr. Brenham told them she likely had a stroke while she slept. Though it was especially hard losing another family member so soon after losing her own parents, JoBeth had undergone significant changes. Her faith rekindled and recharged, she had friends, both old and new, and a fresh, new perspective. And Sam.

She stared ahead. The door smelled like fresh paint — a bright, pleasant green. Inviting.

Sam took her arm and they walked across the threshold. The absence of a tinkle-y bell did not go unnoticed. The interior, festooned with pink ribbons and streamers, Bobby and Candy looked up as they entered. Their baby girl, cradled in Big Grizz's arms, cooed as JoBeth kissed her doting grandfather's cheek.

Instead of romantic songs and ballads playing on the jukebox, sweet lullabies and kid's songs played on an ancient boom box set on the counter. A dazzling array of food and pies spread across a large banquet table in the center of the room. Covered with a white tablecloth, fresh quirky bouquets of tiny pepper plants, zinnias, tiger lilies, ferns and mulberry bush cuttings decorated the table at intervals. She wondered who did the arrangements, and what was going on in their head at the time.

Rayne would have said something funny about the centerpieces. That's for sure. She'd invited her, but Rayne was on a date — an actual date. She met a drummer at the church of all places. Said she liked the music and started coming on Wednesdays, then Sundays too. Seemed like they had a lot in common. Rayne looked pretty mainstream now, except for the nose piercing.

Grizz held court in his wheelchair. "JoBeth, Sam." Grandfather Grizz tucked the blanket around the infant's tiny feet. "Isn't she a doll?"

The word "doll" threw her off for a minute. She hadn't thought about the dream dollies in a while.

"What's her name?" Sam asked, a bright twinkle in his eyes.

"Callie," Bobby answered. "Candy and Cassie favor names that begin with C."

"She's adorable." JoBeth smiled.

Grizz glanced up. "So how's the job at the TV station going?"

"I love working there."

He winked. "If you ever get tired of that glamorous TV job, you can always come back here and wait tables or cook."

She looked around the place, lips curled up. "Producing isn't exactly glamorous. And it's a tempting offer, but I don't think you need me here anymore."

He reached for her hand and kissed it. "Then you have to promise to visit more often."

"I will." She leaned in and gave him a gentle hug, then noticed Seth at the far end of the room.

Grizz's eyes darted toward him. "A couple of months ago, I found out he was in town visiting the plant and invited him to dinner. That's how he and Cassie met. As for the two of us, we're getting to know each other. What can I say? It's a start." A pained expression transformed his face. "Ada would have been pleased."

Sam held out his pinky finger and the baby promptly curled her tiny hand around it. "She's beautiful."

Grizz laughed. "Of course. She's a Herschelstein."

Kit squealed and ran over to JoBeth. "You look great."

"I concur." Delia smiled her approval.

JoBeth twirled. "Size eight, my new personal goal. No higher, no lower."

Candy tugged on Delia's blouse. "You need to help me get my figure back too."

"Sure, but you only have a few post partum pounds to get rid of, that's easy."

She seemed confused, her lips repeating the post partum part like a foreign language word.

Delia put a hand on her back. "I'll explain it all to you later, Candy. Come by the shop."

Officers Hank and Ken joined them, wearing their Sunday best. Ken had his wife with him and Officer Hunk had a girlfriend.

Kit pulled JoBeth aside and lowered her voice. "I want you to know. I finally got up the nerve to tell Grizz how I felt."

"And?" JoBeth held her breath.

"We're spending a lot of time together." Kit smiled.

"What did he say when you told him?"

"Between the heart attack, and not being able to work, and losing Ada—his life isn't what it was. I don't know how much time Grizz has, but I want to be a part of his life."

JoBeth wrapped her arms around Kit. "I wish you the best, my friend."

Kit pulled away and brushed her eyes with a napkin. "You too, honey."

Sam and Grizz were deep in conversation so she decided to go talk to her cousin. Seth was sitting in a booth with Cassie. He slid out the booth to greet her.

"It's good to see you, JoBeth. I hope you're glad to see me."

She leaned to shake Cassie's hand first, then her cousin's. "I am."

He cast a sideways glance to Cassie, who nodded her encouragement. Then Seth did something surprising. He leaned forward and wrapped his arms around JoBeth. Stiff as a board at first, he loosened slightly as they embraced. "I love you, Jo."

She backed away and studied his face. Was this the same man?

His mouth opened like he wanted to say something, but he swallowed instead, nearly choking on his own saliva. Like Ada said, Seth had a good heart, probably a bison-sized one.

"I love you too, Seth."

"I have something to say." He paused. "Jo, you helped me and mom more than you know. I appreciate everything you did for us."

Ada's last prayer on earth for her son Seth to change had come to pass. Her aunt's words resonated through her spirit. *God always answers my prayers.*

Then something amazing happened. Seth's statement seemed to take on a life of its own.

"Amen to that." Delia and Peter looked at one another and held up their punch cups. Bobby and Candy joined them.

Kit began to weep. "JoBeth, you helped all of us."

And one by one, from Grizz to Betty and Cecelia, even the Grumbles, they all held up their punch cups to JoBeth in an impromptu toast.

Sam, the last to do so, held up his. "To JoBeth."

* * *

Dear Mom and Dad,

I'm writing this more for me than for you. Since you're already in heaven, I'm pretty sure you know what's going on in my life. But I miss you both so much!

For a while, things weren't going so well. The truth is, my life pretty much fell apart. But I'm doing much better now. A lot has changed.

You'll be happy to know I'm back in the newly refurbished rent house. And Mom, it's not dumpy anymore! For some reason though, there are lots of plumbing issues. Probably due to Shiner, a cute little dog I rescued a while back. He's fond of dropping his chew toys in the toilet. Of course he has plenty of accomplices, what with Roscoe, Petey and Zoomba around to help.

As a matter of fact, there are so many plumbing issues lately, I have to call a plumber at least twice a week to come and fix things. And I'm spending so much money, I'll either have to keep him on retainer or marry him, which, I think you would agree would certainly be more economical. (I'm just kidding about the money).

And speaking of money, guess what? I finally have a bit of a nest egg saved up in the event things go south financially again. You never know when a "Jobette" moment is going to happen.

Cousin Seth and I made our peace and we actually get along now. He even gave me Ada's doll collection. After a lot of prayer and soul-searching, I had a few of the dolls refurbished and sold most of the others to serious collectors. I made sure the ones I sold went to good homes though.

I was surprised when I got the call to come back for a second interview at the TV station, but floored when they offered me the job. The assistant producer position is everything I ever wanted in a job. Except producer, of course! But I know if I work hard at what I do and give it my very best; the opportunity might one day come. Kit's words still ring clear and true to me. (She's a waitress I used to work with. I took a job for a while waiting tables, and in retrospect, it was the best move I ever made). Anyway, Kit told me once that my job doesn't have to define who I am. A job is what you do. But I happen to love what I do.

I guess one of the main things I've learned about suffering is that everybody goes through it. We all have seasons of hurt, loss, betrayal, and doubt. I was mad at God for a while and I'm ashamed to say that I blamed Him for all the bad things that happened. But you know what I found out? Everybody's going through something. Most of us deal with things one at a time, but when a bunch of things happen all at once, it's overwhelming.

The most important thing I learned through my experiences is that God won't give you anything until He gives you everything. And He is everything. With God and Sam and good friends, a job I love and my faith renewed stronger than before, I feel like I have everything and more.

I have to be completely honest with you about the weight issue. Sometimes I still have a little bit of a food baby thing going on, and sometimes I don't. But I don't binge any more. I exercise and eat normal, sensible meals. Food is just food, not my enemy or my idol. And if I put on a few pounds now and then, I don't freak. When things go wrong in life, and they often do, I turn to Christ instead of a cupcake.

Well, that's about it. I'm a work-in-progress as you well know. I never thought I'd be happy again, but I am. Someday we'll meet up again, and what a reunion that will be!

Love,
Your little girl, forever,
JoBeth

* * *

JoBeth closed her journal and yawned. Journaling was the best suggestion her new counselor had recommended.

She padded to the kitchen, slippers scuffing across the smooth floor. She filled a glass with water and shut the lights off in each room on the way to her bedroom.

A small lamp on her nightstand cast spikes of light up and down the wall by her bed. Her eyes followed the light to a slender curio cabinet next to the nightstand, one of the pieces of furniture she'd retrieved from storage. And she smiled.

Cleaned and refurbished, the piggy-tail doll and the Victorian dolly resided on the top shelf inside the glass cabinet. She'd kept the two for sentimental reasons, a reminder of her food baby days.

JoBeth turned off the lamp and slid under the covers. In the veil between wake and sleep, as her body began to float against the mattress, certain thoughts began to beckon. Whispers. *Siren songs.*

There were times — mostly in the quiet echo of the night, when shadows danced off the ceiling a certain way, or a glint off a metal doorknob reminded her of an agate eye clicking open.

Long, meandering evenings when she craved a salty bag of chips, or an ice cream sandwich.

She could almost swear she heard them again. Tiny, distant voices calling her name over and over. "JoBeth. JoBeth."

But she squeezed her eyes shut, and cocooned the covers around her securely.

Not tonight.

The End

Enjoy the

WHEN THE FAT LADIES SING COZY MYSTERY SERIES

By Linda Kozar

NOW AVAILABLE ON AUDIBLE!

Misfortune Cookies –Book One

A Tisket, A Casket — Book Two

Dead As A Doornail — Book Three

Felony Fruitcake — Book Four

That Wasn't Chicken — Book Five

And coming soon

Weighty Matters — Book Six

Custard's Last Stand — Book Seven

Want to see a sneak preview of the Weighty Matters

cover?

Coming in July 2015!

LISTEN TO ME ON THE RADIO! I'M A HOST ON "ALONG CAME A WRITER" ON THE RED RIVER NETWORK, ON BLOGTALK RADIO!

Linda Kozar is the co-author of <u>Babes With A Beatitude — Devotions For Smart, Savvy Women of Faith</u> (Hardcover/eBook, Howard/Simon & Schuster 2009), <u>Misfortune Cookies</u> and <u>Just Desserts</u> ("When The Fat Ladies Sing" cozy mystery series, Print, Barbour Publishing 2008), and <u>Strands of Fate</u> (Hardcover/eBook, Creative Woman Mysteries 2012). Her cozy mystery series again published and expanded as eBooks at Spyglass Lane Mysteries, MacGregor Literary from 2012-2014, and in September of 2014 Linda indie-published and the continues the series: <u>Misfortune Cookies</u>, <u>A Tisket, A Casket</u>, <u>Dead As A Doornail</u>, <u>That Wasn't Chicken</u>, and <u>Felony Fruitcake</u>. Her latest foray into indie publishing, produced Food Baby (contemporary women's 2015), <u>Alligator Pear</u>, (gothic historical romance, 2013), <u>Moving Tales, Adventures in Relocation</u>, (a nonfiction anthology 2013), and <u>Doomsday Devotions</u> (an end times devotional 2014). Linda is an active member of Cozy Mystery Magazine, which publishes an annual Christmas anthology of its contributing authors, <u>A Cup of Cozy</u> (Short Mysteries and Holiday Recipes, 2013) and <u>A Cup of Cozy 2</u> (Short Mysteries and Holiday Recipes 2014). Her speculative fiction story, <u>Aperture</u>, will release in an anthology book titled <u>Out of the Storm</u> (HopeSprings Books 2015), the proceeds of which will be donated to the ACFW Scholarship Fund. In 2003, she co-founded, co-directed, and later served as Southwest Texas Director of *Words For The Journey Christian Writers Guild*. She received the ACFW Mentor of the Year Award in 2007, founded and served as president of *Writers On The Storm*, The Woodlands, Texas ACFW chapter for three years and continues on the board. In addition to writing, Linda has served as Lead Host of the Gate Beautiful Radio Show, on the Red River Radio Network/BlogTalk Radio since 2010. She and her husband Michael, married for over 25 years, have two lovely daughters, Katie and Lauren and a Rat Terrier princess named Patches. In addition to writing Linda is Lead Host of the Gate Beautiful Radio Show, part of the Red River Network on Blog Talk Radio—interviewing Christian authors from Debut to Bestselling, airing the 3rd Thursday of every month.

Member of: AWSA (Advanced Writers and Speakers Association), CAN (Christian Authors Network), RWA (Romance Writers of American), NHRWA (North Houston Romance Writers of America), ACFW (American Christian Fiction Writers), Writers On The Storm, The Woodlands, Texas Chapter of ACFW, Toastmasters (Area 56) The Woodlands, Texas, The Woodlands Church, The Woodlands, TX.

Linda's Website: http://www.lindakozar.com
Gate Beautiful Radio Show:
http://www.blogtalkradio.com/search?q=gate-beautiful
Babes With A Beatitude Blog:
http://www.babeswithabeatitude.blogspot.com
Bookish Desires Blog: http://bookishdesires.blogspot.com
Cozy Mystery Magazine Blog:
http://cozymysterymagazine.blogspot.com
Twitter: https://twitter.com/LindaKozar

Facebook: https://www.facebook.com/linda.kozar
Pinterest: http://pinterest.com/lindakozar/boards/
Linked-in: http://tinyurl.com/m8vspxu

42989254R00221

Made in the USA
Lexington, KY
14 July 2015